DRAGON PLAY

The dragon leveled off her flight, banked one wing again, and turned in a lazy arc.

"Look down!" she called out.

Rhodry, astride her, saw far below a line of horsemen marching. Leading them was a huge raven.

"Horseskin!" Rhodry yelled.

"And Raena with them! Let's have a bit of sport!"

With a roar, the dragon plunged down.

Kicking, plunging, bucking, the horses tried to bolt. The Horseskin riders were yelling and clutching their saddle peaks to keep from being thrown. The dragon ignored them and swooped after the raven.

Shrieking, the raven dodged, darting this way and that, but steadily the dragon gained. With one last shriek the raven disappeared, bursting through some invisible gate to another world.

Arzosah turned in a wild arc. "Shall we go after them again?"

She skimmed the ground and charged them one more time. The men screamed, wrenched their horses' heads around, and let them run where they would. The dragon pulled up, gained height in a mad flap of wings, and flew fast away, chortling to herself. Rhodry tipped back his head and howled in berserk laughter.

By Katharine Kerr

Her novels of Deverry and the Westlands

DAGGERSPELL
DARKSPELL
THE BRISTLING WOOD
THE DRAGON REVENANT
A TIME OF EXILE
A TIME OF OMENS
DAYS OF BLOOD AND FIRE
DAYS OF AIR AND DARKNESS
THE RED WYVERN
THE BLACK RAVEN
THE FIRE DRAGON

Her works of science fiction

RESURRECTION
PALACE
(with Mark Kreighbaum)

✤ BOOK THREE OF THE DRAGON MAGE ✤

THE ✦ FIRE
Dragon

KATHARINE
KERR

BANTAM BOOKS

NEW YORK TORONTO LONDON SYDNEY AUCKLAND

THE FIRE DRAGON
A Bantam Spectra Book / January 2001

SPECTRA and the portrayal of a boxed "s" are trademarks of Bantam
Books, a division of Random House, Inc.

Copyright © 2001 by Katharine Kerr
Cover art copyright © 2001 by Paul Youll.

ISBN 978-0-553-58247-5

Published simultaneously in the United States and Canada

Bantam Books are published by Bantam Books, a division of Random
House, Inc. Its trademark, consisting of the words "Bantam Books" and
the portrayal of a rooster, is Registered in U.S. Patent and Trademark
Office and in other countries. Marca Registrada. Bantam Books, 1540
Broadway, New York, New York 10036.

PRINTED IN THE UNITED STATES OF AMERICA

11

For my grandfather,
John Brahtin.
He gave me my social
conscience.

✧ C O N T E N T S ✧

TABLE OF
INCARNATIONS

THE CIVIL WARS	EARLY 1100s	MID-1060s
Anasyn	Kiel	
Bevyan	Dera	
Bellyra	Carramaena	Jill
Branoic	(yet to appear)	Blaen of Cwm Pecl
Caradoc	(yet to appear)	
Lillorigga	Niffa	Rhodry
Maddyn	Rhodry	
Peddyc	Jahdo	Mallona
Merodda	Raena	Sarcyn
Burcan	Verrarc	Cullyn of Cerrmor
Owaen	(yet to appear)	Rhodda as a child
Pertyc Maelwaedd (in 918)	Lady Rhodda	

The Roof of the World

N

To the High Plains (Horse Kin)

The Fire Mountain

Haen Marn?

Haen Marn?

To Dwarveholt

Cerr Cawnen

Penli

Lin Serr

The Rhiddaer

Cengarn

Arcodd Province

To the Seven Cities (Gel da'Thae)

To Deverry (Humans)

To the Grasslands (Elves)

0   300

Miles

©1993 A. Karl / J. Kemp

Cities

Capital

Hills

Mountains

Deverry

The year 850. The gods saw fit to give our prince the victory, but never had we dreamt how high a price they would set for it.

—The Holy Chronicles of Lughcarn

$\mathcal{S}$unlight streamed into the tower room and pooled on the wooden floor. Grey gnomes with spindle legs and warty faces materialized in the warmth and lolled like cats. Despite his great age, Nevyn felt tempted to join them. He sat in the chamber's only chair and considered his apprentice, who was sitting cross-legged among the gnomes. She turned her face up to the sun and ran one hand through her blonde hair, which fell to her shoulders in a ragged wave.

"Spring's truly here," Lilli said. "I'm so glad of it, and yet I dread summer. You must, too."

"I do," Nevyn said. "It won't be long now before the army rides out, and the gods only know what the battles will bring."

"Just so. All I can do is pray that Branoic rides home safely."

"You've grown truly fond of Branoic, haven't you?"

"I have. The prince doesn't like it much." Lilli opened her eyes and turned to look up at him. "You don't think he'd do anything dishonorable, would you?"

"Prince Maryn, you mean? What sort of dishonor—"

"Letting Branno be killed in battle. Putting him in harm's way somehow. It sounds so horrid when I say it aloud. I can't imagine Maryn doing such a thing, truly. I'm just frightened, I suppose, and it's coloring my fancies."

"No doubt." Nevyn hesitated, wondering if her fear were only fancy or some half-seen omen. As apprentices so often did, she picked up his thought.

"I've been meaning to ask you somewhat," Lilli went

on. "You know how the omens used to come to me? I'd be sewing or thinking of some ordinary thing, and then all of a sudden the words would come bursting out of my mouth?"

"I remember it well."

"It doesn't happen anymore."

"Good." Nevyn smiled at her. "It's a common thing, that a person marked for the dweomer will have some wild gift, but when she starts a proper course of study, she loses the knack. Later, once you truly understand what you're doing, the gift will return to you."

"I see. To tell you the truth, I'm just as glad. I'd be terrified if I could see—well, you know—someone's death."

"Just so." Nevyn hesitated, thinking. It was likely that if grave harm befell either the prince or her betrothed, she would know, no matter how far away she was. He decided that worrying her the more would serve no purpose and changed the subject. "I need to be on my way. The prince is holding a council—at noon, he said, so I suppose I'd better get myself there." He stood up, stretching his arms above his head. "You may finish the lesson I set you from the dweomer book."

"Those awful lists?"

"I realize that the memory work is tedious." Nevyn arranged a mock-fierce expression. "But those calls and invocations will come in handy some fine day. Learn that first page for today."

"I do understand. I've got part of them off by heart already."

"Splendid. Keep at it. But if you finish before I get back, there's no need for you to stay shut up inside. The more sun you get, the better."

Nevyn hurried down the stone stairs, which still exuded a wintry chill, and walked out to the sunlight and the main ward of Dun Deverry and the looming towers of the dun itself. Not even the bright spring day could turn the smoke-blackened stone cheerful. The fortress spread out over the top of a hill, bound by six high stone walls, lying at intervals down the hill like chains upon the earth. Tall towers, squat brochs, wooden sheds, long barracks, and sta-

bles—they sprawled in a plan turned random by hundreds
of years of decay, the fires of war, and the disasters of siege,
followed by what new building and fortifying the kings had
been able to afford. In among the buildings lay cobbled
wards and plain dirt yards, cut up by stone walls, some isolated, all confusing.

In the center of this tangle, however, lay a proper ward,
and in its center rose the tidy cluster of brochs and towers that
housed the prince, his family, his personal guards, and the
many officials and servants that made up his court. Against the
black stone, bright banners displayed a red wyvern on a cream
ground, lifting and trembling in the breeze. As Nevyn was
crossing this ward, he saw Princess Bellyra just leaving the
main broch tower. With two pages and one of her husband's
bards in attendance, she was heading for the door of one of the
side buildings. Dressed in blue linen, she walked slowly, her
hands resting on her belly, heavy with her third child. Her
honey-colored hair was bound up in a scarf stiff with embroidery, as befitted a married woman of her rank.

"Nevyn!" she called out. "Are you off to the high council?"

"I am, Your Highness. Why are you going inside in this
lovely weather?"

"It's that bit of old map you found for me. I simply have
to go see the room it refers to."

"Ah, indeed. I'm curious about it myself, actually. If
you could let me know what you find?"

"I will. But you'd best hurry. Maryn's been looking for
you."

Nevyn bowed, then hurried through the double doors
of the central broch. The great hall covered the entire
ground floor, a huge round room scattered with wooden tables, benches, and a small collection of chairs at the table
reserved for the prince himself. At either side stood enormous stone hearths, one for the prince's riders and the servants, the other, far grander, for the noble-born. Despite
the spring warmth outside, fires smoldered in each to drive
off the damp.

Nevyn wove his way through the tables and the dogs

scattered on the straw-strewn floor. About halfway between doors and hearths a stone staircase spiralled up the wall. He'd climbed only a few steps when someone hailed him from below. He turned to see Councillor Oggyn just mounting the stairs himself. He was a stout man, Oggyn, and egg-bald, though he sported a bristling black beard. He was carrying an armful of rolled parchments.

"Good day," Nevyn said. "Are those the ledgers?"

"They are, my lord," Oggyn said. "I've recorded all the dues and taxes owed our prince by the royal demesne. I'm cursed glad he can count on the Cerrmor taxes for a while longer."

"So am I. Getting the army fit to march would strip his local holdings bare."

"Just so. We'll have to wait for provisions from the south, and that's that. I just hope our prince sees reason. I know he's impatient to be on the move."

"Oh, I'm sure he will. I'm hoping that our enemies are as badly off as we are."

They climbed in silence to the first landing, where Oggyn paused to catch his breath. He looked out over the great hall below while he mopped his bald head with a rag.

"Somewhat else I wanted to lay before you, my lord," Oggyn said. "I saw our princess going about her investigations just now. Is that wise?"

"Well, the midwives all swear that the walking will do her naught but good."

"Splendid, but that's not quite my meaning. That bard. Is he fit company for her?"

"Ah. I see."

Nevyn considered his answer. During the winter past, Maddyn, the bard in question, had caught Oggyn out in some shameful doings and written a flyting song about them. It was his right as a bard to do so, but in his shame Oggyn wouldn't be caring about rights and duties.

"He is, truly." Nevyn decided that brevity was best. "I've never met a man more aware of his station in life. If anything, he's perhaps too modest for a bard."

Oggyn set his lips together hard and stared for a moment more.

"Ah well," Oggyn said at last. "None of my affair, anyway. Shall we go up?"

"By all means. We should find the prince and his brother there before us."

"I shan't be able to climb around like this much longer." Bellyra laid both hands on her swollen belly. "But I couldn't stand not knowing. I wonder if there truly is a secret passage. Tell me, Maddo. Doesn't that mark look like it means a doorway of some kind?"

Maddyn held the fragment of mouldy parchment up to an arrow slit for the sunlight. They were standing in a wedge-shaped chamber partway up one of the half-brochs, which joined the central tower like petals round the center of a daisy. According to the piece of map, this chamber should have had two doors, the one by which they'd entered and another directly across. Yet the inward bulge of the stone wall opposite showed nothing.

"It does," Maddyn said at last. "Perhaps the door's been walled up."

The princess's pages, however, gave up less easily. The two boys began poking at the mortar and pushing rather randomly on the stones. All at once the wall groaned, or so it sounded, a long sigh of pain. The boys yelped and jumped back.

"So!" Bellyra said. "I'll wager we have a spy's hole or suchlike here. The royal council chamber, the one on the second floor of the main broch, should be right near here."

The pages set to again. Dark-haired and hazel-eyed, they were Gwerbret Ammerwdd's sons, and apparently they had inherited that great lord's stubbornness. They pushed, prodded, laid their backs against the wall, and shoved until, all at once, a section of wall swung inward with an alarming collection of squeaks, groans, and rumbles.

"Look, Your Highness!" said Vertyc, the elder of the pair. "Here's the door!"

"Not a very secret one, I must say, with a noise like

that." Bellyra took a few steps forward to peer through the opening. "It wants oiling, most like."

Maddyn joined her and peered through the opening.

"It's more a passageway than a room inside," Maddyn said.

"It might lead to the council chamber. I wonder if the kings had this made to eavesdrop on their councillors. There was a hidden chamber like this in Dun Cerrmor. By the end my father didn't trust anyone, and so he had one built."

"Shall we find out?" Maddyn said.

"By all means!" Bellyra gestured at the pages. "You two stay out here. If that door swings shut, we could be trapped. Don't look so disappointed! You can explore it once we come out again, and we'll watch the door for you."

The narrow passage smelled heavily of mice. Some twenty feet along they heard voices: Nevyn and Councillor Oggyn. Grinning, Bellyra held a finger to her lips. When they stopped to listen, the sound came clearly.

"The spring's upon us," Oggyn was saying. "We need to requisition mules and suchlike."

"I've no idea how many we'll need," Nevyn said. "It depends upon the muster."

Bellyra could just make out Maryn's voice. Apparently he was sitting at some distance from the wall. As the two councillors continued talking about provisions and transport, Bellyra felt on the edge of tears. The army would ride out soon, leaving her and the other women behind with only the familiar summer terrors for company.

When she glanced at Maddyn, she found him leaning against the wall with his eyes closed. It never ceased to amaze her how fighting men would sleep whenever they could, no matter how precarious their balance. Grey streaked Maddyn's dark curly hair, and he was weather-beaten and gaunt from his soldier's life, but it was his kindness that had snared her. This summer she would worry doubly, she realized, both for her husband and for the man upon whose devotion she had come to rely when dark moods overtook her. For a moment she found herself tempted to kiss him awake. The feeling brought a cold panic with it. As the queen of all Deverry, she would have to keep her honor as pure as a priest of Bel. She took a sharp step back, kicked a rattling stone, and woke him.

"It's stuffy in here," she whispered. "Let's leave."

Out in the cleaner air of the chamber Maddyn took a few deep breaths and rubbed his eyes. Bellyra sent the boys in for their look around, then watched him while he studied the fragment of map.

"Truly interesting," Maddyn said at last. "So kings eavesdrop like commoners, do they?"

"It looks as if the ones here did. The next time Maryn holds a full council I'll remember this. I always wonder what he's like when there are no women around. He must be quite different."

"One would hope."

Bellyra laughed, and not very decorously, either. There was a time when that jest would have wounded her to the heart, she realized. Maddyn grinned at her.

"Now the real question," she went on, "is when this passage was built. I've not found a thing about it in the records, which makes sense, of course. They could hardly keep it secret if they talked about it. But then, I wonder who did the building?"

"Perhaps the king had them slain afterwards."

"Ych! I hope not. Although—" Bellyra paused, thinking. "Nevyn has an ancient book called *Tales of the Dawntime*. According to that, the earliest brochs in Deverry weren't built with proper floors and chambers and suchlike. They had double walls, with a good-sized space between them, you see, and they were empty like a chimney in the center, because there would only be one big fire at the bottom to keep everyone warm. And in those double walls were little rooms and some sort of corridor called galleries."

"I see. This passage could be a remnant of a gallery, then. The heart of Dun Deverry's very old, after all."

"Just so, and then the only thing the later king would have had to add would have been this door. And he might have been able to have that made secretly, if he paid the mason enough."

"True spoken. And especially if the mason were as close-mouthed as Otho, say."

"Quite so. I wonder if our pages have had enough exploring in there? I hate to admit this, Maddo, but I'm tired, and I want to sit down."

Maddyn called to the boys, and in a few moments they hurried out. Cobwebs glistened in their hair.

"There's a little staircase at the end, Your Highness," Vertyc said. "But it doesn't go up to anything."

"Unless it's a false floor," his brother, Tanno, joined in, "but it would make ever so much noise to find out."

"We'd best wait till the prince's council isn't in session, then," Bellyra said. "But don't worry, we'll come back to look at it."

They all hurried down the staircase and outside to find the sunlight leaving them. From the south, white clouds were gliding in, billowing up into the sky with the promise of a storm. Servants trotted back and forth, fetching firewood for the great hall while they kept an eye out for the rain. Bellyra picked her way slowly over the uneven cobblestones with Vertyc at her elbow to steady her. She was so intent on not falling that they were halfway across before she realized that she was hearing the sound of a man screaming in rage. She stopped walking and looked up, glancing around.

Across the ward by the main gate, two men had faced off. Their white shirts, each embroidered with a grey dagger down one sleeve, marked them as silver daggers, members of the prince's personal guard. They were both of them blond and burly, but one was a good head taller than the other—Branoic, she realized, and facing him Owaen, captain of the troop, pacing back and forth and shouting so angrily that his words made no sense.

"Maddo, what's that all about?" Bellyra said.

"Oh ye gods!" Maddyn said. "I don't know, my lady, but I'd best attend to it."

"By all means. Let's go over. If I'm there Owaen will have to stop screaming like that."

"Truly, and my thanks."

Indeed the royal presence did bring Owaen to his senses. He fell silent and bowed to the princess, but he trembled all over, and his face had gone dead-white. Branoic was smiling, Bellyra suddenly realized, a wicked tight curve of his mouth, as if he were enjoying each and every moment of Owaen's rage.

"Your Highness." Branoic bowed low. "Your husband has given me a splendid boon, and I'll thank you for it as well. I know you must have spoken with him about bestowing land upon me."

"I did, and you're most welcome." She turned to Owaen with as pleasant a smile as she could muster. "But what's so wrong, Captain?"

"Forgive me, Your Highness, but your husband is going to make him a lord as well."

"Of course."

"But the blazon—forgive me—you wouldn't understand, Your Highness."

"Oh ye gods!" Maddyn broke in. "He didn't give Branno the eagles back?"

"He did." Owaen could barely force the words out. "Just that."

Branoic tossed back his head and howled with laughter. With one smooth curve of his body Owaen turned and hit him so hard in the stomach that Branoic doubled over. Maddyn grabbed Owaen's arm, but he could hold him for only a brief moment—just long enough for Branoic to get his wind back.

"You bastard!" Branoic snarled.

Owaen shook Maddyn off and charged. Branoic met him with the slap of one huge hand, then swung on him with the other. Screaming curses, Owaen grabbed his shirt with both hands and shook him like a rat whilst Branoic pounded on his enemy's back. For a moment they swayed back and forth like drunken men; then Owaen tripped, and they both fell. Clasped in each other's arms they rolled around on the cobbles while they swore and kicked and punched each other. All Maddyn could do was dance around them and try to make himself heard.

"Stop it!" Maddyn was screaming. "Not in front of the princess! You cursed hounds, stop it!"

"Here!" It was Nevyn, running with all the speed and grace of a young man. "What—by Lord of Hell!"

Nevyn flung up one hand, then snapped it down with the gesture of a man throwing dice. Silvery-blue flames shot from his fingers and struck the cobbles with a crack like thunder and a burst of light. With a yelp the two wrestlers broke their holds and rolled a little way apart. Owaen sat up, rubbing his right eye, which was swelling shut. Maddyn darted forward and grabbed Branoic to keep him off his prey, but Branoic made no objection. He sat up, rested briefly, then got up and stood rubbing his bloody, bruised knuckles while he panted for breath. Owaen scrambled up after him. Dirt and muck smeared their white shirts and the rest of them as well.

"There," Nevyn said mildly. "That's better. Now what's all this?"

"Prince Maryn gave Branoic his grant of land and letters patent today," Maddyn said. "He gave Branoic the right to use eagles for his blazon."

"And?" Nevyn said. "Oh wait. The feud. Ye gods, lads! When did it start? Over ten years ago at least!"

Branoic nodded, staring at the ground. Owaen started to speak, then suddenly turned to Bellyra and knelt. Blood ran down his cheeks. His face was so pale that it reminded her of a fish's belly.

"My apologies, Your Highness," Owaen stammered. "For losing my temper like this in front of you. I meant no insult. Ye gods, can you find it in your heart to forgive me?"

If she didn't, Bellyra realized, Prince Maryn would have him flogged.

"Of course I forgive you," she said hastily. "Do get up, Owaen! Branoic, I forgive you, too. But I'd much prefer never to see such again."

"My lady is too generous." Branoic ducked his head in

her direction. "I'll do my best not to shame myself in front of her again."

"Good. Don't. And now you owe me an explanation. What eagles?"

"It was my father's blazon, Your Highness," Branoic said. "Not that I was ever a legitimate son of his. But when I joined the silver daggers, Owaen had me take it off my gear. It looked like his mark, says he—that falcon he puts on everything he owns."

Owaen crossed his arms over his chest and glowered at the cobbles.

"And now my husband's given you an eagle blazon?" Bellyra thought for a moment. "Well, make them a different color. That's what the heralds did with the wyvern device, isn't it? The usurper's clan used green for theirs, and so we took the same wyvern but made it red."

"My lady is as clever as she is beautiful," Nevyn said. "Branoic?"

"A wise thought, Your Highness, and do it I will. Here. Owaen's falcon is red. What if I have a silver eagle? And I can have the heralds turn its head in the opposite direction, too."

"Owaen?" Nevyn turned to the captain.

"That will suit, my lord." Owaen looked up at last. "My apologies to you again, Your Highness."

Bellyra collected her pages with a wave and turned to go. In the doorway to the main broch Lilli stood shading her eyes with one hand while she watched the scene in the ward. Yet when she saw Bellyra looking her way, she spun around and ran, disappearing into the shadows inside. Poor child! the princess thought. She's still terrified of me, and here I would have liked her so much if only she weren't Maryn's mistress.

"You've both had a silver dagger's luck," Maddyn said. "The prince could have had you both flogged for this, fighting out in the ward like a pair of drunken bondmen."

"True spoken," Owaen mumbled. He was gingerly exploring his injured eye with dirty fingers. "I didn't know the princess would be right there."

"You might have looked." Maddyn turned to Branoic. "You too."

Branoic shrugged and refused to look at him.

"Owaen?" Nevyn put in. "You'd better stop poking at that eye. Let the chirurgeon look at it. Tell him I said to make you up a poultice to draw the swelling off."

"I will." Owaen hesitated, then turned on his heel and strode off.

"Very well, lads," Nevyn said. "I'd best be getting back to my chamber. I—" He stopped at the sight of Lilli, trotting across the cobblestones toward them. "So you've come down? No doubt you're worried about your betrothed."

"I am, my lord," Lilli said, "if you'll forgive me."

"Of course. The memory work can wait till later."

Nevyn left Branoic in Lilli's care and strode across the ward to the side broch that housed his tower room. He wondered if Lilli realized that Branoic had as much of a gift for dweomer as she did. Once the wars were done, and they married, he was planning on teaching both of them. Normally a dweomermaster could take only one apprentice at a time, but the circumstances were hardly normal. He owed Branoic a deep debt from an earlier life, when the person who was a burly silver dagger now had been not only a woman, but Nevyn's betrothed, Brangwen. *I failed her so badly then,* he thought. *May the Great Ones grant that I may redeem myself now!* Yet even though the thought carried the force of a prayer, no omen came to him, as if the matter lay beyond the power of the Great Ones to control.

Up in the big half-round room of the women's hall, warmth and comfort reigned. When Bellyra walked in, her maidservant took her cloak, curtsied, and hurried off to the bedchamber. Near the hearth, where a fire crackled, the princess's serving women rose to greet her. Through the wickerwork partition that separated the hall from the sleeping rooms, she could hear the nursemaid's voice, singing the two little princes to sleep for their nap.

"Your Highness, you look exhausted," Degwa said. "Do

you think it's wise, the way you climb around the towers and suchlike?"

"Most unwise, I'm sure," Bellyra said. "But it's better than brooding about the baby and wondering what's going to happen to me once it's born."

Degwa winced. Bellyra took her usual chair close to the fire, but she sat spraddled, propped up by cushions. Degwa sat opposite. Elyssa brought a cushioned stool for the princess's feet, then fetched a chair for herself and placed it beside.

"My poor highness!" Degwa said. "You look so uncomfortable."

"I am," Bellyra said. "And tired, too."

"It's all that climbing around in the dun," Elyssa joined in. "Do you truly think you should, my lady?"

"You could quite wear yourself out," Degwa said.

"You're both right enough," Bellyra said. "But it gets tedious, sitting around all day. I don't know what I'm going to do when I finish my book."

"That troubles me, truly," Elyssa said. "But mayhap you'll think up another one. About the Holy City itself, say."

"It's the oldest place in all Deverry, after all," Degwa put in. "There must be splendid tales about it."

"And all the legends, too," Elyssa went on. "About King Bran and how he saw the white sow and all of that. It would make a lovely beginning."

"Now there's a good idea!" Bellyra suddenly smiled. She could just see how to do the opening pages. "My thanks."

Elyssa and Degwa glanced at each other, then away, as if perhaps they had planned this suggestion together. She should be grateful to them, Bellyra supposed. Yet she felt like snarling because they had reminded her of the birthing madness, prowling at the edge of her mind just as Braemys's army prowled at the borders of her husband's lands. It will be different this time, she told herself. She wished she could believe it.

The silence grew heavy around them. With a little

shake of her head, Degwa stood up, stepping toward the hearth. In the firelight a silver brooch pinned to the left shoulder of her dress sparkled with a long glint of light.

"There's not a lot of firewood left, Your Highness. Shall I send one of the servants for more?"

"Please do," Bellyra said. "Or wait! What's that on your dress, Decci?"

"A little gift." Degwa smiled, glancing away. "From an admirer."

"Not Councillor Oggyn?" Bellyra clapped her hands together. "It's quite pretty."

"So it is," Elyssa put in. "Is that real glass set in it?"

"It is." Degwa's face had turned a pleasant shade of pink.

Elyssa and Bellyra exchanged a pointed glance that made Degwa giggle.

"If only he were noble-born!" Degwa said. "As it is, I can hardly count him a true suitor."

"Oh, now here!" Bellyra said briskly. "After all the fine service he's paid our prince, who would scorn you if you should marry him?"

Degwa blushed again. She was no longer a lass, but certainly not an old woman, though she'd been widowed for many years now. With her dark curly hair and fine dark eyes, she was attractive, as well, despite her weak mouth and weaker chin.

"I'll take pity on you, Decci," Elyssa said smiling, "and talk of somewhat else. Speaking of jewelry reminds me, Your Highness. I met Otho the smith down in the great hall this morning, after you'd left. He asked for news of you and sends his humble greetings."

"How kind of him. I hope you told him I was well."

"I did."

"Good. I've always had an easy time of it with the babies. Until afterwards."

"Oh, don't!" Elyssa leaned over and laid her hand on Bellyra's arm. "Don't think about it. Just don't."

"You're right. I'll try not to."

Bellyra wasn't able to say why this mention of Otho

gave her the idea, but it occurred to her that afternoon to give Maddyn a token of some sort, a little trinket such as queens often bestowed upon favored courtiers, to take to the wars and bring him luck. That evening, she had Otho summoned and met him outside the door to the women's hall, while her serving women stood with her for propriety's sake.

"I want to give my bard a pin to match that silver ring," Bellyra told the smith. "One with a rose design."

"Easy enough to do, Your Highness," Otho said. "I've still got a bit of silver left over from the—er well, let's just say I found it, like, after your husband took Dun Deverry."

"I don't want to know any details."

"Just as well, Your Highness. I'll get right to work on that."

"My thanks, good smith."

All smiles, Otho bowed, then stumped down the corridor to the stairway. Degwa waited till he was well out of earshot.

"Your bard, Your Highness?" Degwa raised an eyebrow.

"Well, my husband's, truly, but then, my husband was the one who set him guarding me."

"Of course." All at once Degwa blushed. "Er, ah, I'll just see if the servant girls have swept out your chamber. I asked them rather a long while ago, and they'd best have done it properly."

Degwa turned and rushed back into the women's hall. Bellyra and Elyssa exchanged a weary smile, then followed her inside.

On a wet chilly morning Prince Maryn and his councillors assembled in the main ward. With them stood young Prince Riddmar, Maryn's half brother, who would receive the Cerrmor rhan when Maryn became king. He was a lean child, Riddmar, blonde and grey-eyed like his brother, with the same sunny smile. At Nevyn's urging, Maryn had taken the boy on as an apprentice in the craft of ruling. Riddmar accompanied the prince everywhere these days, listening and watching as Maryn prepared to claim the high kingship of all Deverry.

This particular morning Maryn was sending off a message to the rebel lord, Braemys. For one last time the prince was offering him a pardon if he would only swear fealty—a small price, in the eyes of the prince and his councillors both. Gavlyn, the leader of the prince's heralds, knelt at Maryn's feet; he would be taking this message himself, rather than entrusting it to one of his men.

"His guards are waiting by the gates, my liege," Nevyn said. "I've taken the liberty of providing our herald with an escort. The roads aren't safe."

"I thought Braemys had taken all the bandits into his army," Maryn said.

"He offered. Who knows how many took him up on it?"

"A good point. They may be as suspicious of him as he is of me."

"True spoken." Nevyn held up the long silver tube containing the prince's message and waved it vaguely at the sky. "I'd pray to the gods and ask them to make him take your pardon, but it would be a waste of breath."

A fortnight later Nevyn's remark proved true when the herald returned. After the noon meal Nevyn was sitting at the table of honor with the two princes when Gavlyn strode into the great hall, still carrying his beribboned staff. Maryn rose and beckoned him over.

"I'm too impatient to send a page to summon him," Maryn remarked, grinning. "Once I'm king I'll have to mind my formalities, I suppose."

Nevyn nodded his agreement but said nothing. He was watching Gavlyn make his way through the crowded tables. Gavlyn walked fast, snapping at any servants in his path; he was scowling, Nevyn realized, more furious than he'd ever seen the man. As he passed, the men at each table fell silent so that it seemed he worked some dweomer spell to turn them all mute as he passed. By the time he reached the table of honor, the entire great hall, riders, servants, even the dogs, sat waiting in a deathly stillness to hear his news. When he started to kneel, Maryn waved him up.

"Stand, if you'd not mind it," the prince said. "Your voice will carry better."

"Very well, my liege." Gavlyn turned toward the waiting crowd and cleared his throat.

Maryn picked up his tankard of ale and took a casual sip. Gavlyn raised his staff.

"Lord Braemys, regent to Lwvan, Gwerbret Cantrae in his minority, sends his greetings and this message," Gavlyn paused, as if steadying himself. "He says: my ward, Lwvan of the Boar clan, is the closest living kin of King Olaen, once rightful high king of all Deverry, now dead, murdered by the usurper or mayhap his men. Therefore, Lwvan, Gwerbret Cantrae, is the true heir to Dun Deverry. Lord Braemys requests that Maryn, Gwerbret Cerrmor, keep the holding in good order till Lwvan rides to claim it at Beltane."

Maryn's hand tightened so hard on the tankard that his knuckles went white. "Is there any more?" Maryn's voice held steady.

"None, my liege. I thought it quite enough."

Gavlyn lowered the staff and pounded it once upon the floor. His audience burst out talking, and rage flooded the great hall. The riders were cursing and swearing, the servants gabbled together, the message went round and round, repeated in disbelief. With a final bow, Gavlyn left the prince's presence. Maryn rose, glanced at Nevyn, then strode off, heading for the staircase. Young Riddmar got up and ran after him. More slowly Nevyn followed, and Oggyn joined him at the foot of the stairs.

"The gall," Oggyn snapped. "My prince—"

Maryn pushed past him and started up, taking the stairs two at a time, too fast for Riddmar to keep up. Nevyn let Oggyn and the boy go ahead of him and paused, glancing around the crowd. He finally saw Owaen and Maddyn, standing at the rider's hearth. Getting their attention was even harder, but at last Maddyn did look his way.

"You and Owaen!" Nevyn called out. "Come with me!"

They found the prince in the council chamber, standing at the head of a long table with Oggyn to one side.

Afternoon sun spread over the polished wood and gilded the parchment maps lying upon it. In one smooth motion Maryn drew his table dagger and stabbed it into a map, right through the mark that signified Cantrae.

"That arrogant little pissproud bastard," Maryn said, his voice still level. "I'll have his head on a pike for this."

No one spoke. With a shrug the prince pulled his dagger free and sheathed it, then turned to them with his usual sunny smile.

"No doubt Lord Braemys planned to vex me," Maryn said. "An angry man takes foolish risks."

"Just so, my liege." Oggyn bowed to him. "Most well said."

"What gripes my soul the hardest," Maryn went on, "was that reference to poor little Olaen. Ye gods, if I ever find the man who murdered that child, I'll hang him!"

Nevyn turned his attention to Oggyn, who was struggling to keep his face bland and composed despite its being beaded with sweat. Fortunately for Oggyn, Prince Maryn turned away and started for the door.

"I need some time alone, good councillors," Maryn said, "to compose myself. We shall hold council later this afternoon."

The door slammed behind him. When Riddmar started after, Nevyn caught the lad by the shoulder and kept him back. Oggyn caught his breath with a sob that drew him a curious look from the young prince.

"Ah, er well," Oggyn said, "I never know what to say when His Highness flies into one of his tempers. I'll confess it frightens me."

"Me too," Riddmar said.

"He does it so rarely, is why," Nevyn said. "Well, silver daggers, I'm sorry I took you away from your meal. Prince Riddmar? I suggest you go with your brother's captains."

"I will, my lord," Riddmar said. "Owaen's teaching me swordcraft, anyway. We could have a lesson."

"Good idea," Owaen said. "Maddo, come on."

The silver daggers left, taking the boy with them. Once the door had shut behind them, Oggyn crumpled into a chair and covered his white face with both hands. "If we had let little Olaen live," he said into his palms, "the wars would never have ended."

"I know that as well as you do," Nevyn said.

With a groan Oggyn lowered his hands and stared at the floor. Nevyn itched to point out that Oggyn should have talked the prince round to a legal execution rather than poisoning the lad, but he held his tongue. He had chosen to keep silence at the time. Breaking it now would be unbearably self-righteous.

"We'd best get back to the great hall," Nevyn said. "We both have our duties to attend to."

In her sunny chamber, Lilli was sitting at her table and studying the dweomer book when the prince strode in. He slammed the door, then stood leaning against it with his hands behind his back. He'd set his mouth tight, and his eyes had turned as cold as storm clouds. Lilli shut the book and rose to curtsy to him.

"What troubles your heart, my prince?"

"Your cursed cousin, Braemys." Maryn paused, looking her over with cold eyes. "Your betrothed."

"He's no longer my betrothed."

"He was once. What I wonder is if he ever claimed his rights."

"Never! I never bedded him."

"Unlike—" Maryn broke the saying off.

His eyes had turned cold as steel in winter. Involuntarily Lilli took a step back. He neither moved nor spoke, merely studied her face as if he would flay it to see the soul beneath.

"Were you happy when they betrothed you?" Maryn said at last.

"He was better than the other choice my uncles gave me, was all. Uncle Tibryn wanted to marry me off to Lord Nantyn."

At that Maryn relaxed. "If I were a lass," he said, "I'd marry a kitchen lad before I'd marry Nantyn."

"And so would I have."

"No doubt Braemys looked like a prince by comparison." Maryn pried himself off the door and walked over to her. "But he's refusing my offer of fealty."

"I was rather afraid he would."

"Me too. Of course."

Maryn hesitated, considering her, then put his hands either side of her face. "Do you love me, Lilli?"

"I do."

"With all your heart?"

"Of course."

Maryn bent his head and kissed her. Lilli slipped her arms around his neck and let him take another. When they were together, it seemed to her that she'd never loved anyone or anything as much as she loved her prince.

"Can you stay for a while?" she whispered. "Please?"

"I shouldn't. I meant to ask you about Braemys, is all. Ye gods, I feel half-mad at times, when I think of you."

For a moment she nearly wept, simply because he was leaving, but he bent his head and kissed her.

"I'll return in the evening, my lady," he whispered. "Hold me in your heart till then."

Before Lilli could speak he turned and ran out of the room. The door slammed so hard behind him that it trembled. Despite the spring sun pouring in the window, she felt cold. It's like I'm half-mad, too, she thought. All at once she no longer wanted to be alone.

Lilli left her chamber and headed for the kitchen hut out back of the broch complex. Since she was terrified of meeting Bellyra face-to-face, she'd taken to begging her meals from the cook at odd moments of the day, but the only way out of the central broch lay through the great hall. Lilli paused on the spiral stairs, saw no sign of Bellyra, then crept down, keeping to the shadows near the wall. When she reached the last step, Degwa trotted up, so preoccupied that she nearly ran into Lilli. On the serving woman's dress gleamed a silver brooch, set with glass.

"Pardon," Degwa said briskly.

"Granted," Lilli said. "How fares the princess?"

Degwa looked elsewhere and flounced off without saying a word more. Lilli choked back tears and rushed outside. She was hoping to find Nevyn in his chamber, but just as she reached the side broch she met him coming out, dressed in his best grey brigga and a clean shirt.

"What's wrong?" Nevyn said. "You look ill."

"I feel ill," Lilli said. "But not from my wretched lungs, my lord. It was only a woman's matter. I don't want to keep you. I can see you're off on some important business or suchlike."

"I just came back from a visit to the temple of Bel, if you mean these fancy clothes. Now—what's so wrong?"

"It's Degwa. She just snubbed me in the great hall, but that's not the worst of it. Have you noticed the brooch she's wearing today?"

"I did at that." Nevyn looked puzzled. "What of it?"

"It belonged to my mother."

Nevyn pursed his lips as if he were going to whistle.

"Someone must have looted it when the siege ended," Lilli went on. "And then given it to Decci."

"I'll wager I know who it was," Nevyn said. "Councillor Oggyn kept a number of your mother's things. He returned the dweomer book to me, but no doubt he kept whatever else he looted. Do you want the brooch back?"

"I don't, but do you think it might be cursed or suchlike?"

"It might, at that. It's a nasty thing to speak ill of the dead, but I fear me your mother brings out the worst in me. There are certain workings that can charge an ordinary thing as if it were a talisman. That blasted curse tablet is just such a thing, as no doubt you realize. Your mother might well have set a weaker spell on her jewelry to do harm to any who might steal it."

"I see. But I don't dare ask Decci for it."

"Of course not. Leave it to me, but I can't do it immediately. I'm going to attend upon the prince for a brief while. We'll be writing out the formal declaration of the summer's fighting. Tomorrow at dawn the messengers go out to announce the muster."

"I see." For a moment Lilli felt like vomiting out of simple terror. "Oh ye gods, I hope this summer sees the end to it."

"So do I." Nevyn sighed with a toss of his head. "So do I."

The prince had sent out the call for his vassals to muster for war so often that the meeting went swiftly. Nevyn suggested a final flourish of words, the scribe wrote out the first copy, Nevyn read it aloud, and the prince approved it. Nevyn and Maryn left the scribes at their work of copying the message several dozen times and strolled together out in the ward. The sun was hanging low in the sky and sending a tangle of shadows over the cobbles, and the warm day was turning pleasantly cool. Prince and councillor climbed up to the catwalks that circled the main wall of the inner ward and leaned onto it, looking down the long slope of the grassy hill.

"I need your advice on somewhat," Maryn said. "I didn't want to ask publicly and embarrass the lad, but it's about young Riddmar."

"Let me guess. He wants to ride to war with us."

"Just that." Maryn turned his head and grinned at him. "I like his spirit, but I don't want him dead before he's barely grown."

"A very good point, Your Highness. We need him in Cerrmor. In fact, I suggest you tell him just that."

"His safety's too important to the continuing peace in the kingdom? Somewhat like that?"

"Exactly. It has the virtue of being true. I remember you at about the same age. Whenever someone told you you were too young to do a thing, you wanted to do it three times as badly."

Maryn nodded, smiling in a rueful sort of way. "My old tutor's still giving me grand advice," he said at last. "My thanks."

"Most welcome, I'm sure. I have to confess that I'm not looking forward to riding out, myself."

"Doubtless not. I'll be glad of the distraction."

"Distraction?"

Maryn leaned onto the top of the wall and looked out into nothing. Nevyn waited, considered asking again, then decided that Maryn would tell him about his troubles in his own good time.

When he left the prince, Nevyn went straight to the women's hall, which his great age allowed him to enter. He was lucky enough to find Bellyra alone, sitting on a chair at the window. She'd put her feet up on a footstool and sat spraddled with her hands resting on her swollen belly.

"You're going to have that child soon, from the look of it," Nevyn said.

"The midwife says another turning of the moon, at least—I'd wager on two, myself. It's so big it must be another beastly son. Do sit down, Nevyn. What brings you to me?"

Nevyn perched on the wide stone of the windowsill. "Where's Degwa at the moment?" he said.

"I don't know. If you'll summon a page, I'll have him look for her."

"No need. I wanted to talk with you about her, you see. Or rather, about that brooch Councillor Oggyn gave her."

"You've seen that? It's quite pretty, isn't it?"

"It also belonged to Lady Merodda."

"Who? Oh, wait—you mean the sorceress who poisoned people." Bellyra hesitated briefly. "Lilli's mother."

"Just so. I hate to bring Lilli up—"

"Don't apologize! I'm truly sorry I got so angry with her. It's hardly her fault. Maryn's very charming, and she's very young." She leaned her head against the high back of the chair and seemed to be studying the ceiling beams. "Men are just like that, I suppose."

Nevyn made a noncommittal noise.

"But about that brooch." Bellyra looked at him again. "Does Lilli want it back?"

"Not in the least. I'm just afraid there might be a curse upon it."

"Like that other wretched thing? The lead tablet?"

"Somewhat like that. Not as strong, surely, but even a little evil is too much. I can probably break it, the spell I mean, if Lady Degwa will let me have it for a night or so. That is, if it truly is ensorceled."

Nevyn had his chance to examine the brooch in but a little while, when Degwa returned to the women's hall with a basket of fresh-baked bread and a bowl of butter for the princess. She curtsied to Nevyn as well as she could with her hands full, then set her burdens down on a small table near Bellyra's chair.

"Would you like some of this bread, Lord Nevyn?" Degwa said.

"I wouldn't, but my thanks."

Degwa drew her table dagger and began to cut a chunk off the round loaf. "Your Highness? It's quite warm and nice."

"It smells wonderful," Bellyra said. "Slather on the butter, please. Don't spare it."

Degwa smiled and did as she'd been asked. Once the princess had her chunk of bread, Degwa pulled up another chair and sat down, facing Nevyn.

"Her Highness is looking quite well," Nevyn said. "You and Elyssa are taking splendid care of her."

"My thanks, my lord. We do try."

"Despite my nasty habit of climbing all over the dun?" Bellyra joined in, smiling.

"Er, well, Your Highness, I wouldn't call it nasty. Worrisome, mayhap."

Bellyra laughed and took another bite of bread.

"That's a lovely brooch," Nevyn said to Degwa. "May I see it?"

"Certainly." Degwa unpinned it. "It was a gift from an admirer."

When she handed it over, Nevyn examined it: a flat riband of silver, twisted into a knot and set with two pieces of ruby-red glass. The feel of it bothered him, and while the two women chatted, he opened his dweomer sight. Although metals have no auras, of course, it exuded a faint greyish mist, particularly thick around the glass sets. When he turned it over, he saw a small mark graved at one end of the band: the letter A, the first letter of the word for boar. He'd seen it used before as a clan mark for the Boars of Cantrae.

Although he disliked the idea of spoiling Degwa's pleasure in the gift, he valued her safety more. He shut down the dweomer sight.

"How very odd," Nevyn said. "This seems to have belonged to Lilli's mother at one time."

"What, my lord?" Degwa leaned forward. "How can you tell?"

"Her mark is on the back. It's quite small."

Degwa took the brooch back and made a great show of looking for the mark, but like most women of her class, she'd weakened her eyes with long years of fine needlework. At length she gave it up with a shrug.

"Well, if you say so, my lord," she said, and her disappointment trembled in her voice. "I do wish it hadn't. We've heard far too much about that woman from the servants since we've been here."

"I could be wrong," Nevyn said. "Would you mind if I took it to show Lilli? She'll know for certain."

"If it has the Boar mark upon it, I shan't want it." Degwa held it up, then tossed it to Nevyn. "Have the silversmith melt it down, for all I care."

"Now here," Bellyra joined in. "It's still lovely, and Oggyn—"

"I shall talk to the councillor about this," Degwa said. "I must say it doesn't speak well of the man, that he'd give a woman friend a gift of battle loot and from her long-sworn enemies at that."

"Oh come now," Bellyra said. "I've got lots of lovely things that Maryn got in ransom from some lord or another."

"I assure Her Highness that I meant no insult." Degwa turned slightly pink in the cheeks. "But I'd rather not accept cast-off jewelry from the Boar clan's sty."

With that Degwa got up and swept out, leaving Nevyn with the brooch. When the door slammed behind her, he winced.

"My apologies, Your Highness," Nevyn said. "I seem to have botched that thoroughly."

"Better than letting her wear a thing with a curse on it," Bellyra said. "I take it must be cursed, or you wouldn't have made up that story about wanting Lilli to see it."

"Just so. That's what I get for lying."

"Not exactly lying. Stretching a point, mayhap. But poor Decci! She's really quite demented when it comes to the Boars."

That evening, when Nevyn was leaving the great hall after dinner, Oggyn followed him out, pulling on his beard and harrumphing under his breath. They walked a little way out into the open ward, where they couldn't be overheard.

"A word with you, if I may," Oggyn said.

"Certainly. Did Degwa tell you about the brooch?"

"She most assuredly did. I fear me I've greatly displeased her."

Although Nevyn was expecting the councillor to be angry with him, in the twilight Oggyn looked mostly miserable. He shoved his hands into his brigga pockets and kicked at a loose cobblestone with the toe of his boot.

"I'm sorry," Nevyn said. "But the brooch has some sort of spell on it, and she couldn't go on wearing it."

"By the gods! I never thought of that." Oggyn looked up sharply. "That Merodda woman—"

"Exactly. After this, if I might make a suggestion, could you consult with me before you give away any more of the lady's possessions? They're yours by right of conquest, but just in case—"

"I understand, never fear! I'll do that." Oggyn sighed heavily. "The true trouble is, I'm always short up for coin, and even if I had any, where would I find the smith to make Lady Degwa some new trinket?"

"Otho is quite a bit more skilled than any Cerrmor silversmith."

"I do not traffic with silver daggers." Oggyn's voice turned cold. "Good eve. My thanks for the warning."

Oggyn turned on his heel and strode away, head held high. Ye gods! Nevyn thought. A matched pair!

Nevyn took the brooch up to Lilli's chamber, where he found her sitting at her table. In front of her the open dweomer book lay in a pool of candlelight from a silver candelabrum.

"Is this enough light for you to read?" Nevyn said.

"Not truly." Lilli paused to rub her eyes with both hands. "It's given me a bit of a headache." She shut the book and put it to one side. "What brings you to me?"

"I thought you might want to see this brooch. It does have some sort of weak warding spell upon it."

When he laid it upon the table, Lilli leaned forward to study it, but she left her hands in her lap. "I remember my mother wearing that," she said at length. "It was a gift from Uncle Tibryn."

"Can you see the dweomer upon it?"

"I can. It looks like grease, dirty kitchen grease."

"Ah. I see it as a sort of grey mist. Do you remember what I told you about dark dweomer casting shadows?"

"I do. And how the shadows will look different to different minds. It's a good thing you got this away from Degwa. It must be nasty, though I can't say what it would have done."

"No more can I, but let's be rid of it."

Nevyn raised one hand above his head, then summoned the silver light. In his mind he saw it flow down from the astral like a trickle of water. He concentrated on the image, focused it, strengthened it with his imagination, then with a simple word of power brought it through to the physical. It swirled around his hand and burned like a torch, though without smoke. He heard Lilli gasp and knew she'd seen it.

"Begone!" Nevyn snapped his hand down and pointed at the brooch. Silver fire poured over silver metal, then vanished.

"It's lifted!" Lilli said. "The shadow, I mean."

"Good. It was a weak spell, so it cost very little to banish it. Unlike that wretched curse tablet."

"Just so." Lilli reached for the brooch, then stopped. "May I?"

"By all means. Do you want it back? Degwa refuses to have it, since it once belonged to the Boar clan."

Lilli picked up the brooch and held it up to the candle-light. It gleamed as if it had been newly polished with ash and river sand. Most likely Merodda had cast the spell herself, Nevyn decided. Creating the curse tablet, however, had lain beyond her skill. Only a master of evil could have ensorceled that.

"I think I do want it," Lilli said at last. "Not to wear, but to keep. There were times, you know, when I felt that my mother did love me. She gave me to Lady Bevyan to foster, and she made sure that Uncle Tibryn wouldn't marry me off to Lord Nantyn, if naught else."

"Then keep it in remembrance of her better nature," Nevyn said. "Every soul has one, and it deserves a little honor."

Five days after the call to muster, the first of Maryn's vassals rode in to Dun Deverry. The gathering of the full contingent took some weeks, as Maryn's most loyal—and most prosperous—vassals lived far to the south on the sea-coast. With the lords and their warbands came carts, driven by servants and piled high with provisions, as each vassal owed Maryn not only men for his army but the food for three months' campaigning—not such an easy thing to raise, here in the ravaged north. The long years of civil war had starved a good many farm families and killed their sons in battle as well.

As the fighting men arrived, Branoic started keeping a count by the twenties on a bit of smooth board, but when he got up to a thousand, he stopped. Councillor Oggyn would be doing a better job of it, as he remarked to Maddyn.

"Just so," Maddyn said. "The prince must be happy to see such a good turnout."

"No doubt," Branoic said. "Well, we're cursed near to

the victory. That always inspires a little extra loyalty among the noble-born."

They shared a laugh. Since Maryn could not officially ennoble Branoic until he was proclaimed king, Branoic still lived among the silver daggers, and they were sitting together in the barracks on a blustery morning. As they talked, Branoic was polishing his mail shirt with a bit of rag. All around them other men were working on their gear: cleaning mail, replacing leather straps or wooden toggles wherever they needed fixing, talking together in low voices about the fighting ahead, or boasting about their exploits of the summer past.

"Are you looking forward to riding out?" Maddyn said.

"Not truly," Branoic said. "Odd of me. I used to be eager enough to get free of winter quarters."

"Well, you've got somewhat to stay for now."

"Lilli, you mean?" Branoic concentrated on threading the rag through a rusty ring. "If our prince ever lets her go."

Maddyn said nothing for a long moment. Branoic looked up to find him solemn.

"He promised you," the bard said at length, "that you'd be wed once he had the victory. Our prince doesn't break his promises."

"He's never done it before." Branoic paused, groping for words. "But it's like he's half-mad or somewhat. Lilli tells me he's starting to frighten her. He's jealous, like, and all the time."

Maddyn muttered something foul under his breath.

"And him with his own lady, as beautiful and sweet as ever a man could want." Branoic felt his bitterness rise in his throat like bile. "It gripes my soul, Maddo lad, if you don't mind me saying it."

"Not at all." Maddyn seemed to be measuring each word. "His lady's devoted to him, as well."

"She is that." Branoic was about to continue his tirade, but he could see that Maddyn looked oddly distracted—no doubt all this talk of women was boring him. "Ah well, I don't mean to croak like a frog, the same blasted chorus over and over. We made our bargain, the prince and me, and I've no call to be thinking he'll break it till he does."

Maddyn was about to reply, but from outside they suddenly heard shouting and cheers. Owaen got up and went to look out the window. "It's Glasloc!" he called out. "Gwerbret Daeryc's held loyal to the prince!"

The silver daggers cheered as well, whether anyone could hear them or not, then went back to their work. Maddyn, however, neither spoke nor moved, merely sat staring out at nothing.

"Here," Branoic said, "are you ill?"

"In a way, truly." Maddyn turned to him with an odd twisted smile. "In a way."

Once again Branoic wondered if he was understanding what Maddyn meant. Since his usual way of dealing with things he couldn't understand was to shrug them off, he changed the subject.

Yet speaking of Lilli had brought his feelings for her to mind, and in but a little while he got up and left the barracks. Since Daeryc had just ridden in, no doubt Prince Maryn would be safely occupied by greeting his guest in the great hall. Sure enough, Daeryc's riders and their horses filled the main ward with confusion. Near the gates a line of carts stood waiting to be unloaded. Servants rushed around, leading horses away, inviting the men inside to drink, and in general sorting things out as best they could.

Branoic left the ward proper and ducked around a half-destroyed wall. He knew a back way into the central broch complex. He was picking his way through the clutter of servant huts and animal pens when he caught sight of Councillor Oggyn, leaning against the wall of a shed ever so casually, as if he always took the air among the chickens and the onions. Branoic stopped and waited; Oggyn never looked his way. Slowly Branoic took a few steps to the side until he stood half-concealed behind a big pile of stones kept in case of siege.

Not long after he saw a grey-haired man hobbling along with the aid of a long stick. He wore a stained, torn linen shirt and a filthy pair of brigga that once might have been grey, but for all that he looked like a beggar, Oggyn strode forward to meet him. They spoke just loudly enough for Branoic to catch part of the conversation. Apparently the lame fellow wished to speak with Prince Maryn, and apparently Oggyn was telling him that such was impossible. At length the man produced a silver coin from the pouch at his belt. Oggyn became all smiles as he took the coin; he bit it, then slid it into the pouch at his own belt. For a moment more they talked together; then Oggyn strode off back in the direction of the main broch complex. The other man wiped tears from his face on his dirty sleeve, then began to hobble off. Branoic left his hiding place and ran after him.

"Wait! Good sir!" Branoic caught up with him near the kitchen hut. "You've just been robbed."

Uncomprehending, he stared up at Branoic with rheumy eyes.

"The prince will listen to anyone that comes to him," Branoic said. "You didn't need to give Oggyn a copper, much less a blasted silver piece." He glanced around and saw the councillor lurking in the doorway to the side tower. "Slimy Oggo! Get yourself over here!"

With a toss of his head Oggyn disappeared inside. Branoic laid a friendly hand on the old man's shoulder.

"Just come with me," he said. "We'll get that silver piece back for you at dinner tonight."

"My thanks, my profound thanks," the fellow said. "It's all the coin I have in the world."

Whether or not Maryn officially reigned as king, his decisions were the only justice that Dun Deverry had. Every night after dinner he lingered in the great hall so that suppliants could come to him with disputes and complaints they wished settled. And we'll have a fine show tonight, Branoic thought. Slimy Oggo's gone too far this time.

Just that morning, Otho the silversmith had finished the silver token for Maddyn, and Princess Bellyra took care to present it to her bard as openly as she could. With the muster nearly complete, close to a hundred lords ate in the great hall at the tables of honor. Servants had combed the dun and crammed every table and bench they could find into the riders' side of the hall, but still, most of the men from the warbands ate outside. The prince's silver daggers, however, stayed in his presence, eating just beyond the ranks of the noble-born.

As Maryn's wife, Bellyra ate beside him and shared his trencher. That particular evening, before she and her women withdrew to the quiet safety of their hall, Bellyra took the pin from her kirtle.

"I nearly forgot," she said to Maryn. "I've got a little gift for your bard, to thank him for being so patient all winter."

"Good." Maryn held out his hand. "May I?"

"By all means." Bellyra gave him the pin. "It's awfully nice, I thought."

"It is indeed." Maryn held the slender silver rose, barely an inch long, twixt thumb and forefinger. "Must be Otho's work."

"It is. He looted some silver when you took the dun. Er, or I should say, he miraculously found some silver that no one was using."

Grinning, Maryn handed it back, then got up, glancing around the hall. At length he gestured to one of the waiting pages.

"Maddyn the bard's sitting over by the front door," the prince said. "Go fetch him for me."

With a bow the lad trotted off. Just as Maryn sat back down again, Branoic strode in the back door and headed for the prince's chair. Limping along after him came a grey-haired man, dressed in a linen shirt and wool brigga made of cloth that had been once fine, but now was all frayed and patched. When Branoic knelt at Maryn's side, the elderly man started to follow suit, but the stick he'd been leaning on nearly tripped him. Maryn swung round in his chair and caught his elbow in one hand.

"Don't kneel," the prince said. "My rank can give way to your age, sir."

The prince let him go, then stood up. The man bowed as best he could with both hands clutched on his stick.

"My thanks, my prince." The fellow was stammering. "I have a matter to lay before you, you see, and—"

"Two matters," Branoic interrupted. "Your Highness, Councillor Oggyn demanded a coin from this fellow for the privilege of coming to you for justice."

"Oh by the gods!" Maryn snarled. He rose and spun around, looking out over the hall, then bellowed at the top of his lungs. "Oggyn! Get over here!"

With a tight little smile Branoic rose, dusting off the knees of his brigga, and escorted the old man and his stick out of the way. Bellyra twisted round in her chair and saw Oggyn making his way across the hall. Like a hound with chicken feathers still clinging to his muzzle, Oggyn slunk through the tables. The talk and jesting among the lords died down as they turned, a little puzzled, to see what the prince was up to. Bellyra also noticed Maddyn and the page, stopping a little distance away to wait their turn for the prince's attention. At last Oggyn reached the table of honor and knelt at the prince's feet.

"Branoic tells me you extorted money again," the prince said.

"My liege, I never did such a thing!" Oggyn's voice swooped on an obvious lie. "Truly, I—"

"Can you look me in the face and deny it?"

Oggyn started to speak, then merely sighed and shook his head no.

"I told you, no more of this." Maryn's voice was level but cold. "My justice is free to all who ask. Do you understand that?"

"I do, my prince." Oggyn spoke so softly that Bellyra could hardly hear him. "I welter in apologies. I beg your pardon most humbly."

"Give him the money back," Maryn said.

Slowly and with trembling hands Oggyn fumbled with the pouch at his belt. His lips trembled as well, and his face had turned scarlet all the way up and over his bald skull. When he held out a silver piece, the suppliant snatched it from his sweaty fingers. Oggyn slumped down and stared at the prince's boots.

"Good," Maryn went on. "Now then, what shall we do with you? I made you a threat, the last time I caught you grafting. I think me I'd best live up to my word."

"Not that, my prince." Oggyn looked up, his lips working, his hands trembling. "I beg you—"

"It behooves a noble-born man to carry out what he threatens, councillor, lest his men think him weak-willed. Maddyn! Where's your harp? There's a song I want you to sing."

"My lord." Bellyra got up and laid a hand on the prince's arm. "The poor man! Isn't it a bit much?"

Maryn hesitated, glanced at Oggyn, who was studying the straw on the floor, then back to her. "It's only what he deserves, but your kind heart becomes you, my lady."

With a little sigh Bellyra took her chair again. For a few moments confusion swirled around the table of honor. Nevyn appeared from somewhere and rushed forward to speak with the suppliant. Maddyn and a Cerrmor bard talked earnestly; then the bard's apprentice hurried forward and handed Maddyn a small lap harp. Through it all Oggyn stayed kneeling, folding over himself with his face as low to the floor as he could get it. At length Gwerbret Daeryc, who had been dining across the table from the princess, got up and pulled his chair out of the way so that Maddyn could climb up onto the table and sing.

For a moment or two Maddyn fiddled with the harp while the great hall gradually fell silent. Bellyra studied his face, carefully impassive. She should have known, she felt, that he would refrain from gloating. Maddyn looked up with a polite smile and a nod for the prince, cleared his throat, and began to sing the song of Farmer Owaen and the fox. At first the cheerful little melody and the subject matter made it sound like some sort of children's song, and Bellyra could see Daeryc and the other nearby lords looking puzzled.

As the song progressed, however, and the fox found himself snatched bald by the farmer, the true import became clear. Verse after verse bounced by, and the resemblance to Oggyn grew more and more obvious. A few men snickered, a few others laughed. Bellyra could see some whispering and pointing at the councillor crouched at the prince's feet, as if they were explaining the joke to those around them.

"So a fox went to the henhouse," Maddyn finished, "but he found a wolf on guard. And he ended up as smooth and bald as any stone in the yard." He ran a trill up and down the strings, then struck a chord with a flourish of his wrist.

The great hall cheered and clapped, but Bellyra was watching Oggyn. Tears ran down his face. She leaned over and grabbed her husband's arm.

"It's enough, Marro," Bellyra said in his ear. "Do let him go."

Maryn nodded his agreement and pointed at Oggyn to give him leave to speak.

"My liege!" Oggyn howled, then choked on his words.

"You may leave us, truly," Maryn said. "Don't stand on ceremony."

Blubbering thanks, Oggyn hauled himself to his feet. He turned and headed for the staircase on the other side of the great hall as fast as he could manage—not very, in the clutter of tables and human bodies. Long before he reached it the laughter started, a huge wave of it that followed him up, lapping over the steps as he ran for the safety of the floor above. Scarlet-faced, Oggyn was puffing and panting so badly as he staggered up the staircase that Bellyra felt a sudden concern. She leaned over and yelled so that Maryn could hear.

"What if he has an apoplexy or suchlike?"

"Nevyn's on his way after him," Maryn answered. "Fear not."

Indeed, the dweomermaster had reached the staircase and was bounding up, as vigorously as a young warrior. He caught up with his fellow councillor, and for a moment Bellyra could see them both. Then, somehow, things got confused. She stopped watching the stairs, glanced back, found the two councillors no longer visible, glanced around and saw that no one else in the great hall seemed to be looking at the stairs either. *I must ask Nevyn how he did* that, she thought, but in a few beats of the heart she'd forgotten what she wanted to ask him. Out among the tables, the normal talk picked up again.

Maddyn had climbed down from the table and was handing the harp back to its owner. Bellyra waited till he'd finished, then waved him over. He knelt in front of her and the prince.

"Well sung, Maddo." Maryn was grinning. "Oggyn will think twice before he extorts any more coin from my subjects."

"So we may hope, Your Highness," Maddyn said.

"I've got a little trinket for you," Bellyra said. "May it bring you luck in the wars."

"My lady is too generous," Maddyn said.

"You deserve somewhat for escorting me round to all those dusty rooms all winter."

Smiling, Maryn nodded at Maddyn, as if to say "take it." When Maddyn held out his hand, Bellyra dropped it into his open palm. The bard looked at the rose pin, then grinned up at her.

"It's beautiful, my lady," Maddyn said. "You and your husband have my humble thanks."

"Most welcome," Bellyra said with a little nod.

Maddyn pinned the rose to his shirt collar. "I'll treasure it always, Your Highness."

"That gladdens my heart. And now I think I'd best summon my women and get back to our hall." Bellyra rose, glancing idly away, as if Maddyn's smile meant naught to her.

At the end of the table Elyssa stood waiting for her, but Degwa seemed to have left already. Oh gods! Bellyra thought. Poor Decci, having to watch all that! With a wave to Elyssa to follow, she left the table and hurried for the stairs, but by the time the two women reached the upper landing, neither Nevyn, Oggyn, nor Degwa were anywhere to be seen.

Nevyn had led Oggyn into the first empty chamber they came to, a tiny room containing naught but one chair. Oggyn sank down upon it and allowed himself to sob aloud.

Repeatedly he ran his face over his sleeve, and eventually the tears stopped coming. Nevyn leaned against the wall and waited while Oggyn pulled a rag from his pocket and blew his nose. He shoved the rag back, then sat slumped, his hands hanging limply between his knees.

"Ah ye gods," Oggyn moaned. "My life is over."

"Oh come now!" Nevyn said. "It's not as bad as all that."

"But I'll have to leave court. How can I possibly stay in the prince's service now?"

"The prince will consider you amply punished and forget the matter."

"But the shame! Ye gods, everyone will talk of this for years."

"They won't. You forget their vanity."

Oggyn looked up, startled.

"The noble-born in particular," Nevyn went on, "think of very little but their own doings. The servants will remember for a few days, truly, but with the wars starting, soon everyone will have plenty of gossip, fears, and bereavements to occupy them. Besides, you'll be riding with the army, and you won't even be here to snicker at."

"You're right, truly. My thanks, Nevyn! A thousand thanks and more!" Oggyn sat up, squaring his shoulders like a warrior. "If I can just get through the next few days . . ."

"You'll have plenty to keep you busy, with all the provisions to tally."

"Right again. But I don't think I'll go straight back to the great hall."

"I wouldn't either if I were you." Nevyn stood up. "Shall we go?"

As they were leaving the chamber, they saw Lady Degwa, trotting toward them. Her widow's black head scarf had slipped back, and locks of her curly dark hair dangled free around her face.

"There you are!" she burst out. "My poor Oggo! I simply had to see you. That awful bard, that awful song!"

When Oggyn held out his hands, she took them in hers and stared up at him. From her puffy eyes and trembling lower lip Nevyn could tell she'd been weeping. Nevyn made them both an unobserved bow.

"My pardons," Nevyn said. "I'll just be getting back to the great hall."

He strode off, but at the staircase he paused and turned to look back. Oggyn and Degwa stood just as he'd left them, hands clasped. Oggyn had bent his head to speak to her in what seemed to be an anguished flood of words, while Degwa stared up adoringly, nodding her agreement now and again. For the first time it occurred to Nevyn that his fellow councillor actually cared for the lady as much as he did for her title. The insight made him end his eavesdropping and hurry downstairs.

In the great hall Grodyr was waiting for him, leaning on his stick over by the hearth of honor. The winter had not been kind to the man who had formerly been the head chirurgeon in Dun Deverry. When Maryn's forces had taken the dun the summer past, Grodyr had fled with the other servitors of the Boar clan, only to find that Lord Braemys distrusted him.

"It's been a long walk you've had," Nevyn said. "All the way here from Cantrae."

"I'm surprised I lived through it, good councillor," Grodyr said. "Especially after I ruined my knee in that fall. It gladdens my heart that you'd take an interest in my plight."

"Ah, I take it you don't remember me."

Grodyr blinked, stared at him, then swore under his breath. "The herbman," he said, "that old herbman who came to the dun—ye gods, how many years ago was it?"

"I don't remember either, but a good long while."

"I take it you were a spy?"

"I wasn't, oddly enough. I merely decided that I'd find no place in Dun Deverry, so I moved on to Pyrdon, where the prince's father took me into his service. Here, let's sit down."

At Nevyn's order, a page placed two chairs in the curve of the wall, where they could talk without being easily overheard. Grodyr sat down with a long sigh and propped his stick against the wall near at hand.

"Did you ever get to plead your cause to the prince?" Nevyn said.

"I did, and a well-spoken man he is," Grodyr said. "But alas, he couldn't help me. When I fled the dun, you see, I was forced to leave some books behind, and I was hoping to reclaim them. He knew naught about them."

"I may well have them. Any books came to me as my share of the looting—not that anyone else wanted them. Did yours discuss Bardekian physic and medicinals?"

"They did. With those in hand, I might be able to find a place in some great lord's dun. Without them, well, why should they believe a shabby beggar like me when I tell them I'm a chirurgeon?"

"True spoken. You shall have them back." Nevyn hesitated, considering. "Or even—what would you think about staying here and taking the prince's service?"

"Would he have me?"

"If I recommended you."

Grodyr leaned back and looked out over the great hall. "I served the Boar clan for years," he said at length.

"Not as I remember it. You served the king's clan, when I first met you, and I'm willing to wager high that you hated the Boars then and hated them even more later."

"You have sharp eyes." Grodyr smiled thinly. "Very well. If the prince can forgive me my former service, I'll be glad to have done with all this cursed travelling."

"I'll speak to him in the morning. There's someone else here, by the by, who might well remember you: Caudyr, your young apprentice who got himself run out by the Boars."

"Ye gods! Did he end up in the prince's service, too?"

"He did. He's the chirurgeon for the prince's bodyguard, the silver daggers."

"Ai." Grodyr shook his head. "How the world changes, eh?"

"It does, it does." Nevyn rose and held out a hand. "The stairs to my chambers are a bit steep, but come with me. You can wait down at the foot."

"My thanks."

As they were making their slow way across the ward, Nevyn saw Lilli walking alone and hailed her. "There's my apprentice," he said to Grodyr. "We'll just send her up instead."

Grodyr clasped his stick with both hands and leaned on it while he stared openmouthed at Lilli. "Your apprentice?" he whispered. "Ye gods! That's Lady Lillorigga of the Boar! Apprenticed to a chirurgeon?"

"She's a daughter of the Rams of Hendyr now, and I'm not exactly a chirurgeon."

Smiling, Lilli trotted over, dropped them a curtsy, then suddenly stared at Grodyr in turn.

"It is me," the chirurgeon said. "I fear me your cousin Braemys refused me shelter in Dun Cantrae last autumn, and wintering on the roads has left me changed."

"No doubt it would," Lilli said. "It saddens my heart to think of Braemys being so miserly. That's not like him."

"Wasn't miserliness." Grodyr's voice turned sour. "He accused me of being a poisoner."

Lilli considered him narrow-eyed.

"It's doubtless a long tale," Nevyn broke in. "Lilli, up in my chamber are three books of Bardekian medical lore. Would you bring them down? They belong to Grodyr here."

"I shall, my lord."

Lilli curtsied again, then trotted off on her errand. Just then Branoic popped out of the back door to the great hall, looked around, made a sketchy bow Nevyn's way, and took out running after her—a good thing, since the books were heavy. Nevyn turned back to Grodyr.

"Tell me somewhat," Nevyn said. "This business of poisons. Is Lady Merodda mixed up in this?"

"She was, truly," Grodyr said. "I heard, by the by, that your prince had her hanged. I have to admit that the news didn't ache my heart. Braemys accused me of supplying her with poisons. I did naught of the sort, I assure you."

"Oh, I believe you. Here, why don't you shelter in the dun tonight? The prince is a generous man and won't begrudge you bread and board whether or not you take his service in the morning. I'd like to hear what you know about Lady Merodda."

After he left the great hall, Maddyn considered going back to the barracks, then decided to climb up to the outer wall and make his way along the catwalk for some privacy. By then the sun was just setting, and a soft twilight was gathering over the dun. To the east a few stars gleamed against the darkening sky. With the firelight and lantern light flickering at the windows, the central broch looked for those few moments almost inviting. At the top of the wall Maddyn squeezed himself into a crenel and looked out over the hillside below. Near the bottom of the hill little fires bloomed in the encampment where the assembled warbands sheltered behind the outermost wall. For all its size, Dun Deverry could never have quartered the entire army.

Maddyn's blue sprite materialized in midair, bringing a trace of silvery glow with her.

"Well, there you are," Maddyn said. "I've not seen you in days."

She smiled with a gleam of needle-sharp teeth.

"You weren't in the great hall just now," Maddyn went on. "And a cursed good thing, too. I played a song I wish I'd never composed."

She cocked her head to one side as if she were trying to understand.

"Having a bit of fun with Slimy Oggo is one thing. Tearing the poor bastard's pride to bits was quite another. Ah ye gods! That was the sourest revenge I've ever taken."

The sprite looked at him for a long solemn moment, then shrugged and disappeared. Maddyn climbed back down from the wall and headed for the barracks. He wanted the company of his own kind.

Lilli heard about Oggyn's shaming from her maid, Clodda, who had watched the entire spectacle from the servant's side of the hall. She had, she told Lilli, climbed up onto a table for a good view.

"It was ever so awful, my lady," Clodda said, but she

was grinning, and her eyes snapped with something suspiciously like delight. "Poor old Slimy Oggo. That's what the silver daggers call him, you know."

"Oh really?" Lilli was smiling herself. "And how would you know? You've not been consorting with silver daggers, have you?"

Clodda blushed scarlet and busied herself with straightening the bedclothes. Morning sun poured in the window. Lilli moved her chair round so that she could sit in the warmth.

"It feels so good," she remarked. "Did you see Lord Nevyn in the great hall?"

"I did, my lady. He told me he'd be up in a bit."

Nevyn appeared but a few moments after. Clodda made a hurried excuse and fled the chamber; like most of the servants, she believed him to be a sorcerer of the sort found in bards' tales, who can turn men into frogs and talk with the spirits of the dead—though in a way, Nevyn told Lilli, he'd been if not raising a spirit then at least discussing one.

"Grodyr told me many an interesting tale last night," Nevyn said. "About your mother, that is."

"Indeed?" Lilli shivered, suddenly chilled. "The poor man! Did he truly walk all the way here from Cantrae?"

"He rode at first, but his horse threw a shoe and stumbled badly. That's how he injured the knee. But about your mother, unpleasant subject though she is? He confirmed my suspicions about that woman who died from the tainted meat."

"Lady Caetha?"

"The very one. Grodyr attended both her and your mother when they were both supposedly so ill. Caetha was ill, all right. He caught your mother drinking an infusion of bitter herbs to make herself vomit convincingly. It wasn't the meat they shared that killed Caetha."

Lilli felt as if someone had slapped her. Tears gathered and threatened to fall. Nevyn leaned over and caught her hand in both of his.

"I've upset you badly," Nevyn said. "My apologies."

"Not your fault," Lilli said. "She really was a murderess. Oh gods! My own mother!"

"It's not a pleasant bit of news, is it?" Nevyn stood up. "And I'm afraid I have to leave you with it. The prince is holding a proper council of war this morning. The muster's nearly complete."

One of the last lords to lead his men to Dun Deverry was Tieryn Anasyn, the Ram of Dun Hendyr. A messenger had preceded him to ensure that the prince knew Anasyn was merely late, not traitorous, and that he'd be bringing a contingent of thirty riders, five more than demanded, to make up for his fault. On the day that he was due to arrive, Lilli kept a watch on the gates from her window. As eager as she was to see her foster-brother, she was frightened as well. How would he take the news that she was the prince's mistress? She decided that it might be better to keep it from him, if she possibly could, but if his wife was coming with him to shelter with the princess during the summer's fighting, the cause was hopeless. When it came to gossip, Lady Abrwnna could hunt with the best of them.

Lilli sat at the window with the dweomer book propped against her table. Every time she turned a page, she would pause and look out, watching the shadows of the towers creep across the cobbled ward. The sun had nearly disappeared behind the westernmost broch when she finally heard shouting out in the ward, servants calling, "The Ram, the Ram!" She laid the book on the table and leaned out of her window to see six men riding through the inner gate, each with the ram shield of Hendyr hanging from their saddle peaks.

She left her chamber, rushed down the stairs, and ran out to the ward in time to see Anasyn and his honor guard dismounting. He was a tall man, grown somewhat stouter since last she'd seen him, with a long face and a long thin nose. As well as the extra weight he'd also grown a full moustache, thick enough to hide most of his upper lip.

"Sanno!" Lilli called.

With a laugh he threw his reins to a waiting groom and ran to greet her with a bear hug. She threw her arms around his neck and let him swing her free of the ground, as he used to when they were small children. After a few circles he set her down again.

"You look well, little sister." He was smiling at her. "Still as scrawny as ever, though."

"So do you, brother, though you're getting fat about the middle, I see. Where's your lady?"

"Back in Hendyr." He smiled in an exceedingly sly way. "She's too heavy with child to travel."

"My congratulations to you both!"

"My thanks. It would be a splendid thing if the child were a son." His smile vanished. "I'd ride with a lighter heart if I knew Hendyr had an heir."

"Just so." Lilli felt her voice catch and looked away.

Murmuring among themselves, the grooms were leading away the horses, while Anasyn's guard waited patiently by the door of the main broch. While Lilli watched, the view suddenly blurred. With a muttered oath she reached up and wiped the tears away.

"Don't weep, little sister." Anasyn laid a hand on her shoulder. "It's in the hands of Wyrd, and what man knows the ways of that?" He shrugged the moment away. "I'd best go present myself to the prince, but dine with me tonight, will you? You can tell me how things stand here in the dun."

Thinking of Bellyra, Lilli hesitated, but only briefly. "Of course, gladly. And you can tell me how Hendyr fares."

Since as a mere tieryn Anasyn was seated some distance from the royal table, Lilli managed to keep a safe distance from the prince and princess both, though just as the meal finished, she did see Degwa making her way through the crowded hall. Lilli smiled and waved, but Degwa hurried right past their table without a word.

"And just who was that fine lady," Anasyn muttered, "to treat you so coldly?"

"Someone who's been my enemy from the day we rode into Cerrmor," Lilli said. "She's a daughter of the Wolf clan, and she's never forgiven me for having been born a Boar."

Anasyn was about to reply when Gwerbret Daeryc strolled over. During the muster Lilli had only seen him from a distance, and now she noticed that he'd lost more teeth over the winter—one side of his face looked positively caved in. Anasyn scrambled up and bowed to his overlord, but Daeryc motioned to Lilli to stay seated.

"I only want a word with your brother," Daeryc said. "About this business of the white mare."

"They've not found one, have they?" Anasyn said.

"They've not, or so they say." Daeryc looked profoundly gloomy. "Who can trust what priests say, eh? But without the mare, the temple won't perform the kingship rite before the campaigning begins."

"Indeed?" Lilli put in. "That's a pity, but is it all that important?"

"Important?" Daeryc snorted. "You could say that twice and loudly, too."

"If the wretched priests of Bel," Anasyn said to her, "would condescend to proclaim our liege king before we all rode out, we could count on plenty of deserters from Braemys's army. I'm willing to wager high that a lot of the lords still loyal to the Boars would come over if they had some noble reason to do it. They don't want to besmirch their honor, but if Maryn were the king? Well, then."

"I'd wager along with you," Daeryc said. "Braemys just might have found his army disappearing like food on a glutton's table. But now?" He shrugged. "The good men will hold loyal till the end, most like."

After the meal Lilli went up to Nevyn's tower room, where she discovered that the delay in confirming Maryn's kingship was preying upon her master's mind as well. Nevyn delivered himself of a few choice oaths on the subject before explaining.

"They have their reason all polished and ready, of course. The lack of the proper white mare for the rites. Huh. Let Maryn win the summer's war, and white mares will doubtless pop up all over the landscape."

"There's somewhat I don't understand," Lilli said. "Does great Bel really care about the color of Maryn's horse? Would we really be cursed if he rode a grey mare in the procession?"

"Of course not. But the lords and the priests and perhaps even the common folk would believe that he was

cursed, and they'd look at him with different eyes. And
Maryn himself—he's as pious as any great lord is, which is
to say, as pious as the times are hard, but he truly does believe that the gods have power over him. If he thought
himself cursed, wouldn't he doubt his judgment and his
luck?"

"I see. And he might do a reckless thing, or shrink back
from a fight, and his men would think he'd lost his
dweomer luck."

"Exactly. And they've followed him for many a long
year now, through famine and battle, mostly because they
believe in his luck and the gods both."

Lilli considered this while the old man watched her
from his seat on the windowsill. "But then," she said finally,
"the gods don't truly care what happens to their worshippers. Is that what you mean?"

"Close enough. In time, I'll tell you a great deal more
about the gods—this autumn, when we have more leisure.
But for now, remember that the gods want homage and little else from their ordinary worshippers. Does the high king
care about each and every man who tends his fields? Not so
long as that man hands over his taxes and dues."

"That makes the gods seem so cold, though, and so
very far away."

"They are. Think well on this. Which you'll have
plenty of time to do once I've gone with the prince."

"Anasyn was the last lord to ride in, wasn't he?" Lilli
felt her heart turn over. "You'll all be marching on the morrow."

"I'm afraid so." Nevyn glanced away, abruptly sad.
"And may the gods all grant that this summer sees the end
of it."

As she walked down the stairs of Nevyn's tower, Lilli
was thinking of Branoic. Although she wanted to say
farewell to him, her rank kept her from going to a place as
lowly as the silver daggers' barracks. She stepped inside the
great hall, stood in the doorway on the riders' side, and
tried to catch the attention of one of the servant lasses, who
would be glad to carry a message for her in return for a cop-

per. In the smoky room, crammed with fighting men of every rank, the lasses were trotting back and forth, bringing ale, serving bread, dodging the men's wandering hands, and answering back as smartly as they could to the various remarks they were getting. Lilli found herself thinking that she was as lucky as Prince Maryn. The summer past, her clan had been destroyed, and she herself might have ended up carrying slops in some lord's hall had it not been for Princess Bellyra's generosity.

"Lilli?" A dark voice sounded behind her.

With a little shriek Lilli spun around to find Branoic grinning at her.

"I didn't mean to scare you out of your skin," he said. "I got one of my feelings, like, that mayhap you wanted to talk with me."

"I do." She managed a laugh. "I was just remembering last summer. It seems like a twenty's worth of years ago, not just one."

"The best summer of my life, it was."

"Truly? Why?"

"You silly goose!" Branoic was grinning at her. "Because I met you, of course."

"I don't deserve you, I truly don't."

"Spare me that, if you please." Branoic reached out and engulfed her small soft hands with his, all battle-hard and callused. "If our prince objects to my kissing my betrothed farewell, then bad cess to him."

Clasped tight in his arms she felt safe, as if his embrace could shut out the entire war-torn world around them. Oh dear Goddess! she prayed. Let him come home to me!

On the morrow, Prince Maryn rode out at the head of his army to settle things once and for all with Regent Braemys. At the head of the line of march rode a pair of young lads carrying the red wyvern banner of Dun Deverry and the three ships banner of Cerrmor. Behind them rode Prince Maryn with Nevyn for company, and directly after, his silver daggers. The rest of the army arranged itself behind, each warband headed by its own lord in order of rank.

At the rear came the provision wagons, servants, grooms with extra horses, and chirurgeons, all guarded by the foot soldiers—spearmen, mostly, under Oggyn's command—owed to the prince by the various free cities in his dominions. All in all, they numbered over four thousand men, less than the summer before, but still, one of the largest armies Deverry had ever seen.

Thanks to the carts and their slab wheels, this massive force could make about twelve miles a day on flat terrain. In the hilly country that lay ahead, they would be lucky to manage ten. Since clever maneuvers were out of the question, the prince had decided upon a simple strategy. In his message Braemys had announced his intention of riding to Dun Deverry by Beltane. Maryn saw no reason to doubt him; Braemys had not the men to take the dun or even besiege it successfully. Maryn's vassals had agreed that they should lead their army east toward Cantrae, over two hundred miles away. Somewhere, when the gods and their Wyrd decided the time was right, they would meet Braemys and his men upon the road.

"Which is not to say," Maryn said, "that the little pisspot won't try some sort of trick. Last summer we saw how clever he can be."

"So we did, Your Highness," Nevyn said. "It's a good thing I can scout for you."

"Just so." Maryn turned in the saddle to give him a tight smile. "And I thank the gods for it."

Since Nevyn had never seen Braemys in the flesh, simple scrying was impossible, and he was forced to resort to the etheric plane for his scouting. Every night when the army halted, he would assume the body of light and travel as far east as he dared. Below the land would seem to burn with the vegetable auras of trees and grasses, pulsing with spring life. The streams and rivers swelled up into silver veils of elemental force, glittering and dangerous to a traveller such as he. To avoid them he flew above the dirt roads, but even they sported a faint russet glow. When the astral tides turned with the spring, the very earth came to the edge of life.

Yet, no matter how far Nevyn ranged, he saw nothing of Braemys and his army. He began to wonder if the message had been a ruse, if Braemys intended to stand a siege in Dun Cantrae. If so, taking it would cost another long effort and a good many men's lives. We'll bridge that ditch when we come to it, he told himself. After all, there was naught else he could do but wait.

The army had been gone only a few days when Bellyra went into labor. Lilli waited with the other women—the serving lasses, the cook, the swineherd's wife, and the like—down in the great hall while the midwife and the princess's serving women tended Bellyra during the birth. Out of habit they sat by the riders' hearth, even though with the nobility gone except for young Prince Riddmar, they might have sat where they liked. Despite the size of the hall, the men left on fortguard went back to their barracks, as if they felt themselves in the way of these women's matters. The young prince trailed after them.

"I do hope it goes easy for Her Highness," said the cook.

"She's delivered two before," Lilli said, "and not had trouble."

"Huh!" The cook snorted. "I had my first three easy as boiling barley, but my fourth? A lad, it was, and he cursed near killed me. I told him about it, too, I did, every year after."

Despite the cook's fears, the birth went fast. Bellyra's labor had begun just after dawn, and not long after noon a triumphant Elyssa hurried down the staircase. She paused about halfway and called out, "Another healthy son for the prince! Our lady fares well." Everyone answered with cheers and loud good wishes. Elyssa paused for a moment, smiling at them, then came down to the floor of the hall. She hurried over to the table where Lilli was sitting.

"Lilli?" Elyssa said. "Could you spare me a moment?"

"Of course." Lilli jumped up and curtsied. "What shall I do?"

"Just come walk with me a while."

Elyssa led her outside to the main ward. In the hot spring sun, flies hovered, jewel bright as they darted back and forth. Over by the watering trough a groom curried a dun palfrey, who stamped a lazy hoof and flicked his tail whenever a fly tried to land upon him. Otherwise the dun seemed wrapped in silence like some enchanted fortress. For a moment Elyssa stood staring at the cobbles; then she looked up with a little shrug.

"I see no reason to mince words," Elyssa said. "Are you minded to forgive the princess her fit of temper?"

"Me forgive her?" Lilli heard her voice crack. "I'm the one who's done her harm."

"You're not. It's Maryn who's paid her the hurt she feels. In her worst moments she's blamed you, certainly, but when she's herself again she knows where the fault lies."

"Truly?"

"Truly." Elyssa gave a firm little nod. "Now, you know about the awful sadness that takes her after she's given birth."

"I do. Is it happening again?"

"Not yet. The other two times, at least, she's done well for the first few days." Elyssa looked away, frowning. "I wish the midwife understood it. Neither she nor the herbwoman can say aught but 'it passes, it passes.' So it always does, but ye gods! The cost it takes while it lies upon her!"

"It's terrible, indeed."

"So, I was wondering somewhat. Bellyra told me about that brooch of your mother's, the one that had some sort of evil spell upon it. Nevyn said that a thief would feel uneasy or suchlike from the handling of it. Is there such a thing as a spell that would cheer someone up, like, rather than cursing them?"

"There is." Lilli thought for a moment. "I wonder if I could make such a thing? I think I know how, but I'm not sure I have the skill. I'm but an apprentice."

"I know, but I thought mayhap you'd try." Elyssa reached into the folds of her kirtle and drew out a small silver ring brooch. "This belongs to her."

"I'll gladly try." Lilli took the brooch and clasped it in her hand. "The worst I can do is naught. You can't curse someone by accident or suchlike."

"I did wonder about that." Elyssa suddenly smiled. "It's good to talk with you again. If the princess's grief comes upon her, it would be a splendid thing if you'd come to the women's hall. Any distraction would be a boon."

"Even her getting enraged at me?"

"Even that, but I doubt me it would happen." Elyssa paused, glancing at the sky, when the sun had started its slide toward evening. "Is it too late in the day to send the messengers off?"

"To the prince, you mean?"

"Just that. You know the lay of the land around Dun Deverry. Is there a dun nearby that would shelter them for the night?"

"A good day's ride east. Most of the duns near the city have been razed and gone for years."

"That's what I was afraid of. Very well. I'll have the scribe compose the messages today, and we'll get the men on the road tomorrow at dawn."

They walked inside together and climbed the staircase, but when Elyssa went to the women's hall, Lilli returned to her chamber. She laid the little brooch upon her table beside the book and for a moment gloated over the task ahead of her. She too needed a distraction from her worrying over Branoic and the prince both. It did occur to her to wonder if Nevyn would approve this independent foray into dweomerwork, but since he wasn't there to ask, she went ahead with the job.

Nevyn's dweomer book devoted a page to the process of charging a talisman, and Lilli had seen Nevyn work its opposite twice now as well. She would need to cleanse the brooch first of any and all evil influences it might have been exposed to over the years. That very evening, by candlelight she drew a magic circle around her table and chair to mark it as her place of working. The brooch she laid in the center of the round table. Next, she sat down and meditated upon the Light to clear her own mind of troubled thoughts. That done, she rose and stood as she'd seen Nevyn stand, one hand in the air.

"Lords of Light," she called out. "May my work be true."

In her mind she visualized the Light, streaming across the starry sky. She imagined light pouring down like water to drench her, light swirling round her upraised arm, light gathering at her fingertips. With a snap she brought her arm down and washed the little brooch in a beam of silver light.

"Begone!"

To her altered sight the brooch gleamed, as bright as molten silver from the jeweller's ladle. The light flickered, then vanished. She broke the magic circle with a ceremonious stamp of her foot.

"And any spirits trapped by this ceremony, go free!"

The chamber once again was an ordinary room, lit only by dim candlelight. She stamped again to earth herself with the feel of solid things, then let out her breath in a long sigh. She was trembling and sweaty, she realized. When she took a step, she nearly stumbled; she had to catch the back of the chair to steady herself, an effort that left her gasping for breath. There will be plenty of time, she told herself. You'll simply have to work slowly, in stages. She wrapped the newly purified brooch up in a bit of cloth to protect it, then went to bed.

Over the next few days Lilli worked on the talisman, stopping often to rest. The work was making her so tired, in fact, that she thought of leaving it undone, but she couldn't bear to disappoint Elyssa. She saw the serving woman often, generally in the great hall, where Elyssa would always stop to chat and let her know how the princess fared. Finally, on the morning that she finished the talisman, Elyssa told her the news they'd both been dreading.

"When the princess woke this morning," Elyssa said, "she wasn't herself. She wept so piteously that it wrung my heart."

"Ah ye gods! It aches my heart just to hear of it," Lilli

said. "Her brooch is finished, by the by. Come up to my chamber with me, and I'll give it to you."

Wrapped in cloth, the brooch lay on Lilli's table by the window. Lilli took it out and handed it to Elyssa.

"Well, this is a pretty thing!" Elyssa said, smiling. "Did you have Otho polish it, too?"

"I didn't."

"But see how it glitters in the sun! I don't remember it being so lovely."

Lilli knew then that her working had succeeded. Elyssa took the brooch and hurried off to the women's hall to give it to the princess. Lilli sat down to her studies, but her mind kept wandering to Bellyra's plight and the brooch. Finally, when the morning was well advanced, Elyssa returned to the chamber.

"How does she fare?" Lilli blurted.

"A bit better, though the sadness still grips her," Elyssa said. "The brooch did please her, though. She pinned it to her dress and swore she'd wear it always."

"That gladdens my heart!" Lilli tapped the book with her fingers. "It says in here that sometimes talismans work slowly. Maybe it will help in a few days."

"I'll pray so." Elyssa sighed, glancing out the window with exhausted eyes. "Anything for a little hope."

"Should we send off another messenger? Nevyn will want to know that she's—" Lilli could not bring herself to use the word mad. "—unwell."

"That's true." Elyssa considered this for a moment. "But even if he does know, what can he do? He won't be leaving the prince's side."

"He can't, truly. I suppose we'll just have to wait till the men ride home again."

"Just so." Elyssa looked up, studying the sky as if it could report the prince's progress. "Now, the messengers we sent off about the new baby? They should be reaching Maryn soon. He'll send them back to us with news."

"And then I can write Nevyn a letter to go back with them. Well and good, then. Do you want me to come visit Her Highness?"

"In a few days. This—this illness always seems to affect her the worst at the very beginning. In about an eightnight she settles down, like."

After Elyssa left, Lilli spent some time trying to think of other ways she might help Bellyra. She failed, except for the one obvious course of action: end her love affair with the prince. That, she felt, would be a harder thing for her to work than the mightiest dweomer in the world.

The princess's messengers caught up with the army just at sunset, as it was making camp in a grassy meadow beside a stream. In the midst of the purposeful confusion Nevyn was standing with the prince, waiting for the servants to finish setting up their tents. A sentry led up the two men, all dusty from the road.

"Messages, Your Highness. From your lady."

The messengers knelt to the prince. Maryn grabbed the silver tube and shook out the tightly rolled letter inside. He glanced at it, laughed, then began to read it aloud.

"To my husband, greetings. I was delivered of yet another wretched son, who now awaits your choosing of a name. I had my heart so set upon a daughter that I neglected to think of any suitable for a lad. At the moment my women are calling him Dumpling, which—while plebeian—will serve until the end of your campaigning."

At that point Maryn began reading to himself, a rare trick in those days and one he had learned from Nevyn. From his smile, Nevyn could guess that the message was unfit for public ears. At last Maryn looked up and turned to the messengers. "You must be hungry," the prince said. "My apologies for forgetting you. Here, sentry! Get these men fed, and then spread the news of the new prince among the noble-born."

Soon enough, Maryn's vassals began appearing in twos and threes to congratulate him on the new prince's birth, but none of them lingered. The smell of cooking in the camp drew them quickly back to their own fires. When Gwerbret Daeryc arrived, though, Maryn bade him stay a while. The servants brought out a wooden stool, and he sat down by the fire with the prince and Nevyn.

"From the maps I have," Maryn said, "we're nearly to Glasloc. Do you think that's correct?"

"I do, my liege," Daeryc said. "Once we reach the lake, and that'll be in about two more days, we'll have arrived at the edge of the Boar clan's holdings. If I remember rightly, Glasloc marks half the distance twixt the Holy City and Cantrae town."

"I see," Maryn said with a nod. "I'll wager Braemys will meet us before we start trampling on his lands." He glanced at Nevyn. "Do you know the lay of the land twixt here and Glasloc? Is it flat?"

"Mostly, my liege." Nevyn turned to Daeryc to explain. "When I was younger, Your Grace, I lived near Cantrae."

"Good, good," the gwerbret said. "I haven't been there since I was but a little lad, and we'll need someone who knows the lie of things better than I do." He rose with a bow Maryn's way. "If you'll forgive me, Your Highness, I'll be leaving you. I'm hungry enough to eat a wolf, pelt and all."

Provisions for the silver daggers travelled in their own cart, tended by a stout carter and his skinny son. That particular night, Maddyn was sitting with Owaen when the son, young Garro, brought the two captains a chunk of salt pork impaled on a stick. Green mold marbled the fat.

"My da," Garro announced, "says it been in the barrel too long. Weren't salted enough, either, Da says."

"Your da's no doubt right." Maddyn took the stick from the boy. "Owaen, what do you think?"

"We've had worse," Owaen said. "Any maggots?"

Maddyn twirled the stick this way and that to catch the sunset light. "None that I can see."

"Weren't none in the barrel, neither," Garro said.

"Then it should do. Let's see." Maddyn drew his dagger. He cut off the green streaks and took a few bites of the rest. "It's not bad but it's not good, either. It wouldn't be worth fretting about, except I'll wager this is Oggyn's doing."

Owaen swore so furiously that Garro cringed.

"I'm not angry with you," Owaen snapped. "Go thank your da for us. Now. Give me that, Maddo. Let's go shove it up the bald bastard's arse."

Unfortunately for Owaen's plans, they found Oggyn attending upon the prince in front of the royal tent. Since not even Owaen could get away with violence there, the two silver daggers knelt not far from the prince's chair and waited. Oggyn was congratulating Maryn for the birth of the new son in all sorts of long words and fulsome metaphors—as if, Maddyn thought bitterly, Bellyra had naught to do with it. Exposed to the open air, the pork began to announce that truly, it was rotten. Once Oggyn paused for breath, the two silver daggers, or their complaint, caught Maryn's attention.

"What's that stench?" Maryn glanced around. "Ye gods, Owaen! What have you brought me, a dead rat?"

"I've not, my liege," Owaen said. "The rat is kneeling there beside you."

In the firelight Maddyn could see Oggyn's face blanch.

"Spoiled rations, my liege," Owaen went on, waving the bit of pork. "Your councillor there assigns the provisions, and I think me he gave the silver daggers the last of the winter's stores."

"What?" Oggyn squeaked. "No such thing! If you received spoiled food, then one of the servants made a mistake." He glanced at Maryn. "Your Highness, if you'll release me, I'd best go have a look at the barrel that meat came from. I'll wager it doesn't have my mark upon it."

"I'll do better than that," Maryn said, grinning. "I'll come with you. Lead on, captains."

Maddyn received a sudden portent of futility. No doubt Oggyn had been too clever to leave evidence lying about. The two silver daggers led the prince and his councillor back to their camp and the provision cart, where Garro and his da hauled down the offending barrel. By the light of a lantern Oggyn examined the lid with Maryn looking on.

"Not a mark on it," Oggyn said triumphantly. "This

barrel should have been emptied for the dun's dogs, not carted for the army."

"Well, make sure it's dumped now," Maryn said. "But a fair bit away. I don't like the smell of it."

"Of course, Your Highness," Oggyn said. "I'll have a replacement sent round from my personal stores."

All at once Maddyn wondered if he should have sampled the pork. Too late now, he thought, and truly, we've eaten worse over the years. He put the matter out of his mind, but it remained, alas, in his stomach. He woke well before dawn, rolled out of his blankets, and rushed for the latrine ditch just beyond the encampment. He managed to reach it before the flux overwhelmed his self-control.

"Nevyn, my lord Nevyn!" The voice sounded both loud and urgent. "Your aid!"

Through the tent wall a dim light shone.

"What's all this?" Nevyn sat up and yawned. "Who is it?"

"Branoic, my lord. Maddyn's been poisoned."

Nevyn found himself both wide-awake and standing. He pulled on his brigga, grabbed his sack of medicinals in one hand and a shirt in the other, and ducked through the tent flap. Branoic stood outside with a lantern raised in one hand.

"He ate a bit of spoiled pork, Owaen told me," Branoic said. "But it came from a barrel that Oggyn gave us."

Branoic led Nevyn to the bard's tent. Just outside, his clothes lay stinking in a soiled heap. Inside Nevyn found Maddyn lying naked on a blanket. The tent smelled of vomit and diarrhea. Owaen knelt beside him with a wet rag in one hand.

"I've been wiping his face off," Owaen said. "I don't think he's going to heave anymore."

"Naught left," Maddyn whispered.

"How do you feel?" Nevyn said.

"Wrung out. My guts are cramping."

The effort of talking was making him shiver. Nevyn grabbed a clean blanket and laid it over him. In the lantern light his white face, marked with dark circles under his eyes, shone with cold sweat. Nevyn sent Owaen off to wake a servant to heat some water, then knelt beside his patient. Branoic hung the lantern from the tent pole and retreated.

"Gods," Maddyn mumbled. "I stink."

"Good," Nevyn said. "Your body's flushing the contagion out. I'm going to make you drink herbwater, though, to ensure that every last bit's gone. It won't be pleasant, I'm afraid."

"Better than dying."

"Exactly."

Maddyn sighed and turned his face away. The stench hanging in the tent was free of the taint of poison, or at least, Nevyn thought, free of any poison he'd recognize. While he waited for the hot water to arrive, Nevyn sat back on his heels and opened his dweomer sight. Maddyn's aura curled tight around him, all shrunken and flabby, a pale brownish color shot with sickly green. Yet it pulsed, as if it fought to regain its normal size, and brightened close to the skin. Nevyn closed his sight.

"You'll live," Nevyn announced.

"Good." All at once Maddyn tried to sit up. "The rose pin."

"What?" Nevyn pushed him down again. "Lie still!"

"I've got to find the rose pin. On my shirt."

All at once Nevyn remembered. "The token the princess gave you, you mean?"

"It was on my shirt."

"All your clothes are right outside. It can wait."

Maddyn shook his head and tried to sit up again. Fortunately, a servant provided a distraction when he came in, carrying in one hand a black kettle filled with steaming water.

"My thanks," Nevyn said. "Put that down over there by the big cloth sack. I've got another errand for you. On the bard's shirt outside—"

"The rose pin, my lord?" The servant held out his other hand. "Branoic told me to bring it to him."

On his palm lay the token. Nevyn plucked it off and showed it to Maddyn, who lay back down.

"I'll pin this on my own shirt," Nevyn said, "so it won't get lost."

Maddyn smiled, his eyes closed. Nevyn set a packet of emetics to steeping, then called in Branoic. Together they carried Maddyn and the kettle outside, where the herbwater could do its work while sparing the tent. The rest of the night passed unpleasantly, but toward dawn Nevyn realized that Maddyn was on the mend when the bard managed to drink some well-watered ale and keep it down. He sent young Garro off to wash Maddyn's clothes and told Branoic to try feeding Maddyn a little bread soaked in ale the next time he woke.

"I've got an errand to run," Nevyn said. "I wonder where Oggyn's had his servant pitch his tent?"

"Just back of the prince's own," Branoic said. "He's put a red pennant upon it."

"Just like the lord he wants to be, eh? Very well then."

In the silver light of approaching dawn the tent proved easy enough to find. Nevyn lifted the flap and spoke Oggyn's name.

"I'm awake, my lord," Oggyn said, and he sounded exhausted. "Come in."

Nevyn ducked through the tent flap and found Oggyn fully dressed, sitting on a little stool in the semidarkness. Nevyn called upon the spirits of Aethyr and set a ball of dweomer light glowing. When he stuck it to the canvas Oggyn barely seemed to notice.

"I've been expecting you," Oggyn said. "I heard what happened to Maddyn. The gossip's all over the camp. I suppose you think I made that wretched bard ill on purpose."

"I had thoughts that way, truly," Nevyn said. "Was it only the spoiled pork, or did you use a bit of Lady Merodda's poisons?"

"Neither, I swear it!" Oggyn began to tremble, and by the dweomer light Nevyn could see that his face had gone pasty white around the eyes. "Even if I had given them that barrel, how could I ensure that only Maddyn would eat the stuff? Nevyn, do you truly think I'd poison the entire troop to get at him?"

"Shame is a bitter thing," Nevyn said, "and you had a score or two to settle with Owaen and Branoic as well."

Oggyn slid off the stool and dropped to his knees. "Ah ye gods! Do you think I'd do anything that would harm our prince?"

"What? Of course not!"

"He depends upon the silver daggers." Oggyn looked up. Big drops of sweat ran down his face. "Think you I'd poison his guards?"

"Well." Nevyn considered for a long moment. "Truly, I have to give you that. And there's no doubt that spoiled meat will give a man the flux as surely as Merodda's poisons would."

Oggyn nodded repeatedly, as if urging him along this line of thought. Nevyn opened his dweomer sight and considered Oggyn's aura, dancing a pale sickly grey in terror but free of guile.

"Will you swear to me again?" Nevyn said.

"I will," Oggyn said. "May Great Bel strike me dead if I lie. I did not try to poison Maddyn or anyone else. That salt pork should have been left at the dun for the dogs."

The aura pulsated with fear but fear alone.

"Very well," Nevyn said at last. "You have my apology."

Oggyn got up and ran a shaking hand over his face. "I can see why you'd suspect me," he whispered. "But I swear to you, I did no such thing. I'm just cursed glad you came to me in private and didn't just blurt this in front of the prince."

"I did have my doubts."

"Ah ye gods! I'll never be safe again. Anytime the least little harm befalls that wretched bard, I'll be blamed."

"Truly, you might devote some time to thinking up ways to keep him safe."

Oggyn gave him a sickly smile. Without another word, Nevyn left him to recover his composure.

There remained the problem of what to do with Maddyn. He was too weak to ride with the army; jouncing around in a cart would only weaken him further. This deep into enemy territory leaving him behind would be a death sentence. The morning's council of war, however, solved the problem. Gwerbret Ammerwdd pointed out that Braemys was most likely laying a trap or, at the least, leading them into some weak position.

"He knows this country well," Ammerwdd said. "I've no doubt he's got some trick in mind, or some battlefield that will be to his liking but not to ours."

"I agree," Maryn said. "I suggest we camp here today and send out scouts. They can cover a good deal of territory once they're free of the army."

After a great deal of discussion, the rest of the lords went along with the plan. All that morning the army waited as horsemen came and went, fanning out into the countryside in the hopes of getting a glimpse of Braemys's position.

Nevyn spent much of the wait with Maddyn in his tent. Although the herbs had purged the worst of the contagion, the bard still lay ill, so exhausted he was cold and shivering despite the afternoon warmth. From the vomiting, his lips and the skin around them were cracking. When Nevyn rubbed herbed lard into them, he noticed that his skin had no resilience. Nevyn pinched a bit twixt thumb and forefinger so gently that Maddyn never noticed, but the little ridge of skin persisted rather than smoothing itself out.

Fortunately, near to camp some of the men had found a spring of pure water; Nevyn sent Branoic off with a clean bucket to fetch some back.

"The contagion has depleted his watery humors," Nevyn told him. "We've got to replenish them."

Sometimes Maddyn could keep the pure water down, and sometimes it came back up again, but eventually he did manage to drink enough to allay the worst of Nevyn's fears. Through all of this Branoic hovered miserably outside, glad for every little errand that Nevyn found for him to do.

"He's been my friend from the day I joined the daggers," Branoic said. "I'll do anything I can, my lord."

"Good," Nevyn said. "He needs water and food both, but he won't be able to keep down more than a bite or swallow at a time."

"If all that arse-ugly pork's gone, why is he still so sick?"

"I wish I knew. Men who've eaten spoiled food often stay ill for a long time after, but I've no idea why."

Branoic stared wide-eyed.

"There's a cursed lot of things I don't know," Nevyn went on. "No other herbman I've ever met knows them either. Why contagion lingers is one of them, and how it spreads is another."

"I see." Branoic rubbed the back of his hand against his chin. "That's not what I'd call reassuring, my lord."

"Honesty rarely is. Now, go tend Maddyn. I've got to make myself presentable for the prince's council of war."

In a darkening twilight two of Daeryc's men galloped in with news. A herald led them to the prince, who was sitting in front of his tent with Nevyn and some of his vassals around him. In the firelight they knelt to him and told their tale. They'd ridden directly east—or so they'd reckoned from the position of the sun. Their shadows were stretching long in front of them by the time they topped a low rise and saw, some miles farther off, a huge cloud of dust drifting at the horizon.

"It had to be the Cantrae men, Your Highness," one of the scouts said. "Naught but an army could raise that dust, and the gods all know there's not enough men left for more than one."

"Just so," Maryn said, grinning. "How far away were they?"

"From our camp, Your Highness?" The scout thought for a moment. "Well, at least a day's travel for an army that size, but not a cursed lot more, I'd say. We watched for a bit longer, too. The dust didn't seem to come nearer."

"Looked like it were shrinking a bit," the second scout volunteered. "And I thought, I did, they be settling down for the night's camp."

"Good." Maryn stood up and glanced at the noblemen. "I doubt me if we'll see battle on the morrow."

"Most likely not," Gwerbret Ammerwdd said. "But I say we should stand ready for it anyway."

The rest of the noble-born nodded, muttered a few words, and glanced back and forth among themselves. Nevyn was aware of Gwerbret Daeryc, watching him with one eyebrow raised. Nevyn smiled blandly in return. He had nothing to add to the scouts' report, not at the moment, at least.

Late that night, when the camp lay asleep except for the night sentries, Nevyn went into his tent and summoned his body of light. He rose straight out through the tent's roof into the etheric plane, where the stars hung down close, it seemed, as huge glittering silver spheres. With the scout's report to guide him, he travelled fast over the red and glowing countryside below. Eventually he saw on the horizon a strange light, a flickering expanse of yellows and oranges, shot through with dancing reds, that looked just like a wildfire burning across a grassy plain would have looked in the physical world. He knew, however, that here on the etheric he was seeing the massed auras of Braemys's army.

Although he now had a reasonable idea of their distance, he decided to risk going closer. The army had set up camp on his side of Loc Glas and the river that flowed south from it. He could approach them with no danger from the seething water veils, and Braemys had no dweomermaster in his retinue. Unchallenged, Nevyn floated over the horse herd, drowsing at tether in a meadow. The tents lay just beyond. Nevyn rose up high for an overview; while he had no time to count them, he could tell that this force was a good bit smaller than Maryn's.

Something about the camp struck him as odd. He let himself drift on the etheric flow, hovered like a hawk on the wind while he tried to think. The rational faculties function sluggishly, if at all, out on the etheric. Still, he studied the camp and stored up images of it before he turned back and returned to his tent.

As soon as he was back in his body and fully awake, he understood what he'd seen. No carts. No packsaddles, either, stacked at the edge of the meadow. With the first streak of grey dawn, he got up and trotted through the sleeping camp to Maryn's tent. He found the prince awake, standing outside and yawning.

"News, Your Highness," Nevyn said. "Braemys has left his baggage train behind. His men must be carrying what food they can in their saddlebags. He's marching for a quick strike."

Maryn tossed back his head and laughed. "Good," the prince said at last. "Today might see the end of this, then."

"Perhaps. I can't help but wonder if Braemys has some tricky maneuver in mind."

The camp went on armed alert. Under Oggyn's command, the contingent of spearmen assembled the provision wagons, extra horses, servants, struck tents, bedrolls, and suchlike out in a meadow, then stood guard round the perimeter. The army saddled and bridled their horses, then donned armor, but rather than tire their mounts, they sat on the ground beside them to wait. Since the prince had sent some of his silver daggers out as scouts, they would have ample warning should Braemys be making a fast march to battle. In the dust and shouting that accompanied all these preparations Nevyn slipped away from camp. He walked about a mile back west to a copse of trees he'd spotted earlier. The matter of Braemys's missing wagon train irked him.

In the shelter of an oak he lay down on the ground, crossed his arms over his chest, and went into trance. During daylight the etheric world glowed, pulsing with life, and the blue light shimmered and trembled all round him. The sun, a vast blazing sphere, shot huge arrows of gold down upon the earth. The reddish auras of grass and trees writhed and stretched out long tendrils of etheric substance to capture the gold and feed upon it. In all this confusion Nevyn could barely sort out east from west. He rose up high, where he could comprehend the view and pick out roads and rivers from the general splendor. With the silver cord paying out behind him, he travelled back east, heading for the spot where he'd seen Braemys's army.

Nevyn was expecting to meet up with the enemy, and indeed, he overtook them some miles closer to Maryn than he'd left them the night past. The army straggled over a long stretch of road, and thanks to this loose formation he could see that not a single wagon followed the riders. He swung north to keep clear of the tangled mass of auras and physical dust, rose higher in the blue light, and saw off on the horizon northward a glow. It appeared as a dome of pale light, mostly yellow, shot here and there with red. On the etheric, with his physical body and its correlates far behind him, he was hard-pressed to tell just how close it might have been.

Isn't this interesting? Nevyn thought. A second force, perhaps. He angled away from the road and headed toward the pulsing dome of light. As he travelled, he noted landmarks below that might, once he'd returned to his normal intellect, give him some idea of distance and location. The dome itself never seemed to move or change its size. Once he drew close, he could see why. Not a second force, but Braemys's missing baggage train spread out over long-deserted fields. It was enormous, as well, a good many times larger than Maryn's—even though Braemys was leading a far smaller army. When Nevyn dropped down closer for a look, he saw many small auras, pale and trembling, among the larger glows: frightened children, he realized with a shock. Many of the large auras belonged to women, as well. What were they doing there? And why north, what must have been a good long distance north? A puzzle, all of it.

Nevyn hovered for a few moments, memorizing the lay of the camp and the land around it both, then turned and headed back south. Sped by his curiosity, he saw the landscape below unrolling as fast as a Bardek scroll dropped by a careless scribe. In what seemed like a few moments he once again hovered above Braemys's army, which had stopped marching and stood in the road. Nevyn could feel the tug of the silver cord that connected him to his body; he was tiring fast, and staying too long in the etheric offered danger even to a master of dweomer such as he. But at the same time he felt an urgency to stay, some deep intuition from his innermost being. Like a hawk on the wind he hovered above the army and saw a small group of men sitting on horseback out in a meadow. *Braemys and his lords, I'll wager!*

The thought caught him like a gust of wind and blew him to the cluster of men on horseback, but he was too late to join their conference. The lords all drew their swords, black smears of death in the golden auras, clashed them together as if sealing an oath, then turned their horses and trotted back to the waiting army. Once again Nevyn felt the tug of his silver cord. When he glanced down he saw his body of light growing dangerously thin. He focused his will and began to capture etheric light, wrapping it in long silvery blue strands around himself. His simulacrum soaked it up as cloth soaks water, and once again he felt strong and solid.

By that time the army below had begun to move. In an instant Nevyn understood why he'd forced himself to stay: the column was splitting itself into two parts. One, with the Boar banners at its head, was heading fast off to the southwest—to circle round from the Red Wyvern's flank? Most likely. Only when that second column was well under way did the remains of the army set out westward again. At its head fluttered banners carrying the crossed sword device of Lughcarn. This time, when Nevyn felt the silver cord hauling at his body of light, he gave in to the impulse and sped back west to his body and Prince Maryn. He had some news for the council of war now, good and proper.

All that same day, Lilli had been restless. She would read a page in the book only to realize that she'd comprehended not one word of it. In the middle of the morning she gave up on her studies and headed downstairs. She was crossing the great hall when a boyish voice hailed her, and she turned to see Prince Riddmar trotting over to her. His pale-haired resemblance to Maryn struck her like an omen. If one day she had a son by the prince, he would look much like this, no doubt.

"Good morrow, Lady Lilli," Riddmar said. "Are you going out for a ride or suchlike?"

"I thought I'd just have a bit of a walk. Why?"

"Oh, I'm bored." The boy pulled a long face. "It's so wretched, not getting to go to the war. I wanted to ride down to the lake, but Lady Elyssa told me I couldn't go alone."

"And quite rightly, too. You're too valuable to risk to some traitor or Cantrae spy."

"That's what my brother said." Riddmar sighed with deep drama. "May I walk with you?"

"Of course. I'm just going for a stroll."

Although Riddmar had lived in the dun for some months, he still had a great deal of trouble sorting out the warren of walls and towers that made up Dun Deverry. As they walked, Lilli pointed out various landmarks and showed him the main paths through the confusion.

"Some of these buildings and suchlike look so clumsy," Riddmar remarked at one point. "Like that odd tower you can see from the main ward."

"The one that leans so badly? Your brother told me that it was built that way on purpose, so defenders could drop rocks down on attackers."

"Oh. That makes sense, truly."

All at once Riddmar blushed and looked away.

"What's wrong?" Lilli said.

"Er, ah, well, I was just—well, remembering somewhat my brother told me."

"About me?"

The boy blushed again, betraying the answer.

"What was it?" Lilli said. "Everyone knows I'm his mistress. You don't need to be embarrassed."

"I know that." Riddmar looked down at the hard-packed dirt of the ward. "It was just an odd thing."

"What?"

"Well." Riddmar began drawing lines in the dirt with the toe of one boot. "He said he hoped that I never loved a woman the way he loves you." He looked up. "I don't understand that."

"He should be more careful of what he tells you."

"I've not made you angry, have I? I'm sorry. He sort of

blurted it out one night when he wanted me to go away so he could—could visit you."

"I'm not angry. Just weary all of a sudden. Here, let's go back to the great hall. I need to rest."

As they were walking up to the main broch complex, Elyssa came trotting out, lifting her skirts free of the muck as she hurried across the cobbles. She saw them, waved, and waited for them to catch up to her.

"There you are, Your Highness," Elyssa said to Riddmar.

"I stayed in the dun," Riddmar said. "Just like you told me."

"My thanks for that. The captain of the fortguard's looking for you. He wants to give you another lesson in swordcraft."

"Splendid!" Riddmar broke into a grin.

"He's down at the royal stables, the one the silver daggers use when they're here."

"My thanks." Riddmar made her a sketchy bow and did the same to Lilli. "I'll be in his company if you have need of me."

The young prince turned on his heel and ran off, heading across the ward to the stable complex. Elyssa watched him go with a shake of her head.

"He's a fiery young colt," Elyssa said at last. "Which is all to the good."

"He'll need that spirit when he's Gwerbret Cerrmor. He's so awfully young. Shouldn't there be a regent for him?"

"Well, Prince Maryn will hold that rank formally, but of course, he'll be here in Dun Deverry. No doubt one of the councillors will go."

"It would be splendid if Nevyn were appointed to Cerrmor. Then I could go with him."

"Away from the prince?"

"Just that." Lilli laid her hand at her throat. "Don't you think I know the grief I'm causing our princess?"

"It's not you who's doing the causing. But it's honorable of you to consider her grief. Not many lasses would." She paused, her mouth twisting. "None of the others did."

"No doubt. But it's not just the princess. Sometimes I want naught more than to get free of Maryn."

Elyssa made an odd little gasp—out of surprise, Lilli assumed.

"Lyss, I feel like I've got a fever, and it's burning me up. No doubt if I had to go to Cerrmor I'd weep and carry on for days, but then I could recover."

"I see." Elyssa studied her for a long moment. "You truly mean that, don't you? You know, the prince is not a man to force himself upon a woman who refuses him."

"I know that. It's just when I see him, I can't think of anything but him. It's horrid, actually."

"It must be, at that." Elyssa considered for a moment. "Would you like to see the princess?"

"I would, truly. How is she?"

"Much the same. Every little thing makes her weep, and she's so tired, so tired. Not even her needlework distracts her, and she's not been able to put one word into her book. A visit might cheer her a bit."

They went inside and climbed the staircase up to the women's hall, but Degwa met them at the door and motioned for silence.

"She's sleeping," Degwa whispered. "At last, and I'd not wake her."

"Of course not," Elyssa said. "Lilli can come again later."

Degwa stepped out and shut the door to the hall behind her. For a moment they all stood together out in the corridor. Degwa cocked her head to one side and considered Lilli with a nasty little smile.

"I gather," Degwa said, "that you have a brooch that once belonged to me."

Elyssa waved a hand and made a little clucking sound, which Degwa ignored.

"I do," Lilli said. "But you may have it back, if you'd like. I took it only because I thought you didn't want it."

"Well, I don't, at that." Degwa held her head high in the air. "The Boar's leavings should go to a Boar, no doubt."

Degwa stomped off, her wooden clogs loud on the

stone floor, and hurried down the staircase. Elyssa rolled her eyes to the heavens.

"Ye gods!" Elyssa whispered. "My apologies, Lilli."

"There's no need for *you* to apologize. Ah well, Decci is what she is, and that's true for all of us."

When she returned to her chamber, Lilli opened her wooden chest and found the brooch that had once been her mother's. She sat down in her chair and held the silver knot up, letting it catch the sunlight. Why was she keeping it? she wondered. Her mother—a murderess, a sorceress who had used Lilli's own gifts ruthlessly for the clan's advantage. And yet Merodda had put out considerable effort to save Lilli from a horrible marriage; at times she had been kind as well, for no reason other than that Lilli was her daughter. A token for those good things, Lilli decided. That's why I keep it.

Thinking of her blood-kin made Lilli remember Braemys, her cousin, her half brother, and once, too, her betrothed. Dark thoughts gathered, that he was likely to die in the coming fighting. But what if he won the battle? What if Maryn were killed instead? One or the other of them would have to die to settle the feud between them. Deverry men always settled feuds that way, with the death of one or the other. With the brooch clasped tight in one hand, she rose and walked to the window. Outside the sky blazed with gold light, streaked with pink and orange against the darkening blue.

"Dear Goddess," Lilli whispered. "Let Maryn be the victor. I beg you."

And she wondered if she would ever get free of him.

Just at sunset the scouting parties returned to Maryn's camp. Armed with Nevyn's report, Maryn had sent Branoic with some of the silver daggers to the southeast, while a squad from Daeryc's men had ridden straight east. Neither party had seen either half of Braemys's army, which meant that the enemy was, most likely, making camp for the night.

"I'll wager they march here tomorrow, Your Highness,"

Branoic said. "This Braemys—he's young, but he's got a good head on his shoulders."

"So your betrothed told me once," Maryn said. "She knew him well, after all."

"I take it His Highness discussed the matter with her?"

"I did, truly. Why wouldn't I?"

Branoic said nothing more, but his slight smile had turned dangerous. For a moment the two men stared at each other, their eyes narrow, their jaws tight-set, Maryn standing with his plaid cloak draped over one shoulder and his hands set on his hips, while Branoic, his clothes dust-stained, knelt at his feet. The other scouts, waiting behind Branoic, took a step back, but Maryn's servant stopped, dead-still, at the mouth of the tent behind him. Nevyn felt a cold warning run down his back and strode forward, ready to intervene. His movement brought them both to their senses. Maryn forced out a smile and turned it impartially upon all of the waiting men, including Branoic.

"Well done," the prince said. "Don't let me keep you from your fires."

"My thanks, Your Highness." Branoic rose and bowed. "It's been a long day's ride."

In the company of the other scouts Branoic strode off into the sea of tents. Maryn's servant sighed aloud and darted away. Nevyn raised an eyebrow at Maryn, who shrugged.

"My apologies," Maryn said. "I need to watch my tongue."

"A wise thought," Nevyn said.

"That's the worst of it, isn't it? Being the prince, I mean. I'm not allowed to lapse like ordinary men."

"Even ordinary men need to watch their tongues now and again."

Maryn gave him a sour smile, then turned and without another word ducked into his tent. In the gathering twilight Nevyn walked back to his own. The worst danger for the kingdom would arrive tomorrow with Braemys's army, but the worst danger for the prince and those who loved him was waiting back in Dun Deverry.

Deep in the night, once the astral tide of Earth had settled into a steady flow, Nevyn scried again, and once again he found the two halves of Braemys's army, one to the south, one to the east, camped under the stars without tents or campfires. They had sacrificed everything for speed. If Maryn had lacked the presence of a dweomermaster, he and his army would have found themselves caught between two forces like a bite of meat between two jaws.

As it was, of course, they were warned.

Well before dawn Maddyn woke. He sat up in the silent darkness of his tent and considered the odd sensation troubling him. In a few moments he realized that, for the first time in days, he felt hungry. Somewhere near at hand Branoic had left him a chunk of bread on just this chance, but he could see nothing but a triangle of lighter dark at the tent's mouth.

"Curse it all!"

Cautiously he got to his knees and began feeling the ground at the head of his blankets. Behind him he heard a rustling and a sound that might have been a whisper. A silver glow cast sudden shadows. When he twisted round he saw his blue sprite, glowing like the moon and grinning at him.

"My thanks," he said. "And there's the bread."

Branoic had left it wrapped in cloth upon his saddle, the only thing in the tent that would serve as a shelf. Maddyn found a covered tankard of watered ale nearby as well. With his sprite for company, Maddyn began dipping the bread in the ale and eating the moist bits, but he'd not got far into the chunk before he realized he was making a mistake. He tried a sip of plain ale and felt his stomach burn and twist.

"So much for that."

Maddyn wrapped the bread back up, then lay down again, but it took him a long while to sleep with his stomach cramping and complaining. When he finally dozed off, he dreamt of Aethan, lying dead on the battlefield, and woke in a cold sweat. This time, at least, dawnlight streamed into the tent. From outside he heard voices, talking softly; then someone pulled the tent flap to one side and stuck his head in: Nevyn.

"Ah," Nevyn said. "You're awake."

"More or less, my lord." Maddyn sat up, then clutched his aching stomach with both arms. "I tried to eat somewhat in the night."

"With bad result, I see. The prince wants to see you."

"I'll come out."

Much to his relief, Maddyn found that he could crawl out of the tent with some effort and then, with Nevyn's help, stand up. The prince had already donned his chainmail shirt, but the hood lay on his shoulders, and he wore no helm. In the dawnlight his hair gleamed as if the sun itself were honoring him.

"Don't try to kneel or bow," Maryn said. "How do you fare?"

"Not so well, Your Highness, I'm afraid."

"You look pale about the mouth still," Nevyn put in. "After the army rides out, I'll have a better look at you."

"My thanks, my lord."

"Mine, too," the prince said, nodding Nevyn's way. "I wanted to see you, Maddo, because I was just remembering how you and the silver daggers smuggled me from Pyrdon to Cerrmor, all those years ago. We had so little then, do you remember? And we hadn't the slightest idea of what we were riding into."

"So we hadn't." Maddyn smiled, the first time he'd felt like doing so in some days. "And you slept on the ground like an ordinary rider."

"I did." The prince smiled in return. "I remember sharing a fire with you and Branoic." The smile vanished, and for a moment the prince was silent. "Ah well," he said at last, "long time ago now, but that ride began everything. And so I wanted to come thank you now that we're about to end the matter." Maryn held out his hand. "I only wish that Caradoc were here."

"So do I, my liege, so do I."

As he shook hands with the prince, Maddyn felt tears

in his eyes, mourning not only Caradoc but all the men the silver daggers had lost in one battle or another. It had been a long road that they'd travelled to bring the prince to his rightful Wyrd.

"Well," the prince said, "I'd best be gone and let you rest. It's time to get our men ready to march."

Nevyn left with the prince, and Maddyn crawled back into his tent and lay down. The canvas roof, glowing from the light outside, seemed to spin around him. He'd not eaten a true meal in days, but was it hunger making him so light-headed? He doubted it. More likely it was the grief of war.

Nevyn accompanied the prince back to the royal tent. Out in front of it, his vassals were gathering to receive their orders for the battle ahead. Gwerbret Daeryc and Gwerbret Ammerwdd stood in front of the huge red-and-white banners of the wyvern throne, and the rising sun gilded their mail and glittered on their sword hilts. Behind them stood the tieryns, and behind them, the men who could only claim a lordship for their rank.

"Good morrow, my lords," Maryn said, grinning. "Shall we go for a bit of a ride on this lovely morning?"

Some laughed, some cheered him.

"Very well," Maryn went on. "We're dividing our army to match Lord Braemys's little plan."

Nevyn merely listened as they worked out the battle plan. Gwerbret Ammerwdd would command approximately half the army and station it, looking east, across the main road. The other half, with Maryn in charge, would make its stand facing south at the rear of the other. As an extra precaution, Maryn decided to send some twenty men a few miles north to keep a watch for any further cleverness that Nevyn's night travels might have missed.

"Good idea," Gwerbret Ammerwdd said. "I don't trust this son of a Boar."

"Indeed." Daeryc glanced at Ammerwdd. "The crux is this. Your men have to hold until Braemys charges the prince. We can't be turning our line to join your fight until then."

"I'm well aware of that." Ammerwdd's voice turned flat. "And I think our prince knows he may trust me on the matter."

"Of course!" Maryn stepped in between them. "I have the highest regard for both of you." All at once Maryn grinned. "I think me Lord Braemys is in for a bit of a surprise."

"So we may hope," Nevyn put in. "He's badly outnumbered, and cleverness was the best weapon he had."

"Well, it's blunted now. Still—" Maryn hesitated. "Pray for us, and for the kingdom."

"Always, Your Highness. Always."

When the army rode out, Nevyn stood at the edge of the camp and watched till they were out of sight. The cloud of dust that marked their going hung in the air, as cloying as smoke, for a long time. Perhaps, he told himself, perhaps today will be the last battle ever fought over the kingship. All he could do now to ensure it was to invoke the gods and hope. With a weary shake of his head, he walked over to the circle of wagons to meet with the other chirurgeons. They all needed to ready their supplies for the flood of wounded that would soon deluge them.

Like the others, Nevyn would work on the tailgate of a wagon, sluiced down with a bucket of water between patients. On the wagon bed itself he arranged herbs, tools, and bandages, then put a second set of supplies into a cloth sack. Eventually, if the prince won the battle, Nevyn would go to the battlefield to see what he could do for the wounded left there.

At the wagon to his right, Caudyr was doing the same. He was a stout fellow in the prime of life now, not the frightened lad Nevyn had first met as Grodyr's apprentice all those years ago. Grey laced his blond hair—prematurely, really, but then he was often in pain. He had a clubfoot, which gave him an uneven, rolling gait for one thing but for another threw his entire body out of alignment. His hips and knees protested so badly that as he aged he had more and more trouble standing for any long while.

Today as Caudyr laid out his supplies, he looked so pale, his mouth so twisted, that Nevyn went over to his wagon.

"Are you all right?" Nevyn said.

"I will be." Caudyr paused to stretch his back and grimaced. "I slept wrong or suchlike, is all. It'll loosen up in a bit."

Nevyn considered him, but he had nothing to offer to kill pain but strong drink, an impossibility since Caudyr would need all his wits about him.

"Well," Nevyn said at last. "Try to sit down till the battle joins, at least. Though it won't be long now. The prince will be making his stand only about a mile from here, but it's going to take time for the Boar's army to find us."

"Only a mile?"

"He wants to be close at hand should Braemys decide to raid the camp."

"The wretched young pigling tried it last time, truly. He's a clever man, young Braemys."

"He is. Unfortunately."

Both men turned and looked beyond the huddled wagons. Outside of the ring, Oggyn was marching his company of spearmen into position. Beyond the wooden wall they stood shoulder to shoulder in an overlapping formation three men deep. With long spear and shield they made a living wall and a formidable one against an attack on the baggage train. Let's hope they have naught to do but stand there, Nevyn thought. But who knows what the gods have in store for us?

In the hot spring sun Prince Maryn led his men to the chosen field. The army jounced and jingled down the road in a plume of dust that drifted across green pastures and rose high in the windless air, an invitation to Lord Braemys and his allies. As usual when the army marched to battle, the silver daggers rode at its head with Prince Maryn safely in their midst. As he always did, the prince grumbled and complained, too, as if after all these years of riding to war together he still feared that his men would think him a coward. And as usual, Branoic was the one to reassure him.

"Ah for love of the gods, Your Highness!" Branoic said. "If you fall in battle, all these cursed years of fighting won't have been worth a pig's fart."

"True spoken," Maryn said. "But it gripes my heart all the same."

Not far from camp lay their destination, a stretch of fallow fields beside the east-running road. When they turned off the road they found the grass high enough to swish around their horses' legs. With the silver daggers around him Maryn stationed himself at the road, facing south. As each unit arrived he rose in the stirrups and waved a javelin at the spot where he wanted them. Warband after warband trotted across the field till the grass lay trampled into the dirt. Over a thousand riders waited in a rough formation, a curving line some six men deep, an unpleasant surprise for Lord Braemys.

Acting at the prince's request, Gwerbret Ammerwdd led the other half of the army past them. He arranged his units into a shallow crescent with the embrace facing east and blocking the road to greet their share of the enemy when it appeared. Their line stood at right angles to Maryn's, like a bowstring with Maryn's formation the arrow, nocked and ready. By the time the full army stood disposed, the sun had nearly reached the zenith. Ammerwdd rode up to the prince and made him a bow from the saddle.

"My liege, if I may be so bold, it would be best if you withdrew from the first rank."

"So it would," Maryn said. "Very well, silver daggers, follow me."

Ammerwdd bowed again, then trotted back to his own line. Prince Maryn led his silver daggers through the ranks of the south-facing army and took a place behind the center of the long line. The banners of the red wyvern stood off to one side, billowing as the wind rose.

"Naught to do now but wait," Owaen remarked.

"Not for long." Branoic rose in his stirrups, turned

toward the east, and shaded his eyes with one hand. "I see dust coming. Ammerwdd's men are going on alert."

He heard Maryn burst out laughing, and on that laughter the command travelled through the ranks: draw javelins and stand ready to use them. With a jingle of mail the men leaned down and drew the short war javelins from the sheaths under their right legs. Horses stamped and tossed their heads; some men laughed, while others turned grim and quiet. Branoic was about to make some jest when he saw the ravens, circling high above the assembled armies.

"Look at that," he said to Owaen, "the cursed birds are eager, aren't they? Three big ones!"

"What birds?" Owaen was looking up where Branoic was pointing. "I don't see any birds."

"Oh." Branoic lowered his javelin. "Guess I was imagining things."

He felt very cold, and very still, as if his vision, his mind, his heart, his very soul had all suddenly turned inward away from the world. As he looked out toward the south, where a second plume of dust had just appeared, it seemed that he was seeing not the day and the landscape but a thin grey picture of them. The Three, he thought to himself. Well, lad, you always knew it would come to this. When he looked Owaen's way, he saw him rising in his stirrups and looking toward Ammerwdd's position.

"Here comes the first lot of rebels," Owaen said abruptly. "Hold your position, men! Wait for the Boar and his little pigs to arrive!"

Off to their left, beyond the crescent of Ammerwdd's waiting line, noise exploded, men screaming war cries, galloping hooves, the whinny of frightened horses, and all the jingling chaos of a charge. All along Maryn's line horses stamped and neighed in answer; the men had to fight to keep their mounts in position. Off to the south the plume of dust swelled like smoke high into the crystal-blue sky. A few moments more, and figures appeared under the dust, a lot of them, mailed riders on horseback, following the grey banners of the Boar.

"Here they come," Owaen whispered, then laughed, a little mutter under his breath.

Branoic could hear the horses. With a howl of war cries, Braemys's men started their charge, expecting to slam into the rear of the fighting. Branoic settled his shield on his left arm, raised the javelin in his right, and waited.

At about the time that Braemys was leading his share of the rebel army toward the banners of the Red Wyvern, Lilli was sitting in her window, perched on the sill and looking down on the ward far below. Her intellect seemed to have deserted her—she could neither study nor think clearly thanks to the icy cold fear that gripped her. When she held up a hand, she found it shaking. Somewhat's going to happen, she thought. Some evil thing. She gasped for air; her lungs ached, or so it felt, as if some invisible being was squeezing her ribs with huge hands.

Overhead a flock of little birds flew, chirping and twittering to themselves—sparrows, most likely, but suddenly in her mind they loomed huge and black, shrieking as they wheeled round the dun. The sunlight began to disappear, swallowed up by the black of raven wings. Lilli had just enough presence of mind to twist around and fall inside the chamber rather than out to her death. She lay huddled on the floor and heard herself moan as the vision overwhelmed her.

Over the battlefield she flew among the ravens. To her horror she realized that the birds were as real as the armies, that they rode the wind and waited for the feast being prepared for them below. In the vision state she heard nothing, not war cry nor clash of metal. The sunlight and the silence melted together into something thick and enveloping, as if she were drowning in honey. At first, too, she could barely make sense out of what she saw. The fields below glittered—armed men, she realized—their armor glittered as they charged together, broke apart, spun, rushed this way and that. Surges of movement carried ten, twenty, some uncountable number of horses and men forward, then turned on some tide of their own and swept them back again. At times the mobs below pulled apart, and she could see the ground, all trampled grass and red stain. At other times it seemed to her visionary sight that the red blood rose like a river in spate to pull the men and horses down under its drowning waves.

Slowly she began to pick out details: a sword held high, a javelin gleaming as it sped through the air. Banners rose out of the chaos. She saw the grey Boar of her old clan first, dipping and swaying in the midst of hard fighting. Like the ravens she wheeled and turned. Maryn! she thought. The red wyvern! At her thought she saw his banners, creeping forward in the midst of a tight squad of riders. These horsemen moved together like longtime partners in some well-known dance. When the squad leader turned, they turned smoothly; when he charged, they leapt forward together. Silver daggers, Lilli thought.

"Branoic!"

She heard her own voice speak his name, the first sound in this long ghastly vision. At the sound she saw him, or rather a rider who she somehow knew must be him, up near the front of the squad. Swords flew and horses reared or stumbled. Wyvern shields flashed up, Boar shields answered them. A wedge came cutting its way through from the Boar's side of the melee and slammed into the side of the silver daggers. Lilli heard herself scream and scream again as the wyvern banner swung, dipped, threatened to fall. She could look at nothing else until at last, with a defiant swoop, it straightened itself and soared once more above the melee.

The Boars began to retreat, but one silver dagger had ridden too far out. He was cut off, doomed—but another—Branoic—spurred his horse and came after, swinging hard, yelling a horrible hoarse cry that blended with her own screaming, the only sounds she could hear. Men fought and died in silence; horses wrenched their mouths open in agony; she heard nothing but Branoic's berserk howl and her own terror matching it. It seemed to her that she hovered low over him as he swung and cut and shoved his way to the isolated rider's side. For a moment the two held position, doomed together, it seemed.

Sudden flashes of metal filled her vision. Prince Maryn himself came charging in to the rescue with the other silver daggers right behind him.

She saw blood. Saw a sword rise and fall. Saw Branoic's face run with blood. Heard his howl cut off, heard nothing but her own sobbing. Saw nothing but his face, slashed half-open like a torn mask hanging in blackness. Saw nothing.

"My lady, oh my lady!" Clodda's voice sobbed in the blackness. "My lady, oh by the Goddess!"

Lilli opened her eyes and saw her maidservant's face, perfectly sound and whole, leaning over her. She was lying on the floor, Clodda was kneeling next to her, they were in her chamber.

"Oh thank the gods! My lady, I thought you were dying."

"Here." Elyssa's voice came from some near distance. "Give her some water."

Clodda put an arm around Lilli's shoulders and helped her sit up enough to lean against the wall, then held the wooden cup while Lilli drank. Elyssa knelt down beside the maidservant.

"What is it?" Elyssa said. "Did you fall? Are you in pain?"

"Should we get old Grodyr to attend you?" Clodda said.

Lilli shook her head and took the cup, then gulped more water. The two women sat back on their heels and waited till she finished.

"I had a vision." Lilli could hear her voice croak, all hoarse. "Branoic's been wounded. Badly."

They stared at her for a long silent moment. She braced herself against meaningless reassurances, but none came.

"Oh gods, how horrible!" Elyssa said. "I'll pray for him, then."

"And so will I," Clodda said. "There's not much else we can do."

"That's true," Lilli whispered. "I wish it weren't, but it is."

• • •

The chirurgeons back in camp heard the battle begin, a distant shouting on the wind. For some while they paced back and forth beside their readied wagons, but soon enough the wounded began to arrive. Some men could still ride, others came in the company of friends who left them to rush back to the slaughter. With them came news: the Boar forces had received the shock of their life to see Maryn waiting for them. The other part of the enemy army, that under the command of Braemys's allies, had broken fast—its men had been bandits, mostly, was the judgment of those men who could talk well enough to consider the matter.

The sun was still fairly high in the sky when the tide of wounded began to swell. This time the slightly wounded men brought in the badly wounded, and most of those died while the chirurgeons were trying to help them. Yet their presence meant that some troops had the leisure to help their comrades, that the battle was turning Maryn's way. Distantly on the wind came the sound of silver horns, screeching for a retreat. Nevyn prayed that it was the Boars pulling back. A man with a bloody scrape down one arm confirmed Nevyn's guess while he waited his turn.

"The Boars are running like a lot of scared pigs," the rider said. "I'm no captain, my lord, but I think me they were only planning on making one try on the prince and then retreating if they couldn't kill him straightaway."

"What?" Nevyn turned briefly away from the patient lying on the wagon bed. "They were making straight for the prince?"

"They were, my lord, but the silver daggers, they were right around him."

For a moment Nevyn felt fear like a cold stone in his stomach. If the prince were slain? Yet he had only a little while to wait before he learned that Maryn was safe. He had just finished binding his informant's arm when he heard someone yelling his name. He turned and saw the prince himself, his mail hood pushed back, his pale hair plastered to his skull with sweat, running toward him.

"It's Branoic! He's bleeding too badly for us to bring him all the way in."

Nevyn grabbed his readied sack of supplies and raced after Maryn as he led the way back. By then the tide of wounded had turned to a flood. Men brought them in fast, dumped them near the wagons, then rushed back to their horses to return to the field. Together Nevyn and Maryn picked their way across the camp, strewn with the dead and dying, horses and men both. In the middle of the worst of it they found Caudyr and a little clot of silver daggers clustered around someone who lay on ground turned muddy with blood. At the prince's order, the men parted to let Nevyn through. He saw Branoic with Caudyr kneeling beside him, pressing a wad of bandages to Branoic's face. Red oozed through the pale linen. Branoic struggled to sit up.

"Lie still!" Caudyr snarled.

Maryn fell to his knees behind Branoic's head and shoved him back down by the shoulders. Caudyr gasped out a thanks.

"Where is it?" Nevyn knelt beside his fellow chirurgeon.

"Cut his mouth in two," Caudyr said. "A lucky stroke just under the nasal of his helmet. It's deep, and it won't staunch."

Caudyr lifted the wad quickly and pressed it back even quicker, but Nevyn had seen what he needed to. The blow had split both lips, shattered teeth, then bitten deep on either cheek, almost to the ear on the left side of his face. No doubt the skull lay cracked under that part of the wound as well. Branoic's eyes sought him out, and in them Nevyn read a desperate resignation. *He knows he's going to die,* Nevyn thought. Aloud he said, "Let's get it stitched up. We daren't move him till we do."

Prince Maryn rose, glancing around him. "Well, don't just stand there, you pissproud lot of slackers! Get out there and find the rest of our wounded!"

The men rushed off at his order, but the prince himself lingered, staring down at his rival. Nevyn had no time to wonder if Maryn were glad or sorry to see Branoic at the gates of the Otherlands, and in a moment, the prince turned and walked away. Nevyn rummaged in his sack and found a long needle, threaded and ready.

"Nevyn, your aid!" Caudyr yelped.

Nevyn turned back to Branoic and found him choking on his own blood. Caudyr had put one arm under his massive shoulders and was trying to raise them whilst keeping the bandages pressed on the wound. Nevyn grabbed the wad and let Caudyr lift. Branoic's face was dead-white and sweating; the skin of his eyelids stretched thin, a pale bluish white. Suddenly his cloudy eyes rolled back in his head. He coughed, spasmed, flailing with one arm and waving it near his head, as if he were trying to find his face.

"It's no use," Nevyn whispered.

Caudyr nodded. Branoic convulsed again, both arms working, and somehow managed to pull himself up to a sitting position. For the briefest of moments he stared unspeaking at Nevyn's face; then he arched his back and fell in an oddly graceful gesture to die against Caudyr. With a sigh the chirurgeon laid the body down upon the ground and crossed its arms over its chest. Nevyn felt his cold skin crawl with the presence of spirits close at hand, clustering on the etheric plane.

"Ah horseshit!" Caudyr muttered. "That's one death I'd hoped never to see."

"Me either." Nevyn could barely speak. "Well, there's naught to be done here. You'd best get back to work. I'll follow in a moment."

Caudyr nodded, then got up, shaking his head, and hurried off, heading back to the circled wagons and his improvised surgery. Still kneeling, Nevyn opened his dweomer sight and looked up, searching for Branoic's etheric double. Dimly he saw great shafts of silver light, vaguely manshaped, surrounding the pale blue form that once had been Branoic's soul. The Lords of the Elements had come to guide him—no, her—to the Light that lies beyond death. In her true female form she was staring down at the male body she had worn, as if perhaps in disbelief.

"My thanks," he whispered to the lords. "My solemn thanks."

They nodded his way. Nevyn closed down the sight and scrambled to his feet, grabbing his sack of supplies. There were other men dying on this field, and his duty lay with them, no matter how badly he wished he could say farewell to the soul that he would always think of as his Brangwen.

Maddyn had spent the battle lying under one of the wagons and cursing himself for a weakling for being unable to fight. Finally, when he heard men yelling, others sobbing or crying out, the hurrying of horses and the curses, he knew that the wounded were being brought in. He went out, found a couple of waterskins, and made himself useful as a water carrier for the wounded men. He had just refilled the skins for the fifth time when Caudyr hailed him.

"Maddo, Maddo! Branoic's dead."

Maddyn turned fast to see the chirurgeon limping over. He felt nothing but a chill that seemed to have frozen his mouth shut. He shrugged, tried to speak, then merely stared at Caudyr in a blind hope that he'd misheard.

"I thought mayhap we could dig him a proper grave," Caudyr went on. "When there's time."

Maddyn nodded to show that he understood, then turned on his heel and walked away. By then the men of the army were reclaiming their possessions from the heap in the middle of the protective wagons. Tents were already rising, men were talking about finding provisions and firewood. Maddyn found his own bedroll with Branoic's piled under it. For a moment he nearly wept. He grabbed one of Branoic's blankets, then headed for the long sprawl of dead men brought back to camp. He could see their friends wrapping them in blankets like the one he held to lay them out for the morrow's burying. By then the sun hung low and striped the sky with pale gold at the horizon. As he walked down the long grim lines, Maddyn began to wonder if he'd be able to find Branoic's body, but at length he saw Owaen, standing next to one of the dead.

"Over here," Owaen called out. "I can guess who you're looking for."

Maddyn joined him. Owaen had cast off his mail to reveal his rust-stained and filthy shirt; his hair lay plastered against his skull with sweat. Branoic lay on the ground, stripped of his mail and sword. Maddyn swore at the sight of the wound, a ghastly gape of red as if Death herself smiled up at them. When he knelt, he threw the blanket over Branoic's face first. With Owaen's help he wrapped Branoic up. For a moment they knelt at his side.

"Remember us in the Otherlands," Maddyn whispered. "The gods all know we'll be joining you soon enough."

Together they rose, then stood together, shoulders touching. Maddyn looked down at the old blue blanket wound round what was left of a man he'd known for more years than he could remember. He felt his grief like a blanket pressed into his face, smothering him. Involuntarily he shuddered, tossing his head as if to throw it off. He heard Owaen step back.

"Did you see it happen?" Maddyn said.

When Owaen didn't answer, Maddyn looked up to find him staring off at the sunset, his head thrown a little back, his jaw set tight.

"Ah well," Maddyn said. "See that stone wall over there, across the pasture? On the morrow, when they bury him, I'll be wanting to haul some stones to set up a cairn. Will you help?"

Owaen nodded.

"And what about his poor lass?" Maddyn went on. "It aches my heart, thinking of her praying he'll ride home soon, and here he's already ridden through the gates of the Otherlands."

"Just so." Owaen kicked the ground hard with the toe of his boot. "Oh horseshit and a warm tub of it!" He turned and ran, trotting down the long line of their dead.

Despite the warmth of the night, Lilli had her maid build a small fire in the hearth in her chamber. She wanted light, and lanterns would, she felt, cast only shadows. As she sat in her chair and tried to read, her mind kept turning to the war and to Branoic. No matter how hard she concentrated on the book in front of her, the horrors she'd seen earlier kept breaking into her studies. Finally she laid the book aside and stared into the flames. She found herself thinking of Branoic, remembering the blood sheeting from his face. Nevyn will save him—she told herself this repeatedly but didn't believe it once.

Suddenly in the glowing coals she could see Nevyn, a tiny figure, it seemed, walking among the ashes. She leaned forward in her chair, concentrated on the image, saw the embers turn into the image of another fire as the darkness of a night camp appeared through the flames. The fire faded away, and it seemed to her that she walked beside Nevyn, who was carrying a cloth sack as he threaded his way through the tents. At length he returned to the tent she recognized as his from the past summer's expedition. In a stone circle a tidy stack of wood waited for him. When Nevyn snapped his fingers, salamanders rushed forward to light it. He tossed the sack into his tent, then sat down on a stool in front of the fire. Lilli saw him lean forward—the view changed. It seemed to her that she sat on the other side of fire and looked across at him.

"Lilli!" Nevyn's voice sounded in her mind. "How did you reach me?"

"I don't know, my lord."

"Think to me, don't speak aloud. I can't hear you when you actually talk."

"Well and good, then. I was looking into the fire, and then I saw you. Can you hear me now?"

"I can. You must be badly troubled, to reach me this way."

"It's Branoic. I saw it—I mean, I had one of my visions, and I saw him take that wound. How does he fare?"

"Oh my poor child! I'm afraid he died soon after."

A flood of tears washed the vision away. Lilli covered

her face with her hands and sobbed, rocking back and forth on the edge of her chair.

Although Nevyn tried for some while to reach Lilli again, he failed, picking up only her grief like the sound of distant keening. Finally, he broke the link and threw a few more sticks onto his sputtering fire. As the flames leapt, he became aware that someone was standing in the shadows beyond the pool of light and watching him.

"Who is it?" Nevyn snapped. "How long have you been standing there?"

"Owaen, my lord, and not long at all." The silver dagger captain took a few steps forward. "I—er, well—I wanted a bit of a talk with you."

"Very well. Come sit down."

Owaen sat down on the ground about an arm's length away. For a few moments they stared into the fire together. Owaen's face was as expressionless as a mask.

"Ah well," Owaen said at last. "It's about Branoic."

"I see. You're surprised that you're sorry he's dead. You thought you'd be glad, but you're not."

"Just that!" Owaen looked up sharply. "Ye gods, you truly can see into a man's soul, can't you?"

"Only when his feelings are obvious."

Owaen tried to smile but failed. "He got that wound saving my worthless life. I got cut off at the head of our countercharge, and he came up to pull me out of a mob. Ye gods! I thought he hated me. Why would he do it?"

"You're a silver dagger and the captain," Nevyn said. "That's reason enough."

Abruptly Owaen raised one arm and buried his face in the crook, but in a brief moment he lowered it again. His voice shook. "I was thinking about his woman. She's left with no one to protect her, if our prince tires of her, I mean. Do you think I should offer to marry her?"

Nevyn's first impulse, quickly stifled, was to laugh.

"That's an honorable thought," he said instead. "But she has me and her studies. The prince would know better than to try to send her away from court or some such thing."

"True spoken." Owaen smiled, relieved. "I wouldn't have made her much of a husband, anyway. But I felt I should offer."

It seemed that the prince was worried about Lilli as well. The next morning, when the army was digging trenches to bury its dead, Maryn summoned Nevyn to his side. They escaped the noise and confusion by walking clear of the encampment. Out in the middle of what had once been a field, they could see a pair of men pulling stones off its boundary wall and carrying them out onto the grass.

The prince shaded his eyes with one hand. "That's Maddyn and Owaen. I wonder what they're doing."

"Building Branoic a cairn, most like," Nevyn said. "I saw Maddo earlier, and he said that he and a couple of the lads had dug him a proper grave."

"Oh." Maryn lowered his hand and looked at him with bleak eyes. "I thought I'd got used to men dying for my sake. I was wrong."

"Well, Your Highness, this particular death—" Nevyn let his words trail away.

"Indeed. Do you want me to find Lilli some other husband?"

"I don't. I think me the dweomer will give her all the position in court that she'll need."

Maryn nodded, staring at the ground. "I'm sending messengers back this morning. I tried to write her a letter, but I couldn't. I just couldn't. I don't know why. I felt as if I'd never known how to read and write."

Nevyn choked back his own words: it's because this death gladdens your secret heart. "Well, you could send a special messenger," he said instead.

"Good thought. I know! Maddyn. He's still blasted weak from that spoiled pork. We're sending the wounded back to Dun Deverry, and he can join the escort."

For a moment Nevyn felt struck dumb. The dweomer-cold seemed to freeze his lips and fill his mouth with ice.

Maryn glanced his way and considered him with narrow eyes.

"What's so wrong?"

"My apologies, my liege." Nevyn had to force out the first few words; then his voice steadied. "That escort? Will it be substantial? I have the oddest feeling that Maddyn and the wounded will be in some sort of danger."

"I'll double it, then." Maryn smiled briefly. "I know those odd feelings of yours by now."

Lilli woke and found her chamber filled with cold grey light. For a moment she lay in bed. Her eyes burned, and her head throbbed with pain. Did I sleep? she wondered. Did I sleep at all? I must have. All at once, she remembered.

"Branno," she whispered.

Her hot and swollen eyes refused to deliver more tears. She sat up, pushing the blankets back. She had wept for half the night, or so it seemed as she looked back upon it. In her hearth a pile of ash testified to the fire in which she had seen Nevyn's face and heard him speaking. It was odd, she realized, but never once, not even in the depths of her grief, had she tried to pretend to herself that the vision had been merely some unreal dream. She knew it beyond doubting. Branoic was dead.

Someone pounded on the door.

"Who is it?" Lilli called out.

"Just me, my lady." Clodda's normally cheerful voice trembled. "You've barred the door, and I can't get in."

"I'm sorry." Lilli got up and went to the door. "I didn't mean to worry you."

She unbarred the door, opened it wide, and let Clodda come in. The maidservant dropped her a brief curtsy.

"I was ever so afraid you'd been taken ill," Clodda said.

"Not ill, truly." Lilli hesitated. Telling someone about Branoic's death would make it horribly real—but it's real anyway, she told herself. "Branoic's dead. Nevyn told me last night. He used dweomer."

Clodda's face turned pale. "Oh my lady!" Her voice shook with tears. "That wrings my heart."

"Mine too."

"No doubt." Clodda pulled up a corner of her dirty apron and wiped her eyes. "Oh, it's so sad. My poor lady."

With a sigh Lilli sat down on the edge of the bed. "It must be well into the morning. Why is the light so cold?"

"Clouds, my lady." Clodda looked at her sharply, as if wondering if Lilli had gone mad with grief. "It's going to rain, I wager."

"Oh. Rain. Could you go to the great hall and find me somewhat to eat? Bread would do."

"I will. Lady Elyssa has been asking for you. That's why I came up and knocked."

"I'll dress, then. If you see her, ask her if she'd just come to my chamber."

Clodda must have seen the lady in the great hall, because Elyssa herself brought Lilli a basket of bread and butter in but a little while, just as Lilli had finished combing her hair. Elyssa set the basket on the table and considered Lilli for a moment in the harsh grey light streaming in the window.

"Clodda's right," Elyssa said. "You do look ill. Your cheeks—they're all red and raw!"

"I'm always a little bit ill."

"Or is it from tears? She told me that you're convinced Branoic's dead."

"Don't you believe me?"

"It was Clodda I was doubting, not you. I suppose you must have been—er, what does Nevyn call that?"

"Scrying."

"My heart goes out to you, lass." Elyssa looked away, biting her lower lip. "Another good man gone."

"Oh ye gods, I wish I could weep some more. I feel like a bit of old rag the cook used to scrub a pot or suchlike. All soiled and wrung out and twisted."

Elyssa nodded. She seemed to be searching for words, then sighed and held out the basket of bread.

"Here. Do eat."

Lilli took a piece of bread and bit into it. Her grief robbed it of all its savor, but she forced herself to keep eating to reassure Elyssa.

"You look more than a little unwell," Elyssa said, watching her. "I was going to ask if you'd like to visit us up in the women's hall, but I think me you'd best stay here and rest."

After Elyssa left, Lilli threw the half-eaten chunk of bread back into the basket. She went to the wooden chest at the foot of the bed, knelt, and opened it. Right on top lay the pieces of Branoic's wedding shirt, which she'd not quite finished embroidering. He'd never wear it now. He had died too far away to even be buried in it. Next to it lay the little knife she used for cutting thread, a short blade but sharp. She took it out and her little mirror with it.

She propped the mirror up on the mantel, and by twisting this way and that, she could see well enough to chop off her hair, a twist at a time, sawing it short with the sewing knife as a sign of her mourning for her betrothed. She'd heard bards recite old tales from back in the Dawntime, when mourning women gashed their faces as well. For a moment she was tempted—not to mourn Branoic but to keep Maryn away. With a shudder she laid the knife down. In the mirror her face looked back, puffy-eyed, pinched, the short hair all ragged. She turned away, remembering how he looked, sitting on the edge of her bed.

"I did love you," she whispered. "I'll pray to the Goddess that you believed me."

Lilli put the mirror and knife away, then wrapped up the cut-off hair in the sleeve of the shirt that would have been Branoic's. She put the shirt away, then returned to her chair and stared out the window. Every breath she drew made her chest ache, as if her grief had filled her lungs and turned them heavy.

The sun had barely started to climb into the sky when Nevyn left his tent and went to tend the wounded. He found Caudyr there ahead of him, and as they started their

work, other chirurgeons came to join them and some of the
servants as well. As Nevyn had feared, several men had
died in the night. The servants wrapped them in blankets
and carried them away. Nevyn had finished his rounds and
was just washing the gore off his hands and arms when
Gavlyn, the prince's chief herald, came running, carrying a
long staff bound with ribands.

"My lord Nevyn!" Gavlyn called out. "Lord Braemys
wants to parley."

"Indeed?" Nevyn said. "Well, that's welcome news!"

Together they hurried across the camp. The night before, servants had pitched Maryn's tent apart from those of
the other noble-born; a good ten feet of bare ground surrounded it. Out in front a groom waited with Gavlyn's dun
gelding, saddled and bridled. In the horse's black mane
hung ribands of red and yellow. Maryn himself came out of
the tent just as Nevyn arrived; he wore the red-and-white
plaid of Cerrmor, pinned at one shoulder with the huge silver brooch that marked him as a prince.

"This is good news," Maryn remarked to Nevyn. "I'm
hoping and praying that Braemys wants to swear fealty and
end this thing."

"So am I, Your Highness," Nevyn said, "so am I."

"We should know soon. Gavlyn, you have my leave
to go."

But in the end they waited a good long while to hear
Lord Braemys's decision. All that morning, while Maryn
paced, stewing with impatience in front of his tent, the heralds rode back and forth, negotiating the conditions for the
meeting between Prince Maryn and Lord Braemys. Each
side suspected the other of having treachery in mind, and as
Maryn remarked to Nevyn, he could understand why.

"The war's been hard enough fought," the prince said,
"and my men did kill his father."

"And his men did his best to kill you," Nevyn said, "by
a ruse."

Over the next long while, Maryn's vassals strolled over
to join him in ones and twos. Daeryc and Ammerwdd paced
up and down with him. The lower-ranked men sat on the

ground and talked among themselves in low voices. Finally, not long before noon, Gavlyn returned, leading his horse with one hand and carrying the staff in the other. Everyone got up fast, but no one spoke, not even the prince. The groom trotted forward and took the dun gelding's reins, but when he started to lead the horse away, Gavlyn stopped him.

"I'll be going back out, lad," Gavlyn said. He turned to the prince and bowed. "Your Highness, this is going to be a long slow thing. We've spent what, half the morning? And we've only got this far: Braemys wishes to discuss terms, but he'll only do so under certain conditions."

A good many of the lords swore, muttering among themselves. When Maryn raised a hand, they fell silent.

"Oh ye gods!" Maryn said. "And does he think he's in any position to dictate these conditions?"

"He doesn't, Your Highness," Gavlyn said. "There's no arrogance here, just fear. Their herald's going to ride back to their camp when he gets my answer. A long ride, he said, but he refused to tell me the slightest thing that might tell me where the camp was. I take it that Lord Braemys's army is much depleted."

Everyone turned to look at Nevyn. Since he'd scryed on the etheric during the night past, he had answer for them.

"It is," Nevyn said. "I'd say he has no more than a thousand men, and that's a very generous guess. A good many of his allies must have deserted him."

"Indeed?" Ammerwdd stepped forward. "If we were to hunt him down, we'd have an easy victory and end the Boar clan forever."

"Your Grace!" Gavlyn turned dead-white. "The man's asked for parley."

"Just so." Maryn smiled in a wry sort of way. "We've done our best to conduct ourselves honorably all through the war, and I've no desire to dishonor myself and my vassals now."

Ammerwdd started to speak, then caught himself with a shrug.

"Very well," Maryn went on. "What are these conditions?"

"I've no idea, Your Highness. We've not got that far."

"Ye gods!" Ammerwdd muttered. "How long will the little bastard weasel? It's an insult, Your Highness, for a man to drag these things out. How long are we going to put up with him mocking our honor?"

"Consider this, Your Grace," Maryn said. "Suppose we cut the parley short. Braemys and his men will flee. If they reach Cantrae safely, we could spend a year digging them out of it."

"True spoken." Ammerwdd gave in with a bow in the prince's direction. "He won't talk as long as all that."

"Just so." Maryn smiled, then turned to Gavlyn. "Tell the Boar clan's herald that we'll parley till we reach an honorable conclusion to the matter."

"My thanks, Your Highness. I'll just be on my way, then."

To pass the time till Gavlyn returned, Nevyn organized the wagon train that would carry the wounded home to Dun Deverry. Maryn designated fifty sound men for an escort, and Oggyn handed over supplies for everyone. By then the army had eaten enough of their supplies to free up six wagons. Others of the wounded men would be able to ride.

"Just keep the pace slow," Nevyn told Maddyn. "Not that you'll have much choice in that."

"True spoken," Maddyn said. "Do you have private letters you want delivered, my lord?"

"I do." Nevyn reached into his shirt and handed him two silver message tubes. "One for Bellyra, one for Lilli. Go to Lilli first. She'll read the headings and tell you which is which."

"The princess can read, too."

"I know, but I don't want her getting a look at Lilli's letter."

"I see." Maddyn smiled briefly. "Very well, my lord. Lilli first it is."

Maddyn put the letters into his own shirt for safekeeping. Nevyn considered him: still pale and visibly thinner, but he had managed to keep some porridge down that morning.

"Be careful of what you eat and drink," Nevyn said. "No dried beef and suchlike for you, bard."

"Oh, have no fear of that, my lord! One round of spoiled food is enough to last me for life."

The wounded men left camp at noon. Nevyn stood in the road and watched them go until the dust cloud shrank to a smear on the distant view. He could only hope that they'd all reach the dun alive, but for many of them, he feared.

All that afternoon Gavlyn and the Boar's herald held their talks out in a green pasture to the north of the camp. By evening, nothing had been truly settled, but Gavlyn felt confident that the herald was bargaining in good faith.

"We'll reach an end to this eventually," Gavlyn told Nevyn. "Not soon, but eventually."

"What exactly is Braemys so afraid of?" Nevyn said. "Do you know?"

"From what his herald told me, I'm guessing he fears capture more than death. He suspects our prince of wanting to hang him."

"Ah. That would explain it, then. It's a terrible death for a fighting man."

"I don't know how convincing I am, but I've tried to make clear to the herald that Maryn is the soul of honor."

"Well and good, then. There's not much else you can do."

On the morrow the negotiations started again. Soon after Gavlyn rode out, Nevyn noticed a few wisps of cloud streaking the western quadrant of the sky. A west wind picked up, and all morning the clouds came in, a few stipples at first, then a sky-spanning reach of them, like a spill of clabbered milk against a blue dish. Oh splendid! Nevyn thought. The most important parley in a hundred years, and it's going to rain! Unless, of course, he did something about it. He left the prince to his vassals and hurried to his tent.

Outside the noisy life of the camp strolled by: men laughing and jesting, or mourning some dead friend in an outburst of rage. Thanks to long practice Nevyn could withdraw his attention from it all. He sat down cross-legged, let his breathing calm, then visualized a ray of silver light circling him deosil, that is, in the direction of the sun's travel through the sky. At each cardinal point he placed, again in his imagination, a five-pointed star of blue fire. When he spoke a word of power, the imaginary circle sprang into life on the etheric plane. While he couldn't see it with his physical eyes, he could feel its energy trembling and surging all round him.

With the place of working prepared, Nevyn called to the Lords of Water. Streaks of silvery-blue light appeared in front of each pentagram, wavering at first, then solid, turning into pillars of light. Within each swam a vaguely human form. Nevyn could hear them as a chorus of thoughts within his own mind. How they might hear him lay beyond his knowledge. Yet they understood when he asked them to prevent the storm, and he understood when they told him it was impossible. They could, however, bring the storm to a head early, so that after a night's rain the next day would dawn clear.

"I thank you for that," Nevyn told them. "It will do splendidly."

With a murmur of assent, they disappeared.

By sunset the iron-dark clouds seemed to hang so close to earth that it seemed one could reach up and touch them. The setting sun could do no more than stain the west with a sullen orange. Just before the night smothered even that faint glow, a weary Gavlyn returned to camp. After the evening meal, when Maryn's vassals joined him around the fire in front of the royal tent, Gavlyn delivered his report.

"Lord Braemys insists that Prince Maryn meet him in open country. He suggests that each side bring a personal guard of twenty men, a councillor, and a herald. The guards must stay some thirty yards away from the parley itself. Braemys has a field in mind, some ways from our camp, that's free of trees and suchlike. He says that each side will be able to see the surrounding countryside clearly and thus be assured that no ambuscade has been laid by the other."

"Very well," Maryn said. "This all sounds fair to me. Nevyn, will you be able to tell if he has some treachery in mind?"

"Most likely, Your Highness," Nevyn said. "But truly, think of the situation. Braemys is badly outnumbered. If he chose treachery, he'd lose the subsequent battle and his life."

"True spoken. Gavlyn, meet the herald tomorrow as early as you can and tell him we accept these conditions."

"I'll ride out at first light, Your Highness." Gavlyn bowed to him. "I think he's as eager to get this done as I am."

A sudden flash of silver burst overhead. For the briefest of moments Nevyn wondered if Braemys had dark dweomer on his side after all, but he caught himself with a laugh. The promised storm had begun. Thunder boomed and rolled, and as it died away Nevyn could hear the whinnies of frightened horses and the yells of the men rushing out to calm them. The lords gathered around Maryn as if to protect him and braced themselves as a second bolt split the sky. The rain broke and fell in a downpour. The fire hissed, fought, and died. All through the camp, fires drowned until the only light was the occasional flicker of a sheltered lantern.

"Get back to your men!" Maryn called out. "There's naught more to be said here."

Again the lightning, and again the thunder.

"Except by the gods," Maryn added, and fast. "And by their will and the power of Tarn the Thunderer."

Apparently his tribute appeased them, because the next flash of lightning shone less brightly, and it took a brief while after before the thunder sounded. Even though the lightning moved away fast, heading for the east, the camp spent a wet and miserable night. Still, when they woke the next morning, the rain had stopped, just as the Lords of Water had promised. In the cold grey light, men pulled wet clothes from soggy saddlebags and spread them out to dry, then lined up at the provision wagons for clammy flatbread and sopping strips of dried beef.

After he ate, Nevyn picked his way through the mud to Maryn's tent. The prince was standing outside with a fistful of soggy bread in one hand and a tankard of ale in the other.

"There you are," Maryn said with his mouth full. He swallowed hastily. "Gavlyn's already ridden out."

"Good," Nevyn said. "I hope the other herald's there to meet him."

"Me too. I'll just send my manservant to see if Owaen's picked our twenty guards. If he has, let's ride."

The location of the parley proved to be some five miles north of the Wyvern camp. With ten silver daggers riding in front and ten more behind, Nevyn, Maryn, and Gavlyn followed a narrow dirt track that led through flat green fields where weeds and brambles grew as high as their horses' chests. The track brought them to a road of packed earth, and there they paused. Some distance ahead, in a long stretch of flat pasture where, just as Braemys had promised, there was neither wall nor copse to hide so much as one traitorous swordsmen, they could see a gathering of men on horseback. Owaen rose in his stirrups and shaded his eyes with one hand while he counted. He sat back down with a satisfied grunt.

"Just twenty, Your Highness," Owaen said, "and one man well out in front. Braemys, I'd say, but there's no sign of his councillor or herald."

"It matters not to me," Maryn said. "He's the one who asked for them." With a wave to Nevyn to follow, Maryn turned his horse and headed in the direction of the waiting riders.

By then the wind was driving the storm away, but while the western half of the sky shone clear, in the east clouds hung dark like a huge wall, so that it seemed they met outside of some fortress of the gods. On a blood bay gelding with black mane and tail Lord Braemys rode out to meet them. He wore neither helm nor sword, though Nevyn could see the bulky lines of a mail hauberk worn under his shirt. In the flood of sunlight his blond hair gleamed. A wary five yards or so away he stopped his horse and sat, reins in one hand while he looked them over. Braemys was just raising his first beard, Nevyn noticed—a sprinkling of fine hair on his chin and upper lip. Nevyn heard Maryn swear under his breath and glanced at the prince, who was staring at his enemy in a kind of amazement. Only then did it occur to Nevyn that with his fine features and wide blue eyes, Braemys looked very much like Lilli.

With a toss of his head Maryn recovered himself.

"Greetings, Lord Braemys," Maryn said.

"And mine to you, Your Grace," Braemys said, "Gwerbret Cerrmor."

For a moment they considered each other. When Nevyn opened his etheric sight, he saw the young lord's aura gleaming a steady gold, shot with red. Rage, no doubt, but not treachery. Satisfied, Nevyn closed the sight down.

"Gwerbret I am of that city," Maryn said at last. "But I hold a bit more rank besides. I take it that you refuse to swear fealty to me as the rightful high king in Dun Deverry."

"I do." Braemys looked him straight in the face. "But who reigns in the Holy City is no longer a concern of mine or of those to whom I owe protection."

Maryn blinked, caught off guard. Braemys smiled, just slightly, and went on speaking.

"I wish to remind you of the terms you laid me, Your Grace, before the summer's fighting. You told me that I had two choices, to swear to you or leave your lands forever. Very well. My clan, those few of our vassals who hold loyal, my retainers, the farmers who have served my clan, my artisans and my servants, my warband and the warbands of my vassals—" Braemys paused for breath. "They're all waiting for me to the north of here with their possessions and livestock. We shall quit your lands forever, just as you demand."

"What?" Maryn blurted. "Where will you go?"

"North," Braemys said. "North of Gwaentaer lies unclaimed land. It's rough country, I hear, full of hills and rocks. You need not fear I'll found a rich kingdom there to threaten you or suchlike."

"That's daft!"

Braemys merely smiled for an answer. It was daft, Nevyn thought, but rather splendidly so, a wild gesture of a very young lord. When Maryn glanced his way, as if for advice, Nevyn shrugged.

"Lord Braemys seems to have thought this all out," Nevyn said. "If he wishes to withdraw from your jurisdiction, then no law of the land will stop him."

"Just so." Braemys turned solemn. "Our ancestors left the Homeland, didn't they, rather than wear the harness the Rhwmanes had all laid out for them? Do you think I'm not as brave as they?"

"I know naught about you at all." Maryn had recovered himself and spoke with dignity again. "But you tell the truth about our ancestors."

"Just so. Will you keep to the terms you gave me, or go back on your sworn word and prevent us from leaving?"

"Never will I go back on my sworn word." Maryn sounded on the edge of snarling.

"So I've heard, Your Grace, that you're a man with a fine sense of honor." All at once Braemys tossed his head back and laughed. "I gambled on that, didn't I?"

"Just so," Maryn snapped. "And you've won."

"My thanks." Braemys made him a half bow from the saddle. "There remain, Your Grace, the terms of my clan's withdrawal. Shall we have our heralds and councillors discuss them?"

"By all means, my lord, by all means."

The terms took another full day of negotiations, but in the end things worked out thusly. Gwerbret Ammerwdd with his warband and his direct vassals with their warbands would escort Braemys and his followers north to the border, whilst Maryn and the remainder of his men would push on east. The prince would proclaim Cantrae and the Boar clan lands to be attainted; then he would dispose them upon some loyal vassal of the high king—after Maryn was proclaimed as such. The politicking that winter, Nevyn knew, was going to be nearly as fierce as the battles of the summer, and Maryn agreed.

"We'll fight one war at a time," Maryn said. "That's all any man can do."

"Just so," Nevyn said. "But start weighing every word you speak now. An idle saying can sound like half a promise to a greedy man."

"Unfortunately, that's true spoken. I'll be as cautious as a cat in a bathhouse."

One last request made by Braemys was too honorable to be refused. He had men under his command who had been wounded too badly to travel north. Maryn agreed easily that he would add those men to his own and have their wounds tended.

On the morrow, while the heralds finished the last few details of the settlement, Nevyn set out to fetch the Boar clan's wounded. Tieryn Anasyn of the Ram offered to bring his warband along for an escort. They assembled some wagons for the worst injured and some horses for the rest as well as the usual medical supplies. In the sunny morning, they plodded along a path that ran uphill beside a stream. The foam-flecked water gurgled cheerfully around black rocks. The wagons creaked along behind the riders, and now and again one of the teamsters started a song and his fellows joined in. The sense of peace achieved made Nevyn himself smile, though the task ahead wasn't going to be a pleasant one. If the Boar's herald had given them good directions, they would reach the wounded men's camp in a few miles.

"It's honorable of young Braemys," Anasyn said, "worrying about his wounded this way."

"It is," Nevyn said, "and I was glad to see it in the lad."

"I only wish his honor had taken him off to Cerrgonney before the battle and spared us all such grief."

"Indeed. Some of the dead are men I mourn for."

"My heart grieves for my sister, losing her betrothed."

"So does mine. Branoic's one of the men I was referring to."

"I thought he might be. I only wish I could have broken the news to her myself, but she's a warrior's daughter. She'll heal."

"Just so. At least she has her dweomer studies to keep her position at court secure."

"Oh, I never doubted that it would be." Anasyn turned in the saddle and smiled at him in a weary sort of way. "If naught else, she could serve the princess as one of her women."

Nevyn suddenly realized that Anasyn had no idea that his beloved little sister was the prince's mistress. Some men would have rejoiced at the influence this would give them at court, but Anasyn had been raised to treat his womenfolk with scrupulous honor and respect.

"Did you have much chance to talk with Lilli before we left?" Nevyn said.

"I didn't," Anasyn said. "I rode late to the muster, and she seemed much distracted by somewhat."

"Er, she was, truly."

"Do you know why?"

Nevyn sighed, considering. Anasyn would eventually discover the truth no matter what he did.

"Well, my lord," Nevyn said at last, "her fortunes have become quite complicated. She was betrothed to Branoic, and I truly do think she loved him, but the prince took quite a fancy to her."

Anasyn's face turned scarlet. His hands tightened on his reins so hard that his horse jerked its head up. With a foul oath Anasyn relaxed the reins again.

"I can see why no one told me." Anasyn's voice growled. "Was she willing?"

"Of course! Our prince would never force a woman, never."

"Forgive me. I know that's true."

"Lilli's very young, and she was flattered. Maryn could charm fish out of the sea if he set his mind to it."

"No doubt." Anasyn hesitated, thinking. "I'll discuss it with her when we return to the dun, then. My thanks for the truth."

They rode in silence the rest of the way.

Some miles from the Wyvern camp the path brought them to the grassy rise mentioned by the Boar clan's herald. As they walked their horses up the slope, Nevyn suddenly realized that something was wrong. He could hear birds squawking, and just as he was about to point this out to Anasyn, a flurry of ravens rose, squabbling among themselves as they circled the hill only to settle again out of sight.

"Oh by the gods!" Anasyn snapped. "This bodes ill."

When they crested the rise they could look down the grassy slope to the camp below, or to what once had been a camp. Spread out across the flat lay corpses, all tumbled around, some half-dressed. Nevyn saw not a single wagon or tent, not a horse, either. Anasyn turned in the saddle and called out to the men behind them.

"Don't bring the wagons up! There's no need."

With ten of his men for a guard, Anasyn and Nevyn rode down the slope. Birds rose and a cloud of flies as well. Nevyn dismounted, dropped his horse's reins to make him stand, then jogged into the camp. The stench of rot in the hot sun nearly overwhelmed him, but he steeled himself and went on. He could see that every single man there had had his throat cut, no doubt on the day before, while their lord still bargained for their safety. More slowly Anasyn followed, shaking his head in disbelief.

"What?" Anasyn snapped. "Who did this? Braemys? Was this his idea of a jest or taunt or suchlike?"

"Oh, I doubt that very much," Nevyn said. "It's the bandits, I'd wager. Remember his amnesty to men who'd lost their lords? Some of them doubtless were good men and loyal to their new warband, but others—"

"The ones that broke and ran during the battle. They couldn't loot on the field, so they took what they wanted here." Anasyn shuddered convulsively. "Well, no doubt our liege will be hunting them down soon enough."

When, after their return to camp, Maryn heard the story, he fulfilled Anasyn's prophecy, vowing to round up the bandits as soon as he'd been invested as high king.

"The cowards!" Maryn snarled. "Pisspoor bastards, more

dogs than men! I'll hang the lot if it takes me the rest of the summer."

"Good," Nevyn said. "It turned my stomach. Tieryn Anasyn had his men bury them properly."

"That gladdens my heart. Ye gods, I hope that our own wounded fare well!"

"That thought had crossed my mind. I'm glad Your Highness doubled the size of that escort."

The bandits, however, must have ridden in some other direction, for they spared the Wyvern men. Maddyn had been leading his ragged procession of wounded riders, wounded horses, and wagons as fast as they could go—no more than some ten miles a day, by his rough figuring. No one could stay in the saddle for long, but the men in the carts fared worse, bounced, rattled, and thrown about by every stone in the road. At the end of each day's travelling the healthy men of the escort would bury those who had died, and in the morning, before they set out west again, they would bury anyone who had died in the night.

It was no wonder then that messengers from the prince caught up with them. In the middle of an afternoon Maddyn was riding at the head of the line when he heard someone shouting at the rear of it. He yelled for the halt, then turned his horse and jogged back. By the time he reached the last wagon, the dust around their line of march was beginning to settle. He could see another cloud of dust on the road, coming toward them. The nearest carter leaned over the side of his wagon.

"Be they enemies?" he called out.

"I hope not," Maddyn called back. "Wait—there's just two of them. Can't be enemies."

As the two riders trotted up, Maddyn could see that one of them was wearing, tied over his mail, a tabard appliquéd with the red wyvern, a piece of clothing that identified him and his companion as speeded couriers. A few more yards, and he recognized the men for silver daggers, Alwyn and Tarryc. They trotted up and stopped their horses beside his.

"So," Maddyn said. "You're riding for Dun Deverry, then?"

"We are," Alwyn said. "A cursed strange thing's happened, Maddo."

"Not more fighting?"

"Not that at all."

"What's Braemys doing, then? Running for Cantrae as fast as he can?"

"He's not." Alwyn was trying to suppress a smile, and Maddyn realized that he was building up to some sort of jest. "He's travelling north."

"Oh, is he now? And why might that be?"

Alwyn paused, grinning. By then the other men in the escort had walked their horses back; they all leaned forward in their saddles to listen.

"Lord Braemys," Alwyn said, "is heading for Cerrgonney."

"What? Why?"

"Well, now, it seems that our prince gave him a choice, like, to swear fealty or leave the royal lands forever. So he's packed up his people and women and children, and a lot of cattle and sheep and suchlike, and he's leaving." Alwyn paused for effect. "Gwerbret Ammerwdd's escorting him to the border. Braemys has handed Dun Cantrae over to Prince Maryn, down to the stones and the dungheaps."

"He's daft! There's nothing up there in those hills."

"There will be, and soon enough, most like, when he gets there."

Maddyn shook his head in amazement. Young as he was, Braemys had a touch of genius when it came to tactics. When it came to common sense, however, he seemed more than a bit lacking.

"Ah well," Maddyn said. "The noble-born do what they will, and there's naught for a bard like me to do but remember it for them."

"Just so." Alwyn glanced around at the men crowding in to listen. "Let us through, lads! We've got a fair bit of daylight left, and we need to be on our way."

The couriers walked their horses around the straggling

wagon train, then trotted off fast, heading east to bring this peculiar news to the princess and her fortguard. Maddyn's lot followed at their usual slow pace.

To pass the time for both of them, Lilli had taken to teaching Prince Riddmar how to play carnoic and gwyddbwcl of an afternoon. They would sit at a table in the great hall, empty except for the dogs, circling flies, and a few servants, who generally watched the game and offered bad advice to both of them impartially. When the two silver daggers arrived with messages from the army, the two gamers happened to be the only noble-born persons present. The messengers knelt at Lilli's side and proffered the message tubes.

"From Prince Maryn, my lady," Alwyn said. "Is the princess here?"

"In the women's hall," Lilli said. "I'll take these up." She glanced at a lurking servant lass. "Get these men food and ale."

As she climbed the staircase Lilli looked back and saw that Riddmar had gone to sit with the riders. No doubt he was going to badger them with questions about the fighting.

Lilli was planning on handing the messages to Elyssa or Degwa at the door, but when she knocked on the door of the women's hall, Bellyra herself opened it. She wore only a simple shift, so old that the linen was shiny, and it seemed to Lilli that she could have counted every bone in the princess's body. Bellyra paused, looking her over with dull eyes. Lilli, who was of too low a rank to speak first to a princess, curtsied, then merely waited while her breath caught ragged in her throat.

"What are those?" Bellyra said finally.

"Messages, Your Highness, from your husband." Lilli held out the tubes. "The men that brought them are down in the great hall."

"My thanks." Bellyra took the tubes. "I was sorry to hear about Branoic's death. You have my sympathies."

"My thanks, Your Highness."

"I had hopes that he'd take you away from Dun Deverry. My husband honors his men highly, after all, and what he wouldn't do for us, he might have done for one of them."

Lilli tried to answer, but her mouth had gone too dry. Bellyra continued with her slow scrutiny.

"Oh, I'm sorry, Lilli," the princess said at last. "It's truly not your fault. I just can't stand the sight of you, is all."

With that she slammed the door shut. Lilli stood in the hallway and trembled for some while before she could summon the breath to leave.

Maddyn led his straggling procession into Dun Deverry late on an afternoon when clouds hung heavy in the western sky. Light the color of beaten copper slanted under the swelling thunderheads and made them blaze over the black towers and walls of the dun. As they rode through the last gate into the ward, Maddyn was hoping that the storm would break soon. The heat seemed to have turned the air too thick to breathe.

Servants swarmed out of the broch, and grooms came running. As Maddyn dismounted, he saw Grodyn the chirurgeon limping across the ward with his stick for support. Pages scurried at the old man's orders to help the wounded men down. Lady Lillorigga, with young Prince Riddmar at her side, stood waiting in the doorway of the main broch. As Maddyn hurried over, he noticed that her skin looked oddly pale except for the hectic red upon her cheeks. *I wonder if Nevyn knows about this,* he thought. When he started to kneel, she stopped him.

"Don't, Maddo," Lilli said, and her voice quivered with tears. "If the gods had been kinder I'd have been a silver dagger's wife, and I shan't have his comrade kneeling to me."

"My heart aches for you, my lady," Maddyn said, "and for my own grief as well. I'd ridden with Branno for many a long year."

"I know." Lilli raised one arm and wiped her eyes on

her sleeve. "But it was Wyrd, and what can we do about that?"

"Naught, truly." Maddyn reached into his shirt and brought out the two silver message tubes. "One of these is for you, but I can't read the names upon them."

Lilli took them, slid one parchment out, then handed it and the tube both back to him.

"This is for the princess," she said. "It's odd how when there's a choice of two things, one always chooses the wrong one."

Her voice twisted with such bitterness that Maddyn heard a tale's worth of meanings in her words. "So it is," he said. "Is the princess in the great hall?"

"She's not. I suppose I could take that letter to Elyssa to give to her."

"Or you could just take it up to the women's hall."

"I can't." Lilli looked away. "But you know, I think our princess would like to see you. Maybe you can distract her a bit. Let me just find Elyssa."

While Lilli went upstairs, Maddyn and the rest of the escort sat themselves down on the riders' side of the great hall. Servant lasses brought them ale, then hovered around them, asking after various men who'd gone to the battle. For some it was a sad asking, because their men had been slain, but most could laugh and rest easy, knowing they'd ride home again soon. Maddyn kept watch on the great staircase while he prayed that Bellyra would be well enough to come down.

In but a little while his vigil was rewarded. With Lady Elyssa beside her the princess appeared at the top of the stairs. Bellyra wore a pair of green dresses, and her richly embroidered head scarf pulled her honey-colored hair back from a face gone pale and gaunt. Barely thinking, Maddyn rose and hurried to the foot of the stairs. Bellyra was frowning a little, concentrating on taking each step down as if she were exhausted, so carefully, so sadly, really, that he longed to pick her up and carry her down in his arms. When the women were about halfway down, Elyssa waved, gesturing that he should come up to meet them. He knelt two steps below them and offered Bellyra the message tube.

"From Nevyn, my lady," Maddyn said.

"My thanks." Bellyra took the message, slid it halfway out of the tube, then slid it back. "I'd hoped for a word from my husband."

Maddyn winced. "He was much distracted, Your Highness. The battle wasn't long over."

"I see." She glanced at Elyssa. "You know, I feel rather faint." In a rustle of crisp linen she sat down on the step directly above him. "But I want to hear what Maddyn can tell me about the prince. Is he truly well?"

"He is, my lady. Victory becomes any man."

"The messengers told me about Braemys's withdrawal. I'm so glad there was but the one battle, but they also told me Maryn's going to be chasing down bandits or suchlike."

"Oh, he'll ride home before that campaign, Your Highness. He needs to claim the kingship as soon as he secures Cantrae."

"Ah. That's somewhat to hope for, then. I'll send letters back with you."

Bellyra stared down at her hands, lying in her lap. When Maddyn looked at Elyssa, he found her pointedly looking elsewhere.

"My heart aches to leave you again," he whispered.

Bellyra managed a smile. "I wish you weren't leaving, but the messages—"

"Anyone can carry those. If you want me here, I'll stay. Owaen will be glad to have me gone."

"And what about our prince?"

Maddyn hesitated, searching for words. "Ah well," he said at last. "He gave me leave to stay here, you see, should I want to."

"Why?" Bellyra looked up, her eyes anger-bright. "To comfort his little mistress if *she* needed it?"

Maddyn winced again.

"So I thought." Bellyra's voice trembled. "I'll just steal a little happiness for myself, then, out of his ever-so-generous gift to her. Do stay, Maddo. I'll be glad of your company."

"I will, then."

She smiled, just faintly, then scrambled up and turned to Elyssa with a wave of the letter she held.

"No doubt Nevyn will want a reply," the princess said. "I'll read this and compose an answer."

"Very well, Your Highness," Elyssa said. "The men from the escort can carry it back."

Maddyn stayed kneeling until they'd climbed the stairs and gone. For so many years, through so many dangers, his loyalty to Prince Maryn had shaped his life—his heart and soul, really. It was odd to think that a woman's unhappiness had destroyed it.

After the parley with Braemys, Prince Maryn and Gwerbret Ammerwdd sent some of their weaker vassals home to tend to their own affairs, then divided the remaining forces between them. Maryn ended up with some eight hundred men—his silver daggers, several of the northern lords including Nantyn and his men, the riders due him as Gwerbret Cerrmor, and half the Cerrmor spearmen. With their much-reduced numbers, they could now make better speed, some eighteen miles a day on the flat, though hilly country would take its toll on the wagons when they reached it. The messengers sent by Princess Bellyra caught up with the prince some ten miles east of Glasloc, half a day's march from the lands belonging to the Boar clan.

The army had camped in a stretch of fallow fields just at the edge of a straggling forest. With a few hours of sunlight left in the day, Nevyn took a cloth sack and his digging tools and walked into the young trees to look for herbs, but he found mostly weeds and brambles. In the shade of a few of the larger trees he did see young bracken pushing their curled shoots through the green-covered ground. The land had been cleared once, he supposed, then allowed to go wild again, doubtless as a result of the war. About a quarter mile into the second growth, he found proof of his theory in the form of a remnant of low stone wall, overgrown with mosses.

Beyond stood the last remnant of the wild forest that had covered the entire area back when Nevyn had been young and a prince himself. As he leaned onto the top of the wall and contemplated the ancient oaks, he realized exactly where he must be. Within that forest lay the cairn that marked Brangwen's grave. He'd seen it last some twenty years ago, though he'd approached it from the other side. The shadows lay deep in the forest; sunset lay close at hand. With a shake of his head he turned and made his way back to camp.

As he was walking back to his tent, Owaen hailed him.

"Messengers rode in, my lord," Owaen called out. "The prince has letters for you."

"My thanks!" Nevyn said. "I'll go fetch them."

There turned out to be two personal letters for Nevyn—one from Princess Bellyra, one from Lilli. The princess had sent only the briefest of notes, acknowledging his earlier message. Lilli's letter supplied the reason. She had written it herself in her big blocky letters rather than trust her meaning to a scribe.

"My dear master," it began, "I am writing about the princess. Her illness still lies upon her, and it aches my heart to see. Maddyn the bard did cheer her somewhat upon his return with his songs, but in only a few days she fell into a deeper sadness than ever. Lady Elyssa is beside herself with worry, saying that this fit of madness is worse than the last. Is there some herb I might brew to lift some of her clouds? I would be ever so grateful for any advice upon this matter."

The letter continued with comments upon her studies and some gossip from the dun, then ended with a line that brought tears to his eyes.

"I think about Branoic every night at sunset and weep for him. I understand now why bards call grief a monster that gnaws at your heart."

Nevyn rolled the letter up and slipped it into his shirt to keep it safe. Was there any advice he could give her about helping Bellyra recover? When he did think of a possible remedy, it required no mighty magicks or even herb lore. The next morning, while they waited for the first scouts to return, Nevyn took the prince for a little stroll into the forest edge.

"If I remember rightly, Your Highness," Nevyn said, "there's a proper road just beyond this stretch of forest."

"Splendid!" Maryn said. "I'll send a couple of men to scout it out. Is there a path through here?"

"I think so. I'm fairly sure I know this spot. If I'm right, there's a grave marker along in here somewhere."

Sure enough, in a short walk's space they came to a neat stack of stones, some four feet high, in the midst of a small clearing. Just beyond it they could see a worn dirt path through the trees.

"Is this the grave?" Maryn said. "It looks like a cairn."

"It is, and of a noble-born lady," Nevyn said. "I heard the story from a gamekeeper years and years ago, my liege. The lass was betrothed to a prince, but she died before they could marry."

"A sad Wyrd, then."

"Made sadder because he spurned her, or so the story runs, and there was naught she could do but throw herself away on an unworthy man. Noble-born women have so little power over their own lives."

"True spoken." Maryn nodded absently, looking away into the trees.

Nevyn paused to wonder if he were wasting his breath, but the thing needed saying, he decided, whether the prince chose to listen or not.

"I was remembering the days when I was your tutor," Nevyn said. "We studied the laws, the history of the great clans, the Dawntime. But we never touched upon how a man might comport himself around the women of his household. I begin to think that was an oversight on my part."

Maryn whipped his head around and glared at him, his mouth tight-set.

"I see you see my line of thought," Nevyn said calmly.

"Lady Lillorigga is your apprentice." Maryn's voice grated close to a growl. "I understand that you need to have her welfare at heart."

"I wasn't talking about Lilli."

"Oh." Maryn relaxed. "My apologies."

"The woman I fear for, Your Highness, is your wife. Those fits of madness—"

"Well, they trouble me, too, Ye gods, don't you think I realize that they've appeared after every child? There are three heirs to the throne back in Dun Deverry now. That's enough for safety's sake. I see no reason to put her at risk again." Maryn shook his head sadly. "I'm fond of her, truly I am, but there are other women. I'm not some animal who can't control himself."

It took a moment for Nevyn to parse the prince's meaning—quite the opposite conclusion from the one he wanted drawn. Maryn smiled briefly.

"She need not fear my attentions any longer," Maryn said. "It's a sad thing, because she always seemed to like them well enough. But this madness—" He shuddered, deeply and sincerely. "The poor woman!"

Before Nevyn could gather his wits and speak, Maryn nodded to him and walked away, heading back to camp, leaving him to scowl at the unhearing stones.

"Well, I made a botch out of that!" Nevyn muttered. "Naught to be done about it now, I suppose."

Long shafts of golden sunset fell among the trees and gilded the mossy stones that marked Brangwen's grave, so like the new cairn that marked Branoic's. Nevyn found himself wondering what body this soul would wear in its next life. He could only wait and hope to see, if indeed, the Lords of Wyrd should grant that once again their paths would cross.

Travelling on the Cantrae road did indeed prove faster than picking their way by farmers' paths. The army rode steadily northeast. Every now and then they passed a farm, ringed by ditches and wooden fences, where dogs would bark hysterically from behind closed gates. The owners had fortified themselves against the noble lords more than bandits, Nevyn supposed. They rode through long meadows as well, where in the distance they could see trails of rising dust where the famous horseherders of Cantrae were driving their stock far beyond an army's greedy reach. The one dun they passed stood empty—not a chicken nor a chair remained. Some lord had chosen to follow Braemys, Nevyn assumed.

Some two days later the army rode up to Cantrae, a compact walled town that once had sheltered a thousand souls. Maryn halted the army in a meadow some hundred yards from the stone walls. Nevyn joined him as he and the silver daggers rode a cautious hundred yards farther on. Once they'd left the army's noise behind, they could hear the wind sighing and the river chortling as it ran through the portcullis that guarded its channel through the walls. They rode up to the open gates and paused just outside. In their clear view down the main street of the town, all the way to the market square, no one and nothing moved.

"Ye gods," Maryn said. "I didn't know silence could be so loud."

Since Nevyn had received not the slightest warning of danger, he rode with the silver daggers when they walked their horses through the broad gates of Cantrae. Not one dog barked, not a person called out. The houses still stood, round under their heavy thatched roofs, scattered along curved streets as in any Deverry town. Here and there a wooden shutter banged in the wind.

"Gods protect!" Owaen said. "It creeps a man's flesh, all this quiet."

"So it does," Nevyn said. "They must have taken everything with them, cat and chicken, dog and cow."

Owaen nodded and rose in his stirrups to look down the wide road ahead. The wind blew puffs of dust along in tiny whirlwinds. He sat back down with a shake of his head.

"If anyone were here," Owaen announced, "they'd have come out to curse us by now, if naught else."

"Let's get back to the army," Maryn said. "Braemys was

telling me the truth, all right. Cantrae needs a new gwerbret, but it will take the winter to sort that out."

"So it will, my liege," Nevyn said. "But if we leave it unguarded, it would make a splendid shelter for bandits."

"I was thinking much the same." Maryn considered for a moment. "The vassal of mine who lives the closest is Lord Nantyn. If I left him and his men here, do you think he'd turn against me?"

"What?" Nevyn nearly laughed. "Proclaim himself gwerbret, you mean? With twenty-five riders and a stony field demesne?"

"My worrying sounds stupid now that you say it aloud. Very well. I'll hold a council tonight when we camp, and I'll appoint Nantyn and maybe another northern lord to keep an eye on the town for me."

"Good. And then at last we can ride for home."

"Just so. I'll mount a campaign against those bandits later this summer, but there's no need for you to come with us for that. No doubt you're weary of all this campaigning."

"I am, truly."

They turned their horses and rode slowly back to the waiting army. Nevyn paused for one last look at the open gates of Cantrae. Ye gods, he thought. The Boar threat is truly over. Although he'd been expecting jubilation, he mostly felt exhausted.

"Nevyn?" Maryn said abruptly. "Are you well?"

"I am, my liege. I was just thinking about Eldidd."

"Do you truly think the king will keep pushing his claim now? It was always the weakest of the three."

"It was, and for a hundred years, the Eldidd kings have pushed it anyway."

Maryn nodded, looking ahead of him where his stripped-down force waited for him, the men standing beside their weary horses.

"No doubt he'll attack Pyrdon," Maryn said, "to draw me west. Do you think it will be this summer?"

"I don't. It will take some time for the news of your victory to even reach him. He'll want better information than the tale will carry with it. By the time he gets that, summer will be nearly over."

"Next year, then. There's only one way to ensure the peace, you know."

"What's that, Your Highness?"

"Conquer Eldidd. Put an end to it, turn it into a province."

Nevyn's weariness increased fivefold. But he's right, he told himself. Alas, he's right.

Since Maddyn was the only man sleeping in the silver daggers' barracks, the silence began to trouble him. He took to staying in the great hall as long as possible of an evening, and to rising with the dawn to return there, but unless he wanted to sleep in the straw with the dogs and servants, he had no choice but to spend the night in his lonely bunk. He'd spent his entire adult life sleeping in the midst of a warband. Privacy meant nothing to him but the prospect of bad dreams.

After the first few nights, ghosts came to join him, or so it seemed. He would wake in pitch-darkness because of some sound or other, sit up on his bunk, and listen while he tried to convince himself that he was only hearing the wind at the shutters or a horse moving about in its stall below. Yet he could clearly hear men's voices, soft murmurs of regret, the occasional curse or angry quarrel, the occasional burst of laughter at some jest. He could never quite understand their words. At times he'd see someone out of the corner of his eye, but when he turned to look, they'd be gone. Once, when a drift of moonlight came in an open window, he was sure that he saw Branoic standing beside his old bunk. Maddyn called his name, and the figure turned toward him, but when he sat up, the specter vanished.

It was on his twelfth night back in the barracks that Maddyn heard Caradoc calling him. He woke up, as suddenly as always, to hear that familiar growl of a voice. *Get up, Maddo! I'll kick your arse around the ward, sleeping when you're on guard duty!* Without thinking, Maddyn was on his feet and looking around for his sword, only to realize that he was alone as always, safe in Dun Deverry. Going back to sleep eluded him. He pulled on his brigga and his boots, then walked to the window and looked out in the warm summer night.

In the ward below a tiny dapple of light was moving across the cobbles, a candle in a lantern bobbing as its carrier walked—cautiously, stopping often to look around. When the light came close he realized that the carrier was Princess Bellyra. He leaned half out of the window, stared down, but there was no mistaking her silhouette, her gait. For a moment his heart seemed to freeze. Might she be looking for him? Might she be coming to the barracks? He dismissed the dishonorable hope with an effort of will, but it seemed that his heart stopped beating till she walked on past the barracks' stairs.

Then where was she going? Was her madness giving her spells of aimless wandering? Maddyn had heard of such things. If naught else, she shouldn't be wandering around alone at night. Caradoc had been right. He had been sleeping on guard duty. He grabbed his shirt, pulled it on, then picked up his sword belt and buckled it as he strode down the long room. He hurried down the stairs and trotted off, following her candle through the darkness. She was moving purposefully, and he was still some yards behind when she suddenly turned to knock on a door. The door opened and let a flood of reddish light spill out into the night.

"Who is it?" Otho's voice growled. "Ah, Your Highness! What are you doing here?"

"I was wondering the same," Maddyn called out. "Your Highness!"

She laughed, turning in the light from the door to wave to him. He caught up to her and bowed. Otho stood scowling in the doorway to his forge.

"It's a dangerous thing," Maddyn said, "going out by yourself at night."

"I swear, Maddo, that you must have dweomer or such-like yourself. How did you know I was out and about?"

"Caradoc's ghost told me."

She started to laugh again, then fell silent. "You truly mean that, Maddo, don't you?"

"Well, so it seemed." Maddyn looked down at the ground. "It must have been a dream."

"Ye gods!" Otho snarled. "Come in, then, both of you! I'm in the midst of working, and I'm not going to risk the loss of good silver to humor a pair of the daft. You can prattle about ghosts inside as well as out."

Inside the square room, heat blazed from a central fire pit, which had walls round it, some three feet high and built of brick. The sour thin smoke of glowing charcoal rose in wisps above to an open vent on the roof. The fire cast a fitful light on the clutter heaped up at the edges of the room: tables, chests, a couple of wood benches, racks of tools, piles of rags.

"I don't remember you having all these goods before," Maddyn said.

"The Boar clan's silversmith wasn't going to be using any of them," Otho said. "Or he would have taken them with him, eh? Now here, Your Highness, I don't have a proper chair in the place."

"This will do." Bellyra set her lantern down on the ground, then perched on a three-legged stool. "I couldn't sleep. I wanted to see how the gift was coming along."

"That's right." Otho turned to his forge. "I remember telling you I'd start work tonight. The moon's in a good place for the pouring of silver."

"It's for our prince." Bellyra glanced at Maddyn. "To celebrate his kingship."

"I see, my lady." Maddyn sat down on a bench. When he remembered his brief hope that she was seeking him out, he felt like an utter fool. *A gift for her husband*, he thought bitterly. *Well, you knew you were reaching above yourself.*

Bellyra leaned forward, watching the smith. Maddyn slumped back against the wall and watched her. The dancing shadows played over her face and threw its gaunt hollows into high relief. Her hair was coming free of the silver clasp that kept most of it back, letting tendrils fall across her cheeks. He had never wanted anything so much as he wanted to smooth those strands back and kiss her. He could hear the fire hissing and Otho muttering to himself, but Maddyn never looked round. Had someone asked him later what the smith had been doing, he couldn't have told them one thing.

All at once Bellyra turned her head and caught his stare, looked at him so openly, so boldly, that he was suddenly frightened, thinking perhaps she could read his thoughts. With a shake of his head he stood up.

"I'll wait outside for you, Your Highness. The heat in here—it's a bit much."

Before she could answer, he strode out, shutting the door carefully behind him. Outside, the summer night seemed as cold as autumn after the thick dry heat of the forge. His thin linen shirt was sticking to his back and chest both with sweat. For the fresher air he walked a little way into the ward, then came back to lean against the wall. He yawned, suddenly sleepy, and wondered how long she would stay.

Not very: in a few moments the door creaked open, and Bellyra stepped out, carrying her lantern. Wisps of hair stuck to her wet-shiny face.

"You're right," she said. "The heat's unbearable, and besides, Otho's doing some process I'm not supposed to watch."

"Very well." He smiled at her. "Shall I escort you back to the royal broch?"

"When you smile like that, Maddo, I feel like I'm half-mad."

Puzzled, he made no answer. She stooped, set the lantern down, and walked over to him. He knew he should speak, make some pleasantry, remind her that her presence would be missed back in the women's hall. Instead he waited, unbelieving, afraid to believe and be disappointed yet again. She hesitated, her head thrown back as she looked up at him, then laid her hands on either side of his face and stood on tiptoe to kiss him on the mouth. He wrapped his arms around her, pulled her close, and kissed her again, openmouthed and hungry. How long they stood there, clinging to one another, exchanging long kisses the more arousing because so desperate, he neither knew nor cared.

Yet the danger woke him at last as if from one of Nevyn's dweomer spells. If someone came by, if someone saw them—

"My lady," he whispered. "Your Highness."

The mention of her rank made her go tense in his arms. She pulled back a little and looked up at him.

"More than half-mad," she said. "I could have loved you so much if only we weren't who we are."

He felt the beginnings of tears in his eyes, turned his head fast to hide them, but she reached up with one hand and caught the drops on her fingertips. "Forgive me," she said. "I never should have—"

Distantly, like the cry of a bird, someone was calling her name—Bellyra, Your Highness, Lyrra, Lyrra, where are you?

"Elyssa!" she said. "I should have known they'd hunt. Maddo, quick—go back inside!"

She scooped up her lantern and trotted off, heading toward the main ward. Maddyn opened the door and stepped in to find a furious Otho.

"Ye gods!" the smith whispered. "If any harm comes to our lady over this, bard, you'd best watch your back."

"Ah, curse you!" Maddyn snapped. "Do you think I'm the villain in this? Do you think I wanted to reach above me and fill my days with misery?"

Otho considered him for a long moment. "I don't suppose you did," he said at last. "May the gods have pity on you both!"

Lilli had been sitting up late, studying a page of sigils by candlelight, when Elyssa pounded on her door. She got up just as the serving woman opened it and strode in. She was wearing an ordinary dress over her nightdress, and her blonde hair hung in two tidy braids.

"Forgive me," Elyssa said. "But I saw the light under the door. Would you help us? The princess has disappeared. We need to find her before some wretched servant or stable man sees her."

"Of course!" Lilli snatched the lantern from the table. "What do you mean, disappeared?"

"She's off wandering somewhere. She gets so restless at night, you see. During the day she can't seem to stay awake, but then she can't sleep at night, and at times she just goes off somewhere when we're asleep and can't stop her."

With a second lantern in hand Degwa waited for them out in the hall, and for once she refrained from sneering at Lilli. They hurried down the stairs, then picked their way as quietly as possible through the great hall. A couple of dogs roused themselves, sniffed the air, recognized their scent, and lay back down again. None of the servants woke. They reached the warm night outside safely and put a good distance between themselves and the door before anyone spoke.

"At least the gates are shut," Elyssa said. "She can't have gone outside the walls. That's one blessing, anyway."

"It's bad enough as it is," Degwa said. "Everything's so confusing in this awful old dun, and no one knows the place like she does, either. Well, unless Lilli does."

"Not truly." Lilli held her lantern high and peered across the main ward. "I never cared much about ruins and suchlike."

"I doubt if anyone but our princess ever did or does." Elyssa paused, thinking. "We can get Maddyn the bard to help us look. He'll keep things to himself, and frankly, I want a man along in case some drunken sentry gives us trouble."

"True spoken," Lilli said. "The silver daggers' barracks are over this way. Branoic showed them to me once when the rest of the men were in the great hall."

Lilli led them through the welter of sheds and outbuildings all the way to the stone wall, where the barracks stood. At the bottom of the stairs Degwa balked.

"We can't go up there," Degwa whined. "What will people think?"

"Maddyn's the only man in them," Elyssa said. "If it troubles your heart so much, you can wait down here alone."

"What? I can't do that, either. I at least am mindful of my rank."

Elyssa made a growling sound under her breath and started up the stairs. Lilli followed, and, eventually, so did Degwa. They held their lanterns up while Elyssa first knocked on the door, then pounded on it. No one answered. Elyssa risked pushing it open a few feet.

"Maddyn?" she called out. "Maddo, are you in there?"

No voice answered, not a single sound—Elyssa took Lilli's lantern, opened the door full, and walked a few steps in, holding up the light. The long row of bunks stood empty; only one had blankets upon it, and those had slipped halfway to the floor.

"Well," Elyssa said. "He's not here."

Elyssa turned and rejoined them on the landing. Behind her Lilli heard Degwa gasp as if in sudden pain.

"What is it?" Lilli said.

Degwa laid her hand on her forehead and looked tragically up at the stars. Elyssa shut the door behind her, then scowled at Degwa.

"I know what you're thinking," Elyssa said. "Don't."

"There's some good reason for all of this," Lilli put in. "He may have seen her walking and gone after her to guard her."

Degwa pursed her lips and glared, but she did drop her tragic pose.

"Let's go," Elyssa said briskly. "And let's start calling for her. No one's going to hear us way out here."

They hurried down the stairs, then stood hesitating. Which way to go? Finally Elyssa chose a direction, farther past the barracks into the close-packed outbuildings.

"Lyrra!" she called out. "Bellyra—Your Highness! Lyrra, Lyrra, where are you?"

When no one answered, they walked on. As they turned the corner round a storage shed, they saw bobbing candlelight, hurrying toward them.

"Lyss!" It was the princess's voice. "Is that you?"

"It is!" Elyssa called back. "And thank the Goddess we found you."

In the light of the lanterns, the princess looked exhausted, her face bright as if with fever. She was wearing an old dress, torn down one side, with a sleeveless shift over that, a pairing that made her look like a kitchen lass. Her hair hung down in untidy strands; her silver clasp dangled at her neck, in danger of slipping free entirely.

"My apologies," Bellyra said. "I just had one of my moods. I had to get outside, I simply had to."

"I wish you'd wake us, Your Highness," Degwa said. "We'd be glad to accompany you."

"And ruin your sleep?" Bellyra gave her a watery sort of smile. "But you see, when I go off alone, I can forget for one lovely moment that I'm doomed to be queen."

Lilli stared, openmouthed, then glanced at Degwa and Elyssa to find them doing the same. Bellyra smiled vaguely at them all. She reached up with her free hand and slid the silver clasp out of her hair.

"I was about to lose this, wasn't I?" Bellyra said. "Well, my ladies, let's go back to the women's hall."

Maddyn slept late the next morning. He woke from dreams of holding Bellyra in his arms to find the barracks flooded with the full heat of a summer's day. He sat up, as muzzy-headed as a sot, and remembered that his dreams weren't only idle fancies.

I could have loved you so much if only we weren't who we are. She had in truth said those words; she had said them to him. Had she meant to make him happy by the saying of them? He doubted it. She must have known that they would cut him to the heart, as sharp as a silver dagger. She was too clearheaded not to know. The happiness—if he could call it that—came from realizing that she'd wounded herself just as deep.

Maddyn dressed and went into the great hall. The fortguard had already eaten and gone. He wheedled a bowl of porridge and some ale out of a servant girl and took the food to a table next to the door to eat it, where a slight breeze struggled to lift the worst of the day's heat. He'd just started on the bread when Prince Riddmar came racing down the staircase, leaping from broad stone stair to stair and laughing at nothing in particular. In but a few weeks, if all went well, he'd be invested as Gwerbret Cerrmor. Prince Maryn would have to appoint a regent, of course. Maddyn wondered if it would be Nevyn. The old man had raised one prince. Why not another? Riddmar came skipping up to him and bowed.

"Maddyn the bard," the boy announced. "My lady Princess Bellyra would like you to come play for her and her womenfolk. Well, when you've finished your breakfast."

"That's a great honor, Your Highness." Maddyn busied himself with a spoonful of porridge to give himself time to think. To face her so soon, to face her women while he smiled and sang and acted as if he were but the servant he'd always been—could he? He would have to. He looked up to see the young prince waiting, his hands tucked behind his back, his legs spread a little apart, in clear imitation of his brother.

"It gladdens my heart that my songs please her," Maddyn said. "I can't go into the women's hall, though. Will they come down here?"

"They won't. They want you to come to the council chamber." Riddmar hesitated, his grey eyes gone wide. "Maddyn, do you know why the princess won't eat?"

"It's part of her affliction, Your Highness."

"Lady Elyssa told me that she was ill from childbirth. Is that the affliction?"

"It is."

"It's awfully sad. I wish she'd eat more. Lady Degwa's always coaxing her and suchlike."

"Good. We all have to eat to live."

"That's what Lady Degwa says, too. Anyway, shall I tell them that you'll play for them?"

"Please do, Your Highness. I'll finish this porridge, and then I'll fetch my harp and come to the council chamber."

"Splendid. Oh, and she says, don't sing the fox song."

"I won't, not with Lady Degwa there. Don't worry."

Riddmar turned and ran off, racing up the staircase. Maddyn realized he was no longer hungry. He gulped down the ale in his tankard and left.

By the time Maddyn reached the chamber, the princess and her two serving women were sitting in a curve of chairs by one wall. Their maidservants sat on the floor behind them, while Prince Riddmar sat cross-legged in front of Bellyra. Maddyn set his harp in its leather sack down on a table and bowed to the noble-born. He'd never put on such a skilled performance as he was doing then, he felt, by bowing to the princess in exactly the same way as he always had, by glancing her way with naught but a pleasant courtesy in his eyes. In turn she smiled at him with the same amiable smile that she bestowed upon her pet cats or a gift of flowers.

"I'll tell you why I summoned you, bard," Bellyra said. "It's hot, and we all felt so cross and sullen. I thought that music would distract us."

"A splendid idea, Your Highness," Maddyn said. "But forgive my voice this morning. I've never been much of a singer at the best of times, and it's thick from the heat."

"Oh come now, Maddyn," Elyssa broke in. "No apologies. Just music."

Since he was far more accustomed to singing in a barracks or hall than in private audiences, Maddyn shunned the chairs and sat upon the long council table to play. Once he'd tuned his harp and done a few runs on its dweomer-sweet strings, the Wildfolk began to gather, sprites and gnomes clustering round him on the table. In their comforting presence he could play without thought of either danger or desire.

Late that afternoon, messengers arrived from Prince Maryn. The army would be returning home on the morrow. Maddyn wondered if he were sorry or glad—he could have persuaded himself either way.

By the time the army rode through the gates of the city, Nevyn was so exhausted from the constant travelling that the black and chaotic towers of Dun Deverry looked beautiful to him. For a while, at least, he would sleep in a proper bed and have the leisure to pursue his own dweomerwork as well as the all-important task of training his apprentice. Yet the ruins of the city reminded him that rebuilding the kingdom would take his and more than his energies: the prince's, Oggyn's, and those of the prince's vassals as well. This summer, perhaps, while Maryn was off chasing bandits, he would see to the beginnings of Dun Deverry's rebirth.

In the slanting light of late afternoon the army reached the fortress hill and wound slowly up the spiralling road and its ring after ring of stone walls. They passed through gates they'd fought to open just the summer past, passed the graves of comrades, too, who'd died in that assault. Finally, they reached the last wall, the last gate. To the cheers of servants and servitors, Prince Maryn rode into the main ward with Nevyn at his side and his silver daggers behind him. Most of the army would camp outside in the parkland between the walls, though the noble-born vassals would, of course, shelter with the prince.

As they dismounted, grooms rushed forward to cheer the prince and take their horses. Nevyn worked his way free of the mob and headed for the main broch. In the doorway stood Princess Bellyra with her serving women, all of them dressed in their best dresses of brightly colored Bardek silks. With them stood Prince Riddmar in a clean shirt and a pair of brigga that were almost too small for him. Despite her finery, though, Bellyra looked dead-pale and gaunt. When he bowed to her, she smiled and gave him her hand to kiss, but the entire time she looked over his shoulder at Maryn, working his way free of the well-wishers mobbing him. As Nevyn walked past her, Lady Elyssa caught his glance and mouthed a single word, "Worried." "Me too," he mouthed back. On the morrow, once Bellyra had welcomed home her prince, he would go up to the women's quarters, he decided, and talk with Elyssa in private.

Lilli was waiting for him inside, a few steps up the stone staircase. At the sight of him she broke into a grin and rushed down to meet him. Nevyn caught both her hands in his and squeezed them.

"Oh my poor child," he said. "Your hair."

"It's for Branoic," she said, and the smile vanished. "I wanted to mourn him properly."

"So I assumed." Nevyn paused, studying her pale face. "You've been ill again. Or I should say, you are ill again. Another sign of your mourning?"

"I suppose. I wept and wept so much at first." Lilli looked down at the floor. "I couldn't sleep, and oh, it hurt to breathe! But I've been getting a bit stronger just recently."

"That's good, but I intend to make sure you get a great deal stronger before you do any more dweomerwork. Shall we go up to your chamber? We have much to talk about."

"Let's. I'm not ready to face Maryn just yet."

Nevyn raised an eyebrow at that, but Lilli said nothing more until they were safely in her chamber. She insisted that he take the chair and perched on the edge of the high bed.

"It gladdens my heart to see you, my lord," Lilli said. "I've been so worried."

"About the princess?"

"Indeed. She's so unhappy. I've been thinking, I should give Maryn up. I can't stand being her rival, I just can't. She did so much for me, when I had naught."

"Will he allow that?"

"I don't know." Lilli looked down at her clasped hands. "But he'd never force me, and so if I could just hold firm—" She let her voice trail away.

"If. A rather large *if*, I'd wager. But Lilli, if you do mean to do this, remember what I told you about the glamours I cast over Maryn. You have dweomer, you can see past them if you choose."

"Of course!" She looked up, wide-eyed. "That's the thing I was forgetting. I knew there was somewhat."

"But think well on this decision. After all, even if you do renounce him, Maryn will mope and mourn for a while, but in the end, he'll only find some other lass."

"That's what Elyssa says, too. And I'll admit it vexes me."

They shared a wry laugh.

"Anyway," Lilli went on, "the cooks have prepared an enormous feast to welcome the prince home. It should last all evening."

"Very well. I'd like to talk with you about your studies, but it can wait till tomorrow."

"I don't want to go to the feast. Do you?"

"I hate large grand affairs like that."

"So I thought. May I come to your tower chamber, and we can discuss things there? I've got myself completely confused over these sigils."

"Sounds like a splendid idea. The prince will probably be looking for you, though."

"I know. That's why I asked."

Isn't this interesting? Nevyn thought. She may well be tired of him. How odd! I always thought it would be the other way round.

Carrying their bedrolls, laughing and talking at the tops of their lungs, the silver daggers trooped into their barracks. Maddyn had never been so glad to see his fellow riders. His long ordeal by lonely silence was over at last. He even had to admit that he was glad to see Owaen, who grinned at him and threw a friendly punch his way.

"So, bard," Owaen said. "Here you've been, lapping up the comforts of the dun like the dog you are, and we've been riding all over the blasted kingdom."

"Some comforts!" Maddyn said. "The barracks didn't stink as much with you all out of it, though."

They shared a laugh. Owaen tossed his bedroll down on the bunk and his saddlebags on top of it. "You look well," he said.

"I'm over that cursed poisoning, if that's what you mean," Maddyn said. "I hope to every god I never feel that way again."

"So do I. It wasn't much of a pleasantry to watch, either."

"So will we be in quarters all summer now?"

"We won't." Owaen shook his head. "Once the priests have proclaimed him king, Prince Maryn wants to ride out to deal with those bandits. That's right, you don't know this. You'd left by the time we learned how many of them there are—far too many. They're a vicious lot."

"Then we'd best slaughter them all."

"My thought exactly. Let's head for the great hall. I want ale."

Riders from the various lords' honor guards mobbed the great hall, whilst the lords themselves clustered around the prince over at the table of honor. Owaen and Maddyn stood near the door on the riders' side of the hall and looked around for a servant lass to bring them ale. Or Owaen did; Maddyn was watching Princess Bellyra, sitting next to her husband, one hand on his sleeve, smiling at him as if her face would break from it. With a shrug he turned away in time to see Tieryn Anasyn bearing down on him like a charging warrior, his face set and grim.

"Owaen, Maddyn!" Anasyn called out. "Have you seen my sister?"

"Lady Lillorigga, Your Grace?" Maddyn said. "I've not."

"I just went to her chamber and she wasn't there." Anasyn scowled at the stairway as if to hold it responsible. "I thought she'd be in attendance upon the princess, but she's not there, either."

"Off with old Nevyn, most like, Your Grace," Owaen said. "He hates crowds and suchlike."

"Ah. Of course." Anasyn briefly smiled. "Well, I'll wait, then. I want a word with her, but I'm not going to disturb the old man over it."

The tieryn strolled away, still scowling.

"What was that all about?" Owaen said.

"Cursed if I know."

"Oh." Owaen considered this for a moment. "Who can figure out why the noble-born do what they do?" He shrugged the problem away. "The ice in the hells will melt before one of these scabby lasses gets around to serving us. I'll go fetch the cursed ale myself."

Maddyn leaned back in the curve of the wall and watched him plunge into the crowd like a swimmer into rough water. Across the hall, Bellyra sat gazing up at Maryn in wifely devotion. He tried looking elsewhere, but always, it seemed, some dweomerlike power drew him back to watching her. He considered leaving the great hall, but just as Owaen returned with two tankards of ale, Bellyra stood up, glancing around her. He saw her speak briefly to Maryn, then gather her women around her and head for the staircase.

"What are you looking at?" Owaen said. "Are you going to take this blasted tankard or not?"

"My apologies," Maddyn said. He took the tankard and had a sip. "I just noticed that the princess looks unwell again."

Owaen looked where he pointed. "She does, at that. The noise in here won't help."

"Just so." Maddyn had a long swallow of ale. He would get drunk, he decided. It was as good a way to spend a feast as any, and then perhaps he could stop remembering her mouth on his, and the way she'd clung to him.

Bellyra was expecting that Prince Maryn would preside over the feast until late, but it was still early when he came to the bedchamber he shared with his wife. Bellyra had put on her best nightdress and combed her hair down over her shoulders, the way he liked it. She lit candles in the sconces, then lay down on the bedcover and waited, drowsing against the pillows. When he opened the door, the noise startled her, and she sat up straight, one hand at her throat.

"Oh, my poor Lyrra," Maryn said. "Did I frighten you?"

"Not in the least." She yawned, covering her mouth with both hands. "You just woke me, that's all."

He smiled and sat down on the edge of the bed. When she held out her hand, he took it, patted it, and released it again.

"It saddens my heart to see you so gaunt," Maryn said. "You've not been well, your women tell me."

"I feel a good deal better now, with you here."

"Good. I've been thinking about these—these illnesses of yours. I know full well that they come from giving birth. I can't stand the thought of putting you through this ever again."

All at once the warm night turned cold around her. He was watching her so sadly, so affectionately, really, that she fished for words but caught none.

"You've always been my partner in rulership," Maryn went on, "and truly, how could any man hope for a better one? It's a fine way to repay you, risking your life in childbed, making you suffer afterwards."

"Here! It's not like you've done anything harmful to me. Some women just take childbirth this way."

"If I keep getting you with child, then I will have harmed you. Lyrra, think! How long can you endure all this? You don't eat, you weep all day, you can neither sleep nor wake—it wrings my heart to see it." He was speaking with real feeling, real concern, perhaps the most he'd ever shown her. "We've got three healthy sons. That's enough. The line will stand secure without you going through these torments again."

For a brief moment she tried to do what he wanted, to think calmly, to weigh risks, but the moment broke in a flood of tears.

"But I love you," she sobbed. "Can't you see that?"

He sat so still that even through her tears she realized that he was terrified. Her weeping stopped. She grabbed the hem of her nightdress and wiped her face, snuffled back the rest of the tears, caught her breath in a long deep sigh, and faced him.

"You mean ever so much to me, too," Maryn said. "But that's why I can't risk getting you with child again. There's a bedchamber in my apartments, up at the top of the broch. I'll be sleeping there from now on."

Or in your little mistress's bed, you mean. Aloud, Bellyra said, "Very well, my lord. Far be it for me to say otherwise."

"Oh stop it!" Maryn got up and paced a few steps away, only to turn back. "I'm not handing down a judgment upon you. Lyrra, please, can't you see? I'm frightened for you."

She could see, and the seeing killed her rage. "True spoken," she said. "Some women would thank you for this, Marro. I know that."

"Don't do that either! I—ye gods, this hasn't been an easy decision for me to make."

"Truly?"

"Truly. I honor you more than any woman in the world, Lyrra. I don't know how I'd rule without you."

There were women who would have cut off an arm to hear their husbands say that as well. She forced herself to smile, to murmur thanks, to reassure him by telling him how flattered she was, but by the time he finally left the chamber, she wondered if she hated him as much as ever she'd loved him. The two passions seemed to twine together round her heart and choke it.

"Other women truly would thank the Goddess for a husband like him," she said aloud. "Ah well, I suppose I'll get used to it."

Now that she was alone, she could weep all she wanted, but she no longer felt like tears. She lay back on the pillows and watched the candlelight dancing on the beams until at last she fell asleep. All night she dreamt of Maddyn and the sweaty, desperate kisses they had shared out in the ward.

Lilli stayed late in Nevyn's chamber. She told him of the past few months' happenings in the dun and listened to his tales of the battle and of Braemys's strange withdrawal from the kingdom. It was like Braemys, as she thought about it, to find some third way out of a situation where other men would only see death or victory.

"He's got our mother's craftiness," Lilli said. "but he'd never poison anyone or suchlike."

"He wouldn't need to," Nevyn said. "He was going to be a great lord in his own right."

She nodded, then suddenly yawned with a great gulp for air. She covered her mouth with both hands, then yawned again. Nevyn got up and went to his window. He leaned out, looking up.

"Judging from the stars, it's quite late," Nevyn said. "You'd best go get some sleep, but I'll walk you across the ward. From the sounds of revelry down there, I'd say that a good many of the prince's men are blind drunk."

They crossed the ward safely, and Nevyn insisted on escorting her to the foot of the staircase inside the great hall as well. By then most of the celebration had moved outside, though some riders lay asleep and snoring in the straw under the tables. Across the hall at the table of honor, a few lords sat drinking, but there was no sign of Maryn. Lilli climbed a few steps up, then turned to bid Nevyn good night.

"I'll see you in the morning," he said. "Humph, I hope our prince isn't waiting for you in your chamber."

"Oh ye gods!" Lilli laid a hand at her throat. "Well, I'll pray he's not."

The Goddess apparently heard her prayer, because when she reached her chamber, she found it empty. She barred the door behind her before she went to bed.

Lilli woke suddenly to see sunlight pouring through her window and someone banging on her door. It's Maryn, she thought. For a moment she could neither move nor breathe.

"Lilli?" It was Anasyn's voice. "Aren't you awake yet?"

"I just am." Lilli called out, then laughed in relief. "Here, hold a moment. I'll come unbar the door."

She slipped on a dress, then opened the door. She was smiling, glad to see her brother returned safely, but the anger snapping in his eyes killed her welcome. He strode in, slammed the door shut, and leaned against it with his arms crossed over his chest.

"Your hair," Anasyn snapped. "Well, at least you've had the decency to mourn your betrothed."

Lilli began to tremble. "You know about the prince, then," she whispered.

"I do. Ye gods, Lilli! Betrothed to one man, dishonoring yourself with another! What would Bevva have thought?"

In her mind Lilli could imagine her foster-mother's face: not angry, no, but sad, so sad and disappointed that her beloved foster-daughter had sunk so low. Lilli sobbed aloud, one quick gulp. "I tried to say him nay." She could hear her voice shaking. "Truly I did."

"Oh?" Anasyn peeled himself off the door. "Nevyn told me that the prince hadn't forced you." He laid one hand on his sword hilt. "Did he lie?"

"He didn't! Sanno, please! He just—I mean, the prince just—he kept courting—he wouldn't leave me alone!"

Anasyn caught her by the shoulders so hard that his hands hurt her, but she refused to cry out. He was staring into her eyes, his long thin face set in a scowl.

"What are you thinking of doing?" Lilli gasped. "You can't challenge him to a combat, you just can't! He's got to become high king, or the wars will never end."

Her implication—that of course Anasyn would win such a duel—seemed to soothe him considerably. He let her go and stepped back. Lilli crossed her arms over her chest so she could rub her aching shoulders.

"I'm sorry if I hurt you." Anasyn looked suddenly weary. "And I shan't challenge the prince. You're right enough. Ending the wars means more than your wretched squandered honor."

"I'm sorry. How did you find out?"

"Nevyn told me. No doubt he thought I'd best hear it from him rather than from some drunken rider or servant." Anasyn sighed and ran his hands through his hair. "How am I going to find you a decent husband now?"

"I don't want a husband."

He looked up narrow-eyed, seemed about to speak, but she forestalled him.

"All I want is the dweomer," Lilli said, and her voice had turned firm and clear. "I don't truly even want the prince."

"You don't need to lie to please me."

"I'm not. Telling you—I just saw how true it is."

"Very well, then. But what will he think of this?"

"I don't know. But ye gods, Sanno, half the women in the kingdom will be ever so happy to console him."

Anasyn sighed with a shake of his head. Lilli laid a timid hand on his chest.

"Please forgive me, Sanno? I never meant to dishonor you, truly I didn't. I was half-mad at first, thinking I loved him, and he is the prince. I was flattered, I guess. Truly, truly flattered."

"No doubt any woman would be. Lilli, Lilli! Very well. I won't hold it to your shame, but if you were to renounce him, well, it would make me a happy man. You can always come back to Hendyr, if things turn bad here. Abrwnna and I will gladly take you in."

"My thanks. But with Nevyn on my side, I doubt if it will come to that."

"Just so." All at once he smiled at her. "I was forgetting just how powerful the old man is in the court." He gave her a brotherly kiss on the forehead. "Shall we go down and have breakfast?"

"My thanks. Let me just finish dressing."

It was late in the day before Lilli saw Prince Maryn, and then it was only from a distance. She was walking out in the main ward when he and his vassals rode in, followed by an honor guard. Lilli took shelter in the shadow of one of the outbuildings and watched while the noble-born dismounted. They were laughing, joking with one another, and Maryn himself smiled, happier in a quiet sort of way than she'd ever seen him. She could guess that they'd been to the temple of Bel and been told that soon he would be proclaimed king. She waited till they'd all gone inside before she resumed her walk.

Yet Lilli knew that she would have to confront him, and soon, but for all she knew, it might be days before he could get a moment free to visit her. She spent the evening in her chamber, waiting, mulling over what she might say to him, and above all, reminding herself that the glamours she would see were the result of Nevyn's dweomer and the wild energies it had summoned. Her candles had burned down to the last few inches before she heard his soft knock on the door.

"Come in," she called out. "It's not barred."

Maryn strode in, shut the door, then stood smiling at her. In the soft and dancing light he looked so beautiful that for a moment she forgot her resolve. She rose from her chair, but as she did so, she caught sight of the Wildfolk of the air, hovering around him, showering him with their unnatural beauty, all silver and pale.

"My lady," Maryn said. "I've missed you badly."

"Have you, Your Highness?" Lilli said.

"Don't call me that. I'm just your Marro."

Here was the moment. Lilli forced herself to remember her image of Lady Bevyan's disappointed eyes.

"Not mine any longer," Lilli said. "My prince, the time has come for us to end this thing between us."

He stared, his mouth a little open, eyes narrow with sheer disbelief. Ever so slightly he shook his head in a reflexive no.

"My betrothed is dead," Lilli went on. "I'd honor him decently by mourning him."

Maryn let out his breath in a sharp sigh. "Of course," he said. "I'd forgotten about poor Branoic."

"I've not. I'll never be able to forget him. I loved him, truly loved him."

Again he shook his head. He took one step toward her; she took a step back.

"Losing him made me realize what love is," Lilli said. She paused, gasping for breath. "And, Your Highness, I fear me that I don't love you. I admire you more than any man in the kingdom. I hold you in my heart as high king. I was ever so flattered when you wanted me. But it's not love, and truly, I think me you'd be content with nothing less."

Maryn grunted as if someone had kicked him. He sat down on the edge of the bed and continued staring at her, his grey eyes hard and cold, the color of storm clouds. Lilli had run out of prepared speech. She clasped her shaking hands together and waited.

"I'd hoped for a better welcome than this," he remarked at last. "You can't mean this."

"I do mean it, Your Highness."

"I understand about the grief. It would be truly unseemly for you to fall into my arms with Branoic just gone. But griefs pass, my lady, and your heart will change."

"It won't." Lilli felt oddly calm. "I'm sorry, Your Highness, because I never wanted to wound you. But I've seen the truth of my feelings for you now, and I know them. I cannot love you, I just simply cannot."

"I don't believe it."

"Please try. Ye gods, Maryn, you've got a wife who loves you more than life itself! Why must you have me, too?"

Much to her surprise he considered the question, his eyes grave. "I have the wife the kingdom demanded," he said at length. "But I'm a man like any other. What man do you know who's content with one woman all his life?"

She'd made a tactical mistake, she realized. The only man she'd ever known to be content with one woman was her foster-father. How to turn the prince's thrust aside? She felt her breath halt in her throat, and she gulped for air. Maryn got up and held out his hand.

"Are you all right?" he said. "Come sit down, and I'll stand."

She shook her head no and caught her breath at last. "Maryn, please," she said. "Have all the women you want. I just can't be one of them."

"It's because you pity her, isn't it?" Maryn said. "Bellyra, I mean."

"That's somewhat of it, Your Highness. You're the prince and may do as you like, but I'd not be the woman who adds to the princess's grief."

"Oh come now! Bellyra was raised to be a king's wife. Our marriage was arranged when we were but children."

"So? That means you love her the less, but it's different for her."

"Nevyn's behind this, isn't he? No doubt he thinks you need to concentrate on your studies or some such. Or is he in love with you himself?"

"That thought dishonors you, Your Highness. Of course not!"

Maryn started to answer, then merely scowled with his lower lip stuck out. Lilli suddenly saw him as a child, a big, hulking child in a man's body, not much older than Prince Casyl, perhaps, screaming when his nursemaid took away some dangerous toy. Involuntarily she took a step back.

"Oh ye gods," Maryn said. "Don't fear me! That's the most unkind thing you've done."

Just in time Lilli stopped herself from blurting out the truth of her reaction. Instead she laid a hand on her throat as if, indeed, she feared he'd strike her. Maryn tossed his head and stamped one foot upon the floor.

"Very well," he snarled. "You no longer love me. Far be it from me to force myself upon some unwilling lass. But we'll see, my fine lady, how long your resolve lasts." He bowed to her with a mocking flourish of his hand, then turned and strode out of the chamber.

Lilli listened until his footsteps had died away, then rushed to the door, shut it, and barred it. She leaned her head against its solid wood and concentrated on breathing. In some short while her tormented lungs began to ease. She walked over to her chair and sat down, staring out the window, where the stars glittered, cold and fierce in the warm summer night.

"I'm going to miss him," she said aloud.

The moment she spoke she knew that she'd lied. What she felt was profound relief, that at last her mind and heart belonged to the dweomer alone.

Nevyn was in the great hall, talking with young Prince Riddmar, when Maryn came hurrying down the staircase. Since the Wildfolk lent strength to his every mood, his rage announced itself to everyone around. This late there were few riders or lords about to see the display, and Nevyn was glad of it. Maryn stormed across the hall, yelling at a page who approached him, kicking a dog out of his way, snarling at a servant lass to get him mead and be quick about it. He threw himself into his chair at the table of honor and scowled at Riddmar and Nevyn impartially.

"Get to bed, Riddo," Maryn said. "Now."

All wide eyes, the boy got up and started to bow. Maryn raised himself half out of his chair. Riddmar turned and ran for the staircase. Maryn sat back down. The servant lass crept toward him with a goblet in her hand; Maryn snatched it out of her grasp and let her run, too. Nevyn waited to speak until he'd drunk half the goblet straight off.

"Your Highness seems distressed about somewhat," Nevyn said.

Maryn glared at him over the rim of the goblet, then took another sip.

"Treachery among your vassals?" Nevyn went on.

Maryn lowered the goblet and sighed. "You'll hear the truth of it anyway," he said. "Your apprentice has decided that she loves me no longer."

"Ah. I see."

"She tells me that you had naught to do with this."

"I didn't. I'm as surprised as you are." Nevyn spoke the simple truth. He'd never thought that Lilli would be able to hold to her resolve.

"Very well." Maryn stared into his goblet and swirled the mead. "The kingdom's full of lovely lasses."

"It is."

"Some of them a good bit more womanly than her. Ye gods, people must think I'm a miser. My wife and my mistress both look half-starved." Maryn's mouth twisted. "Forgive me, I mean my former mistress."

Those few people in the great hall had all turned to watch their prince; they stood silently, staring at him. Maryn finished the mead in another long swallow.

"I'm retiring to my apartments." Maryn stood up. "Tomorrow we'll need to meet in council."

"Whenever His Highness commands."

Maryn stalked off, kicking another dog, grabbing a wayward chair and throwing it to the floor. He bounded up the staircase. Nevyn had the feeling that everyone in the hall held their breath until at last he disappeared at the top. It was a lucky thing, he decided, that the prince had a good many urgent affairs of state these days to occupy his mind.

The prince had been gone but a little while, and Nevyn himself was thinking of leaving the great hall, when

Lady Elyssa came hurrying down the staircase. She glanced around, saw Nevyn, and trotted over to him.

"My lord," Elyssa said. "There's somewhat I need to ask you."

"Let me guess. You want to know if it's true that Lilli's ended her affair with the prince."

"Exactly that." Elyssa smiled, but wryly. "Do you know?"

"The prince himself told me, and I see no reason for him to lie."

"Me either." Her smile turned sunny. "I'll just be getting back, then. This will gladden Her Highness's heart."

With Nevyn home, Lilli returned to her habit of fetching them both breakfast on her way to his tower room. When she went down that next morning, she was terrified that Maryn would be in the great hall, but a page told her that the prince had risen early and gone out for a ride on his favorite horse.

"Not alone, surely?" Lilli said.

"Of course not, my lady. His silver daggers went with him."

Lilli got a basket of bread and a chunk of cheese from a servant lass, then carried it to the main door. On the threshold she hesitated, because out in the main ward the grooms, pages, and menservants were leading the stabled horses out to drink in the watering troughs, so many that she might get kicked or stepped upon in the confusion. In the clammy heat, the smell of horse lay thick under a cloudy sky. Lilli turned back, crossed the great hall, and started out the back door in order to go round to Nevyn's broch by another way. Familiar voices stopped her, sounding just outside, talking and laughing together: Degwa and Oggyn. Rather than face Degwa's haughty looks, Lilli waited, hoping they'd just move on.

Degwa was telling Oggyn some long involved anecdote about Bellyra while he encouraged her with questions. Lilli waited, listening to Degwa prattle on about the princess and her doings.

"Well, I'm sure it's all innocent enough," Degwa was saying. "Elyssa tells me I'm a dolt to worry, but really, that awful bard! He seems entirely too devoted to her, if you take my meaning."

"Oh, I think me I do," Oggyn said, and something about his voice made Lilli think of warm grease sliding over meat. "I do indeed."

"I just worry, that's all. Now I really must be going, Oggo dearest. No doubt our princess needs me."

"I'll walk with you, my love."

Lilli waited until they were well past before she stepped outside, but for the rest of that afternoon she kept an eye on Degwa and her doings until at last she could catch her alone. Lilli put some thought into her approach as well. If she admitted that she'd overheard the conversation, Degwa would turn furious and thus avoid what she had to say. Clodda inadvertently gave her the perfect opening. Lilli had gone to her chamber and found her maidservant shaking out the blankets at the open window. They chatted a bit about very little at first.

"My lady," Clodda said after a few moments. "Somewhat's troubling me."

"What?" Lilli said. "You know you can tell me."

"Well, I know I've no call to be speaking ill of the noble-born, but it's Lady Degwa. Some of the princess's servants say that Lady Degwa's been gossiping about Her Highness and that silver dagger bard."

"Oh by the gods!"

"I didn't like it, I didn't, but Lady Degwa won't be listening to the likes of me."

"Oh, don't you worry! I'll speak with her and straightaway."

Lilli stormed out of the chamber. When she went to the women's hall she found Degwa gone, but Lilli discovered her down in the great hall, where she was standing near the wall and looking around as if she were waiting for someone. At the sight of Lilli, Degwa drew back as if she'd seen a poisonous snake, but Lilli planted herself between her and the door.

"I need to talk with you," Lilli said. "About your suitor. Some of the servants have come to me with troubling gossip."

Degwa let her sneer fade.

"They say you tell Oggyn about our princess's doings."

"So?" Degwa said. "The doings of the noble-born are always of interest. Why shouldn't I give him bits of news?"

"News is one thing. Suspicions are another. The servant lasses are gossiping behind Bellyra's back, too."

Degwa stared, honestly puzzled, judging from the look on her face.

"About her escort," Lilli said at last.

"Oh. The bard?"

"Him, truly. They tell me you hint at goings-on."

"What? I never!"

In anyone else, Lilli would have suspected duplicity, but with Degwa?

"Well, then," Lilli went on, "where are they getting these ideas?"

"I might have said a few words about that Maddyn." Degwa suddenly flushed scarlet. "I don't like him, and I don't trust him, and I particularly don't like the way he follows our princess about. But by the Goddess, I'm sure Her Highness never gives him the slightest word of encouragement."

"People often take things in ways you don't mean them. Please, Decci? You shouldn't even be hinting of gossip about our princess. Gossip always works more harm than witchcraft, sooner or later. You've been at court for years. You know it's true."

For a moment Degwa hesitated, thinking; then with a toss of her head she pushed past Lilli and hurried up the stairs.

"Well, I did try," Lilli muttered. She decided that when Nevyn came to her chamber at the dinner hour she'd lay the matter before him.

Unfortunately, she had no way of knowing that evening would be too late.

That afternoon the prince sent pages to fetch Nevyn and Oggyn for an informal council up in his private chambers. They sat around a small table and studied the maps of Deverry laid out there. Through the open windows, Nevyn could see a sky gone dark with rain clouds, but the heat of the day covered the men like an unwelcome blanket. Oggyn kept wiping his bald head with a rag; sweat stuck the prince's shirt to his chest. A circle of flies danced and droned in the center of the room.

"I've called you here to discuss the matter of lands that once belonged to the Boar clan," Maryn said. "In particular, those that rightfully belong to the heirs of the Wolf."

"Indeed," Nevyn said. "The village of Blaeddbyr and the lands around it. I've forgotten how extensive they once were."

"I've got it here, all written out." Oggyn laid a scrap of parchment on the table. "The old records are most reliable. I copied this from an old proclamation of the false king, the one where he was handing the Wolf lands over to the Boar clan."

"Good thinking." Maryn picked it up. "The Boars wouldn't have let an ell's worth of land slip their grasp. No doubt it listed every stile and dungheap."

Oggyn smiled, leaned back in his chair, then rested his clasped hands on his ample stomach. He looked entirely too pleased with himself by Nevyn's standards.

"Now, I'm mindful of the old ruling concerning the Wolf lands," Maryn went on. "They're inherited through the female line, so the new lord of the Wolf will be the husband of Lady Degwa's eldest daughter."

"Just so," Nevyn said. "She's married to the man who's the younger son of Gwerbret Ammerwdd's wife's sister. I think I've got that right, anyhow."

"Any connection with Yvrodur will do." Maryn grinned at him. "Tenuous though it may be. I'll call him to court once I've been proclaimed high king."

"That will be soon, won't it, Your Highness?" Oggyn leaned forward. "I trust the priests won't be raising new obstacles to your kingship."

"None," Nevyn said. "They've even found a white

mare. Just like dweomer, it was, how fast they found her once Braemys had taken himself away."

All three of them laughed.

"Then the omens are all good," Oggyn said. "I'm so pleased. I was afeared that some dark thing might blight them."

"Such as?" Maryn said. "The well-known greed of priests?"

"Just that, Your Highness." Suddenly Oggyn looked away, as if he'd had a troubling thought. He paused for a long moment before he said, "Just that. Naught more."

Maryn's eyes grew narrow as he considered the councillor. Nevyn felt a touch of cold run down his back: danger.

"What troubles you?" Maryn said. "Somewhat does."

"Er, naught, naught." Oggyn was looking at the far wall. "Just an idle fancy. I'm sure it means nothing at all."

"What?" Maryn snapped.

"Uh er, well, the gossip—and I'm sure that's all it is, Your Highness. The silly gossip of women who envy your wife."

"What about my wife?"

"Naught, Your Highness. Not a wrong word about her, truly. But that bard, the silver dagger—well, I've heard that he aims above himself, hanging around her all the time as he does."

"I asked him to guard her myself." Maryn's voice had grown dangerously low. "If you've forgotten that."

"Not at all, Your Highness, and I beg your pardon. It's just that I hear things, his being so much in her company and all. That perhaps he has it in mind to take liberties."

"I can't believe it," Maryn snapped. "Not Maddyn! He's the most loyal man I've ever met."

"I'd not believe it of the princess, either." Nevyn felt himself shaking with sheer rage. "Councillor Oggyn, you'd best have proof of these statements."

"I never meant a word against the princess!"

"Indeed?" Maryn got up from his chair. "Then why have you even brought the matter up?"

Oggyn went dead-white and sat gulping for breath.

Abruptly Maryn stepped forward and leaned over him, braced himself on the arms of the chair, and leaned the more until his face was a few scant inches from the councillor's.

"What made you bring it up?" Maryn growled.

"There was one night." Oggyn was gasping for each word. "Her serving women couldn't find her. They looked all over. No sign of the bard, either. Finally, your lady turned up out in the ward, carrying a lantern, but she wouldn't say where she'd been."

Maryn let go the chair and straightened up, considered Oggyn for a moment, then slapped him so hard across the face that the councillor squealed and writhed.

"I'll ask you again," Maryn said. "Do you swear this is true?"

Tears filled Oggyn's eyes, but he nodded. "I swear it," he whispered.

"Very well." Maryn turned to Nevyn. "Let's have this out right now. Fetch my pages. Get my lady and her women down to the great hall. I want to know the truth of this."

"You're making a grave mistake," Nevyn said. "I'd judge this thing in private if I were you."

"You're not me," Maryn said. "Tell me, is Oggyn lying about this tale?"

Nevyn hesitated, tempted to the very heart of him. He could lie and dismiss Oggyn's story right there and then. Oggyn had slumped down in his chair and was snivelling as if he feared that very thing. But the gossip won't end, Nevyn thought. "Your Highness," Nevyn said. "He's telling the truth that he heard it. This says naught about the truth of the tale itself."

"Very well, then, we'll thrash this out right now. I won't have gossip spreading about my wife. The great hall will witness the true or false of this, and then there won't be any idle gossip."

"But the humiliation—"

"Maybe it will teach her to watch herself better." Maryn's face flushed white, then red. "Running about the ward at night, ye gods! Most likely she was just going to find one of her cursed inscriptions or suchlike, but she should have considered what people would think of it. By all the gods, she's going to be queen! Now go fetch those pages! I'm not going to stand here and argue about it any longer."

Outside the gathering clouds of a summer storm began to darken the afternoon, but Bellyra felt the first small signs that her birthing madness might be leaving her. For the first time in several months, she found herself thinking about the history of the royal dun. The pages of her book-to-be lay on a table by the window, where she'd left them on the day she went into labor. Elyssa had been dusting them daily and straightening the heap of cut parchments.

"You know, Lyss," Bellyra said. "I'm thinking I might read over what I've written so far."

"Splendid!" Elyssa said. "Shall I fetch the pages?"

Before Bellyra could answer, the door banged open, and Nevyn strode in. She had never seen him or any man so angry, his head thrown a little back, his face dead-white with rage, his eyes snapping. It seemed that he exuded rage the way melted iron exudes heat, trembling the air around him.

"My lady," Nevyn snarled. "Your husband is the biggest fool in the whole wide kingdom of Deverry. Brace yourself and remember that I'm on your side in this."

Elyssa gasped, rising from her chair. Bellyra felt her heart start to flutter like a trapped bird. She laid a hand on her throat.

"In what?" she managed to say. "Nevyn, what do you mean?"

"That idiot Oggyn has made your husband suspicious of you. He claims that Maddyn the bard is entirely too fond of you." Nevyn paused, visibly calming himself. "What's this about one night when your women couldn't find you?"

"Oh that!" Bellyra rose, smoothing down her dresses. She found it surprisingly easy to tell a half-truth. "I couldn't sleep. I went to Otho's forge to watch him make a little gift for Maryn. I want to give him somewhat when he becomes king. I'd found Otho the silver, you see, and I gave him a pair of red stones from my mother's legacy. I didn't tell anyone because Degwa would have let it slip, and I wanted it to be a surprise. Is Maryn on the way here?"

Nevyn growled, so doglike and fierce that she stepped back.

"He's not," Nevyn said at last. "He's commanding you to come down to the great hall and explain yourself in front of everyone."

For a moment Bellyra was afraid that she would faint. The room seemed to have grown very large, and herself very small. The light turned painfully bright and harsh. Elyssa sprang forward, caught her arm in one hand, and slipped her other arm around her shoulders to steady her.

"I'm all right," Bellyra whispered. "But how could he shame me this way?"

"Just so," Nevyn said. "That's why I'm calling him a fool."

Elyssa muttered something foul enough for a silver dagger. "My lady," she said to Bellyra, "we'll put on your best dresses, and I'll do your hair as well, so he can see what a beautiful wife he's slandering."

Bellyra looked down at the dress she was wearing and ran her fingers over linen stained and shiny with age. "We shan't," she said. "I cannot bear to wait that long. I'll go as I am, bare feet and all. It's good enough for a suppliant."

The door to the inner chamber opened, and Degwa came out, white and shaking on the edge of tears. "Your Highness," she blurted. "Forgive me! I never thought Oggyn would repeat—"

"You don't think, Decci!" Elyssa snapped. "That's your whole trouble in life, inn't? You just don't think!"

Degwa started to answer, then merely snivelled.

"Redeem yourself," Nevyn snarled. "Go find Otho the smith and bring him to the great hall."

"The silver daggers' smith? I can't go mucking about the ward looking for a smith."

"You can and you will, you empty-headed little dolt!" Nevyn took one step toward her. "And you will do it now."

Degwa shrieked and ran for the door. Nevyn waited till

she'd gone, then offered Bellyra his arm. "Shall we go, Your Highness?"

"We will. I'm so glad you're here."

Elyssa followed as they left. The corridor stretched unnaturally long in front of her. With every step she told herself, "You can do this, you can do this." She would be strong and firm, she decided, puzzled that Maryn would slight her so, but never anger, never tears, not and let him see how deep the wound he'd given her ran. When they reached the staircase, she could hear voices buzzing below in the great hall.

"It's full of people," she whispered. "All come to watch."

"Good," Nevyn said. "They'll see with their own eyes and hear with their own ears that you're innocent of all wrongdoing."

When they started down the stairs she could see that indeed, servants and riders, servitors and noble-born vassals had all crammed themselves into the hall. Most stood for a better view of the table of honor, where Maryn stood waiting, his arms crossed over his chest. At his feet knelt Maddyn, but there was no sign of Otho or Degwa.

They reached the floor of the hall, and the crowd parted to let them through. As they passed, silence fell behind them. Bellyra felt as if the great hall had swollen as large as the dome of the sky; she was tiny, creeping along, all cold and sweaty at the same time. At last they reached the table of honor. Maryn looked at her with eyes as cold as the silver they resembled.

"You may kneel," Maryn said.

"I shan't." Bellyra took a deep breath and spoke as clearly and loudly as she could. "You're not yet high king, but my equal in rank. It's only through me that you even have a claim on Cerrmor."

Behind her she could hear the crowd whispering. When she glanced at Nevyn, she saw him suppressing a smile. She knew that she couldn't risk looking at Maddyn, kneeling with his head down, as if he couldn't risk looking at her. The memories of his mouth on hers, of his hands upon her back—she forced them away.

"That's true spoken." Maryn's voice dipped to a growl. "Very well, stand then."

Her hands were shaking so badly, and so cold, that she clasped her arms over her chest and tucked her hands inside them.

"I want to know, my lady," Maryn said, "about this night when your women could find no trace of you."

"So your councillor told me, my lord. I was in the forge of Otho the smith, where I was watching him make you a gift to celebrate your kingship. I gave him silver and the two rubies I had from that bracelet my mother left me. I told no one because I wanted to surprise you."

Maryn winced. The gesture made her decide that she might perhaps be able to forgive him one day.

"While I was there," Bellyra continued, "the man you'd set to guarding me came in as well. He'd seen me crossing the ward alone and was mindful of his duty to you."

At that Maddyn looked up and caught the prince's eye.

"So I did," Maddyn said, "Your Highness. But when your lady left the forge, she ordered me to stay behind. Her women were coming to fetch her, you see."

The prince glanced at Lady Elyssa.

"We did, Your Highness," Elyssa said. "We called to her, and she answered, and so we hurried over to escort her back to the women's hall."

Caught, the prince opened his mouth and shut it again. He glanced away, glanced back to Nevyn, who merely stood looking back at him.

"Can this be true?" Maryn said at last. "If Otho can confirm—"

"Cursed right I can!" Otho was bellowing at the top of his lungs. He strode into the hall through the doorway behind the prince. "What is all this rot and nonsense?" He was looking at Nevyn as he spoke, not the prince.

"Someone's filled the prince's ear with poison," Nevyn said. "This person wanted him to believe his wife had been unfaithful to him. It's that night she came to your forge."

"Worms and slimes!" Otho spat on the floor, then looked at the crowd, pressing in behind her. "I want everyone to hear this, I do."

Otho bowed to the prince, then climbed up on a chair and from there to the table. He stood with his hands on his hips and glared down at Prince Maryn, who seemed too surprised to protest this unseemly behavior.

"Now then," Otho said. "Your Highness, I was working on a gift for you—for you, I repeat—when the lady came in, much distracted. She couldn't sleep, she said. The silver dagger there came hurrying after her, afraid she'd lost her wits or suchlike, from the pain of birthing your—I repeat, your third son. Or are you daft enough, Your Highness, to think she was dallying with me, four times her age and ten times as ugly?"

"Not in the least." Maryn sounded as if he was choking. "Not in the least."

"Good." Otho paused, thinking. "One more thing, Your Highness. That you'd suspect your lady—ye gods! If this is the kind of wits you have, a fine king you're going to make."

Everyone in the great hall gasped, flinched, so that the crowd seemed like a field of grain, bowing and rustling in a sudden gust of wind. Maryn stared speechless, his mouth a little open. Otho turned his back on him and clambered down from the table. He paused in front of Bellyra and bowed, but he said nothing.

"My thanks," Bellyra whispered, but her dry mouth refused to form any more words.

Otho turned to look at the prince. "Well, Your Highness?" Otho said. "And what is your royal judgment on the matter?"

The hall went dead-silent again. For a long moment Maryn stared at Otho with eyes that revealed nothing. Otho scowled and kept looking him full in the face. At last Maryn smiled, a crooked sort of smile.

"My judgment?" Prince Maryn said. "That I've done my lady a great disservice by listening to foul gossip about her."

Riders, servants, court people—everyone leapt to their feet and cheered. Maddyn sat back on his heels and wiped his eyes on one sleeve. Bellyra felt tears gather, but she forced them under control and looked squarely at her husband. The booming noise, cheer after cheer, sudden laughter, talk and the clapping of hands, rolled around them both like thunder—but of a departing storm. As the noise began to still, Maryn held out his hand to her.

"My lady, can you forgive me?"

Bellyra wanted to blurt, to say "of course" or "I already have," but she forced herself to keep quiet for a long, haughty moment.

"I shall try, my lord," she said at last. "Out of the love I bear you."

"I deserve no better. Let me escort you upstairs."

Bellyra nodded and took his offered arm. Councillor Oggyn stood at the door, plastered against the jamb, half in and half out of the hall. When she caught his glance he turned and rushed outside, disappearing among the clutter of the ward. You swine! she thought. Her anger kept her strong up to the top of the stairs, but there her terror caught up with her. She stumbled, nearly fell, let Maryn put an arm around her shoulders to steady her. She could feel herself trembling, and once again the dim light of the corridor seemed to rise until she could barely see.

"Here," Maryn said, "let's get you to the women's hall, where you can sit down. I've been the biggest fool in all of Deverry, and ye gods, I'll beg you again to forgive me."

She merely nodded, concentrating on putting one foot in front of the other. But I'm safe, she told herself. I'm safe now. Maryn opened the door to the hall and helped her inside. She collapsed in the first chair she came to.

"I'll kneel in front of you," Maryn said and did so, sitting back on his heels. "I don't think you realize what envy you bring out in people."

"Envy of me?" Bellyra said. "They've lost their wits, then."

"Nah, nah, nah, you're about to become the queen, aren't you? And truly, if it weren't for that, I'd not have dragged you down to the great hall. The entire kingdom has to know that you're above reproach."

"I'm tempted to ask why, but I shan't. Don't you see, Marro, why I'm so frightened? I thought you were going to put me aside. The shame of it—ah Goddess, it would be the worst thing in the world."

"Well, I'm certainly not going to do that. But I think you should leave court for a while."

She could not speak, no matter how hard she tried. She raised one hand as if to reach out to him, but her strength failed her, and the hand refused to move.

"Now hear me out," Maryn said. "This scandal—it's no longer deadly but it's not dead, either. I've been thinking. I'm going to send you back to Cerrmor for a while." He held up a hand flat for silence. "Just a little while, mind."

"What? Why? I thought you believed me and Otho if not me."

"Of course I believe you! That's not the point."

"It is for me." Bellyra felt herself tremble again. "Oh by all the gods! Don't send me away!"

"It's for your own good. I don't want servant lasses gossiping about my wife. And you *are* the queen. Your honor—"

"There's naught you can teach me about my honor, my lord. I know it better than you ever can, how it binds me like a rope of thorns."

Maryn stared, caught speechless, for a long moment. Bellyra forced herself to stare back, and eventually he looked away.

"Riddmar will become gwerbret the moment I become king." Maryn's voice was steady, almost calm. "He won't be able to rule there alone. I'm going to name you regent, but in truth, you'll be the gwerbret. Cerrmor should have been yours, if there were any justice in the kingdom. That you're a woman—well, I never could have given you the rhan, but at least this way you'll get the new gwerbret off to a splendid start."

"I see." Yet she realized that she'd barely understood his words: something about Riddmar, something about Cerrmor.

"No one will count you dishonored this way. Everyone knows the lad will need a regent at first."

"Will you send me away before the priests make you high king?" She was surprised to find that she could form a coherent thought. "After all my long years of living in fear for your sake, I'd like to see the end of the wars."

"I won't. You've a part to play in the ritual, and Riddmar can't be invested till after I'm proclaimed, anyway."

"Very well. I'll tell the nursemaids and suchlike to be ready—"

"I'm keeping the children here. It's too dangerous, letting them travel to Cerrmor. We didn't fight these wars to put a man without heirs on the throne."

But not too dangerous to send me, Bellyra thought. I've served my purpose. I've given him his litter of sons, I'll have taken my appointed place during the rituals. "You know somewhat, Maryn?" she said aloud. "It's a pity I wasn't born a broodmare. I wouldn't care if I ever saw the stud who mounted me again."

"Oh for the gods' sake! It's only going to be for a little while. A year, say, to let the talk die down."

She thought of saying more, of letting her anger loose like some savage dog freed from its chain, but she realized that he wanted her to be angry, so that he in turn could grow angry as well. If they fought, he would see her leaving court as a victory, and one that he had every right to claim. Instead she looked at him, kept her face as calm as she could make it, merely looked and had the satisfaction of seeing him toss his head and turn away to escape her stare.

"I've got to get back to the great hall." Maryn got up from the floor. "I'll be back to escort you down to dinner, if you'd care to come."

He strode to the door, strode out of it, slammed it hard behind him. Bellyra leaned back in her chair and watched the cobwebs drifting from the massive beams of the ceiling. She heard the door opening behind her, and heard Elyssa calling her name, but raising her head to look or answer seemed beyond her. Just when I thought I was safe, just when I thought it was over. She felt as if she were a stick of wood that had withstood a hundred blows of an axe, only to break on the hundredth and first.

Although Clodda had told her that the prince was dragging Bellyra into the great hall, Lilli had stayed away. She was beginning to wonder if she was starting to hate Maryn. How could he do such a thing to the wife who loved him beyond everything? Didn't he realize—then she remembered him blithely talking about their political marriage. Of course he didn't realize. He didn't want to, she supposed. She heard the news of how things had resolved from Nevyn, who came straight up to her chamber afterwards. The old man was still angry, but by the end of his recital he managed to share a laugh with Lilli over Otho's remarks to the soon-to-be high king of all Deverry.

"Oh, how splendid of Otho!" Lilli said. "Of course, if Maryn were a less honorable man, he would have thrown Otho in prison or suchlike."

"Perhaps," Nevyn said, still smiling. "But I think Otho would have thought it was worth it."

Someone knocked on the door, then banged on it.

"Lilli?" Elyssa's voice called out. "Is Nevyn there with you?

"He is." Lilli rose from her chair. "Do come in, Lyss."

Elyssa opened the door and stepped in, but only by one pace. "Nevyn, please, can you come attend upon the princess? Her madness—ah ye gods! I've never seen it so strong."

"Of course I will." Nevyn got up hastily. "I suppose this attack must be the result of what happened in the great hall."

"That and worse. The prince is sending her away to Cerrmor. He says it's to stand as regent to young Riddmar, but I doubt me if that's the real reason."

"The little bastard!" Nevyn snarled. "And no doubt she blames herself."

"I don't know." Elyssa spread her hands in a helpless gesture. "She can barely put ten words together."

"Lilli, go to my tower room and fetch the canvas sack. It's under the table. The sack with the medicinals. Then bring it to the women's hall."

"I will, my lord." Lilli took a deep breath. "As fast as I can."

Lilli hurried to the staircase and clattered down in her clogs. By then the storm had turned the sunset hour as dim as twilight, and in the murky great hall she could hope that no one would notice her. From the scraps of conversation she could overhear, everyone was still talking about Bellyra and Otho, how between them they had shown the prince a thing or two. She hurried outside and trotted across the ward to Nevyn's broch. At the entrance she paused and looked back: no one was following her. By the time she reached the top of the stairs she was gasping for breath. Although she found the sack immediately, she was forced to sit down and rest till her pounding heart stilled.

By the time she left, the rain had started. Fat cool drops spattered down, thicker and faster with every moment that passed. She wrapped her arms around the sack to keep it as dry as possible and ran for the great hall. She was so intent on keeping the herbs safe, in fact, that she nearly ran into Maryn. He caught her arm and smiled at her. She could smell mead.

"Why such a hurry, my lady?" Maryn said.

"Your wife, Your Highness, has been taken ill. Nevyn sent me for medicinals."

Maryn let her go and stepped back. Lilli could see the men at the nearby tables turning to watch, but her anger pounded in her blood like the rain on the cobbles.

"How could you!" she hissed. "Send her away, I mean. How could you?"

Maryn froze, staring at her with eyes that revealed nothing. Lilli pushed past him and started up the stairs. Her lungs ached and burned, but she forced herself onward until she gained the safety of the landing above. She staggered down the corridor to the women's hall, pushed open the door, and staggered through it to find Degwa lighting candles with a long splint. In the dancing light tears gleamed on her cheeks.

"My lady and Nevyn are in the bedchamber," Degwa said. "I should have listened to you, Lilli. Ah Goddess, how I wish I'd listened to you!"

"I wish you'd listened, too." Lilli set the sack on a nearby table. "Take this in to Nevyn, will you? I don't want to add to our princess's grief by letting her see me."

Lilli returned to her own chamber. Clodda had set on the table a plate of bread and cheese, a goblet of watered mead, and a lit candle lantern. Lilli sank into her chair and remembered Maryn, standing in the doorway with his eyes suddenly gone dead to all feeling. He sent her away for me. The realization sickened her. He sent her away so I wouldn't see her grief. Did he think I'd fall into his arms again, once Bellyra was out of sight?

"I'd rather die," she whispered. "By the Goddess, I hope he never touches me again."

And as she spoke, she felt an eerie cold wash over her, as if some great presence had walked into the room. She looked around and saw no one, but she knew in a wordless way that her prayer had been accepted.

Bellyra lay on her bed, propped up on pillows, and allowed Nevyn and Elyssa to fuss over her. She listened to Nevyn's talk of finding inner strength, smiled when Elyssa announced that they'd all have a more comfortable life in Cerrmor, and in general pretended that their concern was healing the wounds Maryn had given her. That she acted out lies no longer mattered. Nothing mattered anymore. Their talk went on and on, while the shutters banged at the windows and rain fell. Elyssa hurried around lighting candles. It had grown dark outside.

The nursemaid brought in the children. Bellyra kissed all three and told them she loved them—another lie. The sight of them, little Maryns, all of them, with their pale hair and little grey eyes, made her want to scream with rage. Even the newly named Prince Gwardon, so helpless in his little red blanket—perhaps she hated him most of all. That Maryn would keep the children but send her away—it was unbearable. Every decent woman in Deverry would pity her; the malicious would gloat.

The nursemaid took the children out again. Bellyra lay in a pool of candlelight and listened to the rain.

"It's slacking a bit," she said.

"The storm's moving fast, Your Highness," Nevyn said. "No doubt it will clear by the morning."

"Ah. You know, you could go about your evening. I'll be fine; you don't need to sit with me."

"There's nowhere I'd rather be than here."

They talked some more, Elyssa and Nevyn, talked and talked till Bellyra felt like ordering them away. At moments she thought they were about to mention Maddyn, but one or the other would abruptly change the subject. Finally Nevyn stood up and stretched, yawning.

"Well, I had best be off," Nevyn said. "I'm leaving herbs here with Elyssa. They'll help you sleep. You look exhausted, and I for one don't blame you one bit."

Bellyra nodded and smiled. She felt as if she were playing with a doll, as if she stood beside her body and moved its head and flapped its arms while she pretended it was alive.

"I'll be back later," Nevyn continued. "Just to see how you're bearing up."

"My thanks," Bellyra said.

When he left, Elyssa walked him to the door. Bellyra could hear them murmuring incomprehensibly, talking about her, no doubt. It was a pity she was worrying them so, but then, the worry would end soon. Packed off to Cerrmor like a chest of unwanted clothes—she could not, she would not bear it. For one moment the idea came to her that if she did return to Cerrmor, Maddyn might follow at a decent interval, but immediately she thought of the gossip. It would reach Maryn, and then he would know that he'd been right to send her away.

Wearing a fixed smile, Elyssa returned to the bedchamber. She pulled up a high stool to sit at the bedside.

"Are you really glad to be going back to Cerrmor?" Bellyra said.

"I'd be glad if only you were happy about it."

"Instead of shamed like this?"

"It's his shame, not yours, that he'd treat you this way."

"Then why do I feel it? A cast-off woman, that's what I am. Oh, I know that Maryn's talked of recall. Do you truly think he'll ever want me back? It was noble of little Lilli to end their affair, but he'll find another lass, and another after that. He always does. He has his legitimate heirs now. What would he want with a mare too galled to ride?"

"Oh, don't, Lyrra! Stop it!"

"What? Don't you think it's true?"

"What? The mistresses? Of course it's true spoken, but he'll want you back. He needs your good sense. I hate to see you vexing yourself this way."

Bellyra shrugged and considered the bed hangings. Little red wyverns flew on one side, while the ships of Cerrmor still sailed on the other.

"I never finished the new hangings," Bellyra said. "Oh well, his new mistress can finish the sewing. She's the one who'll be sleeping in this bed."

Elyssa made the choking sound of someone trying to stifle tears.

"Do you remember what they called me when we were little?" Bellyra went on. "The lass who wasn't there. That's what I feel like now, someone who's not really here. The priests say that the Otherlands begin their journey to this world on the day past Beltane. This year I can feel it. It's as if this storm came from there."

"Stop it, stop it!" Tears were running down Elyssa's face. "Please, please don't talk like that."

"My apologies. I'll stop."

"I'm going to wake up the pages." Elyssa slid down from the stool. "They'll fetch water and firewood, and we'll brew you up those herbs Nevyn left to help you sleep."

Elyssa hurried out of the chamber. As soon as the door closed, Bellyra threw back the covers and got up. Carrying her clogs, she went to the door and opened it a bare crack. Outside the dark corridor stretched silent. She left, shutting the door again to give Elyssa an extra moment's delay, and hurried down the corridor to the staircase. The great hall stretched dark; near the banked hearths servants and dogs slept in the straw. Bellyra crept through, then put on the noisy clogs once she'd reached the ward.

In the dark night, most people would have been lost immediately in the madman's maze of the huge broch complex, but Bellyra knew it better than anyone else ever had. She ducked through the servant doors, crawled past the windows of occupied chambers, dashed across internal courtyards, and found her way to the base of the east tower at last. She felt nothing, not the rain, not the night wind, not the feel of rough stone under her hands as she groped her way to the staircase.

Her shame no longer burned; it had receded to a kind of warmth, an anticipation of the pleasure she would gain by being free at last of both her shame and Maryn's coldness. She should blame herself, or so she thought, for being sent away. What man wouldn't want to escape from a woman who kept demanding love from him? It seemed true, at any rate, as she climbed up the long winding stairs, that Maryn had a perfect right to want her gone.

All at once Bellyra heard the strange echo of voices. Where were they? She paused, heard men's voices at the bottom of the stairs, and sobbed once. The servants must have seen her after all. She kicked off her noisy clogs and hurried on, gasping for breath, sweating even in the cold, faster and faster on burning legs and feet. At last she burst free of the stairwell and found herself on the narrow parapet.

Down below in the dark ward, so far below that they looked like flowers of light, torches bloomed. She heard yells, saw men rushing to the tower, heard from behind her another set of yells to match them. She stepped to the edge and expected to feel fear, but when she looked down, she saw not the ward of Dun Deverry but her little garden back in Cerrmor, bright and sunny with summer. All she had to do was step forward and she would fall into summer. She could see this now, so high above the world and the doings of men.

"Lyrra! Don't!" It was Maryn's voice, loud behind her. "Stop!"

She turned and saw him at the top of the stairs, dressed only in a pair of brigga, reaching out to her with naked arms. He's not really there, she told herself. You're seeing things. With that she spun around and took the last step into night. For the briefest of moments she heard him screaming, but the wind grabbed her and washed his voice away. Down and down—it seemed to her that she fell forever, but darkness rose up with a sword of stone and stabbed her. There was pain, and then only the darkness, wailing around her with Maryn's voice.

Half-naked in the rain the prince knelt on the ground and cradled his dead wife in his arms. In the light of the lanterns that servants were holding, Nevyn could see the blood from her smashed face running down his chest and arms, but the prince seemed not to notice, any more than his eyes seemed to see.

"Why?" Maryn whispered. "Why would she do this?"

Nevyn felt his patience shatter. "Because you were sending her away," he snapped. "Right in the midst of her birthing madness, you sent her away."

"It was only for a little while," Maryn said. "I told her that."

"Ye gods! There are times when you're as stupid as mud." Nevyn got up and towered over him. "Think, Marro! Not that it'll do any good. Now."

He was the only man in the kingdom who could address the prince that way and live. The servants gasped and drew back a few steps, as if they feared lightning would strike Nevyn where he stood and they along with him. Maryn flinched and returned his gaze to Bellyra's body.

"I would have recalled her," Maryn said. "Truly I would have. I told her so."

Nevyn restrained himself from calling the prince a murderer. Instead he stepped back and let Maryn's men rush forward to tend him. Owaen threw himself down to a kneel next to his liege, and servants followed.

Nevyn strode across the ward, which was filling with servants and courtiers both, all talking, some weeping. In the darkness he stepped into a nook between two of Dun Deverry's random walls, sat down on the wet ground, and slipped into trance almost before his weight had completely settled. He summoned his body of light, joined to his midriff by a silver cord. First he imagined what it would be like to see out of its eyes; then with the ease of long practice he was indeed looking out of them.

The rainy ward smouldered with silver fire, or so it seemed from his viewpoint on the etheric plane, great columns of mist and drifts of smoke that were both naught more than the elemental force and effluent of the water in the physical ward below. Although none of the outpourings was strong enough to threaten his body of light with harm, they did make it very hard for Nevyn to see. In among the swirling water veils he could pick out the glowing auras of the people clustering around Bellyra's body, but nothing as frail as her etheric form. He rose up some twenty feet above the ground, then drifted over to the cluster of auras, pulsing yellow and red, stippled with dark grief. Inside each one he could see, dimly, the body of the person who wore it.

Bellyra's etheric double would be somewhere near her corpse, he figured, or near Maryn, who was kneeling next to it. The prince's aura wrapped tightly around him, a pale gold throb of light, as if he were frightened or puzzled. When Nevyn dropped down closer, he could see something much like a woman's shadow, fluttering around him. Its hands beat at Maryn's head and shoulders, as if it were trying to touch his warm flesh.

Nevyn sent out a thought, which sounded on this plane as words. "Bellyra, Your Highness! Where are you? It's me, Nevyn!"

In the drifting shadow a pale light shone, a strange ice-blue. Nevyn headed toward it, calling again. All at once her simulacrum appeared. The shadow thickened into the shape of a naked woman, her head thrown back, her arms flailing in panic. Nevyn swooped down and steadied himself in front of her.

"It is you!" Her thought voice wavered and threatened to disappear. "I thought I was dead."

"You are. Come with me. Let's get away from all this wretchedness."

Like a frightened child she grabbed at his hands, but hers passed right through them. She spun around and disappeared into a column of water-force, and for a moment he thought he'd lost her.

"Lyrra, come back!"

He raced after her and finally saw her drifting in midair, high above the dun. He flew up and joined her.

"Am I a ghost?" Bellyra's thoughts came to him on a wave of fear. "Must I stay here forever? Oh gods, forgive me! I thought death would end it. I thought I'd be free."

"You will be," Nevyn said. "You're not a haunt. Do what I say."

"Leave Maryn?" She tossed her head this way and that with a swirl of spectral hair. "Leave Maryn?"

"You must! And in truth, you already have. Look down."

Far below them the dun appeared in the silver mists as dark lumps of stone, dead things heaped up like charcoal near a smelter. Little puffs of light, the auras of those living persons in the ward, hurried back and forth.

"You have a choice," Nevyn said. "You may stay here for some few days in misery and pain, desperately regretting what you've done, trying to make Maryn hear you, or you can come with me and go on."

"Go where?"

"To rest and peace."

For a moment the spirit danced back and forth in the mists. When she steadied herself, the form took on more detail. Bellyra's eyes seemed to look out of the pale blue face.

"Very well," she said. "Of course. Show me."

"Follow me. Don't try to touch me. Just follow me."

"I will."

With one hand he sketched a sigil into the air. Before them a pale lavender slit opened in the dark and swirling mists, like a cut through the rind of a fruit that reveals a different-colored flesh beneath. When Nevyn waved his hand, the slit peeled back and revealed itself as a gate.

"Come with me," he repeated, then flung himself through.

In a tunnel of midnight indigo a purple wind swirled around him. He glanced back and saw Bellyra's shade close behind him.

"Courage!" he called out.

Behind them the gate twisted and sealed itself shut. Her shade spun into the air, caught suddenly by the wind. Although she screamed and flailed, the wind bellied her form out like a sail and drove her onward, whipping her past Nevyn. He called out a reassurance and gave himself over to the wind. They fell, flew, climbed, sailed—all these at once on the violet wind—past images, faces, stars, words, animals, sigils—while the wind howled with a thousand voices, all incomprehensible. Fast, faster—until suddenly they burst out into yet another world, this one quiet and pale, where death-white flowers nodded in a lavender light.

Bellyra's soul had changed its form. As a naked child she waited for him on the banks of a white river, where something much like water yet more like mist purled and slid past in silence. The child was looking around her in gape-mouthed surprise.

"Here you'll have to go on alone," Nevyn said. "You must cross that river."

"I understand." The child turned her face up and studied him for a moment. "Farewell, Nevyn. Will we meet again?"

"We will."

"Will I meet Maryn again?"

"Perhaps. That's not for me to say. I rather hope you don't."

With a sad nod of her head she stepped into the white water. Nevyn saw the white mists rise to cover her—then felt a wave of pain, breaking over him like fire. The scene swirled around his head like a shape painted on clouds, then disappeared. He felt himself falling, too fast, too hard, into the darkness of his body. He felt someone's hands on his face.

"It's Lord Nevyn!" a voice was saying. "The old man's fainted or suchlike."

Every muscle of his body ached. His heart was pounding hard. Nevyn opened his eyes to the blinding light of a double lantern, held up in a manservant's hand. Other voices called out, footsteps came running.

"I'm all right," Nevyn said. His voice rasped in a sore throat. "I'm all right. Help me up!"

The servant handed the lantern to someone in the shadows behind him, then held out both hands. Nevyn grabbed them and let the boy haul him up, then leaned against the wall to catch his breath.

"It's a terrible sad thing," the servant said. "Losing our lady." He burst into sobs and stood helplessly, letting the tears run.

"So it is," Nevyn said. "I was quite overcome."

Nevyn glanced around and saw Maryn still kneeling by Bellyra's body. Someone had brought a wide plank, and it looked as if two men were about to lift Bellyra onto it. Nevyn's entire experience in the Otherlands had taken but a few brief moments, as time runs in the world of men.

"Do you need help, my lord?" the servant said.

"I don't, but my thanks. I see my apprentice there, anyway."

In the doorway to a great hall turned bright with torchlight Lilli stood clutching the doorjamb as if she were afraid of fainting herself. Nevyn hurried over to her, as fast as he could, at any rate, with his bruised body. Lilli looked up at him, tried to speak, and failed.

"It's not your fault in the least," Nevyn snapped. "I know what you're thinking."

She shook her head in a mute no, then turned and ran across the great hall. Nevyn stepped inside and watched her climbing the staircase round the far side. No doubt she was going to throw herself on her bed and weep. She'd feel better for it, too, and he envied her. Later he would go up to see how she fared, but at the moment, he realized, he would be of no use to anyone, since he could barely calm himself.

• • •

Maddyn heard the news from Owaen. He woke from a sound sleep just as his fellow captain came running into the barracks with a candle lantern in his hand.

"Maddo?" Owaen sounded hesitant—an odd thing in itself. "Uh, Maddo, you'd best get up and dress."

"Why? What's happened?"

With a long sigh Owaen sat down on the bunk opposite. The lantern light threw dapples of shadow over his face. Maddyn sat up and threw the blankets back.

"What is it, Owaen? For the love of the gods, tell me!"

"The princess is dead. She threw herself down from the leaning tower."

The shadows danced as Owaen's hand trembled. With an oath he bent down and set the lantern on the floor. Maddyn could only stare at him.

"It's a ghastly thing," Owaen said finally. "Uh, mayhap you'd best—I mean, Nevyn—ah horseshit and a tub of piss, too! I don't know what to say."

"No more do I," Maddyn whispered.

As he got up, Maddyn felt nothing at all, no surprise, no grief, nothing. He dressed, he buckled on his belt, he put on his boots, and felt nothing. All around him Wildfolk materialized, grey gnomes, mostly, who sucked on their fingers while they stared with solemn eyes.

"Maddo?" Owaen said. "Are you all right?"

"Of course not," Maddyn said. "I'll just be off to find Nevyn."

At the mention of Nevyn, the Wildfolk disappeared. Maddyn picked up the candle lantern and took it with him when he left the barracks.

Outside the rain had stopped. When he looked up he could see a tear in the clouds and a glitter of stars for one brief moment; then the wind closed over the brightness. Like her life, he thought. A bright moment, and then it was gone. All at once he could no longer stand. He dropped to his knees, set the lantern down on the cobbles, threw back his head, and howled. It wasn't keening, really, just a howl, more rage than grief—he felt it rock him back and forth as he howled, over and over, without a true word in it.

Dimly he heard a voice, calling his name—a man's voice, Nevyn. The old man knelt and grabbed him by the shoulders.

"Stop it!" Nevyn shook him like a child. "Stop it, Maddo!"

Eventually, Maddyn did. By the lantern light he stared openmouthed at the old man. "Did you hear me?" he said at last.

"The Wildfolk fetched me. Come with me. I don't want the prince to see you in this state."

"Curse the prince!"

"Don't tempt me! Now get up off this wretched wet ground, and let's go up to the women's hall. Her women will have washed her body by now. No one's going to dare begrudge you entry there tonight."

"I don't want—"

"Don't argue!" Nevyn grabbed him by the arm with surprising strength. "Let us go, bard. Now."

In the women's hall candles blazed. The dead thing that once had been Bellyra lay on a trestle table of the sort women set up for finishing bed hangings, and indeed, under her lay a half-finished panel of embroidered red wyverns. She wore only a white shift, clinging to her body here and there with damp. At her head Elyssa stood brushing her lady's hair, her face white and set. She never looked up once.

"You know, Maddo," Elyssa said, "I wish to every god that you and she had ridden off together. I would have helped you leave with my blessings."

Maddyn tried to speak, but his mouth had gone as dry as cold ash in a hearth. Dimly he was aware of someone weeping nearby. He glanced round, expecting to see a servant. In the curve of the wall Lady Degwa sat on the floor. She was curled up, knees to chest, her arms wrapped tight around herself, and she rocked like a terrified child, back and forth as she wept.

"I never meant," she was whispering. "I never meant harm."

Maddyn ignored her and walked over to the improvised bier. Bellyra's face—he stared, shaking, at what was left of her beauty, smashed against stone, purple and red, raw like meat.

"I'll lay a bit of silk over her," Elyssa whispered. "For the burial."

Maddyn nodded and turned away. He had meant to kiss her farewell, but her injuries had made it impossible, a last injustice that made him swear aloud. For a long time he stood staring at the floor, thinking of very little, listening as Degwa wept and Nevyn and Elyssa talked of the children and what must be done to help the lads deal with losing their mother. Finally, he heard a door open behind him. The talk stopped, though Degwa wept the louder. He knew that the prince must have entered even before he turned round to see Maryn, standing bewildered by his wife's dead body.

The prince was unarmed with his back turned. Maddyn felt his hand touch his silver dagger of its own will. Madness rose in his throat like a howl; madness blinded his eyes with a red mist. He could draw, step forward, stab, avenge. The word vengeance throbbed in his blood. Vengeance—and then what? He would have broken every vow he'd sworn to Prince Maryn, shattered the last bit of his honor and ground it underfoot. I'll not, he told himself. The thought seemed to clear his vision, and he could see Nevyn, watching him calmly but for the rise of one bristling eyebrow.

Maryn spun around, his arms held a little out to each side, as if he'd just realized that Maddyn stood behind him. Maddyn forced himself to kneel as the courtesy to his sworn lord demanded.

"Get up," Maryn snarled. "For gods' sake, don't kneel to me tonight. I'm not worthy of it."

Unable to speak, Maddyn nodded and rose. For a long moment they looked at each other, bard and prince; then Maddyn bowed, turned, and strode out of the hall. He trotted down the corridor, clattered down the stairway, and rushed out into the damp night air where at last, it seemed, he could breathe.

All night Lilli lay awake, terrified that Maryn would come to her. If he wanted comfort, what would she say to him? He never opened her door, and toward dawn she fell asleep at last and dreamt of being an exile again. Once again she rode into Cerrmor and stood in the sunny ward, but this time it was the princess who walked up to her and smiled in welcome. She woke in tears, dragged herself up, and dressed. She crept downstairs, afraid at every turn that she'd see Maryn, but the great hall stretched out silent in the grey light. A few servants were just rising from their beds in the straw by the hearths. They ignored her as she hurried outside.

The storm had broken, and brilliant sunshine glittered on the freshly washed cobbles. The blue sky above seemed like some insult to Bellyra, as if the sun himself should have been mourning her. Lilli ran into the shelter of Nevyn's tower and puffed up the stairs. His chamber stood open, and he himself sat on the windowsill.

"I thought you might come here early," Nevyn said. "Did you talk with Maryn last night?"

Lilli shook her head and sat down, panting for breath, on the chair. Nevyn leaned forward in concern.

"You look decidedly unwell."

"I am. I hardly slept."

"No doubt. I didn't either. This is a horrible thing."

With one last gasp, Lilli got her breath back. "And it's my fault," Lilli said. "At least partly."

"It's not," Nevyn snapped. "It's to no one's shame, not even Maryn's, though I must admit I'm feeling very ill disposed toward him this morning."

"You don't understand. He was going to send her to Cerrmor because of me. I mean, because I ended the thing between us." Her eyes filled with tears.

"And he grew furious and decided to send her away, where you'd not worry about her?"

"I think so, truly." Lilli could barely speak. She felt the

tears running down her face and let them. "She was so good to me when I had naught."

In the morning light Nevyn suddenly seemed not merely old but ancient, with every line on his face etched deep, his skin pale around the brown discolorings of old age, his eyes clouded and distant. His hands, all knuckles and wrinkled skin, clasped each other, then relaxed, flaccid on his thighs.

"If Maryn had half your sense of honor," Nevyn said at last, "Bellyra would be alive today. Do *not* blame yourself. As your master in your craft, I forbid it."

"Very well. I—it's just so hateful."

"It is that." Nevyn spoke so softly that she could barely hear him. "It is that, truly."

Lilli managed to return to her chamber without meeting Maryn. The pages all told her that the prince had shut himself up in his apartments and would speak with no one. All morning Lilli lay on her bed, weeping at times, but mostly brooding on the princess's death. Was it truly Maryn's cruelty alone that had driven Bellyra to her death? She found herself remembering her mother, Lady Merodda, and her dark magicks that had caused so many so much harm. Her mother's curse had followed her into the sanctuary of Maryn's domain. Lilli could think of it no other way, that like poison in a well her mother's evil had seeped into all their lives. Could nothing lift it?

"I'm her daughter."

Lilli got up and walked over to the window. Down below she could see the ward, gilded in the sunlight pouring through the remnants of last night's storm. It was falling to her, Merodda's daughter, to lift the curse. In that morning's meditation it came to her, that since the curse had been sealed with the blood of their clan, only blood-kin could lift it.

"Have you seen Councillor Oggyn?" Nevyn said.

"I haven't, my lord," the page said. "Not all this morning."

"No doubt he's sulking in his quarters."

"No doubt." The page turned his head and spat onto the cobbles. "He can stay there forever, for all I care."

Nevyn strode into the great hall and paused just inside the doorway. This late in the morning, the hall stood mostly empty, though a few servants sat at a table and gossiped. When Nevyn asked, they too denied seeing Oggyn anywhere. Nevyn couldn't blame the man for hiding. Fairly or not, half the dun blamed him for Bellyra's death. Nevyn went upstairs to Oggyn's apartments and found the door closed. He knocked, waited, knocked again the harder. Still no answer. A thin line of cold dread ran down his back.

When he pushed on the door, it swung open easily. He stepped in, looked around, looked up, and swore aloud. Oggyn's body was hanging from a ceiling beam. His black tongue protruded from his swollen mouth, and he smelled of excrement. Under his dangling feet, a pile of tables, scattered and broken, showed how he'd managed to get up so high. No doubt he'd kicked them away when the noose tightened and his body spasmed. At least he'd given himself plenty of rope. His neck must have broken immediately and spared him the long slow agony of suffocation.

Nevyn shuddered and stepped back out, closing the door behind him. He should, he supposed, go tell Lady Degwa this news himself, but the thought nauseated him. All at once he smiled, a smile as grim and cold and brutal as any a berserker ever felt on his lips. He would tell Maryn, he decided, and let the prince have the joy of dealing with it.

"Hah!" Owaen said. "Slimy Oggo hanged himself. Have you heard?"

"I hadn't," Maddyn said.

"The prince himself told me. He was pleased as a man can be."

Maddyn shrugged. They were sitting on their bunks, facing each other, in the silver daggers' barracks. All the other men had left, off readying their horses for Bellyra's funeral procession. Bright sun streamed in and turned the straw on the floor to pale gold.

"I take it you're not pleased," Owaen said.

"I'm not. He was trying to get at me with his cursed gossip, not at her. If I'd never composed that wretched song, this never would have happened."

"That's horseshit and a pile of it!"

"Oh, is it now? What do you mean?"

"It's simple. If he hadn't been a grasping greedy swine of a man in the first place, you'd not have made up the song. He deserved every note of it. Ye gods, Maddo! Why in all the hells are you blaming yourself?"

"I don't know, but I am."

Owaen rolled his eyes heavenward and got up, setting his hands on his hips. "Don't," he said. "Are you going to ride with us in the procession?"

The prince had planned a magnificent funeral for his wife: his silver daggers, his lords, their riders, all of them on horseback to follow the litter carrying her body, while the prince himself walked beside it, all humility. Behind the riders would come the servants, walking to pay their last respects. The priests would bury her among the sacred oaks behind the temple of Bel.

"I'm not," Maddyn said. "If he takes offense at that, he can choke on it."

"He won't. Suit yourself, then."

"I refuse to be there and see the earth fall on her."

"You what?" Owaen stared at him for a long moment. "Are you telling me you truly did love her or suchlike?"

"I'm telling you naught."

Owaen shook his head in sadness, then strode out of the barracks. Maddyn lay down on his bunk and stared at the ceiling. In the empty barracks the noise from outside drifted back and forth. Assembling and putting in order such a procession took a lot of shouting and cursing while the jingling of bridles sounded a chorus like tiny bells. At last the noise began to dwindle; the men fell silent, the bells grew faint as the horsemen filed out of the main ward. In the silence Maddyn could let himself weep. He turned over onto his stomach, grabbed his pillow, and punched it with the hardest fist he could make, over and over, while the tears ran down his face.

• • •

Nevyn had forbidden Lilli to attend the funeral—not that she'd been wanting to go. In the silence of that long afternoon, with the dun nearly empty but for her, Lilli walked in the new royal garden among the roses and fresh-planted saplings while she considered plans. Once, quite deliberately, she ran her hand through a rosebush and gashed her flesh on the thorns. She let the blood drops fall into the earth as a sign of her pledge, that she would run any risk to bring peace back to Dun Deverry. All day she brooded over her dweomer learning until at last she had some idea of a ritual that might once and for all exorcise the evil. Although she considered consulting with Nevyn, she knew that he would only forbid her. That evening the servants told her that he was closeted with the prince. She had her chance.

The full moon was swinging over zenith toward the horizon when Lilli went up to Nevyn's chamber. At the door she felt a strange prickly tremble of power in the air— some sort of magical ward, she assumed, and the sensation would have sent an ordinary person running. She opened the door and stepped in. The cluttered little outer room lay silent and dark except for a shaft of moonlight on the floor, where a throng of gnomes sat on silent guard. When Lilli knelt in front of the casket's hiding place, the gnomes merely moved aside to give her the room to work.

Lilli pulled the wooden box out of the hole in the floor, then eased the loose board back into place. Even through the box, magically sealed with sigils and markings, she could feel the lead tablet sucking the warmth out of her hands. Its very malignancy would allow her to destroy it, or so she hoped. She tucked it under a shawl and walked out again. She met no one in the corridor. Back in her own room, she barred the door against interruptions, then lit candles. In their midst she set the box down. For a moment she hesitated, gasping in terror. With one long breath she steadied herself and flipped back the lid. She tipped the box up, dumped the lead tablet into the circle of candles, and tossed the box onto the floor.

In the dancing light the strip of lead glittered like the

eyes of some evil animal crouched in fear of its hunter.
When she touched it, the gashes from the rose thorns
ached with the pain she would have felt from pressing her
wounds against ice. She stepped back, flung her arms over
her head, and invoked the Light. With her inner sight she
saw it fall in answer to her cry, a long shaft of gold that
pierced her from head to foot. She flung her arms out to
the sides and let the Light stabilize within her, then picked
up the tablet.

A faint grey matter oozed from the lead, rising like mist
from a lake. She clutched the strip in one hand, held it out
in the candlelight, and began to pull the slime into herself.
She saw the ooze begin to gather in ugly clots of disgust, as
if it were wool and her body the spindle, gathering it up,
twisting it fine and tight, around and around her until she
felt herself choking and writhing from it. For a moment she
felt all her mother's hatred of the world; she saw, briefly,
with Merodda's desperate eyes; Merodda's smothering re-
sentments clotted in her throat and made her gag.

Once again Lilli called up the Light and felt it burst
upon her as fire, a pale blue purifying fire that swept
through her aura, her body, her very soul. She cried out
once with pain, then set her jaw against it. She tried to
drop the tablet on the floor, but all at once she hated to let
it go. There was power in the thing, power that she could
use against her enemies. I have no enemies! she thought
and flung it from her to fall at her feet. When she stepped
back, the blue fire fell upon it like a ravenous dog. The horrible grey threads blazed with fire, turning to a fine white
ash and drifting to the floor.

"Lords of Air!" Lilli cried out. "Aid me!"

A silver wind swept through the chamber and gathered
the ash, swept it up and scattered it. The fire around her
cooled, then flickered and went out. At the windows the light
was turning grey. Lilli blew out the candles and let dawn seep
into the room. When she picked up the tablet, she found it
only a piece of thin lead, its evil spent and gone. She turned
it over and realized that even the very letters of the curse had
disappeared, melted into a smooth scar upon the metal. With

a laugh she flipped it over again: truly no letters, just a faint bubbling of the lead where once the curse had lain.

"I've won!"

The cough racked up from the bottom of her lungs and bent her double. Choking she spasmed, caught the edge of the table with both hands and steadied herself against the pain. Coughed, coughed, coughed until she felt something tear free inside of her, coughed one more time, and spat up rheum, bright scarlet red. A gobbet of blood and phlegm spattered on the tablet and slid, staining the metal. She felt stickiness around her mouth and on her chin like some poisoned sweetmeat.

"This is the price."

Speaking tore another cough from her lungs. She staggered over to her bed and fell onto it, facedown, to cough and spit until the blanket lay stained red under her. When she tried to sit up, she fell back. Wildfolk manifested around her, reaching out with worried hands as they swarmed around her bed.

"Get Nevyn," she whispered.

When they disappeared, she fainted, her face half-buried in the pillow. It seemed to her that she was floating down a river on a little boat, drifting far from shore toward the sea. Yet on the bank someone was calling to her.

"Lilli!" Nevyn's voice, and Nevyn himself, banging on the door. "Lilli, for the love of the gods! Let me in!"

"I can't—" She tried to call out, but the coughing rose and threatened to drown her.

By an act of sheer will she managed to roll to the side of the bed and stand up, but as she turned toward the door, she fell to her knees. Coughing racked her. She heard him swearing; then all at once the heavy bar across the door slid up, wiggling free of the staple. Gnomes and sylphs were clutching and shoving the thing, until at last it leapt up and fell free onto the floor. Nevyn slammed the door open and rushed in. On her knees Lilli could only stare up at him while blood ran down her chin. He looked at the blood-stained tablet, then back to her.

"You didn't," Nevyn said.

"I had to! My clan—I had to."

The old man nodded, slowly, deliberately while tears glistened in his eyes.

"Let's get you into a proper sickbed," Nevyn said at last. "I'll pull you through yet."

She tried to smile but failed. She could feel her death gnawing at her lungs like a beast desperate in a cage.

For three days Nevyn battled to save Lilli's life, but she slid farther and farther away from him. He knew long before the end came that he'd never win, but he kept on trying to fight consumption with herbs, poultices, and warmed blankets.

"It's like trying to fight an army with sticks," Nevyn said. "But ye gods, how can I surrender?"

Maddyn nodded. They were standing at Lilli's bedside while she slept openmouthed and propped up on bloodstained pillows. Old blood blotched the handful of rags lying beside her as well.

"Is she bleeding to death?" Maddyn whispered.

"She is. And in a way, she's drowning."

"Ah gods. She's so blasted young. I wish it were me. What use am I, a worn-out rider with naught to live for? Better it were me!"

"Oh hold your tongue. This is no time for self-pity, bard."

Maddyn winced and turned away. Nevyn sat down on the edge of the bed and opened his dweomer sight. Her aura looked like wisps of mist clinging to her body.

Long past midnight, Nevyn sat alone at Lilli's bedside. He had hung silver balls of dweomer light around the chamber, but all at once, the room turned oddly dark, as if some lord of shadows had entered and scattered gloom with a careless wave of a hand. Or some lady—the spirit appeared at the foot of Lilli's bed, all draped in black but still wearing her likeness of Lilli's mother, Merodda. Fortunately Lilli lay unconscious on her heap of pillows and could not see.

"What do you want?" Nevyn snapped.

"My daughter," the spirit said. "Let me have my daughter."

"She's not yours, and you're not her mother."

"I shall wait for her all the same, when she crosses over."

Her words raked him like cold claws.

"You shan't," Nevyn said, "because I shall travel with her, and if you try to meddle, I'll blast you with a fire that will burn you to the marrow of your soul."

"You boast, old man, and naught more." She flounced her black robes and smirked at him.

All of Nevyn's rage at the prince, at Lilli's illness, at Merodda and her wretched curse tablet rose up and turned him for that moment into a berserker worse than any warrior. He snapped out a word of power, then raised his arms over his head. He felt the rage materialize as red fire, surging and seething.

"Begone, you fetid bitch!"

With a snap of his wrists he brought his arms down and blasted her with the red fire. Like a cataract it broke over her, foaming like boiling blood. She screamed, staggered, screamed and screamed again as she spun and tossed on the burning torrent.

"Begone!"

With one last howl of agony, she disappeared. Still shaking with rage Nevyn opened his dweomer sight—no trace of her.

"Nevyn?" Lilli's voice choked, a bare whisper.

He spun around and saw her trying to sit up. He perched on the bed next to her and put his arm around her shoulders while she coughed, spitting up more blood, bright and fresh.

"Can't breathe," she gasped, then died in his arms.

Maddyn heard the news early the next morning. When he and Owaen went to the great hall for breakfast, they saw Lilli's maidservant, Clodda, sitting in the ashes of the servants' cold hearth and sobbing, her apron over her face.

"Ah horseshit!" Owaen muttered. "That's a bad omen for our Lilli."

"The worst," Maddyn said. "The poor little lass."

"Just so. I'll wager old Nevyn's all torn up about it."

"No doubt. I'll have to compose her a death song. She was a warrior in her way."

Although Maddyn saw naught of Nevyn all that day, the news went round the dun, that Lady Lillorigga had finally died of her consumption. Toward sunset, to get a little peace and quiet in which to think, Maddyn climbed up the catwalks to the top of the dun's inner wall. He wedged himself between a pair of merlons and looked down at the sprawling disorder of the brochs and walls, wards and ruins, sheds, huts, and pigsties. That wondrous day back in Pyrdon, when the silver daggers had hailed the young Prince Maryn as the true king, none of them had ever dreamt that royal splendor would look like a heap of charcoal scattered among sticks. None of them had ever dreamt how many of them would die, either, he supposed, though they'd all made a brave show of talking about the likelihood.

In the west the sun was sinking in a clear sky. Overhead the dome of heaven shone a painfully bright blue, while below the ward lay already in shadow. Maddyn watched servants walking back and forth, bringing food and firewood to the great hall. In a moment or two the prince himself walked out of the great hall. He moved slowly, as if his grief had turned the air to something nearly solid, and aimlessly. He started toward the stables, then turned back, hesitated at the door of the hall, walked in the other direction, hesitated again, then suddenly strode off round toward the back of the dun. Maddyn lost sight of him among the sheds and clutter.

The morrow came with more rain and a low dark sky. Despite the weather, Prince Maryn decreed that Lilli's body should lie in the sacred grove near his wife's grave. This time there would be no splendid procession, though the prince did accompany her in the ride across town to the temple hill. Nevyn debated, then decided against going, simply because Maryn's grief for his mistress was so much more sincere than that for his wife. There are some things, he told himself, that a man shouldn't watch.

Some while after the small cortege left the gates, Nevyn returned to his tower room. The afternoon seemed so gloomy that he lit a pair of candles as much for company as for light. He was sitting at his table, trying to compose a letter to Tieryn Anasyn, when he heard voices on the stairs.

"Who is it?" Nevyn called out. "I'm busy."

The door opened anyway, and Otho marched in, followed by Maddyn, who was carrying a basket of bread.

"We heard you'd not eaten today." Maddyn set the basket down.

"True spoken," Nevyn said. "My thanks."

"And we need you to settle a quarrel," Maddyn went on. "About those red stones the princess gave our smith here. I say he should return them to the prince."

"And why should I?" Otho snapped. "Her wretched swine of a husband doesn't deserve fine stones like that."

"It's not a matter of deserving," Maddyn said. "It's a matter of rightfully owning."

"He's right," Nevyn broke in. "They belong to her children now."

Otho glowered but said nothing.

"Give them over." Nevyn held out his hand.

Otho made a sound like a dog's growl, but he untied the pouch at his belt, fished in it with two fingers, and handed at last the two small rubies, square cut, over to Nevyn.

"You wretched meddler!" Otho snarled at Maddyn. "Bad cess to you!"

"Come now," Nevyn said. "Is it truly the rubies that are vexing you so badly?"

"Well." Otho paused, considering. "It's them, somewhat, but truly, if this slime-hearted silver dagger had stayed away from our lady, she'd be alive now."

Maddyn winced and turned dead-white. Nevyn got up, ready to intervene.

"And I warn you somewhat, Maddo lad," Otho went on. "No one hates as well as the Mountain Folk. I don't care how long it may be till we meet again. I'll recognize you and I'll remember."

"Otho!" Nevyn snapped. "For the love of the gods, think what you're saying! Think what you're doing to yourself!"

"What, my lord? Binding one of your cursed chains of Wyrd?"

"Just that, and ye gods, you could at least be putting the blame where it belongs."

"Indeed, my lord? On our prince?"

Nevyn said nothing. Otho tore his dagger gaze away from Maddyn.

"You're right enough, Lord Nevyn," the dwarf said. "And I'll just be leaving his court. There's naught to keep me here a day longer."

When he left the chamber Otho slammed the door so hard that the candlesticks on the table bounced in a scatter of scorching wax. Nevyn caught them just in time to prevent the half-finished letter from going up in flames. His arms crossed tight over his chest, Maddyn watched him.

"Do you blame me?" Maddyn said at last.

"What for? Loving a woman honorably and from your distance?"

"I never should have taken her gifts."

"Why not? Royalty shower trinkets upon their favorites all the time. Her feelings would have been hurt had you turned them down."

Maddyn nodded, then strode to the window to slap his palms against the sill and lean out into the rain.

"I used to be the prince's man heart and soul, but no more." He seemed to be talking to the rising moon as much as to Nevyn. "I can't stand it, the thought of her—"

"No more can I. I'll be leaving court myself as soon as I can, though I'll take a more gracious leave than Otho's. Ride with me if you like. In the spring, Maryn will have to ride west to do battle with the king of Eldidd. We'll accompany him, and then just slip away from the army."

Maddyn turned back into the room, then perched on the window sill to consider Nevyn for a long moment.

"Slip away?" Maddyn said at last. "And where shall we go then?"

"Ever have a fancy to see Bardek? I've come to realize that their physicians know a great deal more than ours, or certainly more than I do. Besides—" Nevyn heard his own voice tremble and forced it steady. "Besides, I need to get far far away, where Maryn won't hear of me and my doings."

"The prince was like a son to you. This all must burn like poison."

"It does. And the worst part is thinking that I should have done somewhat to prevent it."

"Ah by the hells, Nevyn! You're only a dweomermaster, not a god!"

Nevyn stared, then suddenly laughed, a bitter creaky noise.

"True spoken, bard. Well, then. Shall we ride west together in the spring?"

"We shall. Here's somewhat I never thought I'd ever say: I'll be cursed glad to leave the king and his court behind me once and for all."

Nevyn nodded in sad agreement, but he knew a thing he could never tell Maddyn. While they could ride away from Maryn and his court in this life, neither of them would be so easily free of the souls involved in this tragedy, not for many a long lifetime ahead.

In 863, King Maryn died. The chirurgeons, who wanted his legend to end with a worthy death, stated that an old wound, never properly healed, had burst open. The tale baffled those who knew him, because thanks to his dweomer luck Maryn had never received a wound in all his long years of battle. But over time these witnesses died themselves, of course, leaving the bards free to put the lie into their songs and the priests to copy it into their chronicles.

In truth, a consumption of the lungs killed Maryn. All unwittingly Lilli had poisoned him when they'd lain in each other's arms—her disease the instrument of her mother's curse fulfilled.

The North Country

The priests say that studying magic drives men mad, but they lie to guard their privileged position. How can they pretend to stand between their people and their gods if other men can work miracles as well or better than they? On the other hand, dabbling in sorcery without plan or principle will expose every fault and weakness in any man's mind. If some break along those hidden cracks, is it the fault of sorcery?

—The Pseudo-Iamblichos Scroll

$\mathcal{O}$n far-off Bardek, where Maddyn the bard had met his death some two centuries before, winter turned into spring by degrees. The rains came less frequently; the sun stayed above the horizon longer each day; muddy tracks dried out and turned once again into roads. Merchants and travelling shows alike began to consider their first long journey of the new season. For their winter camp, Marka and Keeta had chosen the public caravanserai near Myleton. Normally Marka's husband, Ebañy, would have made this decision, but over the winter his madness had burgeoned like the grass, turned green and lush by the rains.

"I can't tell you how glad I am that spring's here," Marka said. "Maybe Ebañy will be more his old self once we're on the road. He always did love to travel."

"That's true," Keeta said. "It's been a long hard winter for you."

"It was the way he kept hearing the voices. It seemed like every time it rained, he'd find some new ones."

"It broke my heart, listening to him babble about water spirits."

"It was worse when he answered them."

They were perched together on the tailgate of an empty wagon, where they could watch the camp around them. The various performers bustled about, whitewashing another wagon, mending horse gear, or practicing their juggling and tumbling out in the bright sun. Marka's oldest son, Kwinto, was leading their elephant, Nila, to the watering trough on the far side of the caravanserai. From the way she curled her trunk and trumpeted, she seemed to be welcoming the spring herself. Dressed in a tunic and a floppy leather hat, Ebañy stood talking to Vinto, the leader of the troop of acrobats—not that Vinto did much performing himself these days. His hair had turned solid grey over the winter, Marka noticed.

"Vinto's so patient with him," Marka said. "I'm so grateful."

"We all cursed well should be patient," Keeta said. "Come now, Marka—your husband has made us all rich. Before we met him, what was our idea of a show? To stand up and do our turns, one after the other with no thought for what went before or came after. Ebañy taught us how to order them, to put a quiet routine before a noisy one, to bring on the best last—to make a real show. I'll be forever grateful for that, and as I said, we all should be." She paused, shaking her head. "And when he talks about the show, he's still almost sane. Maybe that's the saddest thing of all."

From inside one of the tents came a high-pitched squeal of fury. Marka climbed down from the wagon fast.

"That's Zandro," she said. "Something's wrong again."

With Keeta right behind Marka trotted over to the big round tent she shared with Ebañy and their children. Before she reached the tent flap Zandro darted out of it, screaming at the top of his lungs. He was a pretty child, with pale brown skin and pale brown hair that hung in tight curls around his face, but at the moment his dark eyes were screwed up tight and his face had turned an ominous purple color. Right behind him came his oldest sister, Kivva, a lithe, dark girl on the edge of womanhood. Marka scooped him up and held him tightly while he howled and twisted in her grasp. When she nearly dropped him, Keeta grabbed him and clasped him in her arms, as long and heavily muscled as a blacksmith's. In but a moment he stopped struggling, and in a moment more he fell silent. At a nod from Marka, Keeta took him back inside the tent.

"Mama, I tried," Kivva burst out. "But he kept trying to

choke Delya, I mean he'd put his hands on her neck, and she'd yell at him, and he wouldn't stop, so I carried him into the tent, and then he had one of his fits."

"It's not your fault, love," Marka said. "It's just the way he is."

Kivva nodded, staring at the ground.

"Are you frightened?" Marka went on, softly.

"Yes." She looked up, her lips trembling, her eyes full of tears. "He's mad like Papa, isn't he? Is Papa going to get like him, screaming and hitting people?"

"No, of course he's not!" Marka made her voice as strong as she could. "And don't you worry. This summer, when we're going from town to town, we're going to ask everywhere about healers. We'll find someone who can cure them both."

"There wasn't anyone in Myleton." Kivva wiped her eyes on the sleeve of her linen tunic. "The priests all tried and they never drove out any demons or anything."

"We'll find better priests. Or maybe a hermit. Up in the hills they have holy women who live in the woods and know every herb in the world. One of them will help us if the priests can't."

At that Kivva managed a smile, but Marka felt like the worst liar in all of Bardek. In her heart she feared that no one ever would be able to help Ebañy and the little son who had inherited his diseased mind.

And yet, that evening, hope of a sort did arrive. When a cool twilight turned the sky opalescent, and the wind made the plane trees and the palms nod and rustle, she left the children and their father both in the care of the rest of the troupe and went to the edge of the caravanserai for a moment's peace. She walked along the grassy top of the white cliff and looked down at the ocean far below, murmuring on the graveled beach.

"Good evening," a voice said. "May I join you?"

With a yelp of surprise Marka spun around and found herself facing the man she knew as Evandar. Tall, with green eyes and the same pale skin as her husband, he wore a green tunic over narrow trousers made of leather and a leather hat, pulled down over his ears—a costume that, she assumed, came from the barbarian land of Deverry.

"I must have been lost in thought," Marka said, smiling. "I didn't even hear you come up."

"No doubt." Evandar glanced away, back to the camp. "Now tell me, how is Ebañy? Still suffering from madness?"

"Yes, I'm afraid so. If anything, he's got worse since we saw you last. For a while he kept trying to run away to live naked in the hills like a wild man. My thanks to the Star Goddesses, though, because he got over that."

Evandar winced. "Very bad indeed. Well, I haven't forgotten my promise to help you."

"I can't tell you how grateful I am."

"I'm not so sure I can bring the healer I had in mind to Bardek, is the problem. She's rather deeply involved in—well, let's just say in some grave matters in her homeland. But I may well be able to bring you and your man to the healer. I'll warn you, it will be a long journey."

"Oh, my good sir!" Marka said with a little laugh. "We spend most of the year travelling. That won't be a hardship."

"Indeed?" He considered her for a long moment. "Well, I'll hope it won't be when the time comes. If it comes—I warn you, I can't promise anything."

"I understand. I'm grateful just for the hope you've brought us."

"Very well, then. Now I'd best be off, to see what I can do."

Evandar turned and walked briskly away. He'd travelled some ten paces when she realized that she couldn't see him anymore. He was gone, like a pattern in smoke caught by a gust of wind. Marka felt her skin turn cold. Gooseflesh rose all along her arms and neck. With a little gasp she turned and ran back to the camp, where firelight and human warmth beckoned.

When he left Marka, Evandar returned to his own country, which lay far beyond the physical world in those fluid reaches of the universe that dweomermasters term the astral plane. Some thousands of years past, as men and elves reckon time, he had made the image of a country for the wandering souls of his people, just as he had created images of bodies for them to wear. To please them he had created green meadows and rolling hills, beautiful gardens and the images of cities. For thousands of years they had lived in their image of paradise, safe from Time, free from the round of death and birth. But now his people had chosen to be born in the physical world. Without them, the land mourned.

On the brown lawn the tatters of a golden pavilion lay strewn. The dead grass stretched down to a river that oozed with silvery mud. Like rusty sword blades water reeds lay clotted in the shallows. Once Evandar had been able to come to this river to hear omens whispering in the reeds and see glimpses of the future in its clear-flowing water. Now—nothing. The images no longer bubbled to the surface, the voices spoke no more. The dead river oozed like a wound down to a sea turned russet, streaked with black masses of contagion.

With a shudder Evandar turned away from the river. He stretched out his arms, ran a few paces, then leapt into the air. As he leapt he changed, soaring on sudden wings. He called out in the harsh voice of a red hawk and flew, flapping hard to gain height. From his berth high on the wind he could see green meadows beyond his dead country, scattered with streams, dotted with trees. Beyond them, far on the horizon, lay a bank of roiling grey clouds. As he flew toward the mists, it seemed they rose up to meet him, blotting out the illusion of blue sky.

Evandar flew straight into the clouds, then laid back his wings and dove. Cool mist surrounded him as he plunged down. Suddenly, just below, he saw through the remnant of cloud a long stretch of grey stone. Just in time he pulled up and levelled off, flapping hard. Directly ahead stood a tree, green and in full leaf. Sitting under it, his back against the trunk, sat an old man with dark skin; he wore a shapeless robe of some coarse brown cloth. He was slicing an apple with an old knife, but as fast as he cut, the apple grew whole again. Evandar landed nearby and took back his elven form. The old man looked up and smiled.

"Back again, are you?" the old man said.

"I am, good sir. I have a question, if I may ask one."

"You may, indeed, though I may not answer."

"Fair enough." Evandar sat down in front of him. "The last time we met was at the white river."

"True spoken, when your people crossed it to be born into the world of Time."

"And you said to me that I'd not be able to be born. Why?"

"Now that's a question I'll be glad to answer." The old man laid his knife down and considered the apple. "You're a spirit of great power. On the riverbank most souls revert to their true form, you see, but you kept your illusions around you: body, clothes, the whole lot. Could you cast those off if you wanted to?"

"I've never tried. I can change from one thing to another. That I do know."

"Ah. So could you change to your own true form?"

"What is it?"

"I can't tell you because I don't know." The old man picked up the knife again. "If you don't know, you won't be able to change into it. And if you can't let go your power, well, then, you'll be stuck on this side of the white river."

"A wisewoman told me once that if I don't cross that river, I'll just fade away and never be reborn."

"She's doubtless right, which is a sad thing."

"Twice as sad for me as for you, good sir."

"I'll not argue that." The old man cut a slice off the apple and ate it. "What are you going to do about it?"

"I've got no idea." Evandar stood up. "Mayhap I'll think of somewhat."

Evandar turned, took a few steps, then broke into a run. As he ran he leapt, and finally, with one last leap and a flutter of new-grown wings, he changed once again into the hawk.

This time Evandar flew toward the forest that lay beyond his lands at the juncture of more worlds than one. As he travelled he often paused and hovered on the wind while his sharp hawk's eyes searched the wild meadows below. Whenever he came this way, whether he flew or walked the mothers of all roads, he hunted for his brother, who had chosen to work mischief in the lands of men. So far, Shaetano had eluded him.

On this occasion, with his mind full of Salamander's problems, Evandar made only the most desultory of searches. The healer he had in mind, the elven dweomermaster Dallandra, lived at the moment in the north country of Deverry, hundreds of miles from Bardek. Normally Evandar could have taken Salamander and his family directly there on the magical roads that he knew so well, but circumstances were forcing him to postpone the journey. Even if Dallandra could cure Salamander eventually—and she'd warned Evandar that this was no sure thing—at the moment she was hauling a wagonload of other burdens. Bring him in the summer, she'd told Evandar, not before.

Evandar had never told her of his fears that his death lay close at hand, that perhaps it would strike him down long before the summer came. He needed to set in motion some current of events that would, eventually, sweep Ebañy home. As he flew, his mind turned to his fears, just as a man will repeatedly touch a boil upon his neck to make sure that it still torments him. Let his death come, if it must. But first he would keep his promises, to Ebañy's wife, to Dallandra, and especially his promise to Shaetano, his brother, that he would destroy him before he worked further harm.

Up in the north country of Deverry, the tardy spring lagged behind the Bardek season. Snow still streaked the hills round Cengarn and lay in sullen drifts against the stone walls. Yet the sunlight did shine brightly in the afternoons, and night took its time about falling as well. During the days, when the sun struck the window of her tower room, Dallandra would take down the ox hide that covered it and sit on the broad stone sill to let the warmth soak into her bones.

Down below her the ward of Dun Cengarn spread out, cobbled and frosted with half-frozen mud, circled with stone walls. She could smell it, too, even up as high as she was, perfumed by a winter's worth of stable sweepings and human filth, piled up near the main gates. Once spring arrived, some of the local farmers would come up and cart the mess away to spread on their fields. Everyone who'd wintered in the dun would bathe, too, in the spring rivers, and wash the clothes that had grown stiff with dirt. Dallandra could only hope that spring came soon, when she would return to the Westlands and leave the stone tents of humankind behind forever.

On a day when the rain melted off the last of the snows and left the world brown mud as far as Dallandra could see from her perch, she decided that it was time to consider exactly when and how she and the souls in her care would leave Cengarn. Wildfolk, a gaggle of gnomes and a sprite or two, sat on the sill with her and pretended to take the sun. Dallandra picked up the leader of their little pack and set him in her lap.

"I need you to run an errand for me," she said. "Find Evandar and bring him here."

The gnome nodded.

"Are you sure you'll remember? Evandar, and bring him here."

The gnome hopped off her lap and crooked a finger at his fellows, as if he were the cook summoning kitchen boys. They clustered around him, pushing and shoving each other.

"Evandar. Here," Dallandra said for the last time.

In an eddy of breeze they disappeared.

Although Dallandra waited till dark, Evandar never arrived that day, nor on the next, not that she found this alarming. The Wildfolk always took their time about following orders.

"I'm just impatient," she remarked one morning. "I want to be out of here and gone."

"I couldn't agree more," Rhodry said. "But I don't want to leave until Arzosah returns."

"Do you truly think she'll come back? Dragons aren't known for keeping their promises."

"She will. I know it in my heart."

They were sitting together in the tower room, Dallandra in the window, Rhodry in the only chair. He leaned back, his long legs stretched out in front of him. In the morning light she could see that grey brushed his raven-dark hair at the temples, an omen that troubled her. Rhodry was half-elven, and among the elves, signs of age meant a person's death hovered close by, ready to swoop down. And yet, as she reminded herself, he was only a half-breed, and perhaps would age in the human way.

"I've been meaning to ask you," Rhodry said. "Have you had any news of my brother?"

"None, but I'm hoping Evandar will bring some. He promised me that he'd look in on Ebañy now and again."

"Good. I'll admit to being worried. He's the only kinsman I have left." He smiled, but briefly. "Well, the only one that knows I'm still alive."

"Just so. He never should have dropped his dweomer studies the way he did. I can't be certain, but I'd wager high that it caused his madness. You can't just walk away from the dweomer after you've opened your mind to it."

"So you've said." Rhodry shuddered like a wet dog. "Cursed dangerous stuff, dweomer."

"Not dangerous at all if you go about it properly."

"Every time it's touched my life it's brought me sorrow."

"Oh come now! It brought you Jill."

"And took her away again. And it gave me Aberwyn and snatched that from me as well. Oh, I could turn bard and sing you a pretty triad—the three worst sorrows of Rhodry Maelwaedd." He paused for a lopsided grin. "It seems like dweomer's ruled and ruined my whole cursed life, ever since I was a lad in Cannobaen. Long before I met Jill, that was."

"Truly?"

"It was all Nevyn's doing. I fell ill, and my mother summoned him to heal me—I think. I remember naught but waking from a fever dream and seeing the old man at my bedside. When I got well, he told me he'd received an omen, somehow or other. It ran 'Rhodry's Wyrd is Eldidd's Wyrd.' I thought of it often, after Rhys died and I inherited the gwerbretrhyn."

"No doubt."

"And so old Nevyn stayed at my mother's court as one of her servitors until the Wyrd was fulfilled."

Dallandra felt a sudden cold, as if a north wind had suddenly blown through the window. She moved uneasily, as if she could physically shake the omen-warning off.

"What's so wrong?" Rhodry said. "You've gone as white as milk."

"If I knew I'd tell you, but I don't. It probably means something grim."

Rhodry laughed, his high-pitched berserker's chortle. "Let's hope it is," he said at last, and his dark blue eyes looked more than half-mad. "I can't tell you how much I long for the bed of my one true love. Mayhap this will be the summer she takes pity on me, my lady Death."

"Oh do stop! I hate it when you talk like that."

"My apologies." He got up and busied himself with putting the chair back under her little table. "I don't mean to trouble your heart."

Rhodry turned, made her a sweeping bow, and strode out of the chamber. For a long time Dallandra sat looking at the closed door and wondering if she dared search for more omens. The dweomer-cold had warned her that Rhodry's Wyrd still waited, unfulfilled. In the end she decided against scrying further. Wyrd always fell where it would, and there was naught that she or any other dweomermaster could do about it.

The Wildfolk eventually found Evandar on Lina-lantava, the Isle of Regret, but by then they'd forgotten why Dallandra had sent them. He could assume that she wanted to see him. They danced around him in a circle and pointed at the sky with stabs of their warty fingers, their usual way of asking him to follow them. The most intelligent of the pack, a big purplish gnome with scabby wens all over his face, tugged at the edge of Evandar's green tunic as if it were trying to pull him along.

"Tell her you found me," Evandar said. "But I can't leave just now. I'll come soon."

The gnome grabbed his tunic with both hands, this time, and tugged so hard Evandar nearly stumbled.

"Is she in danger?"

The gnome looked up, frowning, and shook its head.

"Is anyone else in danger?"

Again the no.

"Then I'll come when I've finished my business here. Now be gone!"

With a sour and reproachful look, it faded away.

Evandar had just arrived on the island, or, to be precise, on the mountaintop that housed the exiled remnants of the Collegium of Sages, formerly of Rinbaladelan. All round him the wind moaned, unfolding long scarves of dust and wrapping them around stunted trees. In the middle of a stretch of pale coarse grass stood a scatter of wooden buildings. Every inch of them—walls, lintels, doors, shutters—bore words in the elven syllabary, embellished with little birds and animals, all engraved deeply into the wood and then rubbed with red and blue pigments to make them legible. These texts and the similar ones on the interior walls held a volume's worth of history, the story of the fall of Rinbaladelan, placed there so that even the very walls would share in the grief. From one of the distant buildings drifted the sound of chanting in young voices, as a group of pupils recited some lesson in unison with the wind sighing in the grass.

Evandar walked over to the longest of the buildings, but before he could knock, Meranaldar opened the door to him. A tall man and a little too thin, he had stooped shoulders and soft hands stained with black ink. Normally his face showed so little emotion that he seemed perpetually wistful, but today he was grinning, his large violet eyes snapping with delight.

"Come in, come in! Your map is finished! Or did you know that?"

"No, not really, but something did prompt me to visit you." Evandar smiled in return. "Let's have a look at it."

Inside the library, rows of wooden cabinets lined the walls and stood rather randomly in the middle of the room. They housed crumbling relics of the Great Library of Rinbaladelan, books snatched from the death of the city by the armload and thrown into the escaping boats. The smell of mildew hung thick, despite the low fires smouldering in two tiled hearths to dry the air. In an adjoining room stood open shelves filled with the copies that centuries of scribes had made of these treasures.

Close to the hearth stood a long narrow table and upon it, a thick papyrus scroll. Meranaldar untied the blue riband and spread the map out with a flourish. In black and red lay the plan of the city that had been the first earthly thing Evandar had ever loved. For a long time he stared at it without speaking, remembering the rose gardens and the fountains, the marble stairways leading down to the sea, the great observatory where elven sages studied the fixed stars and the wanderers moving through the heavens. All that remained now were ruins upon the land and these black lines of ink upon a map.

"You look sad," Meranaldar remarked at last.

"I am. Roll it back up, will you? It's splendid, and you have my profound thanks."

"You're most welcome. I also have a map case to give you." Meranaldar began to roll the map loosely and gently from the shorter edge. "And I have interesting news, as well. The council is meeting down in Linalandal. They're finally ready to act on this matter of our people out in the Westlands."

"Oh indeed? And what do they propose to do?"

"Nothing, yet." Meranaldar looked up with a grin. "It's taken me twenty years to get them to even consider sending a boat to the old homelands. Surely you don't expect a decision in a day?"

Evandar laughed with a shake of his head.

"Well spoken. But you know, this interests me greatly. Tell me something—why are you so eager to get that boat sent?"

"Oh, my dear Guardian! The lore, of course. You yourself told me that their bards remember all kinds of lore about the loss of the cities." Meranaldar paused to slip the scroll into a silver tube. "Things that we've forgotten here." He looked up with a rueful smile. "I'd risk my life twice over for the chance to copy it down. I'm more than a little deranged, I suppose."

"I wouldn't call you that. You know, this could be very useful. I have another problem in hand, you see, and I've not forgotten our bargain, either. Would you like to gain the favor of the greatest bard in the Westlands—assuming you should be allowed to travel there?"

"Of course I would!"

"Good. His son lives in Bardek in rather difficult straits. If you could get him home, Devaberiel would be most grateful."

"Devaberiel." Meranaldar looked away, smiling a little. "The name of a man I never knew existed till today. A man of our people, in our old homeland."

"And there are a great many others. I—"

Evandar paused; the purplish gnomes had materialized again, standing on the table and looking at him with sad eyes. He was about to banish them when he realized that their persistence might mean Dalla truly did need him.

"What's all this?" Meranaldar frowned at the gnomes, who stuck their tongues out at him.

"A nuisance," Evandar said. "I'd best leave."

"Ai! That's a pity!"

In a crowd of triumphant gnomes they walked outside to a lingering sunset. The wind was scouring up the dust and blowing it in great gusts round the carved wooden huts and longhouses. In the distance the ground fell away fast to the long valley, lost in mists below. Meranaldar shivered and tucked his hands into the long sleeves of his grey robe.

"When will I see you again?"

"As soon as possible." Evandar considered for a moment. "I have another bargain for you. How would you like me to appear before the council to argue your case?"

"That would be splendid!"

"Very well. If you agree to help this fellow, the bard's son who's in Bardek, then I'll speak on your side in council."

"You have my humble thanks. I'll certainly be glad to do what I can about Devaberiel's son. I'll wager you'll tip the scales with the council. They're not so arrogant that they won't listen to a Guardian."

"Good. I'll return in some few days."

Evandar glanced around and saw the glimmer of power in the air that marked an entry to the mother roads. He slipped the map case into his tunic, then walked briskly to the entry line, stepped up into the air, and walked back into his own country in two long strides. No doubt he'd left Meranaldar shivering in awe. Although the elven race never fell down in worship of any being, they considered the race they called the Guardians a species of god.

As a master of illusions and transformations, Evandar had fostered that belief over the long years of his existence. It had amused him at first to terrify and amaze lesser beings with his magicks. Once he became enchanted with the elven race and their culture, he had used his magic to help them in any number of ways. For a time in fact he had believed himself a god. Hadn't they all called him one? Those few others among his kind who had developed a true personality and a mind believed themselves divine as well. But at the siege of Rinbaladelan, Evandar learned that he was just a mere trickster. All of the sorceries he thought so mighty had failed to save the city and its people from the ravaging Horsekin.

"What a pity Alshandra never saw the truth," he said aloud. "She died believing herself a goddess, and by the true gods, the troubles that's caused!"

On a mother road made of twilight, Evandar travelled back to Deverry. Meranaldar had unwittingly handed him a riddle along with the map. When, last summer, Evandar had been laying his plans, he'd assumed that he'd simply keep the map with him until that future time when he would at last be ready to build Rinbaladelan anew. Now, however, with the omens—or rather their lack—gnawing his soul with fear for teeth, he knew that he had best find a place to keep his treasure where eventually someone who'd appreciate it would find it.

He considered Rinbaladelan itself, but the ruins offered no safety to something as fragile as a papyrus scroll. Perhaps the temple of Wmmglaedd, where priests dedicated to learning had assembled hundreds of scrolls and codices of ancient lore? But they were human men, and he hated the thought of entrusting them with this record of elven civilization. He could give it to Dallandra, but that choice struck him as too logical. He knew that he was playing carnoic with Wyrd for the map's survival. Only a spectacular move, something with a touch of wild luck about it, would win him the game. Yet thinking of Dallandra made him think of Rhodry, and there he found an answer.

In those days the border between Eldidd and the lands of the Westfolk lay unmarked for most of its length, but down at the seacoast stood a stream called Y Brog, the Badger, and upon it, the westernmost human settlement, a town called Cannobaen. For hundreds of years this demesne and its dun had belonged to the Maelwaedd clan. Back in the 1040s, the holding had passed briefly into the hands of the Clw Coc, the Red Lion clan, in the form of a dower settlement upon one of its daughters, the lady Lovyan. In her will Lovyan had given it back to the Maelwaedds by settling it upon her granddaughter, Rhodda, the bastard Rhodry had sired on a local lass. In Rhodda's veins, therefore, ran enough elven blood to satisfy Evandar's schemes. He'd used her dun as a treasure-house before, in fact—not that she knew it.

The dun stood on the edge of a cliff behind high stone walls, a typical enough fort, with a round broch rising some four stories at the center of a cobbled ward. Around the broch stood wooden sheds for storage, servants' huts, stables, a pigsty, a smithy, and the like in a disordered profusion. When Evandar turned up at its iron-bound gates, he wore an elven form, but that of an old man, all withered and stooped. He'd made himself illusions of Deverry clothes, and he'd stolen a horse to ride upon. Her gate-keeper told him that the lady was up in her chamber and sent a page to announce this unexpected guest.

"So it's you again, is it?" the gatekeeper said. "Come to sell her more of those cursed books, have you?"

"Oh, I have a thing that might interest her," Evandar said. "But I assure you, it's not cursed."

"Well, it's an eerie thing, our lady always shutting her-self up like she does, up there with all them books. Makes folk talk. Tain't natural."

While he waited, Evandar tipped his head back and considered the stone tower that loomed over the dun. It was a slender thing, and tall, wound round by spiralling stone stairs. He could just see, up at the very top, a shedlike structure: a roof supported by four pillars but no walls. Once Rinbaladelan's harbor had sported a lighthouse like this one, though made of finer stonework and set with brightly colored tiles.

"Had many storms?" Evandar said to the gatekeeper.

"Oh, it's been a powerful bad winter, truly. We had a shipwreck, too. The lighthouse keeper couldn't keep the fire burning in all the wind and wet."

"Tell him he needs a glass wall."

"Oh here!" The gatekeeper spat into the dirt.

"I don't jest, my good man. Put squares of glass into some sort of frame. It lets the light through and keeps out the wind."

"And that would cost our lady what? A year's taxes at the very least! No lord out here could stand the ex-pense."

"Well, I suppose so. I—Ah, here's Lady Rhodda now."

With a wave Rhodda came hurrying across the ward. She was wearing a pair of dresses of the finest blue linen, but she'd pulled up the long loose sleeves and tied them be-hind her neck like a farmwife to leave her tanned arms free. Since last he'd seen her, her dark elven eyes had lost none of their beauty. Her raven hair, though, had grown streaks of silver, and she wore it bound round her head in thick braids. Since she'd never married, she wore no head scarf.

"Well, this is a surprise!" Rhodda said. "I've not seen you in many a year."

"Has it been so long?" Evandar bowed to her. "Well, most likely so, and I'm sorry for that, my lady. But here I am, and I've brought you an interesting thing."

"Oh have you now? Another book from the Holy City?"

"Not quite. Somewhat even rarer. A map, and it's from southern Bardek."

In her study at the very top of the broch they spread the papyrus scroll out on a table. Rhodda whistled under her breath and ran a graceful finger along a line of elven writing.

"This looks new," she said. "Where did you find it?"

"It's a copy, so indeed it's new, but the original is very old. As to where, you know, my lady, that a humble pedlar like myself has to keep his secrets."

"Huh. Was it one of those collegia you keep telling me about?"

"What? Did I—"

"Dropped hints and riddles, that's what you did, about wonderful places in the Southern Isles where people meet to read and talk together. I dream about them sometimes."

"Imph. I'm not going to say."

"Then you stole it somewhere."

"Naught of the sort! My dear Lady Rhodda!"

Rhodda laughed and continued studying the map. Evandar wandered round the room, a full floor of the broch and crammed with oddments. On the wall hung a line of shields, blazoned with the devices of the lords of Cannobaen—the grappling badgers of the original Maelwaedds, the dragon of Aberwyn that had come to them upon their elevation to the gwerbretrhyn, the red lion of Lovyan's clan, and finally, the dragon device yet once again, this one slashed with a bend sinister. Wooden cabinets filled the center of the room, and near the window stood a lectern, carved with badgers.

Over the years Rhodda had collected nearly twenty ancient books and over fifty copies of newer works as well, an absolute fortune's worth of learning in those days. To keep the air dry in Cannobaen's fogs, a peat fire smouldered in the hearth, but a few of the oldest books smelled of mildew nonetheless. One of them lay open on the lectern to a page so faded he could barely make it out: a list of the symbols in the Elvish syllabary, each labelled with its equivalent in Deverry letters. On a table nearby lay cut parchments, ruled and ready for writing—raw material for Rhodda's own book, a history of Eldidd and the Westlands.

"Can this truly be Rinbaladelan?" Rhodda looked up from the map at last. "Or is it just some scribe's fancy?"

Evandar debated. She would believe the truth much less readily than a lie.

"I have my doubts, too." He joined her at the table. "I suspect that it's part fancy but mostly truth. Most likely some fragments of old maps survived, and perhaps an ancient book or two described more of the city, and then some scribe years ago put it all together on a map, which was copied here." He tapped the parchment with one finger.

"That sounds reasonable. How much do you want for it?"

Rhodda straightened up and looked at him, her eyes narrow, her head tilted a little to one side. At that moment she resembled Rhodry so much that he smiled.

"It would gladden my heart," he said, "if you'd take it as a gift."

"What? Now that's a surprise!"

"I mean it truly. I'm on my way west, and I doubt me if I'll ever come here again, and I want you to have this to remember me by, the old book pedlar who came your way now and again."

"How very odd of you!"

"It is, truly, but then, I'm a very odd man."

She considered him a moment more, then laughed.

"Very well, and my thanks," she said. "I'd be a churl indeed to turn down a gift, and especially such an intriguing one. I'm forgetting my hospitality as well. Will you dine with me?"

"I'd be honored, my lady, but I was hoping to reach the Wmmglaedd ferry by nightfall, and so I'd best be on my way."

When he left, Evandar rode west for the look of the thing, but once he was out of sight of the dun, he doubled back east. Just at twilight, he reached the farm where he'd stolen the horse. In the conniving dusk, he turned it back into its pasture, then walked on the twilight back to his country and the mothers of all roads. How long had it been, he wondered, since Dallandra had sent the gnomes to fetch him? Too long, he told himself, and he headed north for Cengarn.

Dallandra had just begun to fear that Evandar had met with harm by the time he finally arrived in Dun Cengarn. Out behind the broch complex stood a little kitchen garden, deserted this time of year and far enough away from the dun's stores of iron—weapons, implements, and suchlike—which caused him great pain. Just at twilight of a day that had seemed almost warm they sat together on a small bench amid the mulched herbs.

"I need to discuss plans with you," Dallandra said. "It's a long road to Cerr Cawnen, and so I was wondering—"

"Of course," Evandar said, grinning. "I'll take you by the mother roads. I'm surprised you can't open them yourself."

"I can to some extent. I can slip through when I need to, but I can't keep the gate open long enough for more than one person to come with me."

"Ah, I see. Well, it took me a good hundred years or so to learn the trick myself. But never fear. Just send the gnomes to fetch me."

"Very well, then, and my thanks. How fares Salamander, do you know? Rhodry was asking me about him the other day."

"The news isn't good. His mind still wanders terribly. Which reminds me. Some while ago I received a vision that showed him sailing into Cannobaen come the height of summer. I'm not sure what this means. Would you and Devaberiel be welcome there? So you could meet his ship, I mean."

"I should think so. After all, the lady of the dun there is Salamander's niece. And, for that matter, Devaberiel's granddaughter."

Evandar blinked at her.

"A niece," Dallandra said, "is the daughter of your brother or sister. Rhodry was her father, you see, and so Salamander's her uncle under Deverry law, even though he's but a half brother. And since Devaberiel is Rhodry's father, then he's her grandfather."

"And isn't that a useful thing?" Evandar said, smiling. "I'm glad that Deverry folk take their kinships so seriously."

"Well, and don't the People cherish ours as well? I've never heard of a race who spurned their kin. How could anyone survive without kin and clan?"

"I seem to remember that you walked away from a husband and a little son."

"Yes, but for the sake of you and your little daughter."

"So it was." His smile vanished. "Did you do the right thing, my love? Or did I seduce you into something wrong?"

"I thought it was right myself, at the time. And I still do."

"Good. This is splendid news, about Rhodda's kinship ties. It gives me exactly what I need to fulfill the omens."

"What? What are you planning now?"

"Only what's best for Ebañy and his wife."

"Indeed? Your plans have a way of turning out to have really wretched consequences. I wish you'd tell me what you have in mind."

"It's simple enough. I've arranged him passage on a ship coming from Bardek to Cannobaen."

"Oh. There shouldn't be any harm in that, then."

And yet she felt a dweomer warning, a bare touch of the usual cold. No harm lurked in Evandar's plans, but they were going to bring trouble with them. When she started to ask him more, he smiled at her and disappeared.

• • •

Up in the Rhiddaer, to the west of the Deverry border, spring came earlier than usual that year—a good omen, or so some said. Early one pleasant day Councilman Verrarc left his house and walked uphill to the plaza on the crest of Citadel. At the end of the path he paused to look down over Cerr Cawnen, the city he loved second only to his new wife. Citadel, the island where he stood, rose steeply from the middle of a lake. Public buildings and the houses of the few wealthy families perched among its rocks and twisting streets. The blue-green lake itself, fed by volcanic springs, lay wreathed with steam in the cool morning air. Across the water on the lakeshore, the town proper sprawled in the shallows—houses and shops built on pilings and crannogs in a welter of roofs and little boats. Beyond them, marking out the boundary of Cerr Cawnen, stood a circle of stone walls and beyond those, the farms and woodlands of the Rhiddaer, all dusted with the green of sprouting leaves and growing things.

Soon Verrarc would ride out with his caravan, as he did every spring, to trade among the dwarven cities in the eastern mountains, but on this particular morning the thought of leaving made him profoundly uneasy. Although he was a young man, Verrarc had spent some years studying books and collecting lore about the witchroad, as the northern folk call the dweomer. At times his studies gave him strange omens and insights, but his random attempt at training himself had left him short of ways to interpret them. His unease might come from his wife's poor health, or it might be a token of danger lurking outside the city gates. Perhaps it meant nothing at all.

Verrarc shrugged the feeling off and strolled across the plaza, paved with stone blocks and bordered with stone buildings and a colonnade. In the middle of the plaza stood a public well, where townsfolk waited in a little crowd to draw water. He noticed his manservant, Harl, talking with young Niffa, the daughter of the town ratters, and waved as he walked past, heading to the Council House. At the door he paused with his hand on the latch. A sound rang in the sky, a distant boom like the slap of a hand on a wooden barrel, perhaps, but loud, growing louder. Verrarc spun around and looked up. Something was flying out of the north and heading for Citadel—a bird, he thought at first, but never had he seen one so big. It took him a few moments before he could allow himself to believe that he was seeing a dragon.

In the sun its scales glittered a greenish-black, tinged with copper about the massive head and talons. Its wings stretched out a good fifty feet on each side, he estimated, and cast huge shadows on the paving stones of the plaza as it approached. It banked one wing and lazily circled, then dropped lower as if it might land. At the well the townsfolk were screaming, except for Niffa. As the wyrm hovered near her, Niffa raised a hand in the sign of peace. With a huge flap of wings the dragon rose and flew off, heading south and east. The townswomen clustered around Niffa, all talking at once.

Verrarc stood transfixed. All his life he'd heard tales of dragons, but never had he actually seen one. And here, in his town? His unease returned in force. On a day touched by a dragon the unease had to be an omen. Verrarc started over to speak to Niffa, but the town's spirit talker, Werda, joined the lass. He watched the old woman lead her away, Werda so tall and fierce, with her mane of silver-grey hair and her white cloak floating around her, Niffa so slight and young in her shabby pair of brown dresses. Harl saw him and came hurrying over.

"Master," Harl said, "the beast spoke to Niffa."

"Did it now? There be a strange thing!"

"So I did think, truly. I did understand not one word of what it did say, and no more did anyone else there, not even Niffa."

"And why did you think she would?"

"She did say the same to me." Harl shrugged, smiling. "It be her second sight. Everyone does know how strange her dreams and suchlike are."

"True spoken. For some while now I've meant to speak with you about somewhat. Is it that you're courting the lass?"

Harl blushed scarlet.

"So I thought." Verrarc smiled at him. "Here, if you wish to marry her proper-like, I'll not say a word against it. But I'd not have you trifle with her."

"Never would I!"

"Well and good then. She be a young widow and lonely. There are some men who'd take advantage of her condition."

"Not me, I swear it. If she'll have me, I'd like naught better than to marry her one fine day."

"If that comes to pass, my blessing upon it. There be plenty of rooms in the house, and no reason you and your wife should lack one."

Harl beamed, as merry as the spring sun.

Beside the common decency of the thing, Verrarc had his own reasons to offer Niffa a place in his house should she want one. Later that day he discussed the matter with his own wife, Raena, when he came home for the noon meal. Since she was recovering from a long illness, Raena lay abed most of the day, propped by pillows so she could look out the window by their bed and see the garden trees windblown in the sunlight. Verrarc brought her food himself on a wooden tray, a big bowl of stew for the pair of them and a fresh-baked loaf of bread as well. When he came in he found her sitting up and awake, her black hair spread over the pillow behind her.

"How do you fare, my love?" Verrarc said.

"Far better than the day before, truly." She smiled at him. "I think me I might eat some of that meal you've so kindly brought me."

"Good." He set the tray down on the little table by the bed. "You've got far too thin."

He sat on the edge of the bed and broke the loaf up, handing her a crust to use as a spoon. She dipped it into the thick sauce and tried a dainty bite.

"Very tempting, truly," Raena said. "And how was your morning, my love?"

"Strange indeed. You know, I think me you're right when you say young Niffa has great powers on the witchroad."

"So she does, but what happened? Somewhat did, if you'd call the morning strange."

"True enough. I went to the Council House to await the others, and whilst I did stand by the door, a dragon did fly over Citadel. Then the beast did stoop and hover like a hawk to speak to Niffa."

Raena let the crust drop from her fingers.

"A dragon?" she whispered. "What sort of beast?"

"A black one, but a greeny sort of black that glittered and changed in the sun. About the head, though, the color was coppery."

"Oh ye gods."

"Is it some terrible omen, do you think?"

Raena shook her head no and took the goblet of water from the tray. She drank before she spoke again. "I fear that dragon, my love." Her face had gone as pale as death. "From what you tell me, I think me I do know her, and she does hate me."

"What? Where would you have met such a beast?"

"When I was about my goddess's service." She leaned back against the pillows. "I be so weary, my love. Leave me, I beg you, and let me rest."

Verrarc did as she asked, but he wondered, off and on throughout the afternoon, if she were speaking the truth or merely suffering from a sick woman's fancies.

As she flew south, Arzosah was grumbling to herself. She had smelled Raena's scent as she circled over Citadel. As much as she wanted to kill the wretched woman and be done with her, she'd been forced to leave her, safe in some hidden house, no doubt, surrounded by her own kind. It was just like a pack of stupid human beings to run around and screech at the very sight of a dragon! At least these particular villagers hadn't started throwing spears and rocks, but they had bad manners all the same.

Arzosah had been so addled by the noise, in fact, that she'd lost her chance to tell Niffa that her brother was safe and would be home soon. The girl herself had been polite, though it was obvious she hadn't understood a word. I should have spoken in Deverrian, Arzosah thought. She so hated using the language of humankind that she'd slipped naturally into Elvish instead. Soon, once she reached Cengarn, she would have to lower herself to using Deverrian exclusively—for a while, she reminded herself, only for a while, until Rori and I leave that stinking heap of a town behind.

At moments like these, when she flew free in a balmy sky, with the world below all green and teeming with prey, Arzosah wondered why she was returning at all. After all, Rhodry Maelwaedd had once enslaved her with a dweomer ring. But he let me go free again, she reminded herself— and the enslaving was Evandar's doing anyway. At the thought of Evandar she hissed aloud. How dare he call her faithless, how dare he insult all Wyrmkind! Well, she was showing him, all right. She was keeping her promise to Rhodry, and Evandar could keep his wretched insults! Perhaps she'd even meet Evandar in Cengarn and finally take her revenge upon him.

Yet deep in her heart, Arzosah knew that she was travelling to see Rhodry again and little more. He was the first friend she'd ever had, and compared to friendship, even revenge paled.

Spring brought warmth to Cengarn and hope with it. The winter wheat had sprouted; soon it would be milk-ripe, fit for porridge if not for bread. This first harvest would be a scant one, since the farmers would hold back plenty of seed grain for the next planting, but still, the prospect of food to come raised everyone's spirits. The hope was rewarded, in fact, when just before the harvest an unexpected surplus arrived at Cadmar's dun. On a sunny noontide, Dallandra was studying one of the Jill's books when she heard shouting from the ward below.

"The wyvern! The wyvern! It's the king's men!"

Servants and noble-born alike poured out of the brochs and into the ward, then flooded like snowmelt down to the gates. Up in her tower room, Dallandra leaned dangerously out of the window to watch. Through the town and up the hill a procession came riding. At its head two heralds, mounted upon white horses, carried staves bound with ribands. Just behind them a lad on a pony held the banner of the Gold Wyvern, and then came a noble lord, whose shield, slung at the saddle peak, bore the same device, proclaiming him one of the king's household men. Behind them rode a squad of forty fighting men of the King's Own on matched bays, and after them creaked and crawled a long procession of wooden carts, loaded to the brim with heaped sacks of . . . of something.

Dallandra left her book and hurried down to the crowded ward. Over by the well stood a gaggle of boys, Jahdo among them. When she waved to him, he bowed to her so awkwardly that all the other boys laughed. In the doorway of the main broch stood Gwerbret Cadmar, leaning on his stick, with Prince Daralanteriel standing at his right hand and Princess Carra, accompanied by her wolfish dog, just behind him. She was carrying her own baby like a maidservant. Cadmar smiled when he saw Dallandra and waved her over to join him.

"Good morrow, Your Grace," Dallandra said. "What is all this?"

"Succor from the high king, I'll wager," Cadmar said. "Our liege is as generous as he should be, eh? You'll remember how I sent him messages at the lifting of the siege."

"Last autumn? I do, truly." Mentally she counted out months—it would have taken the courier a long time to ride to Dun Deverry, so far to the south, and of course, it would have been wasted effort for the king to send wagons north in the winter. "This is as soon as his men could have reached us, then."

"Just that."

"I see they've brought their own provisions. And thank all the gods for that!"

But in the event, the carts proved to hold far more than the necessary provisions for the king's men. The king had sent seed grain of the best kind of wheat from his own stores. His personal envoy, a Lord Yvaedd, announced this as soon as he'd presented himself to the gwerbret. He was a smooth-looking man, Yvaedd, with oiled black hair, pale grey eyes, and the soft lilt of Eldidd in his speech.

"The high king sends you this grain as a gift," Yvaedd said. "Doubtless, Your Grace, you're short up for coin. The farmers will gladly pay for this bounty."

Cadmar considered him for a moment with narrow eyes.

"My lord," the aged gwerbret said finally, "I see you hail from the coast lands. Things are different, up here on the border. My farmers are all freemen. Their grandfathers came here willingly with my grandfather when the high king's grandfather declared Arcodd open for settlement. We don't have much coin, either, up here in the north."

"Ah well, then, some extra labor on your walls—"

"My lord, forgive me for interrupting. I see I haven't expressed myself very well. Every farmer who's my vassal is going to get a sack of this grain the same way I did, as a gift."

Yvaedd stared, then his eyelids fluttered, and he bowed.

"My apologies, Your Grace. The high king sent me here because he wished to know more about the Northlands. I see that I have much to learn. I promise you that you'll find me a willing pupil."

Cadmar smiled with a little twist to his mouth. Yvaedd bowed again, rather randomly, to those standing near the gwerbret. Dallandra was suddenly aware of how clean Yvaedd was, and how clean all his men were, too, with their white shirts, heavy with embroidery, their fine grey brigga, and well-polished gear. What had they done? Carried clean clothes with them all this way for the day when they'd meet the gwerbret, or stopped to wash clothes at some river on their way? It had to be one or the other. She noticed them looking around at Cadmar's dun with faint smiles or a wrinkled nose for the pigsties by the far wall. As much as she hated the place herself, their sneers annoyed her.

"Well, now," Cadmar said briskly. "Please forgive my discourtesy, Lord Yvaedd. Come in and take the hospitality of my hall."

The very next morning messengers rode out to announce the king's boon. The heralds left as well, but they headed back south to the duns of Lord Gwinardd, Cadmar's vassal, and Gwerbret Drwmyc, his ally, to take them a royal command to come testify in Cengarn. Apparently Lord Yvaedd wanted to hear the recent war discussed in some detail and from more mouths than the gwerbret's.

"I don't understand," Dallandra told Rhodry. "Doesn't he believe what Cadmar says?"

"He'll have to pretend to if naught else," Rhodry said, grinning, "or he'll end up facing me on the combat ground."

"What?"

"Well, if Cadmar's honor should be insulted, he can't fight to defend it, not at his age and with that twisted leg and all. I've already won a trial by combat, and I'm a silver dagger, so I'd be the man to represent him."

"Yvaedd wouldn't like that much."

"True spoken. So His Lordship's being circumspect. Strange reports have reached the king, says he, about strange things."

"Huh, I'll just wager they have."

"Our Lordship wants to hear every detail. He brought a scribe, too, to write everything down nice and proper."

"I see." All at once she smiled. "You know, I think I'll see if I can call a witness myself. Evandar would be an interesting man for Lord Yvaedd to meet."

Later that afternoon, when she had a quiet moment to herself, Dallandra sat up in her tower room and let her thoughts reach out to Evandar, but she felt no answering touch of mind on mind.

In the gwerbret's chamber of justice Lord Yvaedd was holding a council of sorts, though he kept to the polite fiction that Gwerbret Cadmar was presiding while he himself merely listened and advised. Under the banners of his rhan the gwerbret sat at an enormous oak table with the golden ceremonial sword of his rank laid crosswise in front of him and a priest of Bel at his right hand. At his left were Prince Daralanteriel and Lord Gwinardd. Although Drwmyc had sent word that he would arrive after his dues and taxes had come in, Yvaedd had been unwilling to wait so long to open his inquiry. Yvaedd himself was seated off to one side, with his scribe at a table behind him. The scribe kept making notes on untidy bits of pale scraped parchment, the trimmings from sheets cut for book pages and proclamations.

Rhodry himself sat cross-legged on the floor in front of the table with Cadmar's captain and Gwinnard's. Why a lowly silver dagger had been summoned puzzled him, and as the council proceeded, no one spoke to him. Sunlight streamed into the room, lazy flies circled; staying awake turned into a major battle. Once, in fact, Cadmar's captain let out a long hard snore, but Rhodry elbowed him awake before the noble-born noticed.

None of the noble-born had any idea of how to make a coherent story out of the complicated events leading up to last summer's siege. Dar was perhaps the best at it, but Cadmar and Gwinardd kept interrupting him to add details and digressions. Yvaedd, however, seemed to find their talk of false goddesses and sorcerers who could turn themselves into birds interesting enough. Though at first he asked various questions, eventually he merely sat and listened. Toward the end Rhodry wondered if Yvaedd realized how bewildered he looked. He supposed not. Finally, Dar described the Horsekin. He rose from his chair to indicate their enormous height while Gwinardd and Cadmar kept interrupting to talk about their horses and long sabers. Yvaedd could take no more.

"My lords!" Yvaedd rose and bowed to Dar. "And Your Highness. Truly, I mean not the slightest insult, but these Horsekin—I've never heard of such a thing, and here I was born in the west myself."

"But in Aberwyn. That's all the way down on the seacoast." Dar considered for a moment. "Here, my lord. If you started telling your friends at court about the Westfolk, would they believe you?"

"They wouldn't," Yvaedd said. "I catch your drift, Your Highness—you're certainly quite real, for all their disbelief. My apologies." He glanced at the scribe. "We will take these Horsekin as described. Make sure you write down every detail. This is troubling news."

The scribe nodded.

"They take slaves, you say?" Yvaedd turned back to Cadmar.

"Just that," Cadmar said. "And I fear me they see Deverry as a fine place to catch some new ones."

"The high king will see the great import in this. Fear not. I'm cursed glad you could hold your own against them, when the time came to face them in the field."

"Imph," Gwinardd said. "We never would have managed that without the dragon's help."

"The dragon?" Yvaedd turned to him. "Does His Grace have an alliance with Aberwyn, then?"

"Not that dragon!" Gwinardd leaned forward, all seriousness. "I don't mean a blazon, I mean a real one. You know, like in the old tales. A scaly sort of beast, black and green, with enormous wings. The enemy mounts couldn't stand the smell of her, and they bolted."

Yvaedd looked at him with his mouth stuck half-open like the lid of a rusty metal chest. Gwerbret Cadmar sighed, then hauled himself up with the aid of his walking stick.

"It's late," Cadmar announced. "We've been at this blasted conference all afternoon, and I for one need some ale. I suggest we convene again tomorrow."

"Very well, Your Grace." Lord Yvaedd's voice sounded as feeble as a man with a fever in his blood. "I wouldn't mind a tankard myself."

As the council was dispersing, Lord Yvaedd caught up with Rhodry just outside the door.

"Come walk with me, silver dagger," the lord said. "I'd like a private word with you, if I may."

"Of course, my lord."

They strolled down to the end of the corridor and stood looking out of a small window, framing the view of the town below the dun. Lord Yvaedd considered Rhodry for a moment, then smiled in a way that was doubtless meant to be pleasant.

"I hear from your way of speaking that you hail from Aberwyn," Yvaedd said.

"I do, my lord. Eldidd marks the way a man speaks for life."

"Just so. I can't help noticing just how much you resemble His Grace Cullyn, Gwerbret Aberwyn. Not to bring up anything painful, of course, but I trust you'll forgive me for wondering about the resemblance."

Rhodry stifled a laugh. Cullyn was his firstborn son, but obviously Yvaedd was thinking this silver dagger one of the great lord's by-blows.

"My father's name was a secret my mother kept, my lord," Rhodry said. "I do know that we never lacked for food or shelter when I was a child."

"Ah." Lord Yvaedd allowed himself a slight smile. "I see."

Rhodry smiled, briefly, in return.

"On the morrow, silver dagger," Yvaedd went on. "We'll need your testimony. Lord Gwinnard's tale of a dragon interests me most greatly."

"No doubt, my lord, but I'll swear it's true, and on my silver dagger at that."

For a moment Yvaedd looked him over with a frozen little smile; then the lord muttered a pleasantry and strolled off.

For some while now, Rhodry had been spending his sunsets on top of the main broch in Dun Cengarn. Arzosah hated flying at night, and so, his reasoning ran, she was likely to turn up at the end of a day. Every night when she failed to return, he would stay on the roof until the ward was dark enough for him to climb down unobserved. He knew perfectly well that Dallandra believed Arzosah faithless; he was working hard at not believing it himself.

By the time he escaped from Lord Yvaedd, afternoon shadows filled the ward. He hurried up the staircase to the top floor of the main broch, pushed open the trapdoor, and clambered out onto the flat roof. What if she never returned? He forced himself to consider how long he would stay in Cengarn to wait. After all, poor little Jahdo was longing for his home and kin. Daralanteriel, too, was eager to take his new lady home to his people. Rhodry walked over to the roof's edge and looked idly down. With his scribe in attendance, Lord Yvaedd stood on the cobbles and questioned the gwerbret's captain. Rhodry was just thinking how lovely it would be to chuck a stone down on top of him when he heard the sound.

He'd heard it before, this faint throbbing in the air, as if some giant hand slapped a distant drum. He spun around and shaded his eyes while he stared off to the north. He could just see a black speck in the sky, could just discern that it was moving and coming toward him. He held his breath, hardly dared to hope as he watched it speeding against the blue. The thwack thwack of wide wings grew louder, the speck grew larger. Rhodry let out his breath with a whoop. It was Arzosah indeed, flying fast and steadily.

Down in the ward someone cried out. Rhodry looked down to see Lord Yvaedd staring at the sky and waving his arms like a madman. From his distance it was hard to be certain, but he thought that perhaps the lord had gone pale. Servants and riders were pouring out of broch and stable to cheer the dragon's approach. Laughing under his breath, Rhodry looked up again as Arzosah circled the dun, then with a magnificent stretch of wing glided down. She looked well fed, and her greenish-black scales gleamed in the afternoon light. Suddenly she curled her wings, hovered in the air, and settled gently onto the roof.

Rhodry ran to her and threw his arms around her neck, which felt as cool as satin to the touch. Although her kind gave out a strong smell much like vinegar, he found it bracing and oddly pleasant. She made the huge rumble that did her for laughter. "I absolutely hate to admit this, Rori, but it gladdens my heart to see you again, too."

"Good. You can't know how welcome you are, my friend. Would you mind carrying me down to the ward? There's a man here who thinks you don't exist."

Arzosah craned her neck and looked down, judging the space. Lord Yvaedd stood where Rhodry had last seen him, but he had tipped his head back and was staring up. His scribe looked up, screamed, and ran back into the broch. The king's men ran out after him. They were made of

sterner stuff—they stayed, clustering round Yvaedd like
children around a father.

"I can land off to one side, I think," the dragon said at
last. "Climb aboard."

Since her harness was lying in a storage chest in
Dallandra's chamber, Rhodry scrambled up inelegantly and
wedged himself between two of the big spiky scales where
her back joined her neck. Arzosah spread her wings, flapped
hard, leapt, then glided down in a long turn to settle on the
cobbles not far from his lordship. The king's men all scattered, leaving their lord alone to face the dragon. Yvaedd's
face had indeed gone pale, and sweat gleamed on his forehead. Rhodry slid down and bowed to him.

"My lord, allow me to present to you Arzosah of the
Lofty Wings, my friend and my companion in the recent
war."

Arzosah stretched out her head and nodded at Yvaedd.

"Charmed, I'm sure," she said, "Your Lordship."

Yvaedd struggled for words. When none came, he
bowed so low he nearly scraped the cobbles. His men must
have remembered their oaths to defend him; they returned,
but one slow step at a time.

"An honor," Yvaedd squeaked. "Quite an honor. Ah,
that is—ah—" He turned and dashed for the broch.

The king's men hesitated, glanced at the dragon, then
raced after their lord. Rhodry began to laugh; he leaned
back against the dragon's foreleg and howled until the tears
came. She let out her breath in a long and meat-scented
sigh.

"I'd forgotten about humans," Arzosah said. "You're the
only brave one I've ever met, Rori Dragonfriend. And
maybe that's why I came back to you."

"I don't think there's any reason for us to stay much
longer," Dallandra said. "Prince Dar tells me that Lord
Yvaedd's gone suddenly tractable."

"Tractable?" Rhodry said.

"He believes everything he's told and has his scribe
write it down most carefully."

They shared a smile, and the dragon rumbled under her breath. They were all sitting on the new grass atop the market hill, where Arzosah could stretch out comfortably and take the sun. Since the townsfolk knew her well from the summer past, they mostly ignored her, although a pair of big tan hounds had taken up a watch at a distance and barked now and again. Arzosah eyed them and licked her lips.

"I suppose those belong to someone," she said.

"No doubt," Rhodry said. "Leave them be."

"Very well." Arzosah yawned and curled a paw to consider her claws. "Now about our journey. No doubt the hatchling wants to get home—young Jahdo. By the by, he polished my scales with a cloth this morning. A very sweet child, he is."

"He is, truly," Dallandra said. "We've got a lot of things to work out yet. You and Rhodry will be able to travel a great deal faster than the rest of us. It's a long way to Cerr Cawnen, judging from what Jahdo's been telling me. We'll need provisions and suchlike."

"But can't Evandar open one of his roads?" Rhodry asked. "They seem to save a good bit of effort, though I can't say the same about the time involved. That always seems to get a bit twisted."

"He told me he'd open a gate for us when I saw him some while ago. I've not seen him since then. I've been trying to call him again, but he's not shown up. I hope he's in no danger."

At that Arzosah hissed, just quietly to herself.

"I know you don't care for him," Dallandra said to her.

"Don't care for him?" Arzosah hissed again, more loudly. "I'd eat him if I could. If there was anything really there to eat, anyway. Nasty bastard, tricking me the way he did. Humph!"

"Not so nice of him, but I can't help but be grateful," Dallandra said. "Without you, we would have lost the war, and the Horsekin would have impaled us all or staked us down to die."

"He might have just asked me for my help."

"Would you have given it?" Rhodry said.

"No, but he might have asked anyway. Then when he ensorceled me it would have been only fair."

"There's a certain logic in that, truly." Dallandra rose, dusting off the seat of her leather trousers. "I need to get back to the dun. I'll talk with Jahdo."

As she walked off, Dallandra glanced back to see Rhodry leaning back comfortably against the dragon's scaly side. Arzosah had curled herself into a semicircle with her head on her paws near him. The man and the dragon made an oddly apt pair, she thought—both of them as cold and hard as winter steel despite their good humor toward those they counted friends.

Evandar turned up that night, finally, near sunset. They met outside the dun and town, down in the meadow to the west where a stream splashed and gurgled, running full of snowmelt. In the last golden light of afternoon they strolled beside trees touched with the green of new leaves.

"Jill died in this spot," Evandar said abruptly.

"I know," Dallandra said. "I rather wondered why you chose it."

He shrugged and walked on, his head bent as if he studied the grass.

"I was worried about you, my love," Dallandra said.

"My apologies. I was off arranging things."

"Things? What do you mean, things?"

"Rhodry's brother, of course, getting him home again."

"Oh, that!"

"What did you think I meant?" Evandar scowled at her.

"That it was another one of your schemes, of course. My apologies, my love, but they get so complicated—"

"Oh, I know, I know, and mayhap this one is, too, but I could think of no other way."

"Way to what?"

"Get Salamander home, of course."

Dallandra waited for him to say more, but he merely turned away with a long, sad sigh and resumed his slow walk along the riverbank. In the west the sunset began to streak the sky with burnished gold.

"We're all going to be leaving soon," Dallandra said. "I

was hoping you'd take us through your Lands to Cerr Cawnen."

"Of course I will. It's a long journey otherwise."

All round them birds sang. Evandar walked as slowly as an old man to the streamside and stared into the water.

"There's somewhat wrong," Dallandra said. "What is it?"

"Naught." He looked up abruptly and forced a smile. "When will you want to go?"

"In a few days. Shall I send the Wildfolk for you when we're ready?"

"Yes, do. I've got so many errands to run that I know not where I'll be. But as for Salamander, he'll be returning to the Westfolk's lands by ship, sometime in the summer. They should put in to shore just west of Cannobaen."

"They? Who?"

"It's a surprise." Evandar grinned at her, and for a moment he looked his usual merry self. "One you'll like. The elephant won't be with him, though—I'll tell you that much."

"That gladdens my heart. But—"

"Ah! No prying! I need to find Devaberiel soon, in fact, and tell him his son's on the way home. He can wait for them down on the coast and get word to you, I suppose, somehow or other. No, wait, I've a better idea. I'll get Salamander's old dweomer teacher to go with Devaberiel, and then she can call you through the fire."

"Valandario? Yes, she'll do that if you ask. But I thought you'd be the one bringing him home."

"I may not be able to, what with Shaetano working harm. Do you see, my love? I'm learning the lessons you've tried so hard to teach me—thinking ahead, laying plans, considering how it all fits together."

"Well, truly, I'm proud of you."

"My thanks." He glanced her way, then looked up at the golden sky. Was he near tears? she couldn't tell.

"Evandar, beloved, what's so wrong?"

"Naught." He forced a smile false even for him. "Well,

I'd best be off to Cerr Cawnen. I need to keep an eye on my wretched brother."

Evandar turned and took off running. For a moment it seemed that he would run right into the stream, but at the water's edge he stepped up onto the sunlight and disappeared.

For a long time Niffa kept her conversation with the Spirit Talker locked up in her heart. On the day when the black dragon had flown over Cerr Cawnen, Werda had made her see a hard truth, that Niffa's life work lay upon the witchroad, no matter where it led her. At the time, the road had seemed so clear, but now, days later, Niffa found herself wavering. Never will I leave my home! she would think. I'll marry Harl, mayhap, and live close to my mam and da for always. Yet, even as she treasured her defiance, she knew that she was only postponing the inevitable moment when she would admit that the black dragon had shown her Wyrd.

When she slept, she often dreamt of the dragon, but always she would see the beast from some distance, flying across the sky perhaps, or perched on a high cliff. She could never get close enough to speak to it. Finally, one night when she walked in the green fields of dream, she met Dallandra at the glowing red stars.

"It gladdens my heart to see you!" Dallandra called out. "You've not come in a long while."

"I've not," Niffa said. "But please, think not that it had somewhat to do with you. I've had much to ponder these past days."

"I see. Well, I've got some grand news. We'll be bringing your Jahdo home soon. We leave Cengarn tomorrow."

Joy rushed up and nearly washed away the vision, but over this past winter Niffa had learned to steel her will. In a moment the purple moon held steady over the grass and the warding stars. Dallandra's image returned, smiling at her.

"That gladdens my heart beyond all else," Niffa said. "My thanks! But who will come with you, then?"

"Rather a lot of people, and an escort of armed men, but all of them friends."

"Then welcome they'll all be. Will the black dragon be with you?"

"Here! How do you know about Arzosah?"

"Be that her name? One of the great wyrms did speak to me, some days just past, and somehow I—" Niffa hesitated, puzzled. "I know not how I know, but somehow I do feel in my heart that the beast be tied to you in some way."

"Your heart is right. She'll be coming with us. You know, lass, it's time we spoke of your future. Do you know what the dweomer lore is?"

Again Niffa nearly lost the vision, but she steadied it so easily that she knew her Wyrd had come upon her.

"I think me I do," Niffa said. "Be it what we call the witchroad here?"

"Just so. Do you realize how strong a gift you have?"

"The Spirit Talker did say somewhat about it, truly."

"Well, I want you to think very carefully about that while you wait for us. If you want to follow the witchroad, the dweomer road, then I'll take you on as an apprentice." Dallandra held up one hand for silence. "Say naught now. Think upon it most carefully. This is no light decision to make."

"That I do understand. And my thanks from the bottom of my heart."

"Splendid! Now, I've no real idea how long it will take us to reach Cengarn, but we'll be there as soon as we can. Fare thee well for now."

Dallandra waved her hand, and the vision seemed to roll up like a blanket from one edge to the other. All at once Niffa lay awake in her bed, with dawnlight silvering the room. She got up, and as she dressed she could hear her mother and father, speaking in low voices. I'd best tell Mam, she thought. But not today—I'll wait till Jahdo's home. There be no use in her losing me till our lad be back to give her joy.

On the day of their departure, Jahdo woke long before dawn. For a while he lay awake in the straw by the dragon hearth in the great hall—the bed he shared with the other boys in the dun. He tried to get back to sleep, but finally, when windows turned grey with the dawn outside, the excitement drove him up. Since he slept fully dressed, all he needed to do was pull on his boots, and he was ready. The night before he'd made his meager possessions into a bundle. By the light coming from the main door he wrapped them in his blanket and tied the corners to secure them.

By the hearth one of the boys sat up, looked around, and then got up to join him: Cae, the only real friend he'd made in the dun. For a moment Cae stood rubbing the sleep from his eyes on the sleeve of his torn and dirty shirt.

"Ah well," Cae said finally. "You'll be off, then?"

"I will, truly."

Cae stooped and took one end of the bundle. Jahdo took the other, and together they carried it out to the stables. In the grey dawnlight Cae's dark eyes brimmed with tears.

"I wish I had a home to go to." His voice ached with them, too. "Think of me now and again, will you?"

"I will." Jahdo hesitated, wishing he could think of something to say. "Uh, I'll pray to the gods that you fare well."

Cae turned and ran for the great hall. His day of hard work in the kitchens would begin soon. Jahdo took a few steps after him, then stopped, knowing that there was nothing he could say that would ease the loss for either of them.

He went into the gwerbret's stables for the last time and led Gidro, the brown mule, and Bahkti, the white packhorse, out of their stalls. Gidro belonged to the town council of Cerr Cawnen, but Bahkti had come with Meer the bard from the lands of the Gel da'Thae. Although Jahdo had inherited all of Meer's worldly goods, he thought that the horse perhaps still belonged to Meer's tribe or mother—no one had been able to tell him.

"We're going home," Jahdo said to them. "Well, it's home for you anyway, Gidro."

The mule tossed its head as if it understood. Jahdo led them out to the watering trough and let them drink while he watched the eastern sky silvering with the first of dawn. Home. Soon he would be home. Over the past year he had longed for home so often that he refused to let himself believe that this time his hope would come true.

"Meer did promise us," Jahdo said to the mule. "And he were killed by that demon-get archer. Then did Jill say the same, and she died. I do wonder, truly, if we be some sort of curse."

Gidro snorted in a blow of water drops, as if to tell him to stop talking nonsense.

Sure enough, some hours before the sun hit its zenith the travellers assembled in the ward or above it, in the case of Rhodry and Arzosah, who stood ready to fly on the roof of the main broch. The dun turned out in force to see them off. Gwerbret Cadmar and his lady stood in the doorway; the servants and the warband clustered round out in the ward. Prince Dalanteriel on a splendid black horse headed the line of march. Beside him, riding Gwerlas, her dun gelding, Princess Carra held the baby in a leather sling across her chest. Behind them came an escort of ten mounted archers leading pack mules with supplies for the journey, Dallandra mounted on a grey palfrey, and Jahdo himself, riding his mule and leading a laden Bahkti—all in all they made an impressive expedition, as Dallandra remarked.

"I'm so glad we're leaving," she told Jahdo. "I hope I never spend another winter in a stone tent."

"And so do I hope, my lady," Jahdo said. "And I'll pray we don't go meeting any Horsekin on the road, too."

"We'll have the best scout in the world to protect us."

Dallandra pointed at the dragon and her rider. As if in answer, Arzosah spread her wings, leapt, and flew, circling the dun once and heading off to the west.

"They'll keep circling round us," Dallandra went on. "And then they'll join us for the evening camps. Any stray Horsekin will be sorry they rode our way if Arzosah gets hold of them."

Up at the head of the line, Prince Daralanteriel raised his silver horn and blew one long note. The horses tossed their heads and danced in anticipation.

"Farewell to Cengarn!" he called out. "Men, ready and march!"

In a flood of laughter and farewells, the travellers set out, walking their horses sedately through the dun's great iron-bound gates and down the twisty streets of the city beyond. Jahdo felt as if they were creeping like snails, but they reached the towering walls and the open gates at last. With one final round of waves and farewells, they rode out into the green countryside. Jahdo laughed aloud in sheer relief.

"So far so good," he said to Dallandra.

The western road ran across the flat grassy meadows at the foot of Dun Cengarn's cliffs. They rode past the mass graves from last summer's fighting, long low mounds like welts from a flogging on the grassy skin of the earth. Jahdo was glad to leave them behind, but one more grim memory awaited him. When they splashed across the ford of the stream where Jill had died, he had to swallow hard to choke back tears.

"We all miss her." Dallandra had noticed. "It's no wrong thing to weep, you know."

"I do know. But truly, I've had so much to weep over this year past that I be sick to my gullet of tears."

"No doubt! Well, let's hope that better times are coming for you."

"I do hope so every day. Tell me, my lady, if it be no burden upon you, will Evandar come and make our journey shorter?"

"He will, but not till tomorrow. We want to be well clear of settled country first."

They did indeed travel through farmland for most of that day. Out in the fields the farmers were planting the seed corn from the king's own stock, and Jahdo noticed how carefully they went about it. No broadcasting by the handfuls here—men and women stooped to trickle a line of the precious seeds into plowed furrows while the children followed along, covering the grains with earth and driving off the circling birds.

By twilight they'd left the farms behind. Dar called for a halt in a last stretch of meadow near the forest edge, where a stream ran clean for water. The men were unloading the packhorses when Arzosah returned, gliding down to settle some distance away. Jahdo saw Rhodry slide gracefully from her back, but he was too busy with his horse and mule to pay much attention. He'd gotten his stock tethered out with the rest by the time that Rhodry returned to camp, carrying the heavy coils of Arzosah's harness. Jewels glinted here and there on the black leather.

"She's gone to hunt," Rhodry said. "And the harness gets in her way."

"Tell me somewhat, Rori. Be it a splendid thing to fly?"

"It is, once you get used to it, like. At first—well, I have to confess that I was sore afraid, looking down from so far, and then the way she rocked on the air under her wings was enough to lose a man his stomach. But after a bit, I grew to love the freedom of it." Rhodry paused, smiling. "Would you like to come with us on the morrow?"

"I would, but I'd best not. I have Gidro and Bahkti under my care. Mayhap one day though she'd take me just a little way, just so I'll ken what flying means."

"I think that could be arranged, truly."

"Oh, that would be splendid! To fly above the earth—" Jahdo could think of no word for it. "But often do I wonder why she does obey you, since no longer do you have that dweomer ring."

"I'm surprised myself, truly."

"And she be so strong, so dangerous. Why would such as she stay with us?"

"I think we must amuse her, for now anyway. We're like the minstrels the high king keeps at his court. No doubt one day she'll get tired of bothering about us and fly off." Rhodry looked away, suddenly melancholy. "I hope she stays with us a good long time."

"So do I."

As they walked into the camp together, Jahdo began to sing, and Rhodry joined him, improvising harmony in his clear tenor. Jahdo was so intent on their song that he forgot to look where he was going. All at once he felt his foot kick a stone and trip him. He flailed, nearly fell, then caught himself with a laugh.

"Ye gods, lad!" Rhodry said. "Pick up your feet!"

"I do try." Jahdo tried to look humble but failed. "Ah, Rori, tonight I cannot care if I be clumsy or no. We're going home!"

That night Niffa dreamt that a caravan came through the gates of the city. When she woke, she pulled on her pair of dresses, grabbed a chunk of bread and some cheese, then rushed out of the house. She ate while she walked down the twisting streets of Citadel. At the lakeshore, a scatter of little leather coracles sat drawn up, waiting for any citizen who needed one. For a moment she stood finishing the last of her bread and watching mist tendrils wreathe upon the water. Not since Demet died had she gone across to the town, and she hesitated now, her grief a thong that seemed to bind her hands. What if she should meet his mother or some other of his kin, who all looked so much like him?

"Oh come now!" she told herself. "T'would be a wrong thing to hide on Citadel all your born days!"

Yet it was a moment more before she could make herself choose a coracle. She hiked her skirts up, shoved the boat out into the shallow water, then scrambled aboard. While she paddled across, she concentrated on the town looming out of the mists on its crannogs and pilings, and she took care to land her little boat far away from the weavers' compound as well.

Cerr Cawnen sported two sets of gates in its high stone wall, a grand pair looking south and a smaller set facing east. Although logically Jahdo should return by the east gate, her dream had shown her the southern pair, Niffa realized—something of a puzzlement, and perhaps a disappointment as well, if the dream failed to prove a true one. Well, I'm across now, she told herself. We'll just wait and see. As she made her way through the jumble of wood piers, houses, stairways, shops, and rickety bridges, the various towns-women she knew stuck their heads out of windows to hail her or came out to stand in their doorways and wave.

"Niffa, 'tis so good to see you, lass! How do you fare, my friend? Ah, it warms my heart to see you out and about!"

The greetings were so cheerful, so sincere, that she suddenly realized that indeed, she had missed them too, shut up with only her grief for a companion. Laughing and smiling, she waved back, but with the dream urging her on, she had no time to stop and gossip. She hurried to the south gates, where running parallel to the wall stretched a narrow but long commons, pale green with new grass and dotted white with the first daisies. Niffa sat down cross-legged on the green to wait.

Some long while later a caravan did indeed turn up. Niffa was ready to give up her vigil and go home when she saw through the open gates travellers coming. First she saw dust pluming at the horizon. Slowly the cloud approached and finally resolved itself into packhorses, led by tall figures sporting masses of dark hair. Farther back in the cloud she could see riders as well.

"Gel da'Thae!" The men on watch sang out the name. "Gel da'Thae merchants!"

Silver horns rang out in greeting. A militiaman hurried down the ladder from the catwalk and raced for the lakeshore. The members of the Council of Five would need to know about this arrival. Niffa got up and stood watching the caravan come closer and closer, leisurely in the hot sun. Why had her dream foretold this? Surely it had naught to do with her. A crowd began to form behind her, as the town turned out to watch the first real event of the spring. She could hear the people murmuring to themselves, studying the caravan as it drew near and wondering if this arrival meant trouble or trade.

Calling out to each other, the council members hurried past, their streaky-red cloaks flapping behind them. First came Burra, a merchant not much older than Verrarc, with yellow hair and a thick yellow moustache to match. Stocky Frie hurried after, his shirtsleeves rolled up and his arms black with charcoal up to his elbows—he must have come straight from his forge. When Niffa saw Verrarc she started to turn away, but too late—he saw her, waved at her, then trotted on past. Last of all came the two elders, skinny grey Hennis and stout bald Admi, puffing in the hot sun. By then the caravan was ambling through the gates.

At its head rode two Gel da'Thae warriors, dressed in leather trousers, carrying spears, their bare chests covered with blue tattoos. Behind them came a long line of pack-horses, led by human men wearing cloth trousers, each with an iron ring around one ankle—slaves, Niffa realized, not that they or their Gel da'Thae owners would ever admit such a thing whilst they were staying in this free city. In the middle of the line rode a richly dressed Gel da'Thae man on a roan gelding, most likely the merchant who owned this caravan. His huge mane of black hair, all braided and hung with little charms and talismans, fell past his waist.

Following him on pure white horses came two women of his kind. Niffa caught her breath at a cold stab of magical certainty: here was the reason that her dream had driven her down to the gates. While the Gel da'Thae men wore their hair in braided manes, the women shaved every bit of theirs. This pair wore close-fitting leather caps, covered with little rounds of metal and glass, then a scant wrap of pale linen cloth about their upper bodies that left their arms bare, and leather trousers like the men. Where their eyebrows should have been they wore tattoos of flowering vines. Green tattoos covered the rest of their milk-white skin with pictures of animals, flowers, and landscapes in marked contrast to the abstract blue patterns decorating the men.

The gear their horses carried dripped with metal talismans, strands of beads, and leather ribands stamped with the same patterns as their tattoos. Niffa could hear the people in the crowd murmuring in surprise at their presence. When she turned to glance around, she saw Raena, resplendent in a fine green dress and a gold necklace, working her way through the townsfolk, while a disgusted-looking Harl walked behind her with a staff. Her position as a rich man's wife demanded a guard whenever she walked abroad.

The caravan turned to follow the inside wall. The grassy commons formed the only caravanserai Cerr Cawnen could offer. The merchant, however, swung his horse out of line, then dismounted to bow to the Council of Five, who clustered round him to bow in return. Niffa ignored them and watched the two women. Often her bent toward the witchroad gave her warnings of danger, but at the sight of the pair something in her mind seemed to say "good! they got here safely." Who "they" were lay hidden, but not for long.

"Niffa!" It was Verrarc, striding up to her. "A good thing it is that you be here. The older woman there, do you see? She be the mother of that Gel da'Thae bard who did take your brother off to the Slavers' country. Her protector"—he gestured vaguely at the Gel da'Thae merchant—"did tell us that she did come here to find news of her son, if there be any such."

"It be a long way she's come, then, for disappointment." Niffa kept her voice as bland as she could.

"Ah. No news, then, of Jahdo?"

"Had there been, Councilman, you would have heard it long ere I did."

For a moment Verrarc lingered, seemingly on the edge of prying. With a little shrug he turned away and walked off to join Raena, who was watching the Gel da'Thae women. Never had Niffa seen such hatred in another's eyes. Raena's skin had gone pale and her mouth twisted as she stared at the two women, her lips working as if to mutter an evil spell. Niffa stepped back into the crowd to lose herself among them before Raena could notice her. She nearly bumped into Harl.

"My apologies!" Niffa said. "But here, be there not a need upon you to tend your master's woman?"

"Let the bitch sniff the grass and squat on her own." Harl spat on the ground. "If she gets herself kicked by a horse, so much the better."

"Indeed." Niffa smiled briefly. "Well, fare thee well, I be on my way home."

"If it please you, I'll row you across."

"My thanks. And that will give you some excuse for your master, too, if the bitch should complain about your leaving her."

It was late in the day before Niffa heard more about the caravan and the two women. Kiel, her elder brother, was serving with the town militia, which Councilman Verrarc commanded. Kiel had stuck close to his commander all day, gathering gossip, and he brought a full basket of it home to share as they sat round the table at dinner.

"Her name's Zatcheka, Meer's mother that be," Kiel said. "The lass with her, and the councilman did say that she be young, not that I could tell just from the looking at her, but anyway, the lass be her adopted daughter and her heir. Grallezar be her name."

"Her heir?" Lael said. "Does this mean her son be dead?"

"Not at all. Among them the lasses do inherit their mother's holdings, have she any."

"Sensible of them." Dera was laying a big round loaf of bread on the table. "Is there a want on you all for ale with this?"

"Me, for one," Kiel said. "I did ask about the inheritance, for fear that if Meer were dead, so would our Jahdo be."

"Our lad be safe," Niffa put in. "Have no fear. He'll be home soon."

"One of your dreams, lass?" Lael raised a bushy eyebrow.

"It was, Da."

Lael smiled, then picked up the loaf and began tearing it into chunks.

"So then," Kiel went on, "I did hear Verrarc talking with Chief Speaker Admi. There be more to this visit than a mother's worried heart, he did say. Zatcheka be a prominent citizen among her kind, and she did hint of some portentous matter for her town and ours. And Admi did answer Verro, we'll hold council on the morrow to hear her out."

"Ah," Lael said. "No doubt they'll put out the call for a town meeting at the end of the morrow, like."

"So Admi did mention." Kiel took the tankard from Dera. "My thanks, Mam. But here be the strangest thing of all. Verrarc did tell us, the militia, I mean, and he waited till Admi did get himself gone, but then he did tell us that we'd be guarding the Gel da'Thae camp, taking turns in pairs, all through the night. And why is this, says Sergeant Gart? Think you they be up to trouble?" Kiel paused for a sip of ale. "Not them, Verro did say. I fear that someone in the town may bear them ill, and I'd not have them harmed."

"Raena!" Niffa blurted before she could stop herself. "It be Raena that makes him fear so."

"Raena?" Dera interrupted with a little laugh. "And what harm could one sickly woman do to a campful of Gel da'Thae?"

"I know not, Mam," Kiel said. "But truly, Verrarc did warn us. If you see my lady near the camp, said he, escort her home."

For a brief moment Niffa felt her breath catch ragged in her throat. She recovered with a little gasp and found Dera and Lael both staring at her.

"There be dark times," Niffa said. "And that be all I know."

Lael muttered a brief prayer to the gods, then handed her a chunk of bread. While she ate, Niffa found herself thinking about Zatcheka, come so far to look for her son. Was Meer still alive? She'd never thought to ask Dallandra, not once in all their conversations in the Gatelands of Sleep. It seemed a selfish omission, all of a sudden. I'll ask tonight, she thought. Surely Dalla will know if he walks on the earth or under it.

When Verrarc arrived home, he found Raena there before him, pacing back and forth in front of the empty hearth. The last of the sunlight poured through the window and caught the gold necklace. Its dangling teardrops gleamed like flames.

"That necklace does look splendid upon you, my love," he said. "It gladdens my heart that you do like it. It did belong to my mother."

"It be a lovely piece." Raena put her hands on his shoulders. "You have my thanks."

When he kissed her, she smiled but moved a step away.

"Those Gel da'Thae," she said. "Do you know what might bring them here?"

"I don't. The woman Zatcheka? When we did escort her to the campsite, she kept her mouth as tight shut as a miser keeps his purse. And the lass and the merchant both say naught unless she does give them leave."

Raena muttered a foul oath and flung herself into a chair. Verrarc sat down more slowly across from her.

"What troubles you so badly?" he said.

"I know not yet. Some dweomer-cold lies round my heart, that they mean harm for me and mine."

"Harm for the town?"

"Nah nah nah, for you and me. The town—" Raena caught herself and forced a smile. "The town lies dear to your heart, I know. But somehow I ken not its omens. If I could but go to the ruins and summon Lord Havoc, I—"

"I'll not have you risking that! Ye gods, if Werda found out, she'd rouse the town against you."

"True." Raena sat thinking for a long moment. "It behooves me to be as cunning as a weasel, then, and find some other way to read the omens."

"That might be a useful thing indeed."

Niffa woke heartsick at first light. In her dreams she had met Dallandra, and indeed, Meer lay buried back in the country of the Slavers. Even though Dallandra had offered to do the telling once she arrived in Cerr Cawnen, it seemed only kind to inform Zatcheka now instead of letting her hope in vain for days more. Niffa had to admit that she was frightened. How could she, the ratters' lass, approach such an important guest?

As soon as the sun had risen, Niffa took her yoke and buckets and went to fetch the day's clean water. Maneuvering them through the narrow passage outside the ratters' door took all her concentration, but once she reached the path proper, she became aware of a flurry of noise and bustle just downhill. She stepped to one side and saw the Council of Five coming up, moving slowly so that

Admi, who was quite stout, could keep up without undignified puffing and panting. Striding along in their midst was Zatcheka, wearing the same leather cap but a full-length straight-cut dress of doeskin, decorated with beads and metal disks, that left her hairless arms bare. This close, Niffa could see that each disk bore a symbol stamped on it, and that some of the beads seemed to be little rolled-up scraps of parchment or cloth. At her waist she wore a loose-fitting belt of copper chain, from which hung either a very long knife or a very short sword in a leather sheath. The climb apparently bothered her not at all, because she was singing some long wail of a Gel da'Thae song under her breath. Bringing up the rear came Grallezar, carrying a small leather sack and dressed much like her adopted mother, and two Gel da'Thae warriors carrying slender staves—ceremonial weapons, Niffa could guess, because they were so deeply carved into vaguely floral forms that they would have snapped on any impact.

As this procession went past, Niffa flattened herself against the retaining wall on the uphill side. None of the men deigned to acknowledge her, but Zatcheka looked her way, nodded pleasantly, and smiled, revealing a mouthful of long needle teeth, most likely filed into that shape, since none of the Gel da'Thae men had teeth like them. Niffa curtsied, which brought another smile. The procession went on past, leaving Niffa to follow after. There be a need on me to tell her about her son, Niffa was thinking. Zatcheka seemed much less frightening than she'd thought.

Niffa followed the Council of Five all the way to the top of Citadel and the public plaza, but they crossed it and went into the Council House at the far side while Niffa, of course, stopped at the public well. She watched as the council and their guests entered the colonnade and disappeared into an open door. Already the usual crowd had gathered at the well to wait their turns to draw, though Niffa noticed that there was more gawking than dipping going on. Harl hurried over to join her.

"The master's sore troubled," Harl said. "There be some great thing afoot, I think me."

"The Gel da'Thae always mean trouble," Niffa said. "Bain't?"

"True spoken, but better they are than the Horsekin. That be what the master did say to me, when I was a-bringing him his cloak. Ah well, better them than Horsekin, though I fear me that this visit does concern them somehow."

Niffa felt as if someone had grabbed her lungs with cold hands and made her gasp, just from the witchcertainty of it.

"I do agree with you," she said. "But ai! There's a hope on me that I be wrong."

"The wild Horsekin, they be on the move," Zatcheka said. "I come with warnings."

"A great fear did lie on me that such was true," Admi said. "I thank you for the town's sake."

She inclined her head in his direction, a move that made the talismans on her cap dance and glint in the sunlight streaming through the window. The council was meeting in its usual chamber, a great high-ceilinged stone room with a low dais at one end. On the dais, in front of a long window, stood a round wood table and plain wood chairs; the rest of the room stood empty. With the table round there could be no question of precedent, an arrangement that had pleased Zatcheka. She lounged at ease in one of the chairs, while her adopted daughter sat on the floor beside her and her two guards stood behind. The five councilmen sat in their usual places, but none of them looked in the least bit calm. Verrarc felt as tight-wound as new rope.

"Honored Zatcheka," Admi went on. "Is it that you do know why the savages are ready for war?"

"I do, and a sinful thing it be." Zatcheka laid a pale hand over the clutch of talismans at her throat. "An impiety of the worst sort, a blasphemy to all the true gods and their servants. They claim they serve a new goddess. Some call her The Hidden One; others, Alshandra, Mistress of Storm. I call her fraud."

The entire council gawked like children. Zatcheka smiled, but she kept her lips tightly drawn over her pointed teeth. Old Hennis, a skinny stick of a man with no teeth at all and precious little respect for gods of any kind, gave Verrarc a sideways glance that came too close to a dismissive smile. Verrarc scowled at him. He knew the Gel da'Thae way of telling stories; they always began with gods and ended with them, too. What counted was the middle.

"Honored council, I had two sons once," she went on. "One of them was a great warrior, but he brought naught but shame to his people. He too did serve this foul demoness, this Alshandra. I foreswore him, I cast him out of my heart. My second son be, as you do know, Meer the Bard, and him I did send after his brother to bring back news of him."

"Just so," Admi said. "A sad thing, truly."

"It was. And I hope and pray to the true gods that I have not a second sadness waiting me. I do fear in the depth of my heart that Meer no longer walks the earth, and if so, that be an evil omen for all of us."

"Er, my apologies," Admi said. "I see not why—"

"You see not because I've yet to finish." Her voice, still low, snapped with command. "Hear me out, and you will know what I know."

"Just so, just so," Verrarc broke in. "Forgive us, Honored One. We beg you to enlighten us in our ignorance."

"Very well then." Zatcheka leaned back in her chair again. Her dark green eyes flicked from one to the other of the councilmen. "Because my son had brought this shame upon our city, the task of travelling here was given to me. Because such great journeys deserve a reward, I was allowed to take this orphan child into my house. Otherwise my clan would have died with me."

She paused to lay a hand on Grallezar's head. The councilmen all nodded solemnly, even Hennis. He knew the value of heirs no matter what he thought of gods.

"So." Zatcheka folded her hands at her waist. "This false goddess, this putrefying demoness, this walking blasphemy— she did appear to her worshippers some two springs before this spring. A priestess did come into Horsekin lands, and here be a marvel. This priestess, she who claimed to be the goddess's oracle? She were a human woman."

"Ye gods," Admi muttered. "Strange and twice strange, indeed."

Verrarc felt his stomach clench. It couldn't be, he told himself. Not Raena! Yet the warm room seemed to have turned ice-cold around him.

"At first she did but speak for her goddess," Zatcheka went on. "Then the goddess herself did appear to the tribes, and she did make them promises. They be her chosen ones, or so she does tell them, and they shall be kings over the world, all its cities, all its peoples, even unto the lands of Slavers."

"And we," Verrarc blurted, "we do stand right in their path."

"Clever lad." Zatcheka favored him with a nod. "So you do, and so do we."

Admi had turned white. He grabbed a corner of his scarlet cloak and mopped sweat from his massive jowls. The other councilmen, Burra, Hennis, and Frie, all began to talk at once while Zatcheka considered them with narrow eyes. Admi raised his hands and yelled for silence. The babble stopped. Frie had the decency to murmur an apology to their guest, who nodded in return.

"This be a time for cold thought," Verrarc said. "There be no need to panic like ducks at the smell of fox."

"Just so," Zatcheka said. "Though far be it from me to blame any man for feeling fear of the Horsekin. There be a coward's fear, and then there be prudence, and I think me the latter has the truth of it now."

"If they march this summer," Admi began.

"The gods do love us still, Chief Speaker," Zatcheka broke in. "The year past, our spies do tell us, the Horsekin did march into the Land of the Slavers, and there did they suffer defeat. Many men fell before the walls of some town or other. An even greater boon is this: they did lose many horses. For some little while must they lick their wounds and let their herds replenish."

"Which does give us a bit of time," Verrarc said. "I thank all the gods for this."

"Well spoken, though mayhap it's the Slavers we should be thanking." Zatcheka paused for a long moment. "This be the time to discern who be our friends and who our foes."

So! Verrarc thought. There it be, the thing which brought her to us. The council members looked at each other, glanced away. Hennis seemed to be about to speak, then settled back into his chair. Admi mopped his face again.

"I think me you do guess my meaning," Zatcheka said. "For thirty years and more my town and my people have upheld an alliance with you, but that pact does touch upon matters of trade, not of war. It be time, Honored Councilmen, to put steel behind fine words."

When the babble of talk started up again, she held up one hand flat for silence. Verrarc was struck by how oddly long and delicate her pale fingers were. The talk died down.

"I expect no answer right here and now," she said, smiling. "Such would be most unmannerly and impious. I do ken the ways of your town. You must speak of this among yourselves, and then hold council with all your fellow citizens. Bain't?"

"It is, truly," Admi said. "Ah ye gods, this be grievous news!"

Zatcheka rose, nodded all round, then snapped her fingers. Grallezar scrambled up and bowed to the council; the two guards fell in behind her. Without another word or even a wave, Zatcheka led her people out of the chamber.

Admi moaned aloud and tipped his head to rest upon his chair back. Hennis sat rubbing his mouth with the flat of his hand, while Burra and Frie sat like corpses.

"Never did I think such evil as this would come upon Cerr Cawnen," Admi whispered. "Truly, it would be better to have the fire mountain vomiting than this, better to have the earth shake and heave at our feet."

For a long tedious while the council sat, speaking little, staring at one another as if they thought themselves already doomed. Finally Verrarc stood up with a toss of his head.

"Fellow councilmen, I do suggest this. Let us each go

back home to think on this thing in private. Look at us all, sitting here like stones on the hillside! There be a need on us to recover our wits. Then we can come back here and discuss the matter."

"Well spoken, Verro." Admi heaved his bulk out of the chair. "I do agree. And you, my friends?"

The others nodded and rose, shaking out their cloaks or pulling down their tunics, looking at the floor, the table, anywhere but each other.

"I shall send a servant with a message for Zatcheka," Admi went on. "When it be time for her to rejoin us."

Verrarc returned to his house to find everyone assembled in the great room. Harl was restocking the wood bin by the hearth, Korla was sweeping, Magpie sat on the floor in the corner. Raena, the only one who could wait for news without such excuses, sat in her chair with mending in her lap and her work basket beside her. If he told them the truth, Verrarc knew, it would be all over town before the council could make a formal announcement.

"Our meeting this morning did go well," Verrarc said. "The Gel da'Thae woman be here as an ambassador to renegotiate our treaty with her town. It has stood for thirty years, and they hope it to stand for more years yet."

The servants smiled, nodding. Harl stacked the last bit of wood, bowed, and left, with Korla and Magpie hurrying after him. Raena laid the mending back into her basket and watched him silently as he sat down opposite. With a long sigh he stretched out his legs and sank into the familiar comfort.

"There be more, bain't?" Raena said.

"Just so." Verrarc kept his voice low. "The wild Horsekin be on the move, Rae. It bodes ill for all the towns out in the Rhiddaer."

"And so she did come to forge some new alliance for war?"

"Just that."

Raena swore under her breath and leapt up, then paced over to the window and stared out. Verrarc rose and walked over, putting his hands on her shoulders from behind. He could feel her trembling.

"Here, here, Rae, we're not doomed yet," Verrarc said. "Zatcheka did tell of some mighty battle that the Kin did wage in the Slavers' country. They were badly defeated, said she, and lack horses and men both. No doubt by the time they be ready to fight again, we'll have set up our defenses here."

"No doubt." She sounded angry, he realized, not frightened. "The meddling bitch!"

"What?"

"Forgive me, my love. I know not what I did mean by that. But here, on this matter—will it come to a formal Deciding?"

"Of course."

Raena spun round to face him. She was near tears.

"Verro, please, I beg you! Don't let a Deciding be called straightaway. Here, be it not a grave matter? How can the townsfolk make up their minds so quickly?"

"Well, truly, Zatcheka did say some such thing herself."

"She has the right of it. Please, Verro? Just three nights will do."

"Do for what?"

Raena turned pale and stepped back.

"That I cannot say," she whispered. "Please, do it for the love of me?"

Verrarc considered, looking her over coldly, drawing the moment out. Two springs ago, Zatcheka had said—just at the time Raena had disappeared. A single tear ran down her cheek as she waited for his answer.

"A bargain, Rae," Verrarc said. "A bargain for the sake of the love you say you bear me. If I should do this thing for you, will you share the magicks you've gained? For months now you've put me off, saying the time be not ripe or Lord Havoc be not ready. I do wish to ken the lore you ken."

"You will, my love, you will! I swear it to you. Have I not been gathering it for you, to make you a fine gift of magicks understood rather than scraps and bits of knowledge?"

"I know it not. Have you?"

"I have! I swear it to you. Soon you will learn all that I ken, and no holding back of aught."

"Done, then! I'll do my best to hold back the Deciding."

Verrarc gave her a quick kiss, then hurried out. He wanted to be the first man back at the Council House, in order to work on the other members as they came in, one at a time and willing, perhaps, to listen.

In the event, however, his task turned out to be easier than he'd thought. Hennis and Burra had grave doubts about rushing this decision through. Though Admi and Frie held out for speed, they were quite simply outnumbered. Still, the debate went on for much of the afternoon, while Zatcheka sat straight-backed in her chair and merely listened, her mouth frozen, it seemed, in her smooth little smile.

"Ah very well!" Admi snapped at last. "We wait, then, to hold a formal Deciding among the citizenry."

"Three nights would be a good wait," Verrarc said. "Truly, I do agree with you when you say that we dare not postpone it for long."

Admi glanced round at the other council members, who all nodded. Everyone turned to the Gel da'Thae ambassador, who laid a hand on the talismans at her throat.

"Deliberation and patience, they be always good," Zatcheka said. "I have no objections. There be a need on you and me to consider many fine points and details of the treaty, after all."

"Done then!" Admi said. "Tonight we call council fire to tell the town this bitter news. Three days hence, counting the morrow as the first day, we hold the Deciding upon the finished treaty."

Although the other council members escorted Zatcheka back to her caravan's camp, Verrarc begged off and returned home to report his victory to Raena. He was expecting that she'd be waiting for him at the door, but she wasn't there, nor was she in the great room or their bedchamber. What had she done, disappeared again? Cursing a steady stream he looked through the entire house. No sign of Raena, but in the kitchen he found old Korla, pounding herbs in a mortar. Nearby Magpie sat on the floor with her arms round her knees, watching.

"Where be my lady?" Verrarc said.

"I've not seen hide nor hair of her." The satisfaction in Korla's voice was impossible to miss. "Not since you did leave the house for the second meeting."

"Ye gods! What about Harl? Has he seen her?"

Korla shrugged in massive indifference. Magpie unwound her arms and stood up, giggling.

"Did you see her, child?" Verrarc said.

"She did climb to the top of the back wall, and then she turned into a big black raven and flew away."

"Here!" Korla laid down her mortar and turned to face her granddaughter. "No daft fancies, lass!"

"It be no fancy." Magpie stuck her lip out in a pout. "I did see her, I tell you. Not a stitch of clothes did she have on, neither. Then she grew feathers."

When Korla raised her hand for a slap, Verrarc caught the old woman's wrist.

"Leave her be," he said gently. "I shan't hold it against the poor half-wit."

Korla snorted in disgust, but she let the matter drop. Verrarc knew that Magpie might well be telling the plain truth. What if Raena could shape-change? Mazrak. The Gel da'Thae called wizards who could turn themselves into animals by this name. He'd heard stories of such all his life. It would explain so many mysteries if Raena knew the magicks that would let her fly.

"Be you ill, master?" Korla said. "You've gone all white."

"It's naught but weariness."

"You come sit down, then. I've made soup, and I'll ladle you out some. Good for what ails a man, it is."

"So it be." He managed a smile. "And my thanks."

At sunset the enormous bronze gong that hung in front of the Council House began to clang, calling the citizens to Citadel. Ordinarily, when the Chief Speaker called council fire, most families sent only one trusted member to listen and report back. Tonight, however, it seemed that half the town came across the lake and trudged up the hill in a river of citizens that threatened to engulf the plaza. Niffa was glad that her family lived so close; they found a place to stand right in front, where they could hear well. The Council of Five had arrived early to light the ritual bonfire, and off to one side stood Zatcheka in her doeskin dress with her retinue behind her. When she saw Niffa, she waved. Niffa waved back, but she felt half-sick, thinking of Zatcheka's dead son.

"What's this?" Lael said. "Be it that you've made the acquaintance of the Gel da'Thae woman?"

"Not truly, Da," Niffa said. "We did meet upon the path and smile back and forth, 'tis all."

He nodded, satisfied, but Niffa suddenly wondered why such an important person as Zatcheka had acknowledged her. Mayhap she be wonderfully well mannered, she thought, and let the matter rest there.

Servants carried the big round table out of the Council House and stood it up in the pool of light from the blazing bonfire. With some help Admi climbed up on it and stood in the middle to help his voice carry farther. Niffa could see him fidgeting; his eyes darted this way and that, and every now and then he'd grab the hem of his ceremonial cloak to wipe sweat from his face. Finally the plaza held as many of the townsfolk as could possibly cram themselves onto it. Admi raised his arms high for silence, and at length, he got it.

"My fellow citizens!" Admi called out. "I do ask you this night to welcome Zatcheka, ambassador from Braemel, city of the Gel da'Thae. Long have we held alliance with her people."

Most in the crowd clapped politely; a few voices sang out, "welcome!" Zatcheka nodded gravely in their direction.

"Most serious in import be the matters she has laid before your Council of Five," Admi went on. "Meer the Bard did tell us, the summer past, that the wild Horsekin, they be on the move. Now do we know the bitter meaning of that. They do lay claim to all the cities and farms south and east of them, and all those who own and tend them, even unto the lands of the Slavers. A goddess, or so they say, has given them this dominion, to take us and ours and all else in the lands of the Gel da'Thae and the Rhiddaer for their spoils."

No one moved, no one spoke. Niffa glanced around and saw the townsfolk staring at Admi with terrified concentration. The Chief Speaker caught the edge of his scarlet cloak and used it to mop his jowls.

"The Gel da'Thae wish to extend our alliance," Admi went on, "to military aid and mutual succor in time of war."

The noise began at that. A woman sobbed, a man swore, whispers rustled back and forth and swelled to a sound rushing like a winter wind. Admi stood and listened, his arms at his sides, his face glistening in the leaping firelight—whether with sweat or tears, Niffa could not tell—while out on the plaza the townsfolk cursed or wept or merely repeated what he'd said to those too far back to hear. Lael flung an arm around Dera's shoulders and pulled her close, as if to protect her. Niffa herself felt that the world had turned suddenly huge and terrible, as if she had looked up to find the familiar stars changed into the glowing eyes of hungry beasts, ready to spring. Reflexively she moved closer to her father, who laid his other hand on her shoulder and drew her into his embrace.

At length, when the talk threatened to turn into shouting, Admi flung his arms up and bellowed for silence. The crowd quieted as fast it could, from those closest to the back, as if a wave of silence washed over the crowd.

"It be no time for despair," Admi's voice boomed and swelled, "but for vigilance and cunning! We have walls, we have weapons, we have the men to hold those walls. It does behoove us to join our strengths to those who would befriend us." Admi paused, glancing around at the crowd, looking directly at this person or that. "And yet, this be a grave and serious matter. There be a need on us to refrain from haste and a decision made in fear. What the council would ask you be this: think hard and long on what I have said here tonight. Talk among yourselves, come to us, your councilmen, with your queries and doubts, your counsels and thoughts. The town shall not decide this matter till three more nights have passed."

Admi stood for a moment more, looking out over the crowd; then he turned and gestured to his fellow councilman. Burra stepped forward and struck the gong hard thrice with the long brass hammer. Verrarc and burly Frie helped Admi down from the table. The meeting had ended.

It took a long time for the crowd to clear the plaza. At first the townsfolk stood silently, as if they knew not what to think or say, then they began to talk among themselves, forming little clots of neighbors and friends. Although many wished to leave, there were only two ways down, the winding path near the front, where three or four people could walk abreast, and a narrow goat track round the back of the Council House, which at night was too dangerous to be useful.

Those at the very back of the crowd finally began to move toward the wider path and start the long plod downhill. Since Lael was tall enough to see over the crowd, he spotted friends nearby and waved vigorously. Murmuring apologies, he and Dera began to squeeze through the crowd to meet them as they did the same from their side. Niffa lost them after they'd gone barely two yards and turned back toward the bonfire.

The councilmen were huddled, arguing over something, off to one side. With her retinue behind her, Zatcheka had moved out of earshot. In the firelight Niffa could see her looking around with the polite little smile of someone waiting. Now, she thought. I cannot let her go on hoping! She ran a hand through her hair to tidy it a bit and walked over to the Gel da'Thae. At her approach the two warriors stepped forward, staves at the ready, but Zatcheka laughed and spoke to them in her own language. They bowed and moved back to let Niffa approach.

"A good eve to you," Zatcheka said.

"And to you, honored ambassador." Niffa's mouth had turned dry, but she made herself go on. "My name be Niffa, a citizen of this town. I—" All of a sudden she realized that she could never tell her about Meer's death without explaining how she knew.

"Do go on. I bite not, though I have fangs."

"My thanks. I did but wish to greet you and wish your stay here a pleasant one."

"Truly?" Zatcheka was smiling. "I think me you do have more than that in mind. I did wonder if we'd meet, ever since I marked you at the first, when we rode in the gates."

"You did? Why?"

"And why did you come down to the walls to wait for us? I did ask about you and found that you live here on Citadel, a goodly ways away from the gates."

Niffa felt herself blush.

"I will tell you first," Zatcheka said, "as is seemly for a guest. On the night before we reached your city, the gods did send me a dream. At the gates, they did say, you will see this lass. And they did show me your face."

"And I did dream of a caravan! Go wait, my dream told me. I did think it did pertain to someone else, you see, because my brother, he be travelling home too."

"So! The gods have had a hand in this, then. Grave things are on the move."

"Just so, but I do wonder if it be the gods or . . ." Niffa let her voice trail away.

Zatcheka considered her for a moment, then smiled.

"Or the witchlore, child?"

"Just that," Niffa said. "I take it then that you do ken these things yourself."

"I have seen some of the sights along the witchroad. More than that I would not claim."

"I'd not claim more either. But then I may give you the news I carry, though truly, it be sad, and I do wish I had better."

Zatcheka went tense, her lips a little parted, her eyes narrowing.

"Be it about my son?" Zatcheka whispered. "My Meer?"

"I fear so. He—well, he has gone to your gods."

Zatcheka tossed her head back, her mouth open and rigid as if she would wail, but she made no sound. She raised her arms and clasped them across her chest as if to hold in her grief.

"A thousand apologies," Niffa stammered. "I could not

bear it, seeing you hope in vain when I knew he were gone."

"You have my thanks." Zatcheka lowered her head at last to look at her. "And you have done a right thing. It were better I know the truth, no matter that the truth be a burning spear plunged into my heart."

Niffa groped for words, found none, and unthinkingly held out a hand. Zatcheka clasped it in both of hers with a grip almost painful.

"How did you learn of this?" Zatcheka whispered.

"My master in witchlore did tell me in a dream. She be on her way to Cerr Cawnen. I do hope and pray she'll be here soon. She can tell you more."

Zatcheka gave her hand another squeeze, then let her go.

"You have my thanks," she repeated, in a voice that throbbed with tears. "Forgive me. I would be alone now."

Zatcheka glanced back and summoned her people with a wave. Together they strode off across the plaza to the Council House, to wait there, Niffa supposed, till the crowd cleared and they could return to their tents. She herself turned back toward the front of the plaza and found Harl, watching her from some distance away. She walked over to join him.

"By the gods themselves!" Harl said. "And be you not the brave one? Talking with our shaven monster?"

"No monster," Niffa snarled. "But a woman like all others."

"My apologies. I did but jest."

"Oh, mine to you, too. I do feel as if I walked on nails or suchlike tonight."

"Admi's news would turn any heart fretful, bain't?"

"Just so. Here, I saw not your master's lady here tonight."

Harl grinned, then glanced around. Niffa could see that Verrarc still spoke with Admi, both of them a fair way away, too.

"The bitch did run off again," Harl lowered his voice. "I ken not where she be. The master be ever so troubled, too."

The strange cold warning clutched Niffa's heart, or so it seemed, so hard that she couldn't speak.

"And here be a thing most peculiar," Harl went on. "Korla did tell me about it. Our mooncalf swears that she did see Raena standing naked on the back garden wall, and then she turned herself into a big raven and flew off. Raena, I mean, not poor little Magpie."

"Oh come now! That can't be true!"

Yet even as she spoke, Niffa found herself hearing a little voice in her mind, telling her that true it was. Mazrak—she too had heard the old tales. All at once her loathing for the woman came clear in her mind, that someone would work the witchlore to do harm. All ye gods! she prayed. Do let Dalla get herself here straightaway! She remembered what she'd told Zatcheka: my master in the witchlore. It be true, she thought, mayhap the truest thing I've ever spoke. Harl was standing close to her, smiling at her with an unmistakable fondness.

"Harl?" she said. "Do get yourself another lass. In but a little while you'll understand why I do say this."

Niffa turned on her heel and hurried off. Once she'd caught up with the last of the crowd, she looked backed to find him still standing where she'd left him, staring after her.

Evandar being Evandar, Dallandra and her expedition spent two full days, not one, on the west-running road before he finally joined them. On their second night out from Cengarn, they camped in a wild meadow some miles from the last farm of Cadmar's demesne, at about the time that Admi was summoning the citizenry to hear his news. While the men tethered out the horses and mules, Dallandra took Elessario from a weary Carra, whose back ached from a long day of carrying the baby in the sling. Lightning, Carra's wolfish grey dog, padded along behind as they strolled through the camp. By then Elessi could hold her head up, and she sat up in Dallandra's arms, looking round with her big golden eyes.

"Tomorrow Dar can take a turn at carrying her," Carra said.

"Will she be quiet for him?"

"I don't care if she screams the whole way. He can still take a turn. But truly, she does love her da, and I think me she'll be good enough."

Their stroll had led them to the center of the camp, where Jahdo had built the evening's fire out of scrounged wood. He knelt in front of it and began to strike sparks with his flint and steel. As they watched, the tinder finally caught, and flames leapt up in the kindling. Elessi crowed with laughter and twisted in Dalla's arms, leaning down to reach toward the leaping fire.

"Hot!" Dallandra stepped back and put alarm into her voice. "Very hot! Bad for babies!"

Elessi howled—there was no other word for it, howled like an angry banshee and wrenched herself around in the general direction of the fire. So surprising was her strength that Dallandra might have dropped her had Carra not grabbed the child from behind.

"Nah nah nah!" Carra crooned. "Be good now. Don't fuss!"

Her face red as a sunset, Elessi whipped her head around and caught Carra's arm in a toothless bite. Carra slid her flesh free to a cascade of screaming.

"I'll take her inside the tent." Carra was yelling over the noise. "That usually quiets her right down. Mayhap she'll suckle for a while."

Dallandra gladly let go her grip on the child. Elessi continued to scream and howl as Carra carried her at a trot across the camp and ducked into the peaked tent. For some while Dallandra stood outside, listening to Carra talk to her child. Finally Elessario's wails turned to a normal cry, then stopped as Carra managed to get her to nurse. No doubt the tantrum had left her hungry. Dalla turned away and found Jahdo watching her, his head cocked a little to one side.

"Not all babies be so irksome, my lady."

"That's very true. I'll admit I'm worried."

"I did wonder if you were. Ah well, if we get safely to my home, my aunt, Sirri, will ken what to do. No one in our whole town does ken babies as well as she, you see. The other women, they all call her a fair marvel."

"Good! We're going to need her counsel, no doubt of that. I hope Evandar gets himself here soon. The less time we spend on the road, the better."

That night, when she went to the Gatelands of Sleep to look for Evandar, Dallandra found Niffa waiting for her instead. The lass's simulacrum was pacing back and forth by the fiery-red dweomer stars, and she blurted out her news as soon as Dallandra walked up.

"I did speak with Zatcheka! She did thank me for the telling of her son's death."

"Well, that took courage!" Dallandra said. "I'm proud of you, Niffa. And my heart aches for the poor woman."

"She were ever so sad, truly. But here be the strangest thing of all. I did approach her, and she did seem very pleasant, and then all of a sudden I did think, how can I tell her without telling her how I learnt of it?"

"Oh ye gods! Here I never thought of that!"

"But in the end, like, it mattered not. She did make it plain that she did ken witchlore, and that she'd seen me in a dream, so I did tell her."

"The Gel da'Thae have dweomer? Huh, I can't say I'm surprised, after some of the things Meer told us."

"Only a bit, said she. It be good she does, truly, with the times as black as these. Grave things be afoot. That be the reason she did come to our town. The wild Horsekin do gather an army. They do think some goddess or other did grant our lands and people to them to conquer."

Dallandra swore so foully that Niffa gaped at her.

"My apologies," Dallandra said. "I think me I've been spending too much time around soldiers. Do go on."

"There be not much more to tell, truly. Zatcheka's town, Braemel, does wish to ally with us. We shall hold the Deciding in three days."

"Well, I hope to every god we get there before that."

"Do you think this alliance be a bad thing?"

"Not at all. I just happen to know a great deal about this wretched false goddess, that's all, and I think your town should hear it."

"Ah, I do see. But here, there be another strange thing.

Raena, the councilman's woman—she did leave our town this day, and some say she be a mazrak. Know you what that be?"

"I most certainly do, and she is. I've seen her in raven form with my own eyes."

Niffa stared for a long moment.

"Do you know where she went?" Dallandra said.

"Not I. I did but hear the news from the councilman's servant."

"Huh! I wonder if she knows we're coming? But don't you worry about that. I'll do some scrying."

"Well and good, then." The girl's image was wavering and growing thin. "Forgive me, I do be so tired this night."

"Go back to your body, then, child. We could all do with some rest after horrible news like that."

Niffa's image smiled briefly, then disappeared. *Evandar better get himself here,* Dallandra thought. *We need to make some speed.*

With the first grey light of dawn Evandar did indeed arrive. Dallandra was sitting on the ground, eating breakfast with Jahdo while Prince Dar and his guard struck the tent. Off to one side of the confusion Arzosah sat crouched like a cat with her forepaws folded under her chest and her wings neatly furled, while Rhodry stood nearby, eating a chunk of bread. All at once, Arzosah hissed like a thousand snakes and lumbered to her feet. Lightning sprang up and began to bark a deep-throated warning. Dallandra got up herself and turned to see what had so alarmed the dragon: Evandar, striding into camp leading a scruffy-looking grey gelding on a halter rope for want of a bridle. The grey carried no saddle, either. Although the horse rolled an eye at the sight of Arzosah, it stayed remarkably calm. No doubt Evandar had worked his strange horse-dweomer once again.

"My apologies, my love," Evandar said. "I did mean to get here faster than this."

"No harm done, truly," Dallandra said. "I suppose you stole that horse."

"Borrowed it only." He flashed her a grin. "I'll return it to the farmer when I'm done riding, I promise." He glanced

Arzosah's way. "Ah, I see our wyrm is in a sunny mood to match the morning."

"Hold your tongue, you foul clot of ectoplasm," Arzosah growled. "How I wish I could snap you up and crunch you down my gullet!"

"No doubt, but being as I know the dweomer of your true name, I suggest you don't bother trying." Evandar was grinning in a way that must have been infuriating to the dragon. "Be a good little lass and follow us through my country when we go in."

"Your country? Never!"

"And why not? Your poor little wings will have to do less flapping that way."

Arzosah opened her mouth and hissed like water poured on red-hot iron. Rhodry came hurrying up and laid a hand on Evandar's shoulder.

"Here, here, don't tease her," Rhodry said. "For my sake if not for hers."

"Oh very well." Evandar gave him a lazy smile. "But it'll take the pair of you too long to fly all the way to Cerr Cawnen on your own."

"No doubt she'll take the shortcut if I ask her. Just leave her to me."

Rhodry returned to the dragon, who turned her back on him with a great deal of grumbling and swearing. Still, when he trotted round her bulk to face her, she did bend her head to listen as he talked, too softly for the others to hear. Evandar watched him with his head cocked to one side.

"Rori deserves the names she gave him," Dallandra said. "Dragonfriend, dragonmaster."

"For now," Evandar said. "But I hope he can keep on handling her this well. She's a dangerous beast."

"As if I didn't know that."

"I don't mean her teeth and claws, my love. She has dweomer as well."

"Ye gods! I had no idea."

"All of Wyrmkind loves dweomer, and they have workings that pass from mother to hatchling. They dwell in the fire mountains, and the mountains listen to them and obey them."

"Obey them? What—"

"They can call forth the molten blood of the earth, should they want to. Fire and ash and devastation come at their beck and call."

Dallandra wondered if he were having a jest on her, but he seemed solemn enough.

"I've seen it happen," Evandar went on. "Anger a dragon too near its lair, and you'll lose rather a lot of countryside. Why do you think I went to all that trouble to learn her name?"

"Indeed." Dallandra shuddered like a wet dog. "Well, I'll do my best to keep her feeling kindly toward us."

"Do that. I have hopes that the power of her name will work for you even without the ring. But Rhodry will be able to do naught that she doesn't want done."

Once everyone had eaten, the men loaded up the packs and saddled the riding horses. Dallandra and Carra stood off to one side out of the way as Dar and two of the archers packed up the tent. Carra was holding Elessario in her arms, and the baby fretted, not quite crying, refusing to be cheered, until Evandar walked over to them.

"Look, beloved," Carra said. "Look there! It's your grandfather."

When Elessi saw Evandar, she squalled and stretched out her chubby little arms to him. As soon as he'd taken her, she quieted.

"Now that's real dweomer," Carra said, laughing. "Maybe you should carry her from now on."

"If I didn't have a working to do, I would," Evandar said. "Come to think of it, it would be best if she slept on this part of the journey."

As she understood, Dallandra winced and nodded her agreement. If Elessi should see her old homelands, she might well try to leave the body that was proving such a nuisance.

"That's all very well," Carra said. "If I could make her sleep on command, my life would be a good bit easier, good sir."

"Ah. Then I shall sing to her."

Evandar settled the baby at his shoulder, then began to sing in a high-pitched wail that seemed to follow no particular rhythm. At first Elessi laughed, then she yawned, and in a few moments she shut her eyes and slept. When Evandar handed her back to Carra, she barely stirred.

"I'll teach you that song later," he said, "when we have more time. We should be riding out."

"I'd be ever so grateful," Carra said. "And at least she'll sleep today for Dar. He's carrying her, whether he wants to or no."

Dar, however, was perfectly willing to take a turn with his daughter, though Carra had to lengthen the sling with a bit of rope to go over his broader shoulder. Watching them together, fussing over their child, made Dallandra smile. Yet all at once she felt a thin cold line of fear run down her back—the dweomer-cold. There was some danger close at hand, too close, a thing she'd overlooked somehow. In the bustle of leaving she had no chance to meditate upon the warning, but she knew she'd remember it.

Once everyone had mounted up, Evandar led the way back to the path at the far side of the meadow. Dallandra rode next to him while the line straggled out behind. Overhead Arzosah flew in lazy circles with Rhodry on her back. For a few miles they followed a dirt track that wound through wild grasslands. At their approach birds broke cover and flew, grouse with a whir of wings, the occasional lark, winging up on a spiral of song. The sun was well risen by the time they crested a low hill and looked down to see a river where a mist was forming, a strangely opalescent mist, rising in long tendrils. Evandar held up one arm for the halt.

"Is everyone in good order?" Evandar called out.

Dallandra turned in her saddle and looked back. Carra sat on her horse at the head of the line while Prince Dar, one arm around the sling with the baby and the other gesturing as regally as he could manage, arranged his men in a proper two-abreast marching order, followed by Jahdo, leading his white packhorse. Tied down for safety's sake, Carra's dog lay uneasily atop the pack.

"All except Rhodry and the dragon." Dallandra paused, shading her eyes with one hand. "Where—ah, there they are, coming right toward us."

Evandar waited until the dragon had flown close enough to see them and the mist both, then yelled out the order to march. As they rode downhill, the gleaming pearl-shot mist swelled and put out long cool arms to greet them. A few more paces, and the grey covered the sky above, though when she looked back, Dallandra could still see the morning sun in the east. Once they'd ridden well into the grey-and-lavender clouds, they could see naught but mist and a pale strange light that seemed to emanate from inside the water drops rather than from any sun beyond. Dallandra could hear the prince's guard muttering among themselves.

"Hold steady, men!" Daralanteriel called out. "The Wise One knows what she's doing."

Dallandra smiled to herself. It was better to let them think that she was the one working a familiar dweomer, but of course, she understood next to nothing about Evandar's gates between worlds.

At length the mist began to thin in patches, as if invisible fingers were teasing it out the way a woman teases out wool for the carding comb. The sun beyond brightened as the mist finally faded away. In a cool sunlight they found themselves on the bank of a dead river where brown reeds stood crisp and lead-grey water oozed over filthy sands. The bank itself, covered with short dead grass, made a hard road under the horses' hooves. Dallandra turned in the saddle to look at Evandar, whose eyes had gone bleak.

"Oh by the holy stars!" Dallandra whispered. "What's happened, my love?"

"When my people left to cross the white river, they took the life of the Lands with them." Evandar kept his voice flat and steady, but she knew how much losing his creation must have cost him. "I built this world for them, after all."

Dallandra rose in her stirrups and looked round. Her formal garden had disappeared, although a few cracked bricks among dead weeds marked the spot where it had stood. The cloth-of-gold pavilion had disappeared without leaving even that much of a trace behind. She sat back with a shake of her head and leaned forward to pat her nervous horse's neck.

"It's a ghastly change, in't?" Evandar said.

"It is, and I'm so sorry. I know you loved this place."

Evandar shrugged, then turned to call to Daralanteriel. "We're all here? Good! Let's move on."

With a wave of his arm the prince signalled to his caravan, and they set off, following the dead river through desolation. After perhaps a mile's worth of riding, the view around them began to change, burgeoning green and wild, with long meadows sprinkled with white daisies and yellow buttercups. Farther away grew trees in shaggy copses. Here and there Dallandra saw rabbits out in the tall grass. When they passed a stand of trees, squirrels chattered.

"This isn't your doing," Dallandra said. "Where did it come from?"

"I don't know," Evandar said. "I suspect it's the work of an old man who lives out in the further reaches."

"What? Who?"

"Ah, I see I've forgotten to tell you. When I was searching for the hag Alshandra, back last summer, I flew beyond my lands and into a dead place, all barren rock and sand, where ugly creatures lived, mostly under the rocks. You could see their little red eyes, glaring at you. But in the midst of this grim spot I found an old man, sitting and peeling an apple, and every slice he cut turned into the stuff of life, somehow, like the heat of a fire pouring into the dead place. Whenever I visited there, it seemed more alive and larger, and so I think that in the end his work succeeded, even as mine was dying."

"How very odd!"

"And here I was hoping you could tell me what it all meant."

Dallandra merely shook her head. Something of his tale had triggered a memory—no, more a ghost of a memory, deep in her mind. She had heard that place of rock and death described once, some very long time ago, but try as she might, she could not recall when or how.

They were approaching the wild forest that had formerly divided Evandar's lands from those he'd made for his brother and his brother's people. The forest, at least, still flourished, as wild and tangled as she remembered it, but then, it owed its life to older, stranger magicks than Evandar's. As they followed a road into the twisted, moss-covered trees, the sunlight faded, and a huge greenish-silver moon rose off to their left, hanging in the sky just above the treetops. When she turned in the saddle to glance back, she saw that the elven archers had spread out to surround Carra, Dar, and his precious burden. Jahdo seemed to be having no trouble urging his mule and packhorse to trot along quickly. But in the sky—

"We've lost Rhodry!" Dallandra said abruptly.

"Curse that wretched snake of a dragon!" Evandar looked up, searching the narrow stripe of view between the trees. "I saw them fly into the mist."

"But I never saw them after. We should stop and wait—"

"Stop? Here? Under this moon?"

"True enough. Well, maybe they're just circling our line of march."

"So I'll hope." Evandar's voice sounded full of doubt, not hope. "I should never have trusted that slimy little wyrm."

Thanks to Rhodry's coaxing, Arzosah had flown into the dweomer mist readily enough, following the horsemen. Evandar, however, had forgotten that the mist would blind any creature who flew so high above the ground. At first Arzosah flapped along steadily through the light-shot silvery air, and Rhodry thought he could hear the jingle of tack and the clopping of horses' hooves. All at once, though, they burst out of the mist into sunlight and looked down upon open sea, dotted with what seemed to be white islands.

"Ah by the black hairy arse of the Lord of Hell!"

"What?" Arzosah called back. "Speak louder!"

"Doesn't matter!" Rhodry raised his voice over the wind sweeping over him as they flew. "We've lost them."

"I can see that for myself." The dragon dipped one wing and began to turn. "Hang on!"

He clung to the leather straps of her harness as she banked a wing for the wide turn around. When he risked a look at the ocean below, he saw the white islands more closely and realized that they were chunks of ice, exactly like those that form on lakes of a winter but a thousand times the size. The mist rose up all silver and lavender in front of him and swallowed the ice from his view. They swooped into the fog, flew some way in the blind grey, then swooped out again. Below them crawled a lead-colored river, oozing its way through brown reeds.

"Here we are!" Arzosah called back. "I know this place."

"How?"

She ignored him and flew smoothly onward over the grasslands. At the horizon he could see the dark mounds of what appeared to be a forest. Arzosah changed course slightly and headed for it.

"The mother roads go through there," she shouted. "They must have gone that way."

"If you say so, then."

All at once Arzosah flung up her head and sniffed the air like a hunting dog. She let out a screech that made the hair on the back of his neck prickle, then with a huge beat of her wings launched herself upward, flapping hard to gain height. Rhodry clung to the straps for all he was worth.

"What are you doing?" he yelled.

He got no answer until she'd risen so far above the ground that he felt dizzy. She levelled off her flight, banked one wing again, and turned in a lazy arc.

"Look down!" she called out.

Rhodry saw, so far below that they might have been beetles crawling on a dead log, a line of horsemen marching in military order. When Arzosah began a long glide down, he could count about twenty of them, all riding heavy horses and leading pack mules. He could also discern that they had manes as wild and long as those of their mounts. Leading them, flying fairly low to the ground, was a raven the size of a small pony.

"Horsekin!" Rhodry yelled.

"And Raena with them! Let's have a bit of sport!"

With a roar like a river in spate Arzosah plunged down. The raven saw them first; shrieking, she turned tail and flapped away fast. The men looked up just as their horses smelled the dragon. Kicking, plunging, bucking, the horses tried to bolt. The Horsekin riders were yelling and grabbing manes and necks, shortening up on their reins, clutching their saddle peaks—anything to keep from being thrown. Some of the horses did bolt, with cursing riders still clinging to them. Arzosah ignored them and swooped after the raven.

Shrieking, the raven dodged, darting this way and that, but steadily the dragon gained. Arzosah reached out with the full length of her neck and snapped. With one last shriek the raven disappeared, bursting through some invisible gate to another world, but Arzosah had a pair of black feathers in her mouth. She spat them out, then turned in a wide arc. Below the panicked Horsekin were trying to collect their mounts and their marching order.

"Shall we go after them again?" Arzosah cried out.

"No! Do you want to be lost here forever? We've got to find Evandar."

"True!"

Still, she skimmed the ground and charged them one more time. The men screamed, wrenched their horses' heads around, and let them run where they would. Arzosah pulled up, gained height in a mad flap of wings, and flew fast away, chortling to herself. Rhodry tipped back his head and howled in berserk laughter.

To Dallandra it seemed that they travelled through the thick humid air of the forest for only a short space of time, but she knew perfectly well that in the physical world, Time was speeding along. Whenever they came to a clearing, she would look up, hoping to see the dragon, but they had ridden clear of the trees before Arzosah caught up to them. At the edge of the forest grew a tall tree, half of which burned perpetually with golden flames, whilst the other half grew green in full leaf. With a roar of greeting, Arzosah swooped overhead and landed near the living side. Dallandra was relieved to see Rhodry still on her back. She nudged her horse to a jog and trotted over to join them, with Evandar close behind.

"News!" Rhodry called out. "We've seen Raena, leading Horsekin through—well, through wherever this may be."

"Evil news, then! How many of them were there?"

"Not more than a score. A good many found themselves on the ground when their horses got a noseful of Arzosah."

"It was glorious," Arzosah chimed in. "And I nearly caught that rotten-hearted little mazrak, too. She nipped through some sort of gate twixt worlds just ahead of my front teeth. Huh. I wonder if she'll come back for her delightful friends?"

"If she doesn't, I will," Evandar said. "But come along, all of you! We daren't linger here. Move, move!"

With one long grumble of a roar, the dragon flung herself into the air. Dallandra swung her horse's head around and trotted after Evandar down a long dirt path that skirted the forest. She kept looking back and counting, but this time everyone in their ragged procession followed right along. At an enormous pile of grey boulders, they turned away from the forest edge, but still Evandar chivvied them to make speed. Not until they had got well clear did Evandar let them halt.

On the flat crest of a low hill, much like the one from which they'd first seen the dweomer mist, the line fanned out, allowing the horsemen to pull up abreast. The dragon began to circle above. Dallandra noticed that while the archers looked nervously ahead and muttered among themselves, Carra was smiling, all anticipation. Just below them the path ran down the gentle slope into a gathering mist, shot with pale stains of swirling colors on the silver-grey.

"Just go through that mist and you'll find yourself on the road to Cerr Cawnen," Evandar said. "The town's but a few miles on."

"You're not coming with us?" Dallandra said.

"Not just at the moment, not with Raena flying around the Lands as if the stinking bitch owned them!"

"True spoken, but once we're in Cerr Cawnen—"

"I'll never be far away. Shaetano's lurking there, you know, hoping for a chance at mischief. But I'd best be gone. Raena's not going to dawdle around waiting for me."

Evandar swung a leg over his horse's back and slid down to the ground. He tossed her the end of the halter rope.

"Take this poor beast with you, will you? He'll only be a nuisance to me now."

"Very well, but—"

"I know, I know. I'll take him back to his owner later."

With a cheery wave Evandar turned and jogged off. Dallandra watched until he plunged into the forest and disappeared, then rode back to the others.

"We're almost there," she said. "Jahdo, no doubt you can lead us the last few miles home."

Evandar had not gone far into the forest before he changed his form into the red hawk. With a harsh cry he leapt into the air and took to his wings, gliding on the wind over the trees, then flying fast to gain height. As he soared, he looked this way and that, searching for the raven, but if she lurked in the thick cover, he never saw her. Finally he left the forest behind and flew over the green hills of the new Wildlands.

He saw no horses, no riders, no raven, even though he spent a long time searching, crisscrossing back and forth over the meadows. Although he wondered if perhaps Arzosah had lied to him, he knew that Rhodry never would have done so. It was more likely that Shaetano had come to rescue his so-called priestess and her men and lead them back to the physical world by some devious route. He would simply have to search until he found it—and hope that it lay in a different part of the physical plane than the spot where he'd just set Dallandra down.

Riding through the dweomer mist had indeed brought Dallandra and her band of travellers to a place free of

Horsekin. They found themselves ambling west on a dirt road that ran between two fields of pale green grain, rippling in a soft wind. At some distance off to the south stood a blocky square farmhouse with a steep peaked roof. Dallandra could hear a dog barking, faint on the wind. Jahdo turned in the saddle toward Dallandra, but she could see he was having trouble speaking, caught twixt laughter and sobs.

"Oh my lady! It be true! This be the very road that does lead to my city."

"Splendid!"

"But I did think of somewhat. Rori and the dragon. They mayn't land on the streets or suchlike. Everything be too narrow and crowded."

"That's an excellent point. What shall we do with them?"

"There be an open space of sorts on Citadel. If we might fetch them down, I can tell them."

Eventually Dallandra did get the dragon's attention by rising in her stirrups and yelling like a madwoman. Arzosah flapped her wings in answer, sheared off, and glided down some distance ahead. When the rest of the expedition caught up with her, Rhodry dismounted to stand in the dusty road.

"I thought I'd best not land where those farmers could see me," Arzosah said.

"True spoken," Dallandra said. "Jahdo's been thinking ahead to the problem of where you might stay in Cerr Cawnen."

"A good question indeed." Arzosah swung her head Jahdo's way. "You're very astute for a hatchling, I must say."

"My thanks, my lady," Jahdo said. "Now, when you do fly over our town, in the middle of the lake there be an island. Round the west side of that island there be ruins, these big blocks of stone, all tumbled and broken. But there be trees there, too, and you'll not be far from the plaza, where be a well of sweet water."

"Sounds like a good choice, then," Rhodry joined in. "What we'll do is this, if it passes muster with you, Dalla. I think you'd best prepare the town for our coming, like, and so we'd best not turn up till the morrow morning. I'll take some provisions and a blanket and suchlike before we fly off again."

"I think you're right," Dallandra said. "Jahdo, tell me, what will your fellow citizens think about a dragon?"

"Oh, we do see them now and again. They come to steal cattle—"

"I wouldn't call it *stealing*," Arzosah broke in. "More like a tribute to the beauty of dragons."

"The ones who own the cows, they do live in ignorance of your beauty." Jahdo paused to smile at her. "Be that as it may, there be our fire mountain, too, for their resting place. Never before did I know the liking of great wyrms for fire mountains, but now that I do, it does explain why we see them round here."

"So, then," Dallandra said, "they'll not panic or suchlike?"

"Oh well now, we be a hard folk to panic. But truly, it be one thing to see a great wyrm fly past, another to have her land amongst you. But the spot I did tell about, it does lie out of the sight of most of the town."

"Sounds better and better, then," Rhodry said. "Let's be on our way. You don't want to be caught outside the walls tonight, if there are Horsekin prowling around."

Once Rhodry had taken the supplies he needed, he and the dragon flew off, veering away from the road due north. As she watched them disappear into a vastness of sky, Dallandra felt a sudden sadness touch her, as if she were seeing him leave her for the last time. You always knew we'd part, she reminded herself. She shook the feeling off and turned to Jahdo.

"Lead on!" she said. "How far is it?"

"Well, my lady, all we truly have to do is follow this road, but as to how far, I wouldn't know, truly. I did walk this road only once in my life. But not far, that I do know."

With the sun hanging low in the west they set off again at a brisk walk. They'd not gone more than a mile or so when Dallandra smelled rot—manure from a cow pasture, she assumed. As they rode on, though, the smell grew stronger and fouler. If it was a pasture, it had to be hip deep in filth to smell so bad. Jahdo, riding beside her, noticed it too.

"Oh my lady, what can be making that stench? It be worse than the privies in Dun Cengarn."

"A thousand privies wouldn't be as bad, I'd say."

Dallandra glanced back to find that Dar was holding his reins in one hand and a scrap of cloth, of the sort that normally wrapped spare arrowheads, with the other. He kept flicking it in front of Elessi's face to try to waft the stench away. Dallandra doubted that it was doing much good. The farther they rode, the worse the smell became—it had a rich warmth to it, Dallandra decided, as if the filth were being stewed over a slow fire.

"The lake!" she said abruptly. "Jahdo, didn't you tell me that your town's on a lake fed by hot springs? Do your people just toss their garbage and suchlike into it?"

"They do not, but in the river that leads out to the south. I lived there, and never did it smell like this to me."

"That's because you lived there. When we get used to somewhat, be it a smell or a sight, we stop noticing it."

"My town would never—" Jahdo hovered on the edge of indignation. "Although—well, my lady, there be a sudden fear on me, that you be right, especially after the long winter and all."

Sure enough, by the time they saw the towering stone walls of Cerr Cawnen, they could tell that the stench was coming from nowhere else but the city. Enough garbage got into the lake, Dallandra supposed, to add strength to the reek that went out with the warm river. All of the Westfolk men began muttering among themselves, and Dallandra was very glad that Jahdo knew no Elvish to understand their remarks about pigs and carrion crows.

It was close to sunset by the time they reached the east gates. Above them on the wall stood a handful of men wearing chain-mail hauberks—the town watch, Dallandra assumed. When they saw the travellers they began to call out.

"A caravan! Merchants, mayhap! Leave the gates stand open a bit longer there!"

Jahdo tipped his head back and squinted.

"Kiel!" he sang out. "Kiel, it's me!"

Up on the wall a tall guardsman yelled in wordless triumph.

"My brother," Jahdo said, and his voice was trembling.

By the time everyone had ridden through the gates, Kiel was down on the ground and waiting to greet them. Jahdo dismounted and raced to his brother's open arms with his mule and packhorse trailing after him. Dallandra turned in the saddle and waved the prince over.

"We'd best dismount, don't you think?" she said. "I've no idea where to go now."

"It would be polite," Dar said. "Well, if you think Carra will be safe? There's quite a mob gathering."

So there was—maybe a dozen men of the town watch had climbed down from the wall; everyone in earshot was hurrying their way; farther off, townsfolk were yelling out the news to those farther still. Dogs barked and came running, tails wagging, to join the excitement. Daralanteriel had his men dismount, but he handed the baby up to Carra and told her to stay on horseback. His men kept firm hands on the bridles of their horses. The pack mules, held loosely, began to bray and pull at their ropes every time a dog came near them.

Dallandra was just thinking that they were going to lose stock and supplies both when militiamen trotted over to lend a hand. In a flurry of quick greetings they took over the pack animals and allowed the elven men to settle their horses down. From the back of the crowd, Dallandra heard a determined sort of shouting that swept forward from person to person until she could finally understand the words.

"Let the councilmen through! Here, step aside for the councilmen!"

With their streaky-red cloaks billowing around them two men, one skinny and grey, the other blond and good-looking, were working their way through the crowd. From Niffa's descriptions Dallandra could guess that the blond was Verrarc. The older man stopped and began talking to the townsfolk, pointing with one hand and tapping someone here and there on the shoulder with the other to make the crowd move back and thin out. Verrarc, however, strode toward the group at the gates.

While she waited for him to reach her, Dallandra summoned the dweomer sight and studied his aura, an unpleasant greenish color, all shrivelled around him like a wet shirt. So this was the man who'd ensorceled Jahdo. It was hard to imagine him summoning the power to have done such a thing, but when Jahdo looked up and saw him, the boy shrank back against his older brother. Verrarc gave him a look that ached with a fear to match it, and his aura seemed to shred at the edges, suddenly grey. Dallandra hurriedly returned her sight to normal.

"Jahdo!" Verrarc said, and his voice bubbled with false cheer. "Stout lad! It gladdens my heart to see you! And who be your friends?"

As if he smelled danger, Lightning, head down and ruff up, squeezed in between the boy and the councilman and growled with a wrinkle of lip to expose fang. Verrarc stepped back sharply. Jahdo swallowed hard and turned to Dallandra, who arranged a smile and stepped forward.

"Good morrow, Councilman," she said. "My name is Dallandra, and I—"

She stopped. Verrarc was staring at her face while his own went pale around the mouth. All at once she understood: these people had never seen Westfolk before.

"I assure you I'm not a demon or suchlike," she said, laughing. "We come from a country that lies to the south of here, and we're flesh and blood like you despite our ears and eyes."

"My apologies." Verrarc was stammering. "There be a need on me to apologize for all of us. It be a rude thing to mob you like this, but truly, we've not seen your ilk here before."

"My thanks. Is there somewhere we can set up a camp?"

"In truth, there be so. All along the town green here do we allow merchants and other travelling folk to shelter inside our walls. There be a well and fire pits farther along. Shall I lead you there?"

"Thank you very much. That's most hospitable."

Verrarc managed a brief smile, then glanced at Jahdo. She didn't need dweomer sight to see Verrarc's desperation. What would he do, try to murder the boy to keep him silent?

"Jahdo!" Dallandra called out. "You'd best come with—"

Somewhere in the crowd a woman shrieked in piercing joy.

"Mam!" Jahdo called out. "Mam! Da!"

He rushed into the crowd, which parted to let him through. A small woman, far too thin, her blonde hair streaked with grey, ran forward and threw her arms around the boy. Behind her a tall grey-haired man stood beaming at the pair. Verrarc watched the family slack-mouthed. Dallandra realized suddenly that at his belt he carried a long knife in a beaded sheath, as indeed did most of the townsmen. Although ensorceling a person went against all the ethics of dweomer, Dallandra wasn't about to bring Jahdo home only to see him dead by morning. She took a deep breath, summoned power, and laid a gentle hand on Verrarc's arm.

"Councilman?"

When he turned to look at her, she caught his gaze and held it with raw force of will.

"You will never hurt Jahdo. You love him like your own son."

"I'll never hurt him." Verrarc's voice was thick and slurred. "Never hurt him."

With a quick toss of her head she released him. He blinked rapidly for a moment, then smiled.

"There be no words to tell you how glad I be to see Jahdo home," Verrarc said. "I love him like my own son."

"How sweet. Shall we go to the campground?"

"Of course. There be a need on me to warn you, a merchant and his men do camp there already. They be Gel da'Thae. Know you of them?"

"I do indeed. There's no need to worry." Dallandra

turned and waved to the other elves. "Dar! The councilman here will show you where to set up camp."

Dar nodded and waved in return to show her he understood. Verrarc called to the militiamen to follow him, then strode over to the prince. Together they began to sort out the stock and get everyone moving. Dallandra hung back, looking over the crowd around Jahdo. Finally she saw Niffa, standing off to one side and looking over the crowd—probably for her, Dallandra realized. Smiling, Dallandra made her way through the crowd. Niffa laughed and trotted over, holding out her hands. Dallandra clasped them in hers.

"So we meet in the flesh at last!" Dallandra said. "It's good to see you."

"And it gladdens my heart to see you!" Niffa glanced around, then let go Dallandra's hands and lowered her voice. "And for many a reason more than my own. There's been such a fear on me, this past few days."

"No doubt! Here, you'll want to welcome your brother home. We'll be camping on the commons. Will you be able to join us there later?"

"I can, truly. And I will. Have no fear of that."

Laughing and talking, a small crowd of family and friends swept Jahdo down to the lakeshore, where Chief Speaker Admi stood waiting to offer them the use of the council barge. Niffa stayed close to her father, whose sheer size cleared a path through the well-wishers onto the pier and then the barge itself. While the rest of her family came aboard, Niffa found a spot to stand in the bow. The sun was beginning to set, and the mists on the water turned gold, so that when the barge pushed off, they seemed to be gliding into the heart of a fire. Niffa leaned against the railing and wondered why it was suddenly so hard to breathe. For a moment she thought she saw real fire, flames leaping and crackling as the town burned, so vivid that she nearly cried out. She turned the sound into a cough and leaned over the rail to look at the water and hide her face.

Already, she realized, she was beginning to understand how the witchroad would take her farther and farther away from life in Cerr Cawnen. She knew things hidden to her kin and fellow citizens, and she'd learned them by hidden means. Even her joy in her brother's return was blunted simply because she'd known for months that he was safe. She turned round again and watched Jahdo, leaning into their father's embrace. His great adventure had ended. For that moment she envied him.

The barge crept up to its pier on Citadel, disgorged its passengers, then cast off again, heading back to town. On the sandy lakeshore the crowd sorted itself out. As much as friends and neighbors wanted to hear about Jahdo's travels, the less selfish among them pointed out, loudly, that he and his family would be wanting some time to themselves.

"Come later," Lael called out. "Let's all have a bit of dinner, and then we'll hear what my lad has to say for himself."

On a tide of agreement the family started their long trudge up to the granary, Jahdo between his mother and father, Kiel and Niffa bringing up the rear.

"Here, now," Kiel said softly. "Who be that woman? The one with the silver hair. And how be it that you know her?"

"You have sharp eyes."

"Sharp mayhap but not as strange as hers. Ye gods, they do look like a cat's!"

"So they do. Uh well, I know not how to tell you, nor Mam either, but things be on the move for me."

"Indeed?" Kiel hesitated, then shrugged. "No doubt I'll be hearing more than I wish to, and too soon at that."

In the last of the sunset they all hurried up the little alley to their door and climbed into the big room behind the granary. Lael left the door wide open for the light and went to the hearth to lay a fire. Dera stood smiling at her three children.

"We're all here," she said. "At last. All of us be home."

Niffa winced. Though Dera seemed not to notice, Kiel raised one pale eyebrow. Niffa refused to answer. Now that the moment was upon her, she realized that she'd given no thought of how she was going to tell her mother that her daughter was about to leave her hearth.

"The weasels!" Jahdo sang out. "There be a need on me to greet them."

Jahdo dashed into the other room, where the three children had always slept and their ferrets as well. Niffa followed and stood in the doorway to watch. Jahdo went to the wood slat pen and crouched down to lean over the open top. Ambo, their big hob, stood up and sniffed the air, neck stretched high, then chirruped and allowed Jahdo to pick him up. Jahdo held him up to his face to let the hob get his scent. Ambo thrust his face forward and licked the boy's cheek, then his eyelids. The other ferrets climbed over the side or wiggled through the slats to dance around Jahdo's feet and nip his ankles. Jahdo laughed aloud and set Ambo down.

"They remember me, they do remember me!"

He sat on a straw mattress and let the ferrets clamber over him. Smiling, Niffa turned away and went to help her mother lay out dinner.

In the big room the fire was crackling in the hearth, and light danced over the walls. Dera had hung a pot of water from the hook over the hearth; she stood at the table cutting up chunks of salt pork and the flabby last of the winter's carrots. Niffa opened the big standing crock and scooped pounded grains of parched wheat into a bowl. When the water boiled she would slide the grain into the pot for a meal half stew and half porridge. Kiel and Lael sat down at the table, each with a tankard of ale.

"I do suppose we'll have a powerful large crowd in here tonight," Lael remarked.

"Most like, Da," Kiel said.

And once the crowd came, when would she get a private word with her mother? Niffa realized that she could no longer put off the truth.

"Mam?" she said. "There be a need on me to tell you somewhat."

Out of the corner of her eye she saw Kiel put down his tankard and turn on the bench to listen. With a vague smile Dera looked up from her chopping. Niffa saw no way but blurting.

"The time be upon me to leave you," Niffa said, "to follow the witchroad. Werda did tell me this, and ye gods, we all know how strange a child I was, and the dreams I do have and suchlike."

Dera let the knife slip from her fingers and fall onto the table. She looked as if she were about to speak, but she stayed silent, her eyes brimming tears.

"Ah, Mam! I do hate to tell you this!" Niffa felt her own her lips trembling. "But Werda did say that there's a need on me to follow my destiny, and—"

"I care not what Werda told you!" Dera's voice was shaking badly.

"But she speaks true. My heart does shout the same truth. And the woman with silver hair, Dallandra her name be, the gods do mean her for my teacher."

"What? How can you say such things! Have you not but met her? And how do you know she has the lore? Mayhap she be some charlatan—"

"She's not. I did meet her months before this, Mam, in my dreams, my true dreams. Dallandra, she be a master of the witchroad."

"Oh what drivel you speak! I'll not hear it in my house!"

"Mam, she speaks the simple truth." Jahdo was standing in the doorway with Tek-Tek snuggled in his arms. "This year past have I seen things that never did I know existed, and some of them Dallandra did work, spells and suchlike. In the Slavers' country they do call it dweomer."

Dera spun round to glare at him.

"Soon I'll tell you my tales," Jahdo went on, "and then know you'll what I do. I did go a long long way away, and truly, the whole world be a wider place than any of us did ever dream."

Dera turned her back on all of them, her shoulders shaking under her thin dresses. Niffa could keep her composure no longer. She rushed to her mother, threw her arms around her, and wept. Dimly she was aware of Lael getting up and walking over. He laid one gentle hand on Niffa's shoulder and the other on Dera's.

"No man or woman either can argue with their Wyrd,"

Lael said. "Here, here, Dera my love, in our heart of hearts we always did know this day would come."

With that Niffa could choke back her tears. She let her mother go and stepped back, wiping her eyes on her sleeve, while Lael put an arm around Dera's shoulders and led her out into the twilit alleyway. She could hear his soft voice murmuring, but she couldn't make out the words. Kiel sat at the table as if he'd been carved out of the same wood, staring at Jahdo.

"And what's so wrong with you?" Jahdo said.

"Naught," Kiel said. "I did but notice how tall you've grown, this past year while you were gone."

Niffa picked up the knife and returned to chopping up salt pork. The water in the kettle had come to a simmer, and she slid the grain in. Kiel got up and fetched the wooden paddle.

"I'll just be stirring that," Kiel said. "You bring the other stuffs when they be ready."

"I will, and my thanks."

Kiel glanced her way and smiled, a wry twist of his mouth.

"Things be on the move, you did tell me," Kiel said. "Huh. A bit more than that, eh? But Da did speak true. You've always been the peculiar one."

"Beast!" Niffa grabbed a carrot end and tossed it at him.

At that the three of them could laugh. Jahdo carried Tek-Tek over and sat down.

"I swear, you did miss those weasels more than us," Niffa said.

"I did, truly." But he was smiling. "Though I forgot just how strong they stink. On the morrow I'll bathe them."

"I've been lax about it, truly," Niffa said. "And Kiel's been gone a fair bit with the town watch."

In a few moments Lael and Dera returned. Dera stood looking at her brood unsmiling, then sighed.

"Well and good, then," Dera said. "Wyrd is Wyrd. Now give over the knife, Niffa. That pork, it does need to be chopped finer than that."

During the meal they said little. Jahdo knew nothing of her marriage, Niffa realized, or her widowhood either, yet she knew that this was not the night to tell him. By the dancing light of the fire they could pretend that all troubles had fled, at least for this short while, and she refused to break the fragile calm. By the time they finished eating, guests began to arrive, all eager to hear the rare news of faraway lands.

As the crowd grew, Niffa could slip away. When she lit a candle at the hearth, no one seemed to notice; she stuck it in a tin lantern and crept round the edge of the room to the door. For a moment she hesitated, looking back at the family and friends clustered round Jahdo by the hearth; then she stepped out, leaving the door open behind her for the air.

As she was walking down to the lakeshore she saw someone coming up, carrying another lantern. When she held hers away from her eyes, she recognized Verrarc, walking as slowly and hesitantly as an old man. She would have hurried past, but he hailed her, and they met in the pool of light from their lanterns. She was shocked to see how exhausted he looked, with dark circles puffy under his eyes.

"Good morrow, Mistress Niffa. What are you doing away from your hearth?"

"I've an errand to run in the town."

Verrarc seemed to be studying her face. She smiled and waited.

"Ah well," he said finally. "I don't mean to pry. Tell me, do you think it would trouble your mother if I went to hear Jahdo's tales? Curiosity's eating my heart, I'll admit it."

"No doubt, all things considered."

He winced and tossed his head like a fly-stung horse.

"But I know Mam would make you welcome," Niffa went on. "When has she ever turned you away?"

"Just so. My thanks."

He brushed past her and hurried up the path. She turned to watch him go, wondering if it were only some trick of the light that had made him seem on the verge of tears.

Earlier, Councilman Verrarc had led Dallandra and the Westfolk to a camp about halfway around the lake, a stretch of spring grass with a stone well set a long way back from the reeking shore. As the men bustled around, unloading the mules and tethering out the stock, Dallandra walked to the well and looked beyond it to a trio of peaked tents some hundred yards away. Beyond them mules and some heavy horses grazed at tether. In the middle of the tents a group of human men sat around a low fire, but the only Gel da'Thae she saw was a single guard, standing at the door of one tent with a staff at the ready. She could guess that the tent belonged to Zatcheka. The guard seemed to be looking them over in return.

Behind her a dog barked, and when she turned around, Dallandra saw Lightning trotting over the grass with his tail held high and wagging. Right behind him came Carra, carrying the baby, who wore a bit of cloth tied loosely over her mouth and nose.

"Dalla? I'm not interrupting you, am I?"

"You're not," Dallandra said. "Did you think I was casting a spell or suchlike?"

"Well, I didn't know, you see. I wanted to ask you: Lady Ocradda gave me some rose oil when we were leaving, just as a little remembrance. I've put some on this rag for Elessi. The stench here is just so awful. But the rose scent won't be bad for her, will it?"

"I shouldn't imagine it would, and it's bound to be better than the smell of this lake."

Elessi was awake, sitting up in her mother's embrace and looking around her. Since she let the scarf be without fussing, no doubt she agreed with their opinion of the air. Nose down and busy, Lightning trotted back and forth, stopping now and then to roll on the ground. It must have all smelled like delicious carrion to him.

"This is fascinating," Carra said abruptly. "Not the stink, I mean, but everything else. Look at this town! It's half in the water and half out."

"It's a marvel, truly."

"I never knew the Rhiddaer and people like Jahdo existed, and here I've lived my whole life long on the western border!"

Dallandra suppressed a smile. Carra's whole life long amounted to some sixteen winters—at the most.

"I've got to find out when it was built," Carra went on, "Cerr Cawnen, I mean. Jahdo doesn't know, but someone must. And how did the escaped bondsmen build it? Did someone help them? They couldn't have had masons and suchlike when they first came here."

"I'd not thought about all that. It truly does interest you, then."

"It does. When we were all back in Cengarn, Jahdo told me a fair bit, and then poor dear Meer told me what he knew about the history of the Rhiddaer, but neither of them knew how this place was built. I'd love to just poke around here, like, and ask the old people things. Some of them may have been told ancient lore by their grandparents."

The passion in her voice took Dallandra by surprise for a second time.

"I forget how much you love the old lore," Dallandra said at last. "I'll wager that the old people in town will be pleased to talk with you. They probably don't get too many ready listeners."

In the sky the twilight was fading, covering the camp with soft night. The evening star appeared, like a scout beckoning the army of stars to follow it out. When Dallandra glanced back she saw Dar and his men building a fire in their camp. Melimaladar walked a few paces away, saw the evening star, and began to sing. The others took up the music, which drifted like smoke along the lakeshore. From their tents came Gel da'Thae to stand listening in the dusk. The peace of the moment struck Dalla, bringing tears to her eyes, that men of the Westfolk and the Gel da'Thae should camp like this, side by side. But in the morning? she thought.

When someone called her name, Dallandra turned and saw Niffa, walking toward them, carrying a candle lantern. Dallandra hailed her with a wave.

"Who's that?" Carra asked.

"Jahdo's sister. And my new apprentice."

"Truly? Well, that's exciting!"

"It is, indeed."

With a pleasant greeting Niffa strolled over, holding up the lantern. When the pool of light fell on the women's faces, Carra stared, her eyes widening. Niffa started to speak, then fell silent, studying Carra's face in turn. They had recognized each other. Dallandra turned cold with the certain knowledge that in some life or other these two women had been bound together by Wyrd. Yet as those moments do, this one faded fast. Carra stammered out a "good evening," and with a sickly little smile Niffa answered, then looked away, blushing.

"Well, now," Dallandra said briskly. "Let's go back to the fire. I'm hungry enough to eat a wolf, pelt and all."

That evening, as they sat at the campfire with Dar and his men, they talked mostly of ordinary things. Niffa had much to tell them about the situation in the town, and she in turn quite understandably wanted to learn all she could about the Westfolk.

Every now and then Dallandra would notice the young archers eyeing Niffa or grinning at her on the edge of a flirt while she glanced at them sideways, on the edge of a blush. Dallandra would scowl, and they would look away fast. They knew that the lass was her apprentice now, that Niffa's welfare in the world as well as in the dweomerwork lay in her hands, and none of them were eager to cross a dweomermaster. *My first apprentice!* Dallandra thought. *Ye gods, I hope I never fail her!*

Eventually Carra took the baby into the big round tent, then Dar followed her. Out in the forest and in the grasslands the rest of the elves had been sleeping under the stars in this dry weather, but here in this public campground they wanted privacy. Although their party had only the one proper tent, every rider carried a length of Eldidd canvas and a short pole to make a lean-to. Each lashed one end of his canvas to the tent, tied the other to the pole, and drove the pole into the ground like a long tent peg. It was rough, but they each had private shelter of a sort. Niffa watched all of this fascinated.

"The tent does look like a wheel hub now, with all

those spokes! Our Jahdo, he did tell us that the Westfolk ken how to make a home wherever they are, and he did speak true."

"Well, it's home for us," Dallandra said. "I doubt me if you'll find it comfortable at first, but I hope you'll get used to it."

"So do I. From the bottom of my heart."

They shared a laugh. The eleven men spread out their bedrolls under their improvised roofs and turned in to sleep. While she still had the firelight, Dallandra set up her own lean-to, divided her blankets twixt herself and Niffa, and unlaced her pair of saddlebags to make two pillows. Once the fire burned low, the two women strolled down to the lakeside with a fresh candle in the lantern. The night wind had picked up, and Dallandra had got used to the smell to some degree, so that it was pleasant, walking along the shore and watching the silver road that the moon laid upon the water.

"Dalla?" Niffa said abruptly. "The strangest feeling did trouble my heart when I met the princess."

"Did it? I thought I noticed an odd look on your face."

"It were—" Niffa shook her head in confusion. "I could have sworn—well, it did seem that I remembered her. Yet never in our lives could we have met."

"It's impossible, indeed."

They stopped walking at the edge of the tiny waves. When Niffa held up her lantern, the light sparkled on the water as if to mirror the moon's road.

"There be some truth here, bain't?" Niffa said at last.

"There is." Dallandra smiled, waiting.

No good lay in telling unready souls about the wheel of birth and death, but if Niffa asked, she would answer honestly. Niffa lowered the lantern and stood looking out at the dark mass of Citadel, rising from the lake.

"I do hope my mother's heart be not troubled," Niffa said. "But I doubt me if she did notice me gone, we had so many visitors."

So. She was not quite ready.

When they returned to the camp, Dallandra banked the fire with the bricks of sod that one of the men had cut earlier.

She let Niffa have the lean-to and showed her how to wrap her blanket efficiently around herself. She put her own bedroll by the banked fire and lay down, hoping that it wouldn't rain during the night. In the dark she could hear Niffa squirming around, trying to get comfortable whilst fully dressed on hard ground. If she's going to ride with the Westfolk, Dallandra thought, she'd best get used to it. Then she fell straight asleep.

Only to wake to the sound of a scream in what seemed but a moment later, but silver dawn was flooding the east with light. She sat up, unwrapping her blanket. The scream, a dark throaty male voice shrieking in full terror, rang out again. Dallandra shoved her blankets back and leapt to her feet. A quick glance at the camp showed her that most of the men were just waking, swearing and reaching for weapons. Most, but not all—some while earlier Vantalaber had taken a leather bucket and gone to the well to draw water. So, apparently, had one of the Gel da'Thae men, who by the time Dalla fully woke had stopped screaming and was grovelling on his knees in front of the utterly surprised Van.

"Dalla!" he called out in Elvish. "This Mera's gone daft!"

"No," Dallandra called back. "He thinks you're a god."

As Dallandra ran for the well, Niffa caught up with her. The rest of the Gel da'Thae came running from their camp. As soon as they got close enough to see the elves clearly, they all began shouting; most fell to their knees, some even prostrated themselves, hiding their faces in their manes of hair. When the elven men started to laugh, Dallandra snarled them into silence.

"I know it looks like a jest," she said, "but it's deadly serious to them."

Walking slowly from the Gel da'Thae camp came a tall person covered with green tattoos and wearing a leather cap that seemed to hide a hairless head. Rather than screaming, this person paused, arms folded across chest, to consider the tableau near the well. Another, much like the first, hovered uncertainly behind. Both wore white-cloth garments, falling just above the knee, that might have been long shirts or short dresses.

"That be Meer's mother," Niffa said. "Lady Zatcheka."

"My thanks!" Dallandra spoke in Deverrian. "I truly couldn't tell if she were woman or man."

With one hand raised, palm out in the sign of peace, Dallandra slowly walked forward. Niffa accompanied her, but she waved cheerfully to Zatcheka.

"There be no jeopard here!" Niffa called out. "This be my master."

At that Zatcheka came to meet them, but cautiously, gesturing for the other woman to stay back. The elven men stood on their side of the well, while the Gel da'Thae men crouched or knelt on theirs. A few feet apart Zatcheka and Dallandra stopped, considering each other in the brightening light.

"You be the children of the gods," Zatcheka said, and her voice shook. "Come ye back to claim your broken heritage?"

"We come in peace," Dallandra said. "And though we are the children of the gods, we are no more so than you and yours. We are born, we die, and in between we rejoice or suffer just as you do."

Zatcheka thought for a long moment, glancing around her at the men of her kind, crouched immobile, waiting, some staring at her as if begging her to decipher this dangerous situation for them.

"Your son Meer taught me much," Dallandra went on, "about the Gel da'Thae and your ways. I swear to you, we mean you no harm, and we want no tribute or slavery from you. No more do we fear you, because Meer taught us that at the heart we share many things."

Again Zatcheka thought this through.

"What shall we call you?" Zatcheka said at last. "If not children of the gods?"

"The Westfolk," Dallandra said. "The men of Deverry call us that, because we live to the west of them, but it will do."

"I see." Zatcheka hesitated, then made some decision with a firm nod. "Whoever you are, I think me you did come here timely, like, if you would be friends."

"My apprentice told me about the Horsekin."

"Then you did hear the worst of it."

"I can tell you worse than your worst. I was at the siege of Cengarn, when the Horsekin tried to take one of the Slavers' cities. It was a gruesome thing."

Zatcheka let out her breath in a sharp hiss.

"We would be friends, indeed," Dallandra went on, "if we're going to make a stand against such as them."

"Give me leave to speak to my people."

"Of course."

Zatcheka turned and began to speak in a clear, firm voice. Although Dallandra could understand but one word of it, "Westfolk," she could hear the authority in it, the words of a woman who expected to be obeyed. Sure enough, the Gel da'Thae men first listened, then sat back on their heels to look at those they'd thought gods. Some smiled, a few laughed, and at length they all rose, bowing to Dallandra. The elven men they regarded pleasantly enough. Zatcheka turned back to Dallandra.

"Shall we let our people go about their morning?"

"By all means," Dallandra said. "But shall you and I talk more?"

"Such would gladden my heart."

Zatcheka turned, clapped her hands together twice, and called out a few words in her language. The Gel da'Thae bowed, then hurried off, back to their camp. Dallandra turned and waved to Prince Dar, who'd been watching all this with his arms crossed tight over his chest. He nodded to acknowledge her, then called out in Elvish, telling his men to disperse. Dallandra waited until the Westfolk men had all gone back to camp.

"Niffa?" Dallandra said. "You'd best go tell your mother where you've been. Lady Zatcheka and I have much to talk about."

Jahdo woke when the sky was just turning gold with sunrise. For a moment he lay still and luxuriated in the knowledge that he was lying in his own bed, in his own chamber, listening to his own brother snoring nearby. Ambo was sleeping curled beside his head, and Tek-Tek had draped herself across his chest. He picked her up and laid her next to Ambo, got a nip for his pains, then rolled out of bed on the other side. Niffa had never slept in her bed. He sat looking at her empty mattress, then shrugged and got up. He could guess that she'd stayed at the elven camp.

After he dressed, he leaned onto the windowsill and looked out. By craning his neck just right he could get a glimpse of the lake over the houses on the next street down. Home. He really was home. The smell of cooking porridge finally drove him to dress and leave the view. Out in the big room he found a rumpled-looking Niffa, finishing the last of a bowl of porridge at the table while Dera stirred the iron pot at the hearth. Lael was just coming in the door with two buckets of water.

"Good morrow, all," Jahdo said. "Ah, Mam, it be so good to see you there and smell your cooking!"

Dera laughed and waved the long spoon in his direction.

"Never did I think to hear anyone praise my skill at the hearth! It be good to see you in your rightful place, too."

"But your voice, lad!" Lael said, grinning. "You sound hoarse as a frog in winter."

"No doubt, Da. I did talk more last night than I've done in all the rest of my life."

Jahdo sat down next to his sister with a sigh of contentment. Home. At last he could put all the strange and horrible things he'd seen behind him—or so he hoped. Lael emptied the buckets into the big terra-cotta jar by the hearth, then set them down.

"I do be surprised to see you here," Jahdo said to Niffa.

"Well, I did want to let Mam know where I spent the night past."

Dera said nothing, but Jahdo noticed her giving the porridge a slap and a hard stir in the pot. Behind her back Lael sighed with a shake of his head, then came over to the table and sat down.

"I'll be going back later," Niffa went on. "I'd best collect my things here first."

Dera was concentrating on scooping out the porridge.

She set a bowl down in front of Lael first, then Jahdo, and returned to the hearth.

"I did hear last night about your man," Jahdo said to Niffa. "It does sadden my heart. I did count Demet a friend."

"My thanks. I do believe I'll mourn him the rest of my life."

Jahdo pushed out what he meant to be a reassuring smile, then devoted himself to his porridge. He had seen so much death in the past year that he'd thought himself hardened, but his sister's grief cut him nonetheless. Dera brought her own bowl to the table and sat down. For a while they ate in a subdued silence.

"It gladdens my heart to see you safe," Dera said finally. "Ai! I feel such pity for that poor Gel da'Thae woman, losing her sons."

All at once Jahdo realized that he had a task to do, no matter how much he wanted to bask at his family hearth forever. He laid his spoon down in his bowl and stood up.

"Mam, do forgive me," he said, "but it be needful that I run an errand. There be somewhat I carry with me that does belong to Lady Zatcheka."

"Well, have you not the whole long day for errands?" Dera said. "You've not finished your breakfast."

"Dera, hush!" Lael raised one large hand flat for silence. "I think me our Jahdo do know his own concerns best."

Dera sucked her lips into a scowl, but she said nothing more. As he hurried into the bedchamber, Jahdo felt that he just might burst from pride. His father trusted his judgment. While he knew himself not yet a man, he realized that in some important way, he was no longer a mere boy.

A hot sun woke Rhodry some while after dawn. He threw off his unnecessary blanket and lay naked on the grass, contemplating the clear sky. The night before, he and Arzosah had made a rough camp on this hilltop where, as she remarked, they'd have a bit of a view. Behind them rose the dark-timbered flanks of the high mountains, coiffed in white, while in front of their camp the grassy slope led down to the valley below. When he sat up he could see Cerr Cawnen as a circle of turquoise lake among house shapes, wreathed in mist like a city of ghosts.

"You're awake," Arzosah said.

"I am, and I gather you are too."

The dragon yawned for an answer, revealing her enormous grey tongue and fangs the size of sword blades. She was lying some feet away, comfortably curled with her tail lapped over her front paws.

"Do you want to hunt again?" Rhodry said. "Or shall we just go down?"

"I'm still full from last night. That cow was delicious."

"I don't want to know about it. The farmers are going to start badgering me for cattle lwdd if you keep this up. Why don't you just eat the deer? There's plenty of them around here."

"I get tired of venison. A lady likes a little treat now and again."

Rhodry got up and dressed, ate what was left of his bread and cheese, then rolled up his blankets. By the time he had her harnessed and ready to go, the sun had climbed a handbreadth above the horizon. The town would be awake, no doubt, and people out on the streets.

"I hope Dalla got a chance to warn everyone about you," he said.

"They've all seen me before," Arzosah said. "And it's not like I'm going to eat any of them, after all. They haven't angered me or suchlike."

"Well, once they know that, no doubt they'll feel a good bit better."

"You're laughing at me!"

"Am not."

"Humph! You're a fine one to talk about cattle raids. I've seen your Deverry lords close up now, and there's no difference twixt me and them."

"What? Come now!"

"Well, your lordship sits in his hall all day or rides out

and watches the farmers work, and then he steals some of their food. If they tried to stop him, he'd kill them. Just like me, except the lords aren't even beautiful like I am, and there's rather a lot more of them, too."

"Here! It's not stealing. The gods have ordained—"

"Oh indeed? You mean, the priests say that the gods have ordained it, but the priests know which side their bread is buttered on. They steal some of the farmers' food themselves. Can you imagine a priest standing up in one of your courts and announcing that Bel thinks the lords should raise their own food like the farmers do?"

"But the lords have their place. They protect their people."

"From what? Other lords, that's what. If there were none of you, they wouldn't need any of you. Just like here in the Rhiddaer."

Rhodry found himself without a thing to say. Arzosah curled a paw and smugly considered her claws.

"Shall we be going?" he said at last.

"As soon as you admit I've won."

"Huh. I'll admit there's some justice in what you say, and that's all."

"It will do. For now."

Arzosah stretched out her neck and lowered one shoulder, and he swung himself up onto the saddle pad of her harness. Once he was securely aboard, she stretched out her wings and trotted off, bunching her muscles and springing into the air with a few hard wing strokes that took them well clear of the hillside. She allowed herself to glide, spiralling down in long loops while below Cerr Cawnen grew steadily larger. He could see the outer ring of walls, and the untidy town clustering around the lake, while out in the middle of open water Citadel rose with its burden of trees and buildings, whitewashed wood or pale stone, gleaming in the bright morning. As they swooped lower he realized that the lakeshore town extended out into the lake, built up on pilings and tiny islands that, he suspected, were man-made. Steam rose from the warm water, carrying with it the ripe stench of town life.

"Strange place," Rhodry called out.

"It is," Arzosah shouted back. "It's a fire mountain."

"What? You mean a fire mountain made it?"

"No, I mean it is a fire mountain. The corpse of one that blew its head off. But the water's warm, so there must be life way down below somewhere."

They swept down, circling around Citadel, and Rhodry found himself remembering the volcano where he'd trapped Arzosah, and all the lore about volcanoes and dragons both that Enj, his partner in that odd enterprise, had told him as well. He could see that Citadel rose sharply from the water on one side while on the other it sloped gently down—the remains of a cone, he supposed, when the mountain had exploded through a side vent. The land of blood and fire, he thought. That's where we are, the far north, just as old Othara explained to me.

Lower and lower they flew, and at last he could make out the boulders and the remains of some stone structure among trees high on Citadel's cliffs. Nearby, on the plaza, they could see townsfolk, many of whom were looking up and pointing at the sky. He leaned over and yelled to Arzosah.

"Right there! What looks like a roof!"

"I see it!"

She banked her wings, dropped, extended them, curled, and landed lightly on the flat stones among the boulders. Distantly they could hear screaming and shouting—from the crowd on the plaza, no doubt.

"Ah, what a welcome!" Arzosah said. "You'd best leave my harness on, Rori. Let them believe I'm tame."

When the dragon began circling over the town, Dallandra and Zatcheka were walking along the lakeshore. Behind them followed a pair of Zatcheka's guards, each with a ceremonial staff in one hand and a ferocious scowl on his face, which they turned upon any children or dogs foolish enough to come too near. The two women talked around the edges of important matters, exchanging bits of information about the Horsekin while never touching directly on the situation in the Rhiddaer, but even so,

Zatcheka was as wary as a cat walking along a kennel fence and eyeing the hounds below.

"You know," Dallandra said at last, "your son thought I was a demigod at first, too, but he soon came to realize that I was flesh and blood like him."

"It be very kind of you to try to set me at ease. I do believe you, mind," Zatcheka said. "Never think that I would call your words untrue."

"Oh, I wasn't worried about that. I know it must be a hard thing to get used to, after believing your whole life that—"

One of the guards shrieked. The two women spun around to find both men waving their staves in the general direction of the sky. Overhead Arzosah soared, seemingly the size of a big silver owl at her distance, but she spiraled ever closer.

"Ah, it's Rhodry," Dallandra said. "The man I was telling you about."

"He be a mazrak of great power, if he ken the taking of dragon form."

"Nah, nah, nah, I'm sorry! He's not the dragon. He tamed her, and he's riding her. That's all."

"All?" Zatcheka gave her a sickly look that was perhaps meant to be a smile.

"I'll introduce you, and you'll see what I mean," Dallandra said. "We'd best go over to Citadel."

When the dragon dropped out of sight to land, they hurried back to the camp, but there they found Jahdo, standing outside Dallandra's tent, his hands full of charms and talismans, dangling from a pair of leather thongs. Zatcheka considered him with a thoughtful frown.

"Be this the lad who did attend upon my Meer?"

"It is, truly," Dallandra said. "I wonder what he's got."

With a shout Jahdo trotted over to meet them. They all stood just outside the camp down near the lakeshore, while the two guards kept would-be eavesdroppers away.

"Dalla?" he said. "These things do belong to the lady Zatcheka. I mean, they did belong to her sons, and I did save them, and I wager she'll be a-wanting them."

When Zatcheka saw the thongs and their many small

burdens, she sobbed once, then held out her hands. Jahdo bowed to her and laid the thongs carefully on her palms.

"The one in your left hand, my lady? That I did take from Thavrae's body as he lay on the battlefield. The one in your right—" Jahdo's voice dropped sharply, he gulped hard and went on. "That did belong to Meer, and he were slain by a coward's arrow when the Horsekin were a-sieging our walls."

"The blessings of all the gods be upon you." Zatcheka tipped back her enormous head and howled, a long high note that seemed to stick in the wall like a spear. The guards turned, saw the talismans in her hands, and joined her in a second long howl of keening.

"It aches my heart that I did bring you grief," Jahdo went on. "But Meer, he did tell me that there be a need on any man who finds such things to bring them back to the mother who bore the slain."

"You've not brought me grief, young Jahdo, but joy, for if the gods guide me safely home, I shall be able to hang these in the temple, where they belong." Tears welled in her eyes. "And then their souls will rest at last."

"May peace wrap them in soft arms," Dallandra said. "You have my heartfelt sympathy for your loss."

"My lady?" Jahdo bowed to Zatcheka. "I do miss Meer powerful bad. He did treat me like a son, not a servant. I'll not be forgetting him, not if I live to see a hundred winters."

"My thanks to you for that speaking." Zatcheka was staring at the talismans in her hands.

"There be another thing," Jahdo went on. "The white horse over there? See you him, tethered with the others? His name be Bahkti, and he did belong to Meer."

"In truth, the horse be mine." Zatcheka looked up, her face so still that it might have been painted stone. "I did let him but borrow Bahkti for his journey. But my thanks for his safe return. Later, young Jahdo, I think me I shall find a little gift for you to show my gratitude."

"I should be honored, my lady, but truly, I expect naught. Meer was my friend."

For a moment Zatcheka's mask of stone seemed on the verge of shattering, but she spoke in a level voice.

"Here, mazrak, let me not stay you. There be a need on me to remain here with my grief, but truly, you'd best give the townsfolk balm for their fears of that beast."

"True spoken," Dallandra said. "We'll talk more later, if that pleases you. Jahdo, come show me how to get over to the island."

Since Dallandra had never paddled a boat in her life, she was more than thankful that Jahdo rowed them across. Through the mists drifting across the water she saw Citadel looming above them, closer and closer until at last they ran aground at the sandy shore. While Jahdo beached the coracle properly she stood looking up the winding path that led twixt white buildings to the summit. She could hear distant shouting.

"I hope they don't try to hurt Arzosah," she remarked. "Not that they could, but if they provoked her—"

"My people, they be not stupid," Jahdo said. "And Werda does live right nearby the plaza. She'll be holding them off."

"She's your Spirit Talker? Niffa mentioned that name."

"She is that."

After a long climb uphill that left Dallandra panting for breath, they reached the stone-paved plaza and found themselves in the midst of a small crowd of townsfolk, all huddled together. Some of the men carried staves and flails, but they seemed in no hurry to use them. At the far side, where worked stone buildings ended in a tumble of boulders, stood a tall woman with grey hair that hung free to her waist. She was wearing a white cloak thrown back from her shoulders, and she carried a wood staff, bound here and there along its length with flat silver rings—Dallandra could see them winking in the sun as the woman moved.

"That be Werda," Jahdo said. "Let's join her. I doubt me if anyone will mind our pushing in front of them."

Indeed, the crowd seemed more than willing to let Jahdo and Dallandra get between them and the dragon. They worked their way through the muttering townsfolk, then jogged across the open stretch of plaza. By then Werda had climbed a flat-topped boulder and stood, staff in hand, looking toward the crowd. Dallandra saw Niffa, standing on the paving stones just below the Spirit Talker's rocky perch. She could just get a glimpse of Arzosah, sitting behind the boulders, and Rhodry, standing in front of her in an oddly protective stance—just as if Arzosah weren't capable of tearing this crowd to shreds, Dallandra thought.

"Fellow citizens!" Werda called out. "Listen to me, if it pleases you."

The crowd began to hush itself in a murmur like sighs. When most had fallen silent, Werda continued.

"I have spoken to this dragon. She does have words, she be no mindless beast. She may therefore be reasoned with, and truly, she did assure me that she wishes none of us the slightest harm."

The crowd nodded, murmuring in some relief among themselves. Jahdo stood on tiptoe to whisper to Dallandra.

"Then Arzosah does lie a little bit," the boy said. "We all do know she'd gobble Raena down if the gods did but give her a chance."

"True spoken," Dallandra whispered. "But we don't need to tell anyone that right now."

Werda held up her silver-touched staff again, and the crowd once again fell silent.

"Go now about the business of your day," Werda called out, "as I shall do with mine. Fear not! If you wish, come greet her and hear her speak with your own ears."

Many of the townsfolk called out their thanks; others clapped or waved. Slowly, talking among themselves, they began to scatter across the plaza or head back to the downhill path. Since no one seemed to be taking Werda's offer to come meet the dragon, Dallandra and Jahdo hurried over to pay their respects to the Spirit Talker, who with Niffa's help was clambering down from the rocks. Arzosah waddled up the last few feet to the plaza as well. As always Dallandra marvelled at how awkward she was on the ground in contrast to her ease and beauty in the air.

"Dalla!" Rhodry called out. "All's well on our end. How have things been going here?"

"Quiet so far, and my thanks to every god for that."

"Quiet be a lovely thing, truly." Werda joined them. "You must be Dallandra. Young Niffa has told me many a pleasant thing about you."

"My thanks, then," Dallandra said. "And I'm truly glad to meet you. There's rather a lot we need to discuss."

Werda's house stood just downhill from the plaza at the end of a path made of wooden steps, some way from the ruined temple and right beside a little shrine to the gods of the lake. To talk in privacy Werda took Dallandra and Niffa into her house, but Jahdo stayed outside with Rhodry and of course the dragon, who would never have managed to squeeze herself inside even if she had been invited. The shrine itself was a simple thing: four stone pillars held up a wood roof that sheltered a roughly worked block of stone. Bunches of yellow wildflowers lay on this plain altar, and a scatter of little green stones. In front of the shrine stood a wood bench. Jahdo and Rhodry sat there, while Arzosah spread herself out on the cobbles to take the sun.

"Where's Dar and his men?" Rhodry said.

"Camped down by the lake," Jahdo said. "I did see Princess Carra this morning, and she did tell me that the prince be powerful eager to leave here and go back to the grasslands."

"No doubt. But I think me we'd all best stay till this matter of the alliance is settled. If the Horsekin take Cerr Cawnen, it'll be so much the worse for Deverry."

"I'd not thought of that. I—wait. Here comes Verrarc, and we'd best hold our tongues around him."

With a forced smile Councilman Verrarc came striding up to them. He hadn't slept very well, apparently; the dark shadows under his eyes stood out against the pale of his skin.

"Good morrow, Jahdo," he said. "I did wish to thank you for those splendid tales you told last night."

"Well, my thanks. I did feel as if I were stumbling over my own tongue by the end of it, and my throat be a bit sore this morning."

"No doubt."

"And yet I've not told you all of it," Jahdo went on. "I do feel that there be much I've forgotten, or mayhap knew not the meaning of."

Verrarc stepped back with a toss of his head, then forced out a smile.

"All in good time, no doubt." The councilman glanced at Rhodry. "We've not met, good sir."

"So we've not," Rhodry said. "My name is Rhodry from Aberwyn."

"And I be Verrarc, councilman to this town."

The two men shook hands briefly, but it seemed to Jahdo that they would rather have challenged each other.

"It's a strange thing." Verrarc looked away absently. "The world's a cursed sight wider than ever I thought, and here every summer have I ridden into Dwarveholt to trade and suchlike. Tell me somewhat, lad. Think you that you'll find this town tedious from now on?"

Jahdo was about to deny any such thing, but all at once he wondered how he would feel when the relief of being home wore off. Rhodry was watching him with a slight smile that struck him as a challenge.

"Well now," Jahdo said at last. "I truly hope I'll be happy to stay in Cerr Cawnen all my born days, but I do wonder."

"So do I," Verrarc said. "I'm minded to make you an offer, you see. You ken a fair bit about this world of ours, and there be a need on me to take an apprentice soon, someone to learn the trading."

Jahdo stood up, shoving his hands in his pockets, to gain a little time. His first thought was that he was being offered something wonderful; his second, that perhaps Verrarc was trying to buy his silence; and his third, that perhaps Verrarc intended to murder him on the road when they were far from town.

"Do think well on it," Verrarc said. "It'll be needful for us to consult with your mother and suchlike before you can say me yea or nay."

"You do have my thanks, Councilman," Jahdo said. "I promise you that I'll do some hard thinking about your offer."

"And no doubt your father will want to do some of his

own. No rush, lad, no rush for your decision." Verrarc glanced away, paused, then waved to someone up on the plaza. "It be old Hennis, summoning me. I'll just be off, then."

Verrarc turned and climbed up the stairs leading to the plaza. Jahdo stood watching him make his way over to the elderly councilman.

"You look surprised," Rhodry said.

"I am that. Verrarc did his best to send me off to my death with Meer. Though—wait—truly, I do him an injustice. He did save my life, more like, now that I know the truth of it."

"He what?"

"He did save my life by sending me away. I did tell Jill this tale, but mayhap not you. Last summer it was, and I was picking herbs in the water meadows, and I did stumble across Verrarc with this woman, and she did demand he kill me. I think now that she were Raena, for who else would have been working evil near our town? And Verrarc did refuse. He ensorceled me instead."

"That shows he has some heart left, then."

"Truly. And—wait! The talisman!"

"Now what?"

"I did find a little silver disk in the grass that day. I knew not what it might be, back then. But it were a talisman, just like the ones Meer showed me. I gave it to Tek-Tek for her hoard, but Jill did say it were important."

"Then we'd best go fetch it. Are you sure that woman was Raena?"

"Well, not truly. She were all bundled in a cloak, and I do remember seeing her sweat and wondering why she did wear it, but her face was hard to see."

Rhodry swore in Elvish.

"What be so wrong, Rori?"

"I was hoping you could testify that it was Raena in a court of law."

"A court of law?"

"Of course. Jahdo, think! Raena's a traitor to your people. She'd turn you all over to the Horsekin in a heartbeat if she could. We need evidence that will convince the council no matter how hard Verrarc fights to save her."

"Ye gods," Jahdo whispered. "Truly—she were there at the siege! By those hells of yours, Rori! I do be as big a lack-wit as poor Magpie. Not till this very day did I remember that. Why, I wonder?"

"I don't know, but I'd wager a fair bit of coin that it's all part of Verrarc's ensorcelment. No wonder he went so stiff when you spoke of leaving things out of your tales."

Jahdo turned sharply and looked in the direction that Verrarc had taken—no sign of him now.

"Verrarc does have dweomer?"

"He must," Rhodry said. "You'd best talk with Dalla about this."

"True spoken!"

The familiar plaza, empty now under the bright sun, seemed somehow small and strange. Jahdo stood for a long moment, looking around at one of the places that had meant home in his memories. He was beginning to realize that, in truth, he had changed, and irrevocably.

"Here," Rhodry said, "are you all right?"

"I am, my apologies. Just thinking."

"That's a good idea in times like these. But let's go steal Tek-Tek's treasure before you forget again."

"She'll not like that. I'd best find a trinket to give her in return."

"I've got a coin or two. I'll trade her."

With the talisman safe in his coin pouch, Rhodry left Arzosah sleeping in the sun on the ruins of the temple and went down to the lakeshore. Since he'd been raised in Aberwyn, boats held no mysteries for him, and he paddled across fast to the welter of houses on their pilings and crannogs. By asking people here and there for directions, he found his way to the town commons and Daralanteriel's camp. The prince's guard were sitting out in the grass near their horses and squabbling over dice games, while the prince himself paced up and down by the lakeshore. At his throat the gold chain of Ranadar's Eye glinted in the sun, but he'd tucked the actual pendant inside his tunic. There was no sign of Carra and the baby, but Rhodry noticed that the tent-flap hung closed.

"Ah, there you are," Daralanteriel said in Elvish. "Is everything going well up on Citadel?"

"As well as it can be," Rhodry said. "The townsfolk seem to have taken the dragon in their stride. Dalla and the local priestess have shut themselves up for a talk."

"What about Raena?"

"She's not back yet. She may not have been heading for Cerr Cawnen when we saw her. What if she's bolted? If she's off among the Meradan, we'll never be able to fetch her back."

"True, but if she has to live among them for the rest of her life I'll count her well punished. It creeped my flesh, seeing Dalla talking with that wretched Mera woman."

"Well, here, now!" Rhodry made his voice sound as quietly reasonable as he could. "You remember Meer, don't you? He was a man like any other. It behooves us to treat his mother—"

"I never trusted that hairy bastard. How do you know he wasn't sending messages to the Meradan sieging Cengarn?"

"Why would they have killed him if he was their spy?"

"Well, maybe they didn't trust him either. By the Dark Sun! How can you expect me to tolerate these people? Don't you remember that they wanted to kill my Carra and the baby both?"

"Well, that's true, isn't it? But those were Horsekin, not Gel da'Thae."

"I don't care about fine distinctions."

"Only the Horsekin worship Alshandra. She's the one who wanted Carra dead. Well, in truth it was the baby she wanted slain. I doubt if Carra mattered to her one way or the other."

"I don't find that particularly comforting."

"Well, try! The Gel da'Thae wish no harm to you or yours."

Dar set his mouth in a tight line and looked away, glaring at the lake. At his temple one vein throbbed, and he laid a hand on his tunic, rubbing the pendant through the cloth. He was, Rhodry supposed, thinking about the deaths of his royal ancestors.

"Ah well," Rhodry said at last. "Promise me one thing? Don't do anything rash."

"Anything murderous, you mean?"

"Just that."

For a moment Dar scowled down at the grass, then he shrugged and looked up.

"Very well," Dar said. "You have my word on it."

"That's good enough for me."

And yet Rhodry felt trouble gathering. Dar had, after all, been raised for a revenge that had seemed impossible to gain, out on the grasslands. Now here the ancient enemies were, close at hand.

It was late in the day when Raena finally did return, though not in any way that Verrarc might have expected. The councilman had gone down to the walls to discuss with Sergeant Gart the matter of raising and arming a larger militia. Together they climbed a wooden ladder to the catwalks that ran just below the top of the stonework. On folded arms Verrarc leaned onto the stone and looked west across farmland, pale green with new-sprouted grain.

"One good thing about this town," Gart said. "We'll never lack for water no matter how long they besiege us."

"True spoken. With enough food stored up, I think me we could hold off an army. If of course our men have the weaponry."

"Just so. That does trouble my heart. We'd best be taking a good hard look at what we've got in the armory."

Verrarc nodded his agreement. Distantly he heard shouting, and as the sound grew louder he and Gart turned toward the source: the south gate. A sudden horn rang out.

"That be the alarum!" Gart said abruptly. "We'd best hurry."

They set off around the wall as fast as the rickety catwalk would allow—a little less than a brisk walk.

"We'd best get this shored up," Verrarc said.

"Cursed right!" Gart said. "There'll be a need on us to move the men round quickly. Well, if the worst happens."

The news met them halfway when Kiel came striding along from the south gate.

"Horsekin, Sergeant," Kiel blurted. "They do claim they come in peace, but we did shut the gates nonetheless, for there be about a score of them. Uh, Councilman, I ken not how to say this graciously. Your wife be with them, riding at their head bold as brass."

For a moment Verrarc could neither think nor speak. He felt so cold that he was sure his face must have blanched, right there for his men to see. In his mind he could hear Zatcheka's voice, sharp with anger: a human woman at that, come to preach the false goddess. With a shake of his head he forced himself under control.

"It be time I did give her a good talking to," Verrarc said as briskly as he could manage. "Let's go see what silliness she has in hand."

Gart and Kiel were looking at him—oddly, though he couldn't quite read their expressions. He pushed past Kiel and led the way along the catwalks to the gate. Other militiamen met him there, all talking at once. He yelled at them to hold their tongues, then leaned over the wall.

Sure enough, down below, drawn up in tidy pairs, a full score of tall Horsekin warriors stood beside their massive bay or chestnut horses, eighteen hands, some of them, with heavy legs and shaggy fetlocks. At the rear of their line a high-sided mule cart waited, loaded with sacks of supplies and driven by a human man.

At the head stood Raena, dressed in men's clothing and holding the reins of a beautiful grey palfrey, and beside her, with no horse, the strangest Horsekin Verrarc had ever seen. He wore nothing but rags, though a lot of those: three or four tunics of different colors, all ripped and threadbare, piled one on top the other but barely keeping him decent even so. His feet were misshapen masses of calluses and swollen flesh, for he wore no boots. His huge mane of grey hair had not been washed or combed for entirely too long, and his weatherbeaten face sported patterns of scars instead of tattoos. While he waited he leaned on a heavy, long staff of some dark wood, decorated with little metal disks and feathers.

"Verro," Raena called out. "Why will they not let us in?"

At that the wild man raised his staff and grunted a few words, not that Verrarc could understand them.

"Rae!" He heard himself stammering. "What be you doing there?"

"Let us in, and I'll tell you!"

Verrarc turned around and called down to his men to open the gates. None of them moved. He looked at Gart and Kiel and saw mutiny in their eyes.

"Now here!" Verrarc snapped. "Think you we be so weak as all that? Cannot our men fend off a mere score of enemies? If not, we'd best surrender straightaway, but I never thought you both such cowards."

Kiel blushed scarlet. Gart turned away fast and yelled down, "Open the gates, lads! There be naught here that we can't best."

Verrarc went to the ladder and climbed down just as the gates finished squeaking open. He was about to step forward to greet Raena when he saw Dallandra, standing nearby on the green with her arms crossed over her chest and watching him, simply watching with no expression at all, but suddenly he felt like a thief caught with his hand in someone else's money box. For a moment he could neither move nor think, but Raena and the wild man came walking through the gates with their men and horses close behind. Dallandra turned on her heel and strode off, losing herself in a gathering crowd of townsfolk. Men came running with curious children close behind; dogs barked at the newcomers; women strolled up as well and began pulling children back out of the way.

"Come here, my love!" Raena called to Verrarc. She was smirking, her jaw tight with triumph. "I did bring you a peaceable emissary, Lord Kral of the White Bear tribe."

At this one of the warriors stepped forward, a beefy tall man with his waist-length dark hair held back from his face by an arrangement of gold combs. He wore a dirty cloth-of-gold surcoat over his tunic and leather trousers, and at his side hung a sword so long that he had to keep one hand on the hilt to tip it up and prevent it from dragging on the ground.

"Rakzan Kral," Raena said, "this be Councilman Verrarc."

"Honored," Kral grunted.

"Uh, my thanks."

Verrarc was painfully aware of the crowd around them. Some of the militiamen had joined the townsfolk. He felt as if their stares were so many knives, stabbing him and Raena both. The wild man, leaning on his staff, drew his share of ugly looks. This close Verrarc could smell his unwashed flesh and another stink as well—resinous woodsmoke, so pungent it seemed to emanate from his very being.

"We come," Kral went on, "to offer a treaty."

"Indeed? Well, this be interesting news, but truly, there's a need on you to deliver it to the whole council. I be but one of five, and on my own I may say naught."

"Fair enough. My men and I will wait. The priestess did tell us that there be ground where we may pitch our tents."

"The priestess?"

With another grunt Kral gestured at Raena. She caught Verrarc's expression and looked hastily away.

"Just so." Verrarc glanced around. The crowd had swelled and blocked the road. "If you'll follow me, there's a need on us to go that way." He pointed in the opposite direction from that in which Zatcheka's tents stood. "Round the lake a way here."

Kral turned away to give orders to his men. Verrarc was studying Raena, wondering just how furious she would have to make him before—before what? he asked himself. *You know too well you'll not cast her off.* A sudden yell caught him completely off guard—a child shrieked, dogs started barking, a man screamed. Verrarc and Kral both spun around in time to see the wild man grab a little girl by the arm and haul her into the air one-handed. With the other he shook his staff at a pair of big tan hounds who rushed barking to the rescue.

Kral yelled two words in the Horsekin language, but too late. Blue fire sprang from the staff and streamed through the air. The lead dog yelped and flipped over backwards to fall howling and convulsing onto the ground. The other charged, the fire exploded again, and both dogs dropped dead with blood gushing from their mouths and eyes. The child was screaming and kicking. Her mother kept rushing forward, and her husband kept grabbing her back. Yelling at the top of his lungs Kral ran for the wild man. Just as the rakzan reached him, the wild man threw the child at the ground. Kral caught her barely in time.

When the sobbing mother rushed forward, Kral handed her the child while he stammered an apology. The crowd began muttering and pushing closer. Off to one side, the wild man stood laughing softly, a mutter under his breath. Verrarc looked round and saw that Kiel and Gart had drawn their swords.

"Stop!" Verrarc strode forward. "There be no need for steel! Get the crowd to move back, Sergeant! Do it now!"

A white-faced Gart followed orders, and Kiel followed him. Other militiamen stepped out of the crowd and helped form a protective ring around their unwelcome guests. Kral bowed to Verrarc.

"A thousand apologies! We will camp outside your walls."

"That would be best, truly," Verrarc said. "What—why did he seize that child?"

"She insulted him, or so he tells me." In between the lines of tattooing, Kral's face had gone pale, bringing the pattern into high relief. "There be naught I can do to control him, Councilman. He be one of Alshandra's Elect."

Verrarc had no time to ask him to explain. Even though the rest of the town watch had come to help Gart and Kiel, the crowd was refusing to move. Angry faces, bitter voices— some of the men had sticks, others had picked up stones. They had seen too much today; too many terrors had come to them: first the dragon, then the mysterious Westfolk, and finally this dangerous madman and the Horsekin.

"Get your people out, Rakzan," Verrarc said. "For their sake."

Waving his arms and yelling, Kral strode back to the warriors, who began backing and turning their horses. The cart, mercifully, still stood outside on the road. As soon as it became clear that the Horsekin were moving outside the gates, the crowd of citizens began to calm. Gart kept urging, Kiel kept talking, the militiamen slowly moved forward, and at last the citizens began to disperse, walking away slowly, muttering to themselves or shaking the occasional fist in the wild man's general direction. Through all of this Raena had stood off to one side and smirked. Verrarc crossed to her and grabbed her by both arms.

"What be all this?" he snarled. "Ye gods, woman! Who is that filthy warlock?"

"Just that, a warlock indeed. His name be Nag-arshad."

"He may call himself Lord Filth for all I care. You do owe me many a truth, Rae. And I'm taking you home where you may tell them."

She started to speak, then shrugged and pulled her arms free of his lax grasp.

"Move, woman!"

She shrugged again but turned and began walking toward the lakeshore. Verrarc followed close behind, and as they hurried through the scattering crowd, he noticed how all the townsfolk stopped to stare at her with hatred in their eyes.

When she'd left Verrarc at the gates, Dallandra had not gone far. She found a quiet spot near the wall, turned her face to the stone to shut out distractions, and called to Evandar. In her mind she pictured his country, gone dead and brown; she imagined an image of herself there, walking by the leaden river, and she imagined that image calling his name. When she felt an answering touch of his mind, she banished the images and came fully back to the grass and stone of Cerr Cawnen just in time to hear the child shrieking in terror.

Caught at the back of the crowd as she was, she could barely see what was happening, much less reach the scene in time to stop it. Once the crowd began to break up and clear off, she could finally make her way back to the gates. By then the rakzan had managed to get all his men back onto the road outside and the mazrak with them. She only caught a glimpse of him, striding along barefooted and waving his staff above his head as if in celebration. Two young townsmen were carrying the dead dogs away. One of them was weeping.

Verrarc and Raena stood arguing a few paces off. Dallandra was shocked by the change in her. During last summer's siege she'd managed to get a few glimpses of a plump, sleek Raena. Now she'd turned gaunt. Her face and neck showed every tendon and muscle, it seemed, just because her skin was stretched so tight over the bone. Before Dallandra could make up her mind to confront them, Verrarc had grabbed Raena by the arm and hauled her off, heading for the lakeshore.

"Let them be," Evandar murmured.

With a yelp Dallandra spun around. He had either materialized right there or appeared elsewhere and walked up so quietly she hadn't heard him—the latter, she supposed, since none of the townsfolk were paying him any attention.

"This is a bad omen and a worse outcome," Evandar said. "I'm tempted to blast that nasty-looking fellow into ashes and his Horsekin entourage with him."

"Please don't! The Horsekin would only send a bigger and nastier lot here to look for them."

"You speak the truth, so I shan't. But I fear for you, my love. Be on your guard, will you? Better yet, can you and the prince and the rest of you all move onto Citadel and camp near the dragon?"

"I doubt that. We'd have to bring Zatcheka and her people with us, and there's no grass for the horses and suchlike. I wish you could stay with us."

"So do I, but the iron aches my bones, or what would be my bones if I had any. At least there isn't iron binding the walls, but the weapons and such are bad enough."

"They must be, truly."

"And then there's the lake." Evandar sighed, suddenly melancholy. "It's not a running river, my love, but the water veils hang thick above it nonetheless. Should you scry in your body of light, please: Watch every move you make. The springs that feed it run deep, I suppose, and there's more raw power here than you'd think."

"Oh, don't worry about that! I'll stay on my guard. And

truly, I might need to scry on the etheric. Those Horse-kin—why are they here, do you know?"

"I don't. No doubt we'll find out soon enough."

"Sooner than we wanted, most like. That mazrak—Shaetano's not the power behind his magicks, is he?"

"Alas, no. I know not how, but our prophet of filth has true dweomer, my love. That was etheric fire he brought down with his staff. I do know that he's one of the wandering preachers who spread the story of the new goddess."

"I'll talk with Zatcheka. She might know more about these magicks."

"A good thought, that. And I'll be close by, never fear. The iron-touch isn't too bad up on the plaza, so I'll stay close to Rhodry and the dragon."

"Good. I think we're all going to need you."

"So do I." He laughed, a bitter little sound. "And now I've got to get out of here."

Evandar walked a few steps toward the gates. He seemed to melt first into glass, then a man-shaped puff of smoke, and finally, he was gone.

"Tell me, Rae! Tell me the truth and do so now!" Verrarc caught her by both wrists and hauled her close to face him. "That be where you did learn your magicks, bain't? From the Horsekin wizard and his filthy kind!"

"So what if I did?" Her voice wavered, and he could feel her body trembling against his. "Magicks be magicks, bain't? And who else might I find to teach me?"

They were standing in their bedchamber, an imperfect refuge with the servants just on the other side of the door and doubtless trying to hear every word of this quarrel. Verrarc made an effort to keep his voice down.

"Well, true spoken," he went on. "But Horsekin, Rae? I like not this talk of a treaty with such as them. What will it amount to? If we become their slaves now all peaceable-like, they won't burn our city? I'll wager it's no better terms than that."

"You do sound like that shrew Zatcheka!"

"Mayhap because she has the right of this thing." He gave

her a little shake. "You do know as well as I that the Horsekin, they be dangerous enemies and not much better allies."

"Well, they did become my allies, and always have they been fair to me!" With a sudden wrench she pulled her arms free of his grasp. "Without them, what would I be? Naught! They did save me from a drudge life and did call forth the magicks in my soul."

"So! I'm right, am I? And just where did you meet these ever-so-generous witchmen of yours?"

"There be much you know not." Raena smiled, but her cold eyes studied him. "And there's a need on me to hold my tongue on much."

Verrarc took two quick steps forward, grabbed her by the shoulders, and slammed her against the wall.

"The truth, Rae! I'll have the truth out of you and I'll have it now."

"What will you do, beat me?" She was panting for breath. "Your father's son, bain't you?"

Verrarc let her go, turned away, took two steps and burst into tears. He was aware of sitting down on the floor and sobbing, aware suddenly of her kneeling in front of him.

"Nah, nah, weep not!" Raena murmured. "Forgive me, my love! I did speak in fear alone."

The tears stopped. He wiped his face on his sleeve and looked up to find her leaning over him. He cleared his throat hard until at last he could speak.

"You did make me a bargain, Rae, and I did keep my half. I did delay the Deciding upon the Gel da'Thae alliance. In return, said you, there would be no more secrets."

"So I did." She winced and refused to look him in the eye. "Patience, my love. Just a few more days—"

"Here! Be you weaselling out of our bargain?"

"Not I!" Yet she hesitated a long moment before she finally looked at him. "Oh very well! Come with me to the temple. I shall summon Lord Havoc, and together we shall tell you anything you wish."

"What? If Werda—"

"Curse Werda! Surely she does have more than enough

to occupy her mind this day. Come with me, and you shall
have the truth."

"Good." Verrarc smiled at her. "That gladdens my heart."

As they were leaving the house, Verrarc remembered
the dragon. Was it still roosting on the ruins or had it gone
elsewhere? Although he thought of warning Raena, in the
end he said nothing, just as a bit of revenge for her lapsing
back into her secretive ways.

At the crest of Citadel they left the cobbled street and
walked along the dirt path that debouched between a pair
of huge boulders. In their shelter Verrarc paused to look
downhill. Below them in the trees stood the stone slabs of
the temple's broken roof. On the flat the dragon lazed, eyes
shut tight against the hot sun. Raena had apparently seen
it. She had crammed the palm of one hand into her mouth
to stifle a scream. She went dead-pale and began to tremble
so hard that Verrarc regretted his spite. When he tried to
put an arm around her shoulders, she jerked away from him
and stepped back fast into the shelter of the rocks. Tears ran
silently down her face.

"Ah Goddess!" Raena whispered. "Stop, Verro! We
dare not take one step farther."

"Indeed? They do tell me she be a tame dragon, no
threat to any of us here."

"Then they lie! Hush! There be a need on us to make a
quiet retreat."

Raena began edging away, her back to the safety of
stone. Verrarc followed, glancing back often, but Arzosah
was sleeping soundly, lulled no doubt by the warmth of the
day. Once they'd reached the cross street, Raena frankly
ran, pounding down the cobbles and gasping for breath.
Verrarc followed and caught her just outside the back gate
of his compound.

"Rae, Rae, what be so wrong?"

"She'll kill me, you dolt! That wyrm! That first day she
did fly over our town—remember you not? I did tell you
then. She does know me, and she hates me."

The world seemed to jerk under his feet. He was aware
of feeling cold and clammy all over, and for a moment he

wondered if he would vomit. Raena grabbed his arm and steadied him.

"Let's get inside," she whispered. "There we can talk."

When they returned to the compound, Verrarc sent Raena off to their bedroom to change into some proper clothes, then went into the kitchen, where as he'd expected he found the servants waiting for him without any pretense of working.

"It be a long time now since I've given you any leisure," Verrarc said. "I do know full well how your hearts must ache to be going about the town and talking with your friends ar d suchlike. Why not spend the rest of the day doing just that? My woman and I can find some cold meats or suchlike for a supper."

"My thanks," Korla said, yet she looked grim rather than happy. "Be you sure you'll fare well here?"

"Of course!" Verrarc forced a smile. "I be not a little lad."

Korla and Harl exchanged a brief glance. Magpie stood up, chewing on a corner of her dirty apron as she watched her grandmother.

"Ah well," Korla said at last. "It will be a good thing to walk about a bit. Come along, Maggi. We'll have a bit of sun."

"My thanks as well." Harl ducked his head in Verrarc's direction, then hurried out the back door.

When Verrarc returned to the bedchamber, he found Raena standing by the window in her underdress. The sun streaming in made the cloth glow around her gaunt body and washed her face with harsh light.

"You look ill," Verrarc said. "Be there a need on you to rest?"

"None." Raena turned away from the window and stood looking around the chamber. "Tell me somewhat. How long has this dragon infested the town? What did bring it here?"

"Strange things did happen whilst you were gone, and many a strange traveller did arrive. A party of men that call themselves Westfolk—"

Raena swore. For a moment Verrarc thought she was going to spit on the floor, but she stopped herself.

"They did bring Jahdo home," Verrarc went on. "There be two women with them as well."

"Dallandra be one of them?"

"She is. Here! How do you know these things?"

Raena flung herself into a chair and scowled at the far wall.

"Tell me, Rae. You did promise an end to secrets."

"Last summer it were, when I were off about Alshandra's work, I did meet that mincing scum of a woman. And this wyrm as well—blasphemers, all of them! They would deny that my lady be a true goddess. And one more rode in with them, I'll wager. Rhodry Maelwaedd, he who rides the dragon and be the foulest filth of them all."

"Who? There be a Rhodry from Aberwyn among them."

"He be the same."

"He did seem like a well-spoken man to me."

"You know him not, then. He too has sworn my death. He does blame me for the death of a friend of his, you see, but it were the will of my goddess, and none of my doing."

Verrarc felt himself turn cold.

"He'll not slay you here in my town," he growled. "Shall I call the watch and have him put under lock and chain?"

"You tempt me, my love." Raena smiled as delicately as if he'd offered her a plate of sweetmeats. "But do that, and the stinking wyrm will ramp and roar through the town."

Verrarc rubbed his sweaty face with both hands. Aside from Raena the only thing he loved in life was Cerr Cawnen, and now these strangers had brought danger beyond imagining. What should he do? He started to speak, then paused, considering her. She seemed to be suppressing a smile, and he found himself remembering how often she'd lied to him over the years.

"This be a grave thing," Verrarc said. "I'd best lay it before full council."

"Nah nah nah!" She rose from the chair. "I—uh—it were best to not have these lies about me told in public."

"Indeed?"

For a moment her gaze held his, then she looked away.

"The truth of it, Rae!"

"I did tell you the truth! Both Rhodry and the black dragon wish my death."

"Then why will you not let me call the council and decide what we may do to protect you?"

Raena turned away and walked over to the wooden chest at the foot of the bed, which he'd given her for her clothing and suchlike. She rummaged through it for a moment, then brought out a dagger in a worn leather sheath. When she held it up, he recognized the three silver balls on the pommel.

"Rhodry from Aberwyn does have a dagger like that on his belt," Verrarc said.

"Just so." Raena drew the dagger to show him the blade. "That little wyvern graved there? It be the device of his friend, the one who was slain. It were a man in Alshandra's service who did slay him, not me, I swear it!"

On this point Verrarc was inclined to believe her. After all, how could a woman of her stature have killed a fighting man? She sheathed the dagger, laid it back in the chest, then closed the lid.

"Well, then," Verrarc said, "why not convene the council and have this matter out in open court? If you be innocent, then this Rhodry had best stop laying false charges against you."

"You forget the wyrm." Raena laid a dramatic hand at her throat. "I dare not let her see me."

"It be more than the wyrm. There be somewhat you want hidden, Rae."

"Ai! You be a cruel man, my love."

"Not cruel. Sick to my gut of your lies."

"Oh very well! If we did bring this matter to council, would I not have to tell them where the death did happen?"

"Ah, I do see now! It were at the siege of the Slavers' city, bain't? And you did go there with the Horsekin."

Verrarc was mostly guessing, but she turned dead-white.

"How did you—" she whispered, her voice trembling.

"I be not blind, Rae. You'd best remember that from now on."

For a long moment she stood silently, staring down at the floor, until her face regained its normal color.

"Mayhap you'll not believe a word I say," she said at last. "I'd best have a witness. Let me see if Lord Havoc will answer my call. Do come sit you down, my love."

Verrarc took the chair. Raena flung both arms into the air and tipped her head back, her eyes shut tight. For a long moment she held silent; then she began to chant in a high tight voice that seemed to vibrate like a plucked harp string. The chant rose and fell, wailed and sobbed. All at once Verrarc felt rather than saw someone else enter the room. The hair on the back of his neck rose as a cold chill seemed to freeze him to his chair. Out of the sunlight, against the far wall, a different light began to gather, this one silvery and cool. Slowly the silver thickened, swirled, and formed a cylindrical vortex that grew till it reached from ceiling to floor. Inside it Verrarc could just discern a shadowy man-shape.

Raena opened her eyes, gathered her breath for a moment, then began to chant again. The man-shape thickened, turned solid, became as much fox as man with his russet fur and sharp fox's nose. When Lord Havoc stepped out of the silver light, Verrarc could see that he wore black armor and carried in one pawlike hand a plumed helm.

"Greetings, O my priestess!" Havoc said. "Why do you bring me here?"

Raena fell on her knees before the fox-man. All at once Verrarc felt like shouting at her to get up, to stop prostrating herself before this beast-spirit.

"I do beg your aid," Raena was saying. "O great lord of the inner lands! Help one who worships you!"

"I shall listen," Havoc said. "What is it that you desire?"

"In this town I have an enemy who would kill me. Please, please, drive it hence or slay it!"

"Who is this enemy?" Havoc's voice was not quite steady enough for an all-powerful deity. "Where does it reside?"

"Not far from here, on the ruins of the temple in which I once worshipped you. It be a huge black beast, a dragon. Many times has she tried to devour me as I flew on your errands."

"Arzosah?" Havoc yelped. "I'll not be messing about with such as her! Uh, I mean, no doubt the greater gods have sent her to be a great spiritual test for you."

"Oh, have they now?" Verrarc got up, shoving the chair back. "You stink of fear, fox lord!"

Raena screamed and shrank back. Lord Havoc swelled, grew huge, and towered over them both.

"How dare you take me in vain!" the spirit hissed. "I shall destroy you for that!"

In sheer reflex Verrarc drew his long knife. When the steel flashed in the sunlight, Havoc yelped and began to shrink. With two long steps Verrarc charged forward and swung. As the steel approached Havoc's body, the black armor began to crack and melt; Havoc's torso suddenly wavered and bulged away from the blade as if it were a reflection on water, rippled by the wind. Havoc shrieked in agony, made a futile grab at the knife, and disappeared. The silver light vanished with him. Verrarc sheathed his knife and knelt in front of Raena, who sat sobbing on the floor.

"Rae?" Verrarc said. "That be no god."

"So I do see." She was sobbing so hard that her nose ran like a child's. "I should have listened when you told me of his brother. Ah truly, I should have listened!"

Raena dropped her face to her hands and went on weeping, sobbing wet and noisily. Verrarc stroked her hair and tried to think of some comforting words. He could find none. At last her sobbing ended.

"If only Alshandra would come to me," Raena whispered. "If only you might see her. Then would you truly understand."

"Jahdo did tell us all that she were slain."

"Oh, that be drivel! No one can slay a goddess."

"Just so, which is why I doubt me if she were any such thing."

"Hold your tongue!"

She was glaring at him in such utter rage that he sat back on his heels.

"Mock not my lady," Raena snarled. "Mock her not in forfeit of your life. Now let me think. Truly, if I could only reach her—let me think."

Although Jahdo invited Rhodry to eat dinner with his family, and Dallandra suggested he join the elven camp for a meal, Rhodry ate the last of his bread and cheese up at the ruined temple with Arzosah. Why, he couldn't say. She sprawled on the stone roof, and he sat leaning against her vast belly for a backrest while they watched the sun set in a shimmering haze.

"Have you ever been to the mountains in the west?" Rhodry said.

"Beyond the Westlands?" Arzosah said. "I have, on occasion."

"Then you've flown over the Seven Cities."

"There's not much to see of the southern ones. The ruins are mostly covered over with plants and suchlike now."

"And in the north?"

"One city still lives. Bravelmelim, I think it was called in the old days. That's where Meer came from."

"It must have escaped the plague somehow, then. Huh. Interesting. What about beyond the far mountains? Does anything lie beyond them?"

"Some flat plains with trees and suchlike. They looked boring, and so I never flew over them. I've been told that there's an ocean beyond that."

"Told by whom?"

"My poor dear departed mate. He was a great one for exploring." Arzosah sighed with a heave of her sides that nearly toppled Rhodry right over. "When we've finished whatever we're doing here, would you like to fly west?"

"I'd like to, indeed, but I can't. I've got to go back to Dwarveholt. I suppose I'm daft, but I want to find Enj and settle down to wait for Haen Marn. I keep praying Angmar will come back somehow."

"Ah yes, *your* dear departed mate."

there was an odd edge to her voice—mockery, perhaps. He ignored it. The sun lay just on the horizon, all swollen and gold with clouds. When he looked to the east, he could see a single star, shining against the velvet blue of the sky. Angmar! he thought. Can you see it too, my lady, wherever you are?

"Ah well," Rhodry said at last. "If naught else, I promised Enj that I'd return."

"That's true, isn't it?" Arzosah sounded positively gloomy. "I'll carry you there, then."

"My thanks. If you'd rather not fly to the cold north, I can get myself a horse and ride."

"No need, no need. But I shan't be staying there when the nasty snows come."

"Of course." He scrambled up, then turned to look at her massive head. Her eyes were half-closed and unreadable. "Is somewhat wrong?"

"Naught. Thinking about my dead mate makes me sad, is all."

"Well, that I can understand, truly."

He sat down again, leaning back against her flank. Together they watched the stars come out until the Snowy Road hung above them, a vast river of diamonds in the dark sky, flowing to some unknown sea of light.

Long past the zenith of night, when the entire town slept in a wrap of darkness, Verrarc and Raena crept out of the compound. Overheard the wheel of the stars and the waning moon gave them just enough light to make their way uphill. They were headed for the broken temple, but long before they reached it, the wind shifted and brought them the vinegar smell of dragon. Raena clutched Verrarc's arm with both hands, and whispered "I dare not."

"Just so," he murmured. "Let's go back down."

Through the steep little alleys of Citadel he led her to the plaza by a roundabout way. The Council House stood unlocked. They slipped in by a back door. Away from the starlight the room gaped as dark as a cave. He could feel Raena move close to him and shudder. Verrarc opened the door again, and in the faint greying of the dark he could just make out the stairway at the far end of the room.

"Upstairs there be a back room with shutters," he whispered. "None will see if you make your witchlight up there."

"And if we do break our necks upon those stairs, we shan't care if they see or no, bain't? Shut that door, Verro. I'd best risk making a little light."

He could hear the fabric of her dress rustle. She murmured a chant, so softly at first that he could barely hear her, but a spark of silver light appeared in the palm of her hand. He could see, then, that she was holding one cupped hand level with her waist but close to her body. As the chant rose and fell the point swelled to a little pool of silver, casting a faint light around her for a few feet—enough for them to climb the stairs in safety.

Three doors opened off the corridor at the top, meeting rooms for private matters among the Council of Five. Verrarc went into the first one and felt his way over to the window, where heavy wooden shutters hung. He pulled them closed and latched them on the inside.

"It be safe for you to come in now, Rae."

She walked in and stood for a moment looking around. A square table and four chairs stood in the middle of the plain stone room.

"I dare not brighten this light more," she said at last. "But it will do."

With a snap of her wrist she tossed the ball of light to the floor, where it stuck, glowing like a tiny lantern. She sat down cross-legged in front of it, and Verrarc joined her, cursing a little at the hardness of the stone.

"Huh, you be soft, my love," Raena said. "Those who worship Alshandra needs must have souls of steel."

She rose to her knees, then flung her arms above her head and began to chant in a rhythm he'd never heard her use before, slowly at first, then faster. Such melody as there was rose and fell. As she swayed back and forth, sweat broke out on her forehead, then ran down her face. Back and forth, on and on—sweat stuck her dress to her back, and she began to gasp for breath. In the witchlight her face turned as pale and cold-looking as a fish's belly.

"Hold, Rae!" Verrarc laid a heavy hand on her shoulder. "There be a need on you to stop lest you kill yourself."

With one last sob she let her arms fall to her sides. For a

long moment she knelt, her head bowed, her face so wet that he wondered if it were sweat or tears that ran there.

"There be shame so heavy upon me," Raena whispered. "I did fail her. Now she turns her face away from me."

"Be you sure of that? Or could the truth lie in what Jahdo did tell the town, that your Alshandra were but a spirit like Lord Havoc?"

"Never!" She raised her head with a toss of her long hair. "That lying little snake! Truly, you should have slain him, that day in the water meadows."

"Oh here, as if I'd cause Dera and her kin one moment's pain!"

"True spoken. Forgive me, my love, I be so desolate I know not what I say." Raena sat down, crossing her legs, on the floor and wiped both hands across her face. "What did he tell you?"

"That there were a battle in the sky twixt her and a mighty mistress of the witchroad. When Alshandra died, he saw her body break apart, and all the Horsekin did scream and howl in despair, for they did believe her dead."

"And for their sin they did perish, all of them that doubted her. Those who believed came safely through her country to their homes again, just as I did return to the man I love second only to her." She reached out a soft hand and caressed his cheek. "Ah, Verro! Someday I hope and pray that you will see her as I have seen her, in her glory."

"It would be a grand thing."

His voice must have lacked conviction, because she winced and turned her face away. While he sat, trying to think of some comforting words, at the window something rustled. A shutter knocked on stone, then fell silent. Verrarc was on his feet without thinking and running to the window.

"Douse that light!" he hissed.

As soon as the light disappeared Verrarc flung open the shutters. No one was there, and indeed, he felt a sudden fool when he realized that the window opened out on empty air. He stuck his head out and looked straight down to the stone plaza, a hard drop of some two stories below. He closed the shutters again.

"No one here," he said. "And no one could be here lest they could fly."

"Don't mock that idea, my love." She muttered something else that he couldn't quite understand.

In the darkness he could not see Raena's face. It took him several moments before he realized that she wasn't forming words; she was laughing, a choked sort of laughter, brimming with panic.

In the physical world Raena's dweomer light, an extrusion of etheric force, shone brightly, but on the higher planes it appeared as a darkness, marking the spot on the etheric plane from which she'd sucked substance. In hawk form Evandar had been as usual hunting for his brother, first back in the ruins of his Lands, then ranging farther afield, until at last he circled low over Cerr Cawnen, though still in the etheric rather than the physical world. In the shimmering blue light the stone buildings stood black and dead, while the lake seethed with silver energy, reaching dangerous tendrils up high. As he passed over the plaza, a lake of blackness, he could see the dull reddish glow of the trees near the ruined temple, and Arzosah's aura—a huge plumed thing of gold and green, ever shifting and swelling up high only to fall back in ripples.

Nearby he saw the strange little pock of nothingness that marked a dweomer light on the physical plane. Raena? Quite likely. He let himself drop back to the physical and found himself circling the Council House. Wooden shutters covered one window and only one. Sitting on the sill, his ear pressed against the wood, sat Shaetano in the form of a black-and-white shrike. Evandar gained height, then laid back his wings and dove. Shaetano looked up, threw himself from the sill, and disappeared. Cursing under his breath Evandar swerved and burst through the gateway into the sunshine of the Lands, only to find his brother gone.

Yet Shaetano had left tracks behind him: the pawprints of the fox in moist earth, a tuft of russet fur on a bramble, and in the air, an astral essence like crystals shimmering. Following them, Evandar flew steadily and saw at the horizon the green swell of trees. Of course! There was only one place where Shaetano would be able to hide from him, the wild forest under the verdigris moon. He was desperate indeed, then, with no human worshipper to feed upon, but clever still. That forest was the only place on any plane where Evandar feared to hunt.

Evandar flew onward, turning and swooping over the twisted dark below until he saw the beacon tree, green and burning on the boundary. Mayhap those that live in the wild will do my work for me, Evandar thought. Yet he knew beyond knowing how he knew that his brother's Wyrd lay with him and him alone. In time, though, the creatures of the night would flush Shaetano out of the forest again. He knew that for a certainty as well. On long wings he spiralled down to the ground, and as he landed, he changed, taking the form of a massive black hound. He lay down, couchant, under the verdant half of the tree and waited.

A spring dawn was breaking in a clear sky when the Council of Five met up on the plaza, but rather than go to the Council House—and close to the dragon—they stood twixt the well and the head of the path that led down to Citadel. Below them the white buildings gleamed in the rising light, and a breeze stirred the mists of Loc Vaed, gleaming turquoise through the rifts.

"Soon the watch will be opening the gates," Verrarc said. "It behooves us to reach some decision about Rakzan Kral and his embassy."

"Just so." Burra spoke firmly. "I'd not have them in this town again."

"No more I," Hennis put in, "but you do ken the old saw as well as I: Scorn the Horsekin, see harm ride your way."

Frie and Admi stayed silent. Verrarc was painfully aware of the way that his fellow councilmen were watching him: narrow-eyed, unsmiling, arms crossed over their chests.

"When I did take Raena in," Verrarc said, "little did I ken that she'd been consorting with Horsekin."

"And if you had?" Burra snarled. "Would it have made one cursed bit of difference?"

Verrarc felt his fists clench. When he took a step forward, Burra held his ground.

"Stop!" Admi shoved his bulk in between them. "This be no time for fighting amongst ourselves."

"Well by the gods!" Burra stepped back. "There be a passel of secrets that Verrarc does hide, bain't? How did that witchwoman of his get out of the city if he were not the one to help her?"

Like a sheepdog Admi herded Burra a few steps back, but the gesture made Verrarc realize that the four of them stood on one side of an invisible line whilst he stood alone on the other.

"True spoken," old Hennis joined in. "We do need a few answers from you, Verrarc."

Verrarc tried to speak, but he'd gone cold to his very soul. They waited, his accusers, watching with eyes of flint, sharp and glittering. He swallowed hard and found his voice at last.

"I know not how she did leave the city. There be many a lie she's told me. Ye gods! Don't you think I feel the fool, letting a woman lead me about by the nose?"

They considered this, and Hennis at least seemed more thoughtful than angry. Verrarc took a deep breath, then went on.

"But be that as it may, Raena does ken many a thing about the Horsekin and their country. She can help us, not harm us. There be a need on us for such lore, bain't? Consider this: she did tell me that the Horsekin do indeed worship the new goddess of which Zatcheka did tell us, but this goddess did only promise them the Slavers' country. Is there any one of us who loves the Slavers in his heart?"

"Well, now," Frie said, "if it be the Slavers that they've marked out—"

"Don't be a fool!" Burra snapped. "Mayhap they will conquer the Slavers first. Then we'll be next."

"I do agree with that," Admi said, "but it behooves us to give them a hearing before we reach a judgment. As for your woman, Verro, this be not the time to pass a final judging on her deeds, either. She too shall have her chance to speak to us and the town. I'd have you keep her close by until then."

"So would I." Verrarc could hear the rage in his voice. "You have my word on that."

Still they watched him, but perhaps their eyes had softened. He could not be sure, and no more could he be silent.

"I took her in out of the snows," Verrarc went on. "Should I have let her freeze to death? I knew not where she'd been, any more than any of us knew. Lady Zatcheka did bring us the first news any of us heard of this Horsekin war against the Slavers. Would any of you have thought that she'd been among the Horsekin? I doubt me—"

"Hush!" Admi held up one broad hand. "None of that has the least import now."

The other councilmen nodded their agreement. Their expressions had changed to pity, Verrarc realized, a sickening, condescending sort of pity. Involuntarily he took a step back, as if their feeling were a blow.

"Very well." Burra took up the question again. "Let us think on the problem at hand. Remember what that filthy sorcerer did, threatening that little lass? How dare we let them into the town? Do we want our citizens to tear them apart and have the wrath of the Horsekin come down upon us for it?"

"That be a true fear," Admi said.

"What say you all to this?" Burra went on. "We go down to the south gate and meet there, just inside the wall. If the crowd turns ugly, then the Horsekin may flee for their lives whilst we shut the gates."

"Just so." Hennis nodded. "And truly, perhaps we should summon the townsfolk to hear them out. The day for voting draws near, bain't?"

"Tomorrow," Admi said. "I do keep tally."

"Well, then, let the rakzan plead his case for all to hear, to spare us the time and trouble of repeating it at council fire."

"Splendid!" Frie clapped his enormous hands. "I do agree with that."

In general agreement the council meeting broke up, Admi and Hennis to summon the Horsekin emissaries, Burra and Frie to cry the news through the town. Verrarc hurried back to his house.

By then Raena had risen; he found her in the bed-chamber but dressed, sitting by the window while she ate a bowl of milk and bread. When he came in, she laid the spoon in the bowl and put it down on the windowsill. In the sunny light her hair gleamed with bluish highlights like a raven's feather. Once he had loved the midnight color of her hair, but now the thought of ravens made him shudder.

"Good morrow, my love," Raena said. "You be out and about early this morn."

"So I was. The council did need to come to some deci-sion about the Horsekin emissaries. Rae, the mood of the town be ugly about this. We did deem it best that they stay near the gates—for their own sake."

"Once the folk hear Kral out, they'll be less a-feared. Would it be seemly if I did speak to the citizens as well?"

"It wouldn't. I do think it best you stay here at the house and not go down."

"What?" Raena got up with a toss of her long hair. "I do wish to hear the proceedings!"

"Indeed? Why? No doubt you already ken every word this rakzan will be saying."

"And what do you mean by that?"

"What I did say. Or did you talk of naught when you were a-bringing them here?"

She went pale and silent.

"You understand me," Verrarc went on. "Do you be-lieve me blind, that I'd not see which way your loyalty falls?"

"You know not the whole of it!" She laid a soft hand on his arm and looked up, her eyes pleading. "Truly, I be loyal to their cause, but more than any other, I be loyal to you. Verro, if Cerr Cawnen does decide to ally with them, the Horsekin will remember your part in this. You'll be like a lord unto them, a man they can trust. I swear it: the Horsekin repay their friends."

"Oh, do they now? Think you I'll sell them the town? That be where your words are leading."

"Naught of the sort! I only meant they'd honor you."

Verrarc knew she was lying, but for those moments,

when she stared up into his eyes, he felt tempted. He could be Chief Speaker—more! With Horsekin soldiers at his command he could abolish the council. He could rule Cerr Cawnen as its lord. Raena's eyes seemed to turn to mirrors and show him the treasures that would be his. At last he would have his revenge on all those townsmen who'd let him suffer as a boy and who sneered at him now and snubbed his woman. They would pay for it, all of them! They'd all been against him, always—except for Dera and her family.

The thought of Dera struck him like a slap upon the face of a sleeping man. Raena was smiling, staring up at him in triumph. He grabbed her wrists and held her at arm's length.

"Stop it!" Verrarc snarled. "Keep your ugly little ensorcelments for your enemies, Rae! Unless you count me as one of those?"

"Never! What are you saying? I did naught—"

"Hold your lying tongue!" He let her go with a little push.

Panting for breath, she stood rubbing her right wrist with her left hand and staring down at the floor.

"I must be gone," he said. "For your own sake, stay here! Ye gods, have you not seen the way the folk look at you?"

"If only I could tell them of Alshandra," she began.

"This be no day for that! And what about the black wyrm? Dare you go out where she might see you?"

"Ah gods." Her face dead-pale against the raven of her hair, she sat back down.

"Well and good, then. I'll be back as soon as I ever can to tell you how the meeting did proceed. Until then, stay in the compound."

"I will, have no fear."

Verrarc turned and strode out. He was halfway down the hill before he realized he'd not given her a single kiss. No more did he regret it—that was the most shocking realization of all.

As the dawn brightened into day, the morning shift of the town watch tramped across the commons to relieve the night guard. Both contingents shouted back and forth as they changed places upon the catwalks. The noise woke Dallandra, who rolled out of her blankets and got up rather than lie there and curse the louts. She took a bone comb from her saddlebags and stood working the tangles out of her hair whilst she watched the militia manning the winch to open the south gates for the day. When she strolled over and looked out, she could see, some hundreds of yards away, the Horsekin camp of narrow tents. Some of the men were out and about, leading horses to the nearby river to drink, but there was no sign of the rakzan and the mazrak who belonged to Alshandra's Elect.

In a few moments several men came out of the largest tent. With her strong elven eyes Dallandra could see that one of them was human. This fellow, bald and stout, left the camp and came hurrying back to town, waddling rather than running, his scarlet cloak flapping in the morning wind. And just what was the Chief Speaker doing among the enemy? Dallandra wondered. The question was answered innocently enough, however, when Admi walked through the gates and hailed some of the town watch. She was just wondering if she could get close enough to eavesdrop when Admi waved her over with a vigorous pump of his arm.

"I do have a favor to ask of you, my lady," Admi said. "The council did decide that the Horsekin emissaries shall speak their piece here on the commons. We do fear what our fellow citizens might do, should the Horsekin come all the way across to Citadel. I did ask them to appear here when they've broken their fast and suchlike. Could your men move their horses round to the far side of your tent? We do expect a goodly crowd to hear them out."

"We can do that, certainly," Dallandra said. "Or even strike the tent and move it farther along."

"That does seem a great imposition."

"Not to the likes of us. We'll move the camp over to the commons on the far side of the Gel da'Thae."

"My profound thanks." Admi grabbed the hem of his cloak and wiped sweat from his jowls. "Ai! I do fear that this day be an ill-omened one."

Dallandra would have liked to have reassured him, but unfortunately she could only agree.

Moving the camp took a good while, even with the help of the Gel da'Thae men, who appeared silently, bowed to her, and carried whatever gear she indicated to them. Zatcheka, no doubt, had sent them, but she and her daughter stayed in their tent until the dusty, messy job of moving the horses and tethering them out in the fresh grass was over. By then a crowd of townsfolk had started to form in front of the south gates and spill over, just as Admi had predicted, onto the commons to either side of the path. The other four councilmen also appeared and clustered around Admi for what appeared to be an urgent conversation.

The grassy commons sloped slightly down from the walls to the lake, but even so, only those persons well to the front would be able to see and hear the rakzan when he finally arrived. The Council of Five bustled around, giving orders, sending men off to fetch wood and tools, talking anxiously among themselves, until finally workmen appeared and began to improvise a platform out of tables and crates. Dallandra kept an eye on Verrarc, who stood off to one side, leaning back against the wall with his head bowed. When she shifted her vision to the dweomer sight, she saw immediately that someone had tried to ensorcel him. His aura, a sickly grey-green, clung close to his body and in spots had the appearance of stone. No doubt he'd used his own weak magicks to harden it and fight Raena off. If it even was Raena, Dallandra thought. But she knew that if anyone else in Cerr Cawnen had dweomer, she would have spotted them long before this.

Once finished, the platform wobbled to such an alarming degree that the council had the workmen pull it all apart and start over. The crowd grew and began to sort itself out so easily that Dallandra realized the citizens had come to these large assemblies all their lives. The women and children sat down in front, the men gathered in the rear, the town watch turned up on the walls to lean over and listen from there. Dallandra looked back and saw Daralanteriel and his escort coming from their camp, and

Zatcheka leading her people over as well—the Gel da'Thae, that is. None of the human slaves were to be seen. Niffa and Carra, holding the baby, trailed along behind, talking together, while Lightning trotted beside them.

In front of the open gates the platform appeared to be finished and stable at last. The workmen dragged some slab-sided crates into position for stairs, and Chief Speaker Admi climbed them to stand on the platform. The other council-men waited off to the side, all except for Verrarc, who surprised Dallandra thoroughly by walking over to join her.

"Good morrow," Verrarc said. "My thanks for moving your camp."

"You're most welcome."

Dallandra smiled, expecting him to return to the other council members, but he stayed, standing next to her and watching the gates. The Horsekin appeared so promptly that, Dallandra supposed, they must have been waiting nearby for the workmen to finish the platform. Rakzan Kral and ten men for his escort marched in formation through the gates.

"I don't see that mazrak with them," Dallandra remarked.

"No more do I," Verrarc said. "And my thanks to the gods for that."

There was no denying the sincerity in his voice. The other four councilmen greeted Kral, but Verrarc remained where he was. As Kral climbed the steps to the platform, the crowd grew quiet and still. His cloth-of-gold surcoat glittered in the hot morning sun, and the metal talismans braided into his mane of hair winked and glinted. Although he carried no sword or knife, in his left hand he held a long black whip; jewels winked on the handle.

"Greetings, citizens," Kral began. "Many years have your people hated the Slavers. I do come to offer you vengeance. Did they not enslave you? Did they not drive you off the lands of your fathers? Did they not take your sa-cred springs and pollute them? Did they not take the sacred meadows and drive cattle upon them?" He paused to let the crowd murmur its assent. "Among ourselves, we do call those stolen lands the Summer Country. Here the winters be long and harsh, bain't? What man would not trade the winter for summer?" Another pause, and Kral was smiling as he looked over the crowd. "We too do long for the Summer Country. Join with us, and we shall lead your return."

Dallandra caught her breath. Zatcheka, standing just behind her, leaned forward to whisper.

"Never did I think to see a man of the Horsekin with a silver tongue."

"No more I."

Out in the crowd the young men had pressed forward. Up on the town walls the militia were leaning forward as well. Dallandra could read their expressions clearly: a kindling eagerness.

"Vengeance!" Kral howled the word. "Be it not sweeter than water on the hottest day? And riches as well—the Slavers have prospered on their stolen land. Should not this bounty be yours?"

Some of the townsmen called out their agreement. Up on the platform Admi stepped forward.

"I do beg forgiveness, Rakzan, but we would know the price of this vengeance. What shall we do to join you?"

"Why, join us!" Kral laughed, revealing sharp teeth. "Naught more than that. Join with us in alliance!"

A fair many of the younger men cheered.

"But I understand it not," Admi went on. "Your people be mighty warriors, we be but humble farmers. Truly, we could furnish you a company of foot soldiers, good men and true, but we have naught more than that to add to an alliance."

"Ah, but you do." Kral paused, smiling at the crowd. "The Rhiddaer does lie closer to the Summer Country than our own poor lands. Here you do have rich fields. I hear that they do yield grain in a most marvelous abundance. Warhorses do we need, and the grain to feed them upon. Could the Rhiddaer not become famous for its horses, were you to join with us?"

The crowd muttered, suddenly uneasy. No fools here, Dallandra thought.

"And after all," Kral went on, "the lands of the Rhiddaer lie open to the west. There be good pasturing here, and roads to our lands as well. An army might sweep down easily to claim its horses here."

Was it a threat? Dallandra wasn't sure, but she could see that everyone in the crowd but the young men had turned suspicious and narrow-eyed.

"These be dire times," Kral continued. "The day will come when those who are not with us shall be against us. I think me it were best for you and your town to be with us on that day."

"And is that a threat, then?" Admi's jowls were running with sweat, but his voice rang clear and steady.

"What? Never! My apologies!" Kral arranged a jovial smile. "I did mean only that we are many and strong, and in alliance with us so could you be as well. There be many a rich thing to be gained in the Summer Country."

"Mera!" Prince Dar was shouting at the top of his lungs. "You lie!"

With a snarl Kral swung round to look for the speaker just as Daralanteriel pushed his way through the crowd and strode out into the open stretch in front of the platform. Tall, straight-backed, handsome with his dark hair and striking grey-and-purple eyes—his very presence made Kral look suddenly ugly and somehow smaller. At his belt Dar wore an elven long knife, and round his neck hung Ranadar's Eye on its gold chain. His men fell in behind him, but Dar motioned them back and walked on alone.

Kral snarled as he faced this threat. His escort, who had been standing patiently behind the platform, moved forward as if to block Dar's way. For a moment they stared at the approaching Westfolk; then, muttering to each other, the Horsekin began to edge backwards toward the open gates. Caught as he was on the platform, the rakzan held his place, but he clutched the handle of his ceremonial whip so tightly that the hair on his knuckles bristled. A sweating Admi scuttled back out of the prince's way.

"Meradan!" Dar called out. "You come to offer slavery, not an alliance of free men. You want grooms and ostlers, not allies. You'll take those fields and starve their owners to feed your horses. I've met you on the battlefield. I know you through and through."

Kral stood as straight as he could muster, threw his head back, and let the wind catch his mane of hair. He sneered, one lip curled as if he would speak. Dar broke into a brief run, leapt halfway up the stairs, leapt the rest of the way onto the platform, and strode toward Kral. Dangling on his chest the pendant seemed to catch the sunlight and glow—oddly brightly, really, for a single jewel. All at once Dallandra realized that sunlight had nothing to do with it. The enormous sapphire seemed to burst into flame, a cold silver leap and lick of fire that reached out like hands for the Horsekin leader. Kral yelped and staggered back. When Dar followed, the silver fire exploded from the jewel. It leapt up, spread, spiraled round upon itself until it seemed that Dar carried a burning silver shield in front of him. Kral screamed.

"Coward!" Dar snarled. "Kneel before the children of the gods!"

The rakzan knelt so fast and hard that he grunted. Behind the platform his men did the same, dropping into the dirt. Dallandra could see their lips moving; she could guess that they were muttering prayers. The townsfolk went silent; Dallandra had never heard so many persons make so little noise. On the platform, Chief Speaker Admi tried to speak, failed, and seemed about to choke on shock, but he held his ground.

"This town lies under my protection," Dar went on. "Think you to add to the ancient sins of your people?"

"Never, never," Kral said. "Forgive! No curses upon us!"

"If you would be spared Ranadar's curse, then listen to me! The people of Cerr Cawnen will choose their alliances. It's not for the likes of you to force yourselves upon them."

"So it's not, not in the least. I swear to you! I'll not say another angry word."

"Good." Dar smiled, but it was a ghastly sort of smile—tight-lipped and hard. "Then you may live."

Kral touched his forehead to the platform, then scrambled up, yelling to his men. When he jumped down, they flocked around him, muttering and waving helpless hands in the air. From somewhere in the crowd someone laughed; another person took it up, then another, and like a breaking wave the laughter crashed and howled, washing over the Horsekin and flooding them out of the gates. With his men close behind, Kral raced for the safety of their camp.

By then the silver fire had shrunk back into the sapphire and died. Dar waited until the last Horsekin was out of sight, then stalked to the edge of the platform. When he held up both hands, the laughter stilled, running away like the ebbing tide until at length the silence held.

"Citizens of Cerr Cawnen," Dar called out. "My name is Daralanteriel tran Aledeldar, prince of the Westfolk, heir to the Seven Cities of the Far West. We have more reason to hate the Meradan, that is, the Horsekin as you name them, than ever you could know." He paused, glancing around. "But hate them we do. Hear this! I offer you an alliance with me and my people, to stand against the Horsekin in any time of war. Our longbows brought down plenty of their precious horses in last summer's war, and we stand ready to kill more."

The townsfolk roared their approval, stamping their feet, clapping their hands. Once again Dar flung his arms into the air, and once again they quieted.

"Let me warn you," Dar went on, "that if you take my alliance, the Horsekin will hate you doubly. Think well on that before you make your choice on the morrow." He turned on his heel, strode back to the stairway, and came down it in two leaps.

The crowd seemed frozen in a stunned silence. Admi hurried forward again, but when he tried to speak, his voice choked. He looked as if he'd woken from a blow to the skull. With a wave to her guards to follow her up, Zatcheka climbed to the platform.

"Chief Speaker," Zatcheka said, "be it lawful for me to address your people?"

"It is." Admi made her a bow and stepped back.

"I do have but one thing to say." Zatcheka turned to

face the crowd. "There be no need upon you to choose between the alliance my town does offer you and the prince's offer. We would count ourselves honored to join an alliance twixt your people and his."

In the crowd a fair number of people clapped in appreciation. Others nodded, and the talk began, murmuring among the women first, then spreading to the men. Admi raised his hands, got ignored, and called out that the meeting was over in a voice as loud as booming brass. The talk grew loud and anxious as the women stood, collecting children, looking around for their menfolk. In a long slow milling about the crowd began to disperse.

"I'd best join the others," Verrarc said.

Dallandra nearly yelped, she'd forgotten all about the councilman.

"Indeed," she said. "This is quite a turn of events."

Verrarc tried to smile but succeeded only in looking terrified. And with good reason, Dallandra thought. With all the reason in the world.

"The gall!" Raena grabbed a pottery cup from the table and threw it at the wall. "I do hate him! How dare he!"

The cup shattered with a fine spray of dust. Verrarc grabbed her wrist when she reached for another.

"It be needful for you to spare my crockery," he said. "Hush, Rae! Eat your dinner and calm your soul."

With a snarling sound she pulled her hand away, but she let the dinnerware be. They were sitting in the little alcove near the kitchen in Verrarc's house, and before them on the table sat a steaming pot of venison stew, a loaf of bread, and a pitcher of beer. Verrarc ladled the stew onto the trencher they shared while she cut hunks of bread.

"The Prince of the Westfolk be a well-spoken man," Verrarc said. "There be no surprise in my heart that the Horsekin did listen."

"He lied to them! Children of the gods—my arse! They be men like any other, for all their ugly ears."

"So it would seem. Why does Kral think otherwise?"

"It be a legend among the Horsekin, that their ancestors did overthrow the children of the gods long long ago, and because of this sin the gods did send upon them a terrible plague that did slay them by the thousands. If any man, either Gel da'Thae or Horsekin, should ever harm another child of the gods, then the plague will return. Or so they say. They call it Ranadar's curse."

"No wonder then that they did grovel. That jewel, Rae—never did I see such a wondrous thing, the way it burned without true fire."

"Had I been allowed to be there, I might have doused it."

"Had the black dragon eaten you, you'd have doused naught ever again."

She scowled at him, then laid the loaf back in its basket. Verrarc took a chunk and bit into it while she daintily sliced hers thin.

"So, the prince of the Westfolk be here," Raena said at length. "Tell me somewhat, my love. His wife, a pretty blonde lass—be she here with him?"

"She is, truly, and with her their child."

"Ah, truly, the babe would have been born by now." For a long moment she stared at the wall with the bread knife still in her hand.

"What be so wrong?" Verrarc said at last. "Be you well?"

"My apologies, my love." Raena smiled at him and laid the knife down. "I did but remember a thing Nag-arshad did tell me once, about a vow to our goddess that would tame the Horsekin's hearts. There be a need on me to speak with Kral. I swear to you, Verro, if they make this vow to the Great One, that never will they enslave your fellows, they would die rather than break it. Curse that meddling wyrm! Mayhap she'll hunt tonight, and I may leave the house then."

"If you do go to see the rakzan," Verrarc said, "I come with you."

"You'll not! This be my goddess's affair and none of yours!"

"Oh, bain't? You did promise me—"

"I did promise to tell you what I do know and naught more than that!"

"I'll not have you trotting off to the Horsekin camp alone!"

Raena shoved back her chair and stood up, crossing her arms over her chest.

"Sulk all you want," Verrarc said. "I think me it be time for me to be master in my own house again."

Raena turned on her heel and stomped out of the room. When he heard the bedroom door slam behind her, he half rose, thinking he would go calm her, but he made himself sit down. In his mind he was seeing Burra, sneering his scorn at a man who let a woman rule him. He ate a few bites more, felt as if the food would choke him, then got up and left the house. If he stayed, he would weaken, he knew, and besides, he needed to rejoin the council.

The Council of Five had many a grave matter to discuss that afternoon in the cool stone chamber of Council House. At their round table fear took the sixth seat as they argued over details of possible alliances. The prince's offer had rolled an entirely new handful of dice, as Burra remarked.

"True enough," Frie said. "But it be a goodly roll for winning a wager. Two alliances be a fair bit stronger than one."

"If we can trust these Westfolk," Burra broke. "They did turn up what? yesterday, and what ken we about them?"

"The old lore tells us somewhat," Hennis said. "You've heard the tales a hundred times, lad. Think! When our ancestors fled the Slavers, the horsemen of the west did hide them and speed them on their way. Who else would these people be, but the horsemen of the west? The old tales do limn them the same, what with their eyes like cats and strange ears."

"I'd forgotten that." Burra was silent for a long moment. "But could they not have turned to villainy since then? That were many a long year ago."

"So it was." Frie laid his enormous hands, all callused and pitted with tiny burn scars, flat on the edge of the table. "But desperate men needs must take the help they be offered."

The wrangling went on for a long while, though they settled nothing, of course, because until the townspeople voted they were powerless. As Admi remarked in the end, however, none of them could see many citizens choosing the rakzan's proposition.

"Though I do have fears," Admi said, "that the young men among us do see adventure and glory in his words."

"True enough." Hennis heaved a dramatic sigh. "Well, we'll be setting up an urn for Kral at the Deciding nonetheless. He shan't be able to accuse us of working fraud."

"Just so." Admi shoved his chair back and stood up. "I think me we can do more good out in the town, reassuring whom we can, than ever we'll do sitting here."

Silently the five of them filed out of the Council House. Outside, the hot spring sunlight made Verrarc blink. He shaded his eyes with one hand, then glanced sideways at the sky to get some idea of the lateness of the day—midafternoon, about. He was just about to make some comment to Frie when he heard the sound, a flap or thwack like an enormous hand hitting a bigger drumhead.

"Ye gods!" Hennis yelped. "What be making that noise?"

The answer rose suddenly into the sky from the ruined temple. The black dragon had flown, and she was gaining height steadily with each beat of her huge wings. As they watched, she launched herself straight west, heading for the mountains rising just beyond the farmlands.

"She be going to feed, I'll wager," Burra said.

"As good a guess as any." Admi shuddered visibly. "May she stay gone for a good long while! Let's be about our business, lads. It be needful for us to serve our fellow citizens."

Although most of a day had passed in Cerr Cawnen, under the green moon Time crept. As he lay in hound-shape by the beacon tree, Evandar was painfully aware of the discrepancy. What if Dalla needed him down in the city? How long by her reckoning had he been gone? He was just considering leaving his post when he heard the cries.

Deep in among the twisted trees something was hunting. A pair of them, whatever they were—cries like those of gigantic cats called back and forth. Growling under his breath, the black hound rose to his feet and waited. Closer and closer they came, and with them another set of sounds, twigs snapping, branches cracking, leaves rustling. It would be prudent, Evandar decided, to take to the air. He changed into hawk form, then ran a few steps, flapped hard, and rose, circling over the forest edge.

Through the trees he could see someone running, crashing his way through the underbrush. Not so far behind him came the cat-beasts, though all he could see of them was the occasional flash of spotted hide. Evandar flew a little higher and hovered on the wind to look down. The figure burst out of the trees—Shaetano, all right, screaming as he raced for the safety of the boundary. Or was it Shaetano? It seemed to be his usual form of a fox-spirit, but on his head grew a mane of honey-blonde hair. Evandar banked a wing and turned to fly after him just as he leapt up and mutated into bird form. Hair and fox-spirit both vanished in a flutter of black-and-white feathers: a shrike.

Shaetano was panicked enough that Evandar might have been able to dive and catch him from his superior height, but his curiosity had been aroused. Just what was his wretched brother up to now? When Shaetano flew off, heading for a mother road, Evandar trailed behind at a safe distance, just to see where he would lead.

"There goes Arzosah," Rhodry said, "off to hunt, no doubt."

Dallandra looked up in the sky where he pointed and saw the dragon, a tiny figure against the sky, heading straight west.

"It's a good thing she can fetch her own food," Dallandra said. "Keeping her in meat isn't a job I'd want."

"Nor I, either. I blasted well wish she'd lay off the local cattle, though."

They were walking together at the edge of the lake. The sun was beginning to sink toward the western horizon, gilding a long streak of mackerel clouds that arched over the town.

"Looks like rain coming," Rhodry remarked.

"It does. I suppose the townsfolk will come to the Deciding no matter what the weather."

"No doubt. When I was walking through the town, I could hear the people talk about naught else. I hope to the gods that they see the Horsekin alliance for what it is: bait for a trap."

"I think me most of them do." Dallandra paused to look across to Citadel, looming dark against the sky. "They didn't escape your ancestors just to sell themselves into slavery again. Though I wonder, truly, where the Horsekin and the Gel da'Thae both get those human slaves of theirs. I've not wanted to ask Zatcheka right out."

"It might well blight a flowering friendship."

They continued on, walking so close together that their shoulders touched. Rhodry twined his arm through hers.

"Will you miss me?" he said abruptly. "When I leave for the Northlands?"

"I will. And you?"

"I'll think of you often." He was staring down at the ground. "And curse myself for a fool a thousand times over for leaving you behind for naught but a daft hope."

"Oh here, you'd not stay long anyway, even if you did come back to the grass with me. Somewhat else would catch your fancy, and you'd be off. You're that sort of man."

"Well, I was a man like that once."

"Not anymore?"

"I hardly know who I am anymore. I've lived too long, Dalla."

"Oh hush!" She pulled free of him. "Don't! Just don't go on about Lady Death and all the rest of it!"

"Very well." He was smiling at her, but a smile that hovered near tears.

"You're daft, Rori, but truly, in my own way I love you."

"My thanks." His smile changed, to something nearer humor. "Your own way, indeed! You're a fine one, talking about me being fickle and going off somewhere. I've never known a woman more distant than you."

"Well, true spoken. I suppose this is why we've been able to put up with each other as long as we have."

He laughed and caught her hand again. They walked on

a few more yards, then realized that the open lakeshore by the commons was about to come to an end: ahead lay houses, built on pilings out over the water. When they turned back to return to camp, they saw Jahdo, running across the commons toward them. He was waving frantically.

"Slow down!" Rhodry yelled at him. "Or you'll fall flat on your face."

Jahdo did as he was told. He stood panting to catch his breath and waited for them to reach him.

"What's so wrong, lad?" Rhodry said.

"Raena, that's what. Niffa did send me to fetch you. Raena be down by the gates, up on that heap of wood the council did cause to be built, and she be talking nonsense."

Dallandra took off running with Rhodry and Jahdo right behind. As she raced across the commons and through the elven camp, she could see Raena, dressed in her strange black brigga and shirt, standing on the improvised platform. To her right clustered the Horsekin; off to the left stood the Westfolk and the Gel da'Thae at a cautious distance from one another; out in front a crowd of townspeople was gathering.

"I do come to tell you of miracles," Raena was saying. "And a promise of life everlasting."

Some of the townsfolk laughed, and a few others yelled out "She be daft." Raena ignored them. Dallandra reached the Westfolk and stopped beside Niffa, who turned and mouthed "gladdens my heart you be here." When Dallandra glanced back, she saw Rhodry and Jahdo standing with Dar.

"I come to tell you of a goddess that we all may see with our own eyes," Raena went on, "the great Alshandra!"

"And what kind of ale have you been drinking?" a man in the crowd called out.

All the townsfolk laughed and pointed, but Raena held her ground. Dallandra glanced around, but there was no sign of the Horsekin mazrak. Perhaps he knew that his presence would only disrupt Raena's attempt to spread the word about their goddess.

"Our goddess came to us here on Earth," Raena went on. "She did show herself to us, not hide among the rocks and the trees as do those little spirits that you do worship in your ignorance. Miracles did she show us, a thousand of them."

The Horsekin began to chant, as if to agree with her. Rakzan Kral stepped forward and called out to the crowd.

"I did see her myself, and so did all my men here. We will witness."

The townsfolk began to talk among themselves in a current of whispers, but Dallandra hurried forward. She climbed halfway up the stairs leading to the platform and yelled for silence. Slowly they gave it to her.

"This goddess they speak of?" Dallandra said. "She's dead. She died like any creature, because a creature she was."

"She lies!" Raena shrieked. "Look you all there, in the sky!"

Over the commons a sphere of silvery mist was forming, swelling, growing huge as it drifted back and forth on the breeze. All at once it broke in half and the pieces fell away to disappear. Floating above the crowd was Alshandra, dressed in buckskin tunic and trousers, with her long blonde hair braided and hung with little charms in the Horsekin manner. In her hands she held an elven hunting bow.

"So!" Raena turned to Dallandra with a flourish of both arms. "And what say you to this?"

Dallandra goggled, unable to find a single word. Did Alshandra truly live then? Had Jill's sacrifice been in vain? The Horsekin threw back their heads and roared a greeting, then fell to their knees, holding their hands up high to their goddess. Suddenly Dallandra heard a soft chuckle behind her.

"Shaetano makes a better-looking woman than he did a man," Evandar said. "Less fur, shorter snout."

Dallandra let out her breath in a laugh.

"More fool me!" she whispered, then raised her voice. "That's not Alshandra, you fools! It's but a lying image of her."

"Indeed?" Raena snarled. "If you be so sure, then prove it!"

"Fear not!" Evandar called out. "I shall."

Evandar climbed the steps up to the platform and bowed

to Raena, who drew back with hatred etched on her face. He tipped his head back and called to the apparition in the sky.

"Little brother! I've come for you."

The false Alshandra shrieked in fear, a high-pitched yelp that echoed like twisted thunder. Evandar ran forward, leapt off the platform, and flew into the air in the form of an enormous red hawk. Shaetano shrieked again, then flung himself to one side as the hawk swooped past. As he twisted, huge chunks of his illusion tore away and fell, melting like snow in sunlight. First his blonde mane shriveled and died; then the female face dissolved to reveal his vulpine features. The body thickened and his arms grew russet fur. He raised his bow, but the red hawk swooped down upon it, talons extended, and tore it from his grasp. Howling and gibbering, Shaetano fell from the sky, spinning down out of control.

The Horsekin screamed in rage. The townsfolk screamed in terror, then took off running, pushing each other and shrieking as they headed for the safety of their homes. The red hawk swooped and plunged down after the falling Shaetano, but all at once the fox-lord flung his arms out, seemed to grab some invisible thing in his hands, and vanished. The red hawk fluttered to the ground, wavered, and in a pulse of bluish light, transformed into Evandar. With a cackle of laughter he turned toward the Horsekin.

"Meradan!" he howled out. "Vengeance be mine!"

Evandar flung up his hands, but Dallandra was too fast for him. With a yell of "stop! no!" in Elvish, she leapt down from the stairs and grabbed him from behind, throwing her arms around his waist and hauling him around.

"Run!" she yelled in Deverrian. "Kral, get your people out of here! Zatcheka, you too!"

Evandar pulled free of her grasp, but she grabbed him by the wrists. For a moment they struggled back and forth, but he was by far the stronger. In his rage he would have thrown her to the ground, but Rhodry came running.

"Let her go!" Rhodry yelled. "You're not yourself!"

Evandar hesitated long enough for Dalla to get free of him. Rhodry threw his arms around him from behind and pinned him to his chest, talking all the while, his voice soft yet commanding at the same time.

"Nah nah nah, calm down, man! Come with me, and we'll talk this over, come along now."

All at once Evandar surrendered. He went limp, then caught his balance and stood, head bowed, clutched tight in Rhodry's arms.

"Forgive me, my love," Evandar whispered. "I never meant to hurt you."

"There's naught broken," Dallandra said. "I never knew you could be so strong here in this world."

"No more did I!" Evandar threw back his head and laughed. "No more did I."

With that he let Rhodry march him away. Dallandra rubbed her aching wrists, then turned to find Niffa watching her, all eyes.

"And what were all that?" Niffa was stammering. "Never did I dream that I would be seeing marvels such as that."

"No doubt. But here, come with me. I want a word with Raena, I do."

On the grass Raena knelt, doubled over with weeping. She was sobbing so hard that her shoulders heaved. When Dallandra knelt in front of her, Raena raised a face wet with tears. Snot ran down her upper lip.

"Raena, please, listen to me!" Dallandra said. "It's clear that you have dweomer gifts. I can understand how you came to this pass, at the mercy of lying spirits. Ye gods, the thought of being born into some far-off village and married off to some farmer—it would have curdled my blood, too! I would have gone off with Alshandra had she asked me, had I had your Wyrd."

The sobs quieted. Raena rubbed her dirty face on the sleeve of her black shirt, but still she said nothing.

"It's not too late to forswear the darkness," Dallandra went on. "You'll have restitution to make. I can't lie to you and say it will be easy. But at the end, the real dweomer will be yours, and you'll never be powerless again."

Still trembling, her lips a little parted, her eyes wide, Raena slowly looked at her.

"I mean it," Dallandra said. "I offer you my word. If you're willing to make amends, the dweomer of light offers forgiveness to all who ask."

Raena stared, trembling—whether from hope or fear Dallandra couldn't tell. Dallandra got up, holding out her hands. Raena rose as well, and her hands were shaking. It seemed for a moment that she would reach out to Dallandra, but suddenly her eyes filled with tears, and she turned away with a wrench of her entire body.

"My lady, my own true goddess," Raena whispered. "I cannot desert her. You understand naught, naught! She did come to me, she did take me for her own, she did save me. It were like a mother, whose house does burn, and in the house her baby still does lie. Would the mother not rush back into the burning house to save her child? So did Alshandra come to me, when we were a-sieging the city." She turned back, her eyes glowing again with an unnatural light. "Never will I forswear her! Never!"

"But please, talk with me! If I could only help you see—"

"I wish to see naught of your ugly ways! Leave me be, witchwoman!"

With a toss of her head Raena fled, trotting across the commons toward the open gates. Dallandra took a few steps after, then stopped. Out on the road Kral and his men waited. Raena ran straight for them, and they surrounded her like a wall. Dallandra could only watch helplessly while the Horsekin and their priestess hurried down the road to their camp. She had known the truth about the gods for so long that this simple fact had never occurred to her: Raena loved her goddess with a passion straight from the heart.

For want of anywhere else private, Rhodry half shoved half guided Evandar into Dar and Carra's tent. In the diffused light and relative coolness Evandar grew calmer. He ran his hands through his hair and caught his breath with a long hard sigh. Scattered on the painted floor cloth lay blankets, tent bags, saddlebags, and other clutter. Rhodry shoved a mound of it to one side, found a pair of floor cushions, and sat down. Evandar turned his back on him.

"I have to admit it," Rhodry said. "I liked hearing those hairy bastards squeal when you tore their false goddess to shreds."

"I only wish Dalla had let me turn them all into swine," Evandar said.

"Here! Is that what you were up to?"

"It was. I wanted to show them their true natures. Swine! The turds of swine! They killed the first thing I ever loved, and I loved it more than you and Dalla put together."

"Rinbaladelan, you mean?"

"Just that. And they acted like swine, too, rooting in the ruins, leaving their filth and stench everywhere! I laughed when they began to rot, you know. It was a glorious little plague, Ranadar's curse. I only wish it had spread farther and killed every pustule-laden one of them."

"You hate them still? Ye gods! That was over a thousand years ago."

"So what? You can't imagine the havoc they wreaked. It was horrible."

"I can, at that," Rhodry said. "I sieged and killed a city once, myself, back when I was Gwerbret Aberwyn."

Evandar turned and at last looked at him. When Rhodry pointed to the second cushion, he sat down upon it.

"Slaith, was it?" Evandar said. "The pirate harbor? Well, they were stinking foul swine, too, and you did a right thing."

"Mayhap. But I remember how sick I felt when I came to myself after the slaughter and saw the children. Dead children in the ruins, that is, only a few of them stabbed, more of them burnt to death when the buildings collapsed. We fired the place, you see, in the king's name. Once the siege fell, there was no stopping my men. Or me. I laughed when we were burning it. But later, I found the children. And I never laughed over the city again."

Evandar's eyes narrowed.

"And so I think me," Rhodry went on, "that some of

the Meradan did the same as me—thought twice about things when it was too late, I mean. And they're the people we call the Gel da'Thae. Meer's people—Zatcheka's people. Civilized people now."

Evandar growled like a dog, and for a moment his form darkened and wavered, as if he might transform into a hound right there and then. With a little shudder he caught himself and returned to his blond elven self.

"Back then they were filthy savages," Evandar said. "Why did they destroy the cities? There was no why! They swept down from the north with no reason but plunder and killing."

"No reason? Here, don't you know? I learned the lore up in Lin Serr, the Dwarveholt."

"You what?" Evandar stared for a long moment. "I have to know, I must know! Tell me, tell me now."

"Well, the real culprits were my ancestors, the people of Bel, way back in the Dawntime. They made landfall at some harbor far in the north, then rode south, looking for the omens for the right spot to found their kingdom. And as they rode they slaughtered the Horsekin—took their women as slaves, stole their horses, killed any man who dared to fight back. By the hells, the Horsekin were only savages! They knew nothing of the Rhwmanes, nothing of the troubles that had driven my ancestors here. So they— the Hordes, the Meradan—they fled south. When the People tried to stop them, they fought their way through."

Evandar stared at him for a long moment.

"Not what you thought, was it?" Rhodry said.

"No!" Evandar slumped and folded over his own lap until his head nearly touched the floor cloth. "It can't be."

"It can and it is. I saw it all in the pictures on Lin Serr's doors. Go look yourself if you don't believe me."

For a long while Evandar sat still and silent.

"Oh come now!" Rhodry snapped. "What's so wrong?"

"You don't understand." Evandar was whispering. "I brought your ancestors here. The people of Bel. I did it for a friend, my only friend, then, Cadwallinos the Druid. He begged me to save his people when the Rhwmanes moved in for the kill. I led them across the sea and through the mists on the mothers of all roads. I promised them a kingdom of their own. I found them the harbor. Here. Where they—ye gods, forgive me!" Evandar sat up at last. Tears ran down his face.

It was Rhodry's turn for the shock. For a long while they merely sat and stared at each other. From outside they could hear murmurs of conversation, as the men of the People walked back and forth, talking among themselves. At last Evandar wiped his face on his illusion of sleeve, though the wet-looking tears never dampened it.

"Ah well," Evandar said. "You've spoken true, Rori. If a man lights a fire on a floor, the wood's not to blame for burning."

"You'll let the Gel da'Thae be?"

"I will. You have my word on that." All at once he smiled, his usual sunny daft self again. "But what about the Horsekin? It would gladden my heart to crisp a few of those."

"Nah nah nah! None!"

"Oh very well! Though I must say, you can certainly be cold-hearted when you want to be."

"It's a thing I've learned with age. I recommend it to you."

Evandar scowled at him, then disappeared in a puff of pale light like dust. Shaking his head, Rhodry got up and went outside to look for Dallandra.

The strange battle in the sky had left Dallandra mobbed by people who all talked at once. Prince Daralanteriel and his men, Zatcheka and hers, even some of the townsfolk—they all crowded around her, shoving one another and demanding explanations. She could barely pick a single voice out of the uproar.

"Hold your tongues!" Dallandra shouted at last. "And get back! I'm not going to explain anything in the middle of a howling mob."

"Do what she says!" Daralanteriel snapped. "And hurry! I want to know what this all meant, myself."

The crowd grumbled, but they did step back and let her get free of them.

"That's better," Dallandra said. "Now, then. The first thing you've all got to understand is that very little of what you saw was real. The spirits who worked those marvels are masters of the etheric plane. They exist only as spirits, but they can assume many a strange form, and to our eyes they seem to be as solid as ever they can be. But they're not. They belong to another part of the universe and can only visit ours for short spaces of time."

When she paused for a moment, Dallandra realized that most of those listening had the dazed look of persons struggling to extract sense from a foreign language. Niffa was all rapt attention, and Zatcheka nodded as if in agreement, but the others, Westfolk, townsfolk, and Gel da'Thae alike—she realized that she was wasting her breath.

"These spirits aren't gods, but they do have powerful magicks," Dalla went on. "And they can cast glamours. That is, their magic can make them look like another person. But Evandar's magicks are the strongest of all, and so he destroyed their spells. Think of it as a battle, and he won."

In the fading afternoon light a number of the men smiled or nodded to one another. This they could understand.

"But we've not won the war," Dallandra said. "I want everyone to be on their guard. If you see that fox-spirit or that illusion that looks like a giant woman, you come and tell me immediately. Is that clear? Immediately."

Everyone nodded or called out their agreement. The Gel da'Thae men turned to look at Zatcheka. When she waved a hand, they left, bowing to Dallandra as they silently left the gathering. The men of the Westfolk began talking among themselves; someone suggested a song, others went to the tent to bring out food for a meal. Niffa and Carra stood off to one side, talking together while Lightning lay at his mistress's feet. Dallandra hurried over and joined them.

"Where's Elessi?" she said.

"Dar has her." Carra pointed. "I told him I'd carried her all day, and it was his turn, prince or no."

They shared a laugh.

"Lady Zatcheka did invite us to her tent," Niffa said. "I were wondering, be it a right thing for us to go? She does but wish to properly introduce us to her daughter."

"By all means, do go," Dallandra said. "What a courteous gesture, truly!"

Dallandra would have walked over to the Gel da'Thae camp with them, but Rhodry came out of the tent. She sent Niffa and Carra on in her place and stopped to speak with him.

"Where's Evandar?"

"Gone." Rhodry shrugged open-handed. "I never know where he goes to."

"Back to his own lands, I suppose. He doesn't deign to tell me, either. What are you going to do now?"

"Go over to the island and see if Arzosah's returned."

"Won't you stay here and eat with us?"

Rhodry considered this for a moment.

"I will," he said at last. "I've no idea when she'll get back."

"I'd guess that Raena waited for her to go off hunting before she left Verrarc's house."

"No doubt. The stupid meddling bitch!"

"Oh here, she's been thoroughly misled and deceived by her false goddess. You can't lay all the evil at Raena's door."

"I can and I will. I'm half-tempted to drag her into a law court myself."

"For what?"

Rhodry started to answer, then hesitated, thinking.

"I don't know," he said at last. "I just know that I've hated her for a cursed long time now, and I'm as sure as I can be without proof that she's the cause of Yraen's death."

"Well, in a way I suppose she was. And we know she's a traitor to Cerr Cawnen."

"Better yet, everyone in Cerr Cawnen knows it." Rhodry paused for one of his terrifying smiles. "And no doubt they'd like to get their hands on her, too."

"Just so. Most likely that's why she's left the city."

"She what?"

"Didn't you see her? No, of course not—you were in the tent by then. She wouldn't listen to what I was trying to say, and she ran out of the gates. Kral and his hairy pack were waiting for her."

"Indeed? And what will Verrarc think of that? Poor bastard! Ensnared by a bitch like that!"

Together they turned and looked up at the western sky. By then the sunset was gilding Citadel, rising dark from the encircling mists of the lake. And what was the Council of Five thinking of all this commotion, with fake goddesses in the sky and suchlike? Dallandra wondered, but most of all, she wondered about Verrarc.

When the apparitions first appeared in the sky, Verrarc was talking with Cronin and Emla, the weavers who supplied him with most of his trade goods. Although he'd stopped by only for a brief word, Emla had insisted on his coming into their reception chamber, a pleasant room with chairs and a big hearth. They were still in mourning for their second son, Demet, Niffa's late husband; Cronin said little, in fact, merely sat slumped in his wooden chair and stared at the wall while his wife talked with the councilman.

"This be one sorrow too many for my man," Emla said at length. "First the losing of our son, and now the Horsekin. I know not what to think, Verro, except for one thing. I'll not be dropping my shard in that rakzan creature's urn."

"I think me that be wise. Kral did talk about taking over our pasturelands for horses, bain't? There would be precious little left for sheep then."

"Just so. I—" Emla paused at the banging of an outside door. "What be all this?"

Shouting for her mother, young Cotzi came running down the corridor and slammed into the room. At the sight of her, Cronin managed a faint smile.

"Mam, Mam! There were gods in the sky! And the councilman's woman is daft!" At that Cotzi saw Verrarc and blushed deep scarlet.

"Learning to hold your tongue would be a fine thing."
Emla got up, hand raised for a slap.

With a yelp Cotzi dodged back. Verrarc rose from his
chair.

"Here, here," Verrarc broke in. "Punish her not for my
sake. I begin to fear me she does speak the truth. Cotzi,
slowly now: what be all this alarm?"

"Well, I were about in the town when I did hear shouting by the south gate. So I did run there, and your woman,
she were standing up on that wood thing the council did
have builded. She were talking about some goddess, and
then this goddess, she did appear in the sky. But a god came
too and turned into a hawk and chased the goddess away.
But she wasn't truly a goddess, she were a fox. And your
woman did rant and rave, like, and weep."

For a moment Verrarc truly thought he might faint. He
sat down fast and watched the room spin round for a good
turn before it righted itself. He looked up to see anxious
faces leaning over him.

"Fetch the man a bit of mead," Cronin was saying.

"Nah nah nah, I be myself again." But Verrarc postponed
standing for a bit longer. "Cotzi, be you certain of all this?"

"I did see it," the girl said. "And listen—hear you not
the crowds outside, all talking and suchlike?"

Indeed, Verrarc realized that through the open windows of the room he was indeed hearing panic: voices
raised, voices cursing, voices weeping. Moving carefully, he
stood up and crossed to the window. Although the weavers'
compound extended out over the lake, this reception room
stood on solid ground, and he could see a small mob of citizens just at the edge of the green commons.

"Cotzi," Verrarc said. "Where be Raena now? Still on
the green?"

"She be gone. I know not where."

"Home, most like," Verrarc said. "I'd best go after her.
These troubles be my woman's doing, and there be a need
on me to right them."

Before Emla could speak, Verrarc turned and ran out of
the room.

Other than the grassy commons itself, Cerr Cawnen sported no open spaces, no straight streets, and precious few that ran for more than fifty yards. To get to the lakeshore Verrarc had to dodge between houses, take narrow bridges from shop to shop, leap across narrow inlets of open water, and pick his way across pilings. When at last he reached the sandy shoreline, he found not one coracle drawn up. He turned and began running along the lakeside until he found a boat he could commandeer.

By then the last of the day was fading on the water. The shadows gathered and spread over the town until only the peak of Citadel gleamed gold in the sunset light. As he paddled the coracle through the rising mists, Verrarc became obsessed with a fancy, that he absolutely had to reach the peak before the sunset vanished. When he reached the shallows, he leapt out and soaked himself to the knees. He hauled the coracle onto the sand, then deserted it and ran to the path. There his exhaustion got the better of him. He struggled uphill, panting openmouthed, his legs nightmare-heavy and slow. Ahead the golden light gleamed, just beyond his reach. He forced himself to walk faster, though his legs seemed to have caught fire.

Just as he staggered onto the stone-paved plaza, the light faded. He started to sob, but he had no breath for it. Staggering like a drunken man he concentrated on walking, on picking up one foot and putting it down again, until at last he had struggled his way home. Outside the gates of the compound he stood leaning against the wall. The long muscles in his legs burned and throbbed.

"Master!" It was Harl, hurrying to reach him. "Be you ill?"

Verrarc straightened up and tried to make a jest. He could not speak. Harl flung the gate open, then put one arm around his waist.

"Lean on me. We'll get you inside," Harl said, then shouted. "Korla! Come help! The master be powerful ill."

Between them they got Verrarc into the main chamber of the house. He sank into his chair and leaned back. Swinging his legs onto the footstool took a painful while, but once he let his weight relax against the furniture the pain began to ease. When Korla handed him a pottery stoup half-full of mead, he drank as much of it off as he could in one gulp. In the hearth a small fire burned to take off the chill, and the pale greenish light of twilight came in through the windows. He tipped his head back and watched the shadows dance upon the ceiling until at last the burning in his muscles cooled.

"My thanks," Verrarc said. "I be on the mend."

Korla snorted in disbelief. Verrarc sat up straight and glanced around. Where was Raena? He got up fast, though his cramped legs protested.

"Here, here," Korla snapped. "Sit you down and rest!"

"Where be my lady?"

Harl and Korla exchanged a glance that told him everything. He rushed across the room and threw back the door into their bedchamber. In the dim twilight he could see only the vague shapes of furniture. The silence hung in a peculiar emptiness.

"Bring a lantern!" Verrarc called.

Muttering under her breath Korla lit a candle at the hearth, placed it in a pierced tin lantern, and shuffled over to hand it to him. The light fell on what seemed to be answering sparks, gleaming on the floor, but when Verrarc knelt to look more closely, he realized that he was seeing gold. A poker lay nearby. Raena had thrown his mother's necklace onto the floor and smashed each teardrop of soft gold into a shapeless mass.

"Ai!" Korla sobbed. "She did have no call to be doing that!"

Verrarc set the lantern down on the floor and picked up the fragments of gold. The necklace had been his only memento of his mother. For a moment he stroked them between his fingers, as if he could somehow massage them back into the teardrops he remembered gleaming around her neck.

"No call at all," Verrarc whispered. "Here, Korla. Keep these safe for me?"

When she held out her apron Verrarc dropped the golden handful into the cloth. He took his lantern and rose to throw open the lid of the wood chest—nothing remained, not one dress nor trinket of Raena's things.

"She did go back to the Horsekin, bain't?" Verrarc said.

"So I do suppose," Harl said. "I did see her in her strange black clothes just after that there dragon did fly away. She were hurrying down the path to the lake, and she did carry a bundle of cloth and suchlike in her arms."

"I see." Verrarc paused, thinking. "I'd best go see if I can find her. The Chief Speaker did charge me with keeping a watch on her, and here I've gone and failed him."

"Shall I be searching too?" Harl said. "I'll gladly row us across to the town. We have a bit of light left before the night does fall."

"Do that, and my thanks, but do you go alone. I'll follow in a bit. I've an errand to run here."

Just after sunset, Jahdo made his way across the lake to Citadel. Panting for breath, he hurried uphill through the winding streets. His year spent in the flatter lands of Deverry had spoiled his wind, but once he reached his home, he had enough air left to tell his parents the tale of gods in the sky and powerful dweomers. Through the recital Lael listened stone-faced, whilst Dera kept twisting her hands together and pulling them apart, only to twine her fingers once again. Finally, when Jahdo ran out of breath and tale both, Lael got up from his seat at the table.

"I'll be off to find Kiel," he announced. "Mayhap he can make some sense of all this."

Lael strode out, leaving the door half-open to the twilight. The fire in the hearth brightened and set light to dancing in the room. For a long while Dera stared at the worn planks of the table; then she rose, sighing.

"Well, I'll just be making some dinner," she announced. "Life won't stop just because the whole town's gone daft."

From a wooden bin she took a sack of turnips. Jahdo sat down on the straw-heaped floor with Ambo on his lap. The ferret curled and fell asleep, so oblivious of their plight that Jahdo envied him.

"Well," he said, "if the Horsekin do siege us, at least the weasels can eat rats. They be luckier than we."

Dera tried to smile, then turned away sharply, fumbling with the hem of her apron. Jahdo knew that she was crying, but since she'd gone to the trouble of trying to hide it from him, he said nothing. In a moment she went back to trimming the mould off the turnips.

"Dera?"

Jahdo nearly screamed. Verrarc had opened the door and stepped in, so quietly, so suddenly that he'd never noticed the councilman there.

"Well, come you in, Verro," Dera said. "But how you did startle us!"

"My apologies."

Carrying a candle lantern, Verrarc came in very slowly, very carefully, looking round him at each step. In the grey light he seemed grey, himself, his blond hair as dead and matted as the fur of a sick animal, his eyes deep pools of shadow in his pallid face. He sat down on the wooden bench by the table to watch Dera work.

"Be you ill?" she said, and sharply.

"Not truly. I've not slept much, these past nights."

"Have any of us? But you do look like weasel bait."

Something of a smile formed on his mouth, then vanished.

"Mayhap I do," he said. "It weighs on me worse than most, this threat from the Horsekin."

"There be a charge on you to turn it aside, of course."

He winced and began to tremble. Dera put down the knife and shoved a wisp of hair back from her face with her little finger.

"What be so wrong?" she said, softening her voice. "I meant not but that the council's got the responsibility of looking after the town. The charge lies on the whole council, not only you."

"I know." His voice cracked and broke. "Forgive me? Please, Dera. Forgive me?"

He got up, took his lantern, and rushed out. As he turned in the doorway to squeeze his way out of the alley,

Jahdo got a glimpse of his face, dead-white and streaming tears. Dera stared after him a long, long time.

"Now what does lie behind that?" she said. "The poor lad! He did start life wounded, and he be as weak as a split stick. May his father's spirit walk in pain forever!"

"Mam!" Jahdo slung the furious Ambo over one shoulder and scrambled to his feet. "You don't think a madness lies on Verrarc, do you?"

"What? Of course not! Mind your silly tongue!"

But the crack and quaver in her voice told him that she lied.

"Be it a fit thing for me to ask questions?" Niffa blurted.

"It is," Dallandra said, smiling, "and I'll wager you've got a lot of them."

They were standing together at the edge of the elven camp. A pale greenish twilight was gathering in the sky, and mists drifted out on the water as the night cooled. Behind them in the camp firelight suddenly bloomed. They walked only a few yards away in order to stay within reach of the firelight. Dallandra realized that no one was going to follow them to eavesdrop, anyway. No doubt the men had seen too much strange dweomer already to wish to hear of more.

"Now then," Dalla said. "Where do you want me to start?"

"Well," Niffa said, "you did say somewhat about other parts of the universe. I do know this part, where we stand and see and suchlike. What be the others?"

"Ye gods! You don't want to begin with an easy question, do you?"

"My apologies. I be grateful for any lore you do choose to tell me, so there be no need on you to start there if—"

Abruptly Niffa stopped talking. When Dallandra turned, wondering what had silenced her apprentice, she saw Verrarc, walking along the lakeshore and heading for them. He carried a candle lantern as if it were a heavy burden. Something, at least, was making him stagger like an old man.

"I think me," Dallandra said, "that the workings of the universe will have to wait for a bit. Niffa, go back to camp."

Niffa obeyed her without a murmur. Dallandra hurried to meet Verrarc. They stood at the edge of the lake, where the water lapped onto the sand with a noise like drops falling. The speckled light from his lantern danced around them from the shaking of his hand.

"Are you looking for Raena?" Dallandra said.

"I am," Verrarc said. "Though I think me she did go off to the Horsekin camp."

"I saw her run that way, truly, after her false goddess disappeared. You have heard what happened, haven't you?"

"I did." Verrarc hesitated for a long moment. "That thing in the sky—the one she did think was her Alshandra? That were the fox-spirit, bain't?"

"It was. I take it you've seen Lord Havoc before?"

"I have." He paused again, staring at the closed gates on the other side of the commons. "I do wonder if it behooves me to go out to the Horsekin camp."

"To fetch Raena back?"

"She'll not come back." Verrarc's voice suddenly thickened with tears. "That I do know deep in my heart. But to speak with her, like, for a last time."

"I think me that it would be very unwise, Councilman, if not dangerous. What if they took you hostage?"

"I'd not thought of that. Think you they might?"

"I'd not put anything past the Horsekin. At the least, they could disrupt the Deciding that way."

The candlelight danced so wildly that she reached out and took the lantern from him. He seemed not to notice, even when she raised it to look him in the face. Tears glistened in long trails.

"My heart aches for your grief," Dallandra said. "But truly, her staying would only have brought you a greater one."

"I did deem as much. Ah ye gods! I do hope only that the town may forgive me."

"Well, come now! When you took her in, you couldn't have known the truth of all of this."

"Oh, no doubt. But—later did I err, and grievously."

"What? Here, what have you done?"

For a long moment he merely stood, staring down at the water's edge, then raised one arm and wiped the tears from his face. Dallandra waited, fighting the urge to probe.

"It were a thing I did for Raena's sake." Verrarc spoke at last. "When Zatcheka came, asking for alliance, Raena did beg me to put off the Deciding. And I did what she did ask. Ah gods! Had I not, the town would have had its alliance, and I could have spurned the Horsekin at our gates."

"I see."

"But that be the least of it. I did take her in, I did shelter her, I did listen to her lies. This Lord Havoc—I envied her the magicks he did give her. I should have—"

"Should have what?" Dallandra made her voice gentle. "What could you have done about it?"

Startled, Verrarc looked up, blinking in the lantern light.

"Here you were, alone and unmindful," Dallandra went on. "Did she tell you about the war on Cengarn?"

"She didn't. I heard not a word of that till Zatcheka came."

"As for Lord Havoc, how were you to know who he might be?"

"Well, his brother did warn me once."

"Once."

He managed a faint shadow of a smile.

"It's not all lost yet, you know," Dallandra said. "I think me that if your people choose the alliances Dar and Zatcheka offer them, the Horsekin will think more than twice about taking your lands. You can't blame yourself for everything."

"But there be Rae, working more harm, for all I know, and that cursed mazrak too—she did bring him here."

He was quite right, Dallandra realized. She had no idea of what dweomer Raena and her strange priest might be working, off among the Horsekin. Casually she turned a bit away and glanced down at the water's edge, as if she were merely thinking, but in truth she opened her dweomer sight and called up Raena's image. In the dappled light upon the water the scrying came easily, and she saw Raena quite plainly. Inside a tent dimly lit with silver dweomer light Raena lay on a pile of blankets with the mazrak on top of her, both of them naked. Her head was thrown back and her face, beaded with sweat. Even in vision Dallandra could see the streaks of dirt on his back and hairy haunches.

"Oh curse her!" Verrarc snarled. "The lying slut!"

Too late Dallandra realized that he'd been able to follow her mind's lead and see the vision. With a shake of her head she closed down the sight and turned to see Verrarc trembling, his fists clenched at his sides.

"I'll kill her," Verrarc whispered. "May the gods of my people rise up and help me kill her!"

"Leave her to me," Dallandra said. "Leave her to me and the laws of your town!"

"Why? How may I count myself a man if—"

"Hold your tongue!" Dallandra put a snap into her voice. "If you kill a sworn priestess of their goddess, they'll demand retribution. They'll use it to lay a claim on your town, and when the claim's not paid, they'll come back with an army, alliance or no."

Verrarc started to speak, then merely stared at her, his mouth slack.

"Do you understand me?" She softened her voice. "Truly, my heart aches for you, but ye gods, man! Think of your fellow citizens!"

"I swear to you, Mazrak, that my fellow citizens be never far from my heart. But ye gods! You must think me no true man, that I could swallow this bitter ale she poured me and smile when I were done?"

"Naught of the sort!"

Verrarc turned, one hand on the hilt of the long knife at his belt. He was staring at the town wall, where lantern light bloomed on the catwalks as the town watch took up their posts.

"Sergeant Gart be on duty this night." Verrarc spoke so softly that she wondered if he realized he were speaking aloud. "He'll open the gates if I command."

"Don't! What will you do, rush into the camp and try to stab her? The Horsekin would cut you down so fast you'd never even get a strike on her."

That gave him pause. With a long sigh that sounded near a sob he laid his hands over his face. Dallandra wondered if he wanted her to talk him out of his revenge, and if she could, but she had an ally close at hand. From the elven camp Rhodry came striding over, calling out in Elvish.

"Dalla! Are you all right? Who's this?"

"Councilman Verrarc," she called back in the same. "Come talk with him, will you?"

When Rhodry joined them, Verrarc made some effort to pull himself together, but he could not stop shaking, nor could he bring the color back to his face.

"What's so wrong?" Rhodry snapped.

"Raena," Dallandra said. "She's deserted to the enemy."

"Ah horseshit!" Rhodry turned to Verrarc. "My apologies, Councilman, but your woman's a danger to you and the town both."

"I do know that better than you." Verrarc's voice was more a growl. "Tell me somewhat. She did charge you to me with wanting her death, all over the murder of some friend of yours."

"She spoke true for a change, though she didn't kill him with her own hands."

"I did wonder. She did show me a knife such as the one in your belt there and claim that it were your friend's. It did have a wyvern graved upon the blade."

"True again."

Verrarc considered this for a long moment while he went on shaking.

"Do you blame me for hunting her down?" Rhodry said.

"Not anymore," Verrarc snapped. "I think me there be more than one man's death that might be charged against her."

"True spoken indeed. And if she escapes with the Horsekin, she'll work more harm."

"But you can't go charging into their camp!" Dallandra put as much force as she could muster in her words. "I'll not have you start a new war over their wretched priestess."

"Wise counsel as always, my love." Rhodry grinned at her. "But I doubt that we can lure her out of their cursed camp. If she came back inside the walls, she'd be subject to your laws, Councilman, not theirs. And she knows that as well as I do."

"True enough," Verrarc said. "And she knows another thing as well, that I do command the town watch. We could arrest her easily enough."

"We?" Rhodry said. "Are you in this hunt with me, then?"

"I am." Verrarc took a long deep breath. "And what has she done, but betray me and my town to the Horsekin?"

When Rhodry held out his hand, Verrarc took it. Dallandra allowed herself a quick look at his aura: strong and blazing red.

"Well and good, then," Rhodry said. "Dalla, don't you see? If we're going to bring Raena to heel, we have to do it now, and if it takes force, well, I don't see the harm of that. The Horsekin will doubtless attack anyway, sooner or later."

"Better later," Dallandra snapped. "Think! If they thought they could just march down and take Cerr Cawnen, why would they be bothering to ask for an alliance?"

"True spoken," Verrarc said. "There be some sort of constraint upon them. I know not what it may be, but why would they come talking peace and not war?"

"The horses," Rhodry put in. "We killed a fair number of their warhorses last summer."

"That could be," Dallandra went on. "But if you slay Kral and that filthy mazrak, and you'll doubtless have to do that if you want to seize Raena, then the affair will be a matter of honor and revenge. I don't care what's making them hold back. It won't matter anymore. We need time, Rori. Dar's made this offer of alliance on his own, and if the townspeople take it, he'll have to ride back home and find his father and Calonderiel before he can fulfil his obligations."

Rhodry sighed in a gloomy sort of way. "You're right," he said at last. "But ye gods, it would have gladdened my heart to turn Arzosah loose on the bitch." He turned to Verrarc. "My apologies. I should mind my tongue about her."

"Not for my sake." Verrarc turned on his heel and ran, leaving her the lantern.

Dallandra took a few steps after him, but he plunged into the welter of houses and crannogs and disappeared. And what more could I say to him? she thought. Very little. Very little indeed.

"Think he'll hold true?" Rhodry spoke in Elvish. "I can't help but wonder if he's in league with her somehow, laying a trap for us."

"I doubt it. Just now, when I scryed Raena out, I found her wallowing in the blankets with that mazrak, the dirty one. I didn't realize how much dweomer Verrarc has. He saw it, too."

Rhodry laughed his high-pitched berserker's chortle.

"Oh, he'll hold true," Rhodry said, grinning. "I think me we can count on our Verro, truly I do."

"Well, I feel sorry for the poor man."

"So do I." Rhodry suddenly held up a hand for silence. "There she is. Hear that?"

"No. What do you mean? Wait! That drumming sound?"

"That's Arzosah flying."

Sure enough, in but a few moments the thwack of her wings against the air sounded loud and clear over the town. Dallandra set the candle lantern down and walked a few steps away from the pool of light. When she looked to the west, she could see the dragon-shape against the stars.

"I'd best get back to Citadel," Rhodry said. "It wouldn't be prudent, somehow, to have her land right here."

Rhodry trotted off, heading round the lake—to find a coracle, Dallandra supposed. Now if only we could persuade Arzosah to guard the Northlands, Dalla thought. Mayhap for a tax of cows? She giggled aloud, then decided she must be going daft with the strain.

For a long while that night Dallandra sat by the fire and fed it twigs while she scried in the embers. The vision rose of the Horsekin camp and another fire, where Kral, Raena, and the mazrak sat talking quietly among themselves. It seemed that talk was all they did, but Dallandra's blood ran cold with the dweomer warning. They were planning some danger to the town, whether violence or dweomer she could not know. Finally, when they retired to their tents, she let the fire die and went to her own blankets.

"So," Arzosah said, "the stinking bitch has fled, has she? Why don't we fly over the Horsekin camp and scatter their horses? All the men will have to chase after them, and then I can just swoop down and seize Raena."

"Naught would please me more," Rhodry said, "but we can't. There's the small matter of their tribes back at home to consider."

"The only way I choose to consider them is for meals."

"I know, but there are far too many of them in the Northlands for you to eat, not all at once at least. If we harm these Horsekin, their kin will send an army after us."

Arzosah heaved a massive sigh. They were sitting on the roof of the ruined temple, and in the starlight Rhodry could see her examining her claws.

"That beastly stag struggled," she remarked. "I may have chipped a claw on him. But I ate him for his pains."

"The entire Horsekin army will struggle a fair bit harder than one stag."

"Well, true enough. And I won't be able to panic their horses forever. Sooner or later the stupid creatures will recognize my smell and decide their masters can drive me off." She lowered her massive paw. "Pity. It would have been grand to bring Raena back all bloody and dripping."

"Grand till Cerr Cawnen had to pay the price," Rhodry said. "Now look, on the morrow, I want you to fly off again. Hunt or not as you please, but don't come back to the town till well after sunset."

"Gladly, but do we really have to let her escape?"

"Who said anything about letting her run free? I'm thinking up a plan. But if you're here, Raena will be too frightened to walk into the trap."

"Very well then." Arzosah yawned with a shake of her head. "You do the thinking. I'm going to get a good night's sleep."

• • •

For most of the night Verrarc lay awake, alone in the bed he'd grown used to sharing. His mind raced this way and that like a panicked animal, first cursing him for losing Raena, next exulting that she was gone, then worrying about the Horsekin, wondering why he would trust Dallandra and this Rhodry from Aberwyn, and then once again giving in to his grief at losing the only woman he'd ever loved. Finally he did sleep, only to wake when Korla came rushing into a bedchamber bright with sun.

"The Chief Speaker be here, master. It be a good while past dawn."

"Ye gods! Do him tell that I wake and will join him presently. Oh, and tender him my apology for being so lax."

On every day of Deciding, the town council went up to the plaza early to set up the wood booths that would each enclose a set of colored jugs. Near the well stood the big plank table for the stone markers. For this particular election, those citizens who wanted an alliance with Prince Daralanteriel and the Gel da'Thae would put black markers into a black pot. Those who wished to ally with the Horsekin would put red in red, and those who wished no alliance at all, white in white.

Verrarc arrived just as Sergeant Gart came puffing up the path with the militia marching behind him. Ten men would stand behind the table to ensure that the voting proceeded honestly. Other squads would dispose themselves around the plaza, just in case there was trouble, as Sergeant Gart remarked.

"A good thought, Sergeant," Verrarc said. "The whole town's on edge."

Admi himself stood off to one side talking with Zatcheka, who had come to witness the Deciding. She was wearing her long deerskin dress and a tall headdress made of cloth-of-gold, wrapped round itself and piled high. Jewelled stickpins flashed here and there in the folds. Two of her men, armed with solid quarterstaves, stood guard behind her. Verrarc was about to join Admi when he saw the prince of the Westfolk coming with an escort of his own. Against the folds of his grey tunic the sapphire pendant gleamed. Behind his men walked Niffa, Dallandra, and the princess, carrying her baby. Bringing up the rear as a last guard was Rhodry from Aberwyn. Verrarc hurried over and bowed to the prince.

"Good morrow," he said. "I see Niffa told you of our custom."

"So she did," Daralanteriel said. "So I've come to witness, as she suggested. I hope you don't mind my wife coming along. She wanted to see the workings of your Deciding."

"Of course, of course, you're all welcome," Verrarc said. "No doubt Niffa did tell you, though, that you mayn't speak to the citizens as they make their choices."

"She did, and we'll abide by that." Dar paused, glancing around. "Carra, will you be all right? The day's turning out hot, clouds or no."

"The Council House does stand over yonder," Verrarc put in. "Do avail yourself of it should you wish."

"We could take the baby inside for a bit," Carra said to Niffa. "Not much is happening yet."

"We've yet to send out the criers," Verrarc said. "Here be the customs which do rule a Deciding. The Council of Five does prepare all that you see before you. Then do we send out four criers to the town below, to remind all that on a day such as this no one may lift a hand to do any other citizen harm. It be needful for a Deciding to be free of all strife, for who would choose cleanly if he did think himself in danger for it?"

"True spoken." Dar nodded in agreement. "That strikes me as a fine custom."

Talking together, Niffa and Carra took the baby and strolled away in the general direction of the Council House. Verrarc glanced at Rhodry, who had been listening with his thumbs hooked into his sword belt.

"Tell me, Councilman," Rhodry said. "Does Rakzan Kral have the right to witness?"

"I fear me he does." Verrarc felt suddenly sick. "There be a need on us to send a fifth crier to his camp, methinks."

"I'll be glad to take that duty upon myself." Rhodry suddenly smiled, and Verrarc had never seen anyone smile so brightly and yet look so cold. "To spare one of your townsfolk the danger, like."

"Rori!" Dallandra stepped forward. "And what are you planning?"

"To do the council's bidding and naught more." Rhodry's smile turned innocent.

"Will you swear that to me?" Dallandra set her hands on her hips and glared at him.

"I will, on my silver dagger."

"Oh very well, then, if the council wants to take your offer, I shan't stand in your way. But you need to warn Arzosah off, too. She's someone else who needs to hear the customs of this country."

"We discussed it last night. She knows she's not to eat any Horsekin or their mounts." Rhodry turned to Verrarc. "Shall I be a herald or no?"

"I'll take your offer and gladly," Verrarc said. "There were a great trouble on my heart, thinking of who might be willing to go to that camp."

Rhodry started to answer, but suddenly Verrarc heard a sound like thunder, rising behind him. He spun around and saw the black dragon, flying from her perch. With a few wing strokes she gained height, turned, and flew steadily off to the east.

"Good," Rhodry said. "She remembered what I told her. I thought it might ease your citizens' hearts, Councilman, not to have her so close to the Deciding."

"My thanks." Verrarc watched the dark shape dwindling and shuddered. "I think me it be for the best."

In Cerr Cawnen a crier wore long strips of white linen tied round his head and fluttering behind him; he carried a staff bound with more of the same. Since the other men carried no weapons, Rhodry left his sword with Dallandra, but he kept the silver dagger at his belt. Admi repeated the ritual words several times over for Rhodry's sake.

"And do you remember," Admi finished up, "that the town gates will be shut, lest some traveller disturb the proceedings. The witnesses must call up to the guards and state their errand within."

The five criers rode the council's big barge across the lake. By the time they reached the farther shore, dark clouds filled the sky, and the windless day had turned hot and muggy. Rhodry was glad of the chance to get away from the steaming, stinking lake to the clean air of the water meadows beyond the gates.

The Horsekin had set up their peaked tents in a rough circle around a big fire pit. As Rhodry approached, he could see their horses grazing at tether beyond the camp. The camp itself seemed deserted at first, but when he called out a hail, one of the tent flaps opened and Rakzan Kral himself came out, wearing his gold surcoat and carrying his whip. He smiled with a show of fang, yet Rhodry could tell that he meant to be pleasant. Rhodry bowed to him.

"A good morrow to you," Rhodry said. "I understand that you're a plaintiff at Cerr Cawnen's gates?"

"I am, truly," Kral said. "The priestess did tell me that a herald would come unto us."

Rhodry glanced around, but he saw only a pair of human slaves, standing between two tents and watching silently.

"I am enjoined by the Council of Five to invite your witness to the Deciding this day. The public square on Citadel is open to all who would come."

"Good," Kral said, nodding. "I'll just be gathering a few of my men—"

"Wait! It also is my duty to tell you that on the day of a deciding all strife is forbidden. No man or woman either may carry weapons to the council square. Any who raises his hand against a citizen or a fellow plaintiff will be subject to the laws of the town."

"Very well. I pledge that me and mine will abide by this prohibition."

"Well and good, then. When you come to the town, you will find the gates shut. Call up to the guards, and they will admit you and an escort of two."

"I'll do so."

"So be it." Rhodry thumped the ground with the end of his staff. "Be you welcome at your leisure."

As he turned to go, Rhodry saw Raena, peering out of one of the tents. She held the tent-flap just open enough to look out while remaining mostly hidden behind the canvas.

"And will you come to witness," Rhodry said, "priestess?"

Raena went dead-still, staring at him. Rhodry laughed, his high berserker's chortle.

"I'll wager you don't have the guts." He bowed to her in the best courtly manner he could muster, being as he was holding a staff. "Not after our meeting upon the battle plain."

"Curse you!" Raena flung the canvas aside and stepped out. "Kral! Kill this man! I command you!"

"What?" In two long strides Kral joined them. "I grovel before the holy one, but I'll not be killing a herald and an unarmed man. How, think you, would that please the good folk of the town?"

Raena stamped her foot and glared at him. She was wearing a long buckskin dress, painted with blue designs, and her long black hair was piled up on her head and bound with gold bands. The finery, however, seemed to leave Kral unimpressed. He shrugged and turned to Rhodry.

"Good herald, I do suggest that you return to your town."

"My thanks, Rakzan, and I shall."

As he strode off, Rhodry was grinning. Now he had only to wait and see if Raena took his challenge.

All day the dark clouds hung over Citadel. In the heat tempers ran short, especially among the militiamen, who dripped sweat inside their leather armor. Verrarc walked back and forth, speaking as calmly as he could and settling squabbles. He'd never seen the citizenry so edgy, either. With such an important decision at stake, every adult in town turned out to line up and wait on the only path up to the square. Here and there some impatient soul would try to force himself a few paces ahead of where he should be, or some woman would be carrying a baby that squalled and stank, and those standing near these nuisances would turn nasty.

Burra and Frie spent most of the morning walking back and forth along the queue of townsfolk to keep order. A few at a time the citizens left the path and walked onto the public square, where Hennis handed out the three markers, then went singly into one of the booths. Mindful of the crowd, everyone moved briskly past the jugs. On their way out they dropped the unused stones into another pot. It took all of Verrarc's will to keep from peeking into the discards, just to get some vague idea of which way the vote would swing. By noontime, Verrarc estimated that half of those entitled to vote had finished.

"I think me we'd best send out the criers again," Admi said, "to ask the citizens still at home to stay there until this press thins."

"Just so," Verrarc said. "It gladdens my heart to see so many folk come out."

Admi nodded and pulled a rag out of his pocket to mop the sweat from his face.

"Rain would be welcome," Verrarc went on. "Though I do hope it holds off till most have decided."

Admi said nothing. He was staring over Verrarc's shoulder with a peculiar expression on his face, half contempt, half fear. When Verrarc turned around, he saw Raena in a long Horsekin-style leather dress, her head bound in green cloth, walking briskly toward him with Rakzan Kral. Behind them came a Horsekin warrior, carrying a ceremonial staff. Kral himself carried naught but a table dagger at his belt.

"The gall of the bitch," Admi murmured.

Verrarc wondered if he were about to disgrace himself and weep. Fortunately Kral turned and said a few words to Raena that made her stop walking. She and the guard waited a good distance away while Kral hurried over to Admi and Verrarc.

"I mayn't command the priestess," were the first words Kral spoke. "My apologies, Councilman Verrarc."

"No offense taken," Verrarc said. "I never could control her either."

Verrarc turned on his heel and strode off to the other side of the booths. Raena never came near him, not for the entire long afternoon.

Although the clouds grew darker, the rain held off throughout the Deciding. At various times one of the councilmen or some of the militia would slip off to eat, then return. Slowly the line of citizens crept up the hill. Eventually, when the sun was turning the clouds in the west a dull gold, Verrarc realized that the line had become a scatter of citizens, waiting on the plaza edge.

"I do think the most of our folk have cast their markers," Verrarc said. "Good. When the last be done, we'll be moving into the shelter of the Council House to count them, and the rain will be of no import."

Rhodry had spent the day guarding Carra and her child. Early on the princess had grown weary of the stark Council House and the plaza. For a while they visited with Jahdo's mother and her sister, Sirri, the town midwife, until the talk of babies in general and Elessario in particular made Rhodry wonder if men truly could die of boredom. Fortunately for him, both older women had work to attend to, and about midafternoon he escorted Carra back to the elven camp on the lakeshore. Vantalaber, the pale-haired captain of the archers, came hurrying to meet them.

"I kept a watch on the gates," Val said. "Raena and her swinish rakzan came through around noon."

"Did she now?" Rhodry laughed, a hard berserker howl that made Val wince. "I'm looking forward to tonight. Things may turn interesting."

While Carra and the child rested inside the royal tent, Rhodry sat outside the door with Lightning, Carra's dog, for a second guard. The dog slept and Rhodry drowsed, his hand on the hilt of his sword, but neither Raena nor Horsekin came near. Toward sunset Carra carried the baby outside and told him she'd decided to rejoin her husband up on the public square.

"The citizens ought to be all done soon," Carra said. "I want to see how the council members count the markers out."

"With tally marks, I suppose," Rhodry said.

"No doubt, but that's not what I meant." Her pretty little face had gone thoughtful. "I wonder if they count big lots in twenties, as we do, or in twelves."

"Twelves? Who would do that?"

"Farmers and suchlike do it all the time. I've always thought that they must have preserved the ancient customs of their ancestors, who were bondfolk, you see, or truly I mean, the people our ancestors turned into bondfolk. And now I've got a chance to find out. If Cerr Cawnen uses twelves, then I'll know that such was the original way of counting in this country."

Rhodry managed to smile, but he was wondering if she were a bit daft, to trouble herself over such things.

They found a coracle, and he paddled them across the lake under a dark sky. Sylphs emerged from the water, pale blue and green, stretching out slender hands as they crowded around the boat. At the sight Elessi gurgled and flapped her chubby hands in their direction.

"Oh, now, what is it?" Carra said. "There's naught there."

Elessi ignored her and made the little panting sound of a baby just learning to laugh. One bold sylph leaned into the boat and touched a wisp of her golden hair. A drop of water ran down her chubby forehead.

"Ah!" Carra said. "It must be starting to rain. A drop fell on Elessi."

Rhodry smiled and said nothing. In a few moments the sylphs dove back into the lake and disappeared, melding again with the water. Just as they reached the island, however, a few drops of real rain spattered on Citadel's narrow shore.

"We'd best hurry," Rhodry said. "The storm's going to break, I'll wager."

The rain held off for a while more. Rhodry carried the baby as they climbed the steep path to the plaza, and Lightning trotted ahead, tail held high and wagging. When they reached the top, Kiel, still in his militia armor, hurried over to meet them. Only a few townsfolk still waited near the booths. At the public well, Daralanteriel, Dallandra, and Zatcheka stood talking together.

"Rori," Kiel said. "I'll have to ask you for that sword."

"Right you are." Rhodry handed the baby back to Carra. "My apologies. I'm as used to its weight as most men are to their brigga, I suppose." He unbuckled his belt, slid the scabbard off, and handed it to Kiel. "Take good care of that, will you?"

"I'll give it to Dallandra to carry for you."

Carra had kept walking, heading for her husband, but when Rhodry called to her, she waited for him to catch up. The militiamen had gathered round the booths, ready to take the jugs inside and dismantle the shelter. Four council members stood in a little huddle near the table and talked, but Verrarc had gone elsewhere. Rhodry could see the glow of a fire or perhaps lanterns through the windows of the Council House. All at once Carra yelped and pointed. At her side her wolfish dog growled and bared teeth.

About halfway between the well and the Council House stood Rakzan Kral, a Horsekin guard, and Raena, tricked out in Horsekin finery. Although she wore no kirtle round her buckskin dress, Rhodry noticed her green head wrap, so bulky and heavy-seeming that it might well hide more than hair.

"Carra," Rhodry whispered. "Be brave. I think we can catch ourselves a raven if you don't mind pretending to be a little bird on her nest."

"What? I—oh wait! I do see what you mean."

Carra shifted Elessario's weight in her arms and held the child upright. Elessi obliged by grabbing a strand of her mother's hair in one hand and leaning over Carra's shoulder. Rhodry walked a little behind her as she strolled slowly over to the well. He could see Raena, walking a few steps toward Carra, then stopping, watching her from a distance—too far for Rhodry to see her expression, elven sight or no. Rakzan Kral laid a hand on Raena's arm and leaned close to speak to her. Rhodry let Carra get several paces ahead of him. Raena shook Kral's hand off, but she stood where she was.

Someone came out of the Council House and hurried over to the group by the well—Niffa, Rhodry realized, and she was carrying a wooden cup in one hand, as if she were going to fetch someone water. She saw Carra and waved.

"Carra!" Niffa called out. "I did wonder when you'd be back."

Smiling, Carra hurried over to join her friend. Rhodry kept pace at his distance. He saw Raena reach up to her headdress; he went on guard. Sure enough, she pulled something free—or did she? When she lowered her hand it seemed empty, but then, her dress had long sleeves. Did she know that he was watching her? Rhodry wondered. Carra joined her husband, and Raena turned, gesturing to Kral to follow, and walked away from the group round the well.

The rain began, splattering on the stone paving of the square. Distantly lightning flickered, and thunder rolled in the western sky. The councilmen began rushing back and forth, yelling orders at the militiamen, grabbing the jugs full of markers. Dar called to his men and trotted over to help; Zatcheka sent her guards, then hurried toward the Council House and shelter. Another roll of thunder, nearer this time, and the rain began in earnest. Rhodry saw Niffa and Carra, with the baby in her arms, hurrying toward the Council House. He took off running and caught up with them just as Raena made her move.

"Alshandra!" Raena howled out the name, then darted forward. A dagger flashed in her hand. "Take your daughter back!"

Carra screamed and lurched to one side, only to slip on the wet cobbles and fall backwards with the child clasped in her arms. The baby began to howl. Raena leapt, the dagger held high, but the dog could leap faster and high enough. With a low growl Lightning sprang and grabbed her wrist in his jaws. Raena fell half on top of him and began to shriek. The dagger clattered onto the cobbles. Rhodry kicked it out of her reach and seized the dog's collar in both hands.

"Lightning!" Carra yelled. "Down! Let her go!"

The dog obeyed. Rhodry released him, then grabbed Raena's uninjured arm and hauled her up. Blood ran from her gashed wrist, but Lightning's fangs had closed from the side onto bone and missed the big blood vessels. She whimpered, holding up the injured wrist.

"It be broken," Raena whined. "Let me go, for the pain does vex me to the soul."

"Hold still!" Rhodry snapped. He shook her for good measure. "Or you'll bleed the worse."

Raena turned docile, sobbing and gasping for breath, but Rhodry twisted her good arm around behind her back and pinned her against his chest. The militiamen rushed over, the councilmen pushed their way through, Dar fell onto his knees beside Carra. Everyone was talking at once.

"I'm all right," Carra said over and over. "So is Elessi."

Niffa stooped and picked up the dagger.

"She did carry a weapon," Niffa said. "She did wish to murder at the Deciding."

"So she did." Admi took the dagger from her. "This be a grave and serious thing. Inside, everyone! We'll not be able to think in all this rain. Sergeant Gart! The urns! Get your men inside and guard the urns!"

Dar helped Carra up, then took the sobbing Elessi and cradled her in his arms. In the milling confusion Rhodry looked around for Rakzan Kral and found him standing back by the Council House wall. He looked stunned, his mouth half-open, his hands spread wide as if in disbelief. Rhodry was just considering speaking to him when Raena suddenly went limp in his grasp, falling forward as if she were fainting. Without thinking he let go her arm lest he break it. She twisted away, shoved him off-balance, somehow kept her feet and ran.

"Stop her!" Rhodry yelled.

The crowd around began shouting. Rhodry took out after her, but in the driving rain the soles of his riding boots had gone slick as lard. He slipped on the cobbles, righted himself, and realized that he'd lost her. It seemed she'd melted away into the shadows and the gathering twilight.

"Dalla!" Rhodry called out. "Is it dweomer?"

"Of a sort." Dallandra came running up. "But she can't

disappear into Evandar's country without the help of her
beastly fox-spirit. We've got a chance to find her."

Rhodry felt himself howling with laughter. The militia,
the townsfolk, the councilmen—they all mobbed around.
Admi yelled for silence and at last got it.

"If she be a murderess, then our laws have somewhat to
say to her," Admi bellowed to the crowd. "My fellow citizens! Find her! Bring her here to justice!"

The townsfolk cheered with spontaneous joy. Only then
did Rhodry realize just how much they had hated Raena.
Nearby Verrarc stood with his head bowed, praying to some
god, perhaps, or perhaps simply staring at the stones in an utter exhaustion of will. When Rhodry strode over, Verrarc
neither raised his head nor spoke.

"You know where she'll hide, don't you?" Rhodry said.
"Tell me. Spare us all the trouble of tearing this town apart
searching for her, and you'll do yourself a good turn, too. If
you want to stay on the council, that is."

Verrarc raised his head and looked at him with eyes that
might have been made of glass, so little feeling did they show.

"We'll find her in the end anyway," Rhodry went on.
"The gates are closed, and she'll not get out."

Verrarc said nothing. Rhodry was about to argue some
more when Dallandra grabbed his arm.

"Come with me."

"But—"

"Come with me!" Dallandra tossed her head, and her
silvery hair seemed to snap with life and power. "Leave him
alone."

Rhodry allowed himself to be led away out of earshot.
When he glanced back, he saw Verrarc standing where
they'd left him, staring out at nothing.

"Rori, be reasonable!" Dallandra snapped. "He's only
flesh and blood, not steel. Besides, I've scryed her out."

"Oh." Rhodry paused for a smile. "My apologies. I
should have known you'd be able to find her. Where is
she?"

"In the ruins of that temple thing. Where you and
Arzosah were camping."

Yelling at Kiel to follow, Rhodry took off running. At the edge of the plaza he glanced back and saw that Kiel was bringing five more militiamen with him. He paused to let them catch up.

"I hope there's no back way out of the ruins," Rhodry said.

"I ken it not," Kiel said. "But here, Stone! Go round the back and guard any path you find there."

Stumbling on the uneven ground Rhodry hurried downhill to the heap of rubble, then stopped, peering around for an entrance. He found at last what seemed to be a tunnel mouth. As he headed for it, with the militiamen right behind, he heard a strange sound from inside. All at once a shrike burst free in a flash of black-and-white wings. Right behind it came a red hawk that gave one harsh cry as it leapt into the air and flew after. Both birds were so huge that every man there knew that they had to be shape-changers. Kiel swore under his breath.

"The bitch!" Rhodry snarled. "She may have flown, lads."

Still, neither bird had been a raven. He ran over to the entrance gaping between huge stones and peered in. When he saw the firm ground just below, he scrambled inside, half-stepping, half-sliding. Rhodry had always been able to see uncommonly well in the dark, and in a few heartbeats his eyes could pick out the shape of the structure around him. He trotted down the tunnel and heard, off to one side, the sound of a woman weeping. A broken doorway loomed. He stepped in and saw Raena, huddled against the wall in a pool of silver light. She clasped her injured wrist against her chest.

"So," Rhodry said. "The raven can't fly? What a pity."

Raena grabbed something from the floor and hurled, but he ducked and let the clumsy stone miss. Swearing under her breath she scrambled to her feet. Rhodry could hear men running down the tunnel and so, apparently, could she, because she made no try at escape.

"Kiel!" Rhodry called out. "Come here! We've got her penned!"

With a last dignity she straightened up, shaking back her long dark hair, and stood as proudly as a queen while the militiamen rushed in. For a moment they simply stared at her while she scowled with a narrow-eyed hatred that seemed as palpable as the silver light glowing on the stone.

"Take her back to Admi," Rhodry said. "Her Wyrd lies in the hands of your laws."

Up on the etheric Evandar had been waiting near Raena's hiding place, wedged between two black slabs that in the physical world manifested as stones. As he listened to Raena praying, sobbing, calling out for Lord Havoc to rescue her, he felt a brief pang of sympathy for the woman, but to him she meant bait and no more. Sure enough, in a cloud of silver light Shaetano appeared in his rough manshape, but his long face plumed with russet hair, and his ears stood up sharp and vulpine.

"I have come," he intoned. "I—"

His words broke off into a scream as Evandar leapt the gap between the planes and materialized. Before he could speak, Shaetano took off running down the tunnel. Evandar raced after him. As he ran, Shaetano's form began to melt and blur; at the entrance a black-and-white shrike screeched and leapt into the air. Evandar followed in the shape of the red hawk, flapping hard to gain height. Out of the corner of his eye he saw Rhodry racing down the path toward them, but his brother was prey, and the only thing that mattered to him now. His huge wings slashed the air and drew him ever nearer to the shrike laboring below.

They flew free of Cerr Cawnen's walls and out over the fields. Evandar was gaining steadily when Shaetano dove for the earth to land in the shelter of the pale spring grass. Evandar overshot him, cursed, swung back in a wide circle and plummeted earthward. He could see a fox, dashing for the stone wall at the edge of a cow pasture. As he landed he transformed again, this time into the black hound. Barking, he raced forward, gaining on the fox, but just as it seemed he would catch him, Shaetano leapt into the air and disappeared.

Evandar hurled himself through the gate twixt worlds

and found himself in elven form, running across the battle plain. In the hideous copper-colored light dust roiled. Lightning flashed at the horizon, turning the perpetual smoke a pale bluish-silver as ugly as the skin of a corpse. Just ahead of him Shaetano stood waiting in human form and wearing his black armor. He held his sword across his body as he crouched, ready for a fight. Evandar could see the glitter of dark eyes under the low brow of his black helm.

"Get your weapons, brother!" Shaetano called out. "You need them."

"So I do."

Evandar flung both arms into the air and called down Light. Like a bluish spear of lightning it came to him, but he grabbed it and twisted, weaving it back and forth into a huge net of rope. With a yelp Shaetano stepped back, but too late—Evandar swirled the net round his head and threw. The net flew through the air and fell over a screaming Shaetano, who tumbled to the ground and lay still. Evandar ran over, knelt, and reached through the web of ropes to grab him: empty armor rattled and rolled in the dust.

"Clever, brother, cursed clever!"

Evandar pulled the net free and began tossing pieces of armor this way and that. When he picked up the breastplate he saw a grey mouse, scurrying away through the dust. In an instant he became a cat and pounced with all claws, but Shaetano sprang free, spreading the shrike's wings. With a harsh cry the red hawk leapt after him.

The hunt led them on and on, sometimes in the Lands, sometimes in the physical world. Shaetano changed from fox to bird, from bird to mouse or mole, but every time Evandar became his enemy, from hound to hawk, from hawk to cat or ferret. On and on—the constant transformations drained them. The birds flew slowly, drifting close to the Earth, the fox and hound panted as they staggered after each other. At times Evandar had no idea of where they were. Forest and field, glowing etheric light or the blank darkness between the stars—they raced through them all.

Yet each change brought him a little closer to Shaetano, until it seemed that if he could reach a bare few inches farther with teeth or hand or paw, he would have him.

At last, as much by chance as anything, they found themselves on the shores of Cerr Cawnen's lake. Overhead the night had fallen and the rain slacked. The shrike and the hawk settled to the cool sand and stood, wings half-spread and ruffled as they glared at one another.

"Surrender, brother!" Evandar called out. "You're tiring worse than me. The next time you try to change you might well end up trapped halfway twixt fur and feather, and an ugly thing that would be."

"So, you doubt my strength, do you?"

The shrike-form rippled and dissolved, leaving a panting, bedraggled fox in its stead. With a bark the black hound sprang forward, and the fox bolted and ran, yipping under its breath. Through the narrow streets of Citadel they raced and spiralled up the hill. When the fox turned to dart down an alley toward the lake, the hound leapt forward and nearly got him. Evandar's fangs snapped just behind the black brush as the fox twisted away and bounded uphill. Round and round, slower and slower—both of them were panting by the time they gained the crest. When Evandar tried to drive him toward the ruined temple, the fox leapt onto a barrel and up to the top of a thick white wall.

"Leave me be, leave me be!" Shaetano cried out, and his voice yipped and squeaked. "I'll not work more harm!"

Evandar leapt up and as he leapt he changed, felt his legs and paws turn to wings and talons, his fur transform into feathers. The fox crouched, too exhausted to risk another change, until with a squealing little bark he jumped down from the wall and dashed downhill. The hawk was too fast for him. Evandar stooped and dove, striking his brother's vulpine form so hard that an illusion of blood flowed. The fox whimpered and fell, writhing on the rain-slick cobbles.

In front of the full moon clouds scudded on the night wind. Evandar sank his talons into the fox's brush and rose, flapping hard, while Shaetano squealed and twisted in his grip. Below them the town and its steaming lake seemed to swing back and forth.

"Hold still!" Evandar called out. "If I drop you in this form—"

The fox went limp in his talons. Circling to gain height Evandar flew until he saw a shimmering road where moonlight caught the feathered edge of a cloud. He followed it up and out, racing over muddy fields and dark forests. At a twist in the mother road he burst free of the physical world into the silent meadows of life and death. As he and his burden sank in to the lavender light, he felt himself change back to his elven form. Shaetano too stood before him in a vague elf-shape. When he spun around to bolt, Evandar grabbed his arms with both hands and twisted, hauling him back, pinning him against his chest. He could feel Shaetano tremble, then go limp.

All around them, the fields of white lilies nodded in a spectral breeze. Under the violet sky the river ran, more mist than water, it seemed. On its farther bank they could see trees, the dark green twists of young cypress.

"Where are we?" Shaetano whined. "Let me go! What are we doing here?"

"Waiting," Evandar said. "Once before I brought souls here, and they were claimed by those they belonged to."

"What do you mean by that?"

"You'll see."

Through the mists they heard voices that were more howl than words. Silver horns rang out, and a babble of yells and the baying of hounds.

"Horses!" Shaetano wrenched one arm free and pointed. "I beg you, let me go!"

Evandar laughed and gripped him tighter. Out of the mist galloped the Wild Hunt, mounted on silver horses and riding to silver hounds. The death-pale flowers bobbed and swayed as hooves and paws passed noisily above them. Cloaks glimmering with peacock colors wrapped the riders, and glittering hoods hid their faces. At their head, one rider wore her hood pushed back to free her pale gold hair, adorned with feathers and shells tied into a thicket of narrow braids. Her face shone like the moon, all silver, and her huge blue eyes glared under moon-arch brows. She called out a welcome, then turned her horse and rode straight for them with the Hunt flowing after. Shaetano screamed.

"My Lady of the Beasts!" Evandar cried out. "Take him!" He gathered his strength, swept Shaetano off his feet, and hurled him at her horse. With a peal of laughter she bent down and with one arm scooped him up.

"My thanks!" she called out. "Life he shall have, as the wild things know life, till he earns a true soul a-new!"

In the curl of her arm a fox quivered and yelped. With another long laugh she turned her horse and charged off across the river. In a peal of horns and the baying of hounds, the Hunt followed, plunging into the mists, echoing faintly, and then gone.

"That was well-done." The voice sounded directly behind him. "Clever, in fact."

Evandar spun around to find the dark-skinned old man, still carrying his knife and his apple.

"My thanks." Evandar bowed to him. "Though I begin to wonder, good sir, if you've been following me around."

"I've not, at that. It's just that every now and then a thought comes to me, like, saying I might want to go look you up and see what you're about."

"Indeed? And do you come down to the world of men and Time to see what goes on there, too?"

"I don't. I can't." He laughed, but softly. "I'm dead, you see."

"Oh." Evandar stared for a long moment. "I wonder why that never occurred to me. So you must be, good sir."

"Someday I'll be born again, but until then, the physical world's as closed to me as this world is to most living men."

"Well, that makes a twisted kind of sense. Farewell to you, good ghost." Evandar bowed again. "I'm off to settle some other business of mine."

Since it was too hot for a fire, servants filled the hearth with candle lanterns and hung others from the walls. In this flickering light the Council of Five gathered inside the

Council House to count the colored markers. The witnesses, Kral, Zatcheka, and Prince Dar, sat in chairs near the door. The town criers sat on the floor nearby. His morning's service earned Rhodry a place among them. He leaned back against the cool stone wall and watched as one at a time, Verrarc emptied the urns upon a table. Old Hennis sat nearby with a sheet of parchment and ink to record the tally marks. A scatter of red stones, a slightly larger scatter of white—but black stones poured from the urns and mounded on the table. Zatcheka watched with a studied indifference, but Dar was frankly grinning. He turned Rhodry's way, winked, and said in Elvish, "Looks like we've won."

For the honor of the thing, however, the councilmen set about counting the markers. They did indeed tally by twelves, Rhodry noticed, just as Carra had predicted. With practiced hands each councilman would whisk a dozen stones onto the floor, then hold up one finger. Hennis would make a mark, and the process would begin again. The stones drummed on the floor, and the rain on the roof; the candles in the lantern danced in the draughts and sent shadows flying over the walls. Zatcheka and Dar sat comfortably, and every now and then one of them would smile.

Rakzan Kral, however, sat scowling at the scene by the table. He crossed his arms over his chest, then never moved again, never looked at anyone or at anything except the growing heaps of black stones. Finally, when a scant handful of red stones had fallen onto the table from the last red urn, Kral rose to his feet. Chief Speaker Admi left off counting and walked over to face him. At the table the other councilmen let the tally stop and turned to listen.

"Good councilmen," Kral growled. "There be a need on me to spare us all this tedium. I do concede this decision. Your townspeople did foolishly choose to turn their backs on the strong, who would help them, and ally with those as weak as themselves. So be it. When your Wyrd falls upon you, let none say that I refused to warn you."

"Your concession, it be welcome," Admi said. "But this talk about Wyrd—truly, Rakzan, were I you I would watch my words more carefully."

Kral snarled and tossed his head. The charms in his long mane of hair caught the lantern light and glinted. Unsmiling but calm, Admi caught his gaze and held it. Slowly, quietly, Rhodry rose to his feet and waited, but in only a few moments Kral looked away with another snarl.

"So be it," Kral repeated. "I trust that your guards will let me and my man leave?"

"Of course," Admi said. "And if you do wish to attend the trial on the morrow, you may do that as well."

"Trial? And what justice can our priestess expect? It be clear enough, Chief Speaker, that your town did try and condemn her long ago. I do wonder why you waste effort on a trial. Why not kill her now and be done with it?"

"Kill her?" Admi said. "You know naught of our laws, Rakzan. We all did see her draw that dagger and threaten the prince's child. Her other crimes—they be whispers and rumors, not charges. Unless some person step forward with proof, then I'll not allow them into court."

"Oh." Kral paused, thinking. "Well and good, then, and I do apologize for my harsh words. This charge of threatening to do harm—what be the penalty for that?"

Admi hesitated, glanced Verrarc's way, then spoke. "Exile. Never more may she set one foot on Cerr Cawnen and our lands round about."

"Then attend we shall." Kral bowed, smiling. "Since as you say there be many a witness, she shall ride with us at the end of your proceeding."

Rhodry felt his rage as fire, rippling up his spine. He stood, shaking and burning, then reached for his sword—which was, fortunately, still in Dallandra's keeping. Out of the corner of his eye he noticed Prince Dar getting up. Rhodry took one stride toward Admi, but Dar smoothly stepped in front of him.

"No strife at a Deciding, Rhodry," Dar said. "Stand back."

Zatcheka rose and laid a heavy hand on Rhodry's arm.

"The prince, he did speak," she said. "Why are you not obeying him?"

Rhodry shook her hand off, but he did step back,

turned and walked away in fact. He crossed the room in a few quick strides, then stood at an uncovered window and looked out at the night and the rain. Behind him he could hear voices, but the rage had got into his blood and roared in his ears. He clutched the sill with both hands and tried to will himself calm. Outside the rain fell steadily, straight down in a windless summer storm.

"Rhodry?" The voice was Dallandra's. "They sent for me. Are you all right?"

Rhodry turned around. Except for Dallandra, carrying a lantern, the Council House stood empty.

"I'm not," he said. "Where's my sword?"

"Dar's taking it back to camp."

Rhodry swore with every foul oath he knew, but Dallandra merely waited for him to finish.

"I was right," she said. "You were planning on killing Raena straightaway."

"Well, ye gods! These stupid peasants and their stupid laws! They're going to let her go. Just let her ride away with Kral and her filthy sorcerer. May the Lord of Hell curse them all!"

"My heart isn't overflowing with joy, either, but I'll not have you murder her and end up on a gallows. We need you, the princess and I. Didn't you swear an oath to protect her?"

Caught. Rhodry sighed, ran both hands through his hair, and scowled at her.

"Oh, very well," he said. "I may long for my Lady Death, but I'd just as soon not swing her way on a rope."

"So I thought. Now, why don't you go back to the camp? You must be famished."

"I am at that. What about you?"

"I'll be over in a bit. I have one more errand to run on Citadel."

The town guards had locked Raena in the hut that did Cerr Cawnen for a jail. At Dallandra's suggestion, they hung iron chains from the walls—not on her body—to imprison her further by keeping "the spirits" away, as she phrased it for Admi. She had no idea, of course, that at that moment Shaetano was running for his life with Evandar close behind.

"She'll have a proper trial," Admi said. "For Verro's sake if naught else. Eh, the poor lad!"

"You know, Chief Speaker," Dallandra said, "I was wondering if someone ought to sit with Verrarc tonight."

"That's been attended to. Dera—Jahdo's mother—did come fetch him. No doubt she'll not leave him whilst he still might do himself harm."

"Good. Did anyone bind Raena's wrist?"

"Dera did insist on that, never fear." Admi shook his head in amazement. "After all the grief the bitch has brought us all! But that be our Dera's heart, eh? A better woman I've never known."

When Admi left, Dallandra lingered behind. The stone hut held two cells, one on either side of a short corridor. Unlike such buildings in Deverry, it smelled clean. The doors were slabs of wood, each with a small barred opening toward the top. Dallandra held up her lantern and looked into Raena's cell to find the prisoner sitting in a proper chair. At the light Raena looked up, scowled at her, then stood to face her.

"And have you come to mock and revile me?" Raena said.

"Not in the least," Dallandra said. "I came to talk with you about Alshandra's child."

"So! You do admit that the baby be hers?"

"I do but I don't. The soul of that child once was Alshandra's daughter, truly. But the child herself belongs to her mother in this world. She's been born to a new Wyrd. Even if Alshandra still lived, she'd have no further claim on Elessario's soul."

"She does live, you blaspheming bitch! And on the morrow, when they slay me, I shall have my proof of that, for she will come to me and guide me home."

"No one's going to kill you. Admi said that the punishment would be exile."

Raena tossed her head and considered Dallandra with

narrow eyes. "I think me you speak true," Raena said at last. "Well, then, I shall go to my goddess when she wills and not before."

"You sound disappointed."

"I am. It would have been a splendid thing, to be free of this stinking world once and for all. When she calls me, I will dwell with her forever in her green fields and drink from her rivers of life."

"That's not true. Those lands were never hers. She lied to you. I wish I could make you see—"

Raena snarled, pulled back her lips to show her teeth, and growled under her breath. And her eyes—they seemed to burn with a rage that reminded Dallandra of a trapped animal. At that moment Dallandra knew that indeed, Raena stood beyond any rational thought.

"Very well," Dallandra said. "We shall meet again, no doubt, so I'll warn you this. I'll never let you kill that child. Try all you want, raise mighty armies, but if I have to, I'll take her so far away you'll never find her. I'll carry her across the worlds to a land beyond your Lord Havoc's journeying."

Raena snarled with a toss of her head that sent her long hair dancing. Dallandra turned on her heel and strode out into the cool spring rain.

Rhodry spent the rainy night in the elven camp, sharing a canvas lean-to with Dallandra. He woke at first light, a sullen line of silver in the east. Although the rain had stopped, the dark clouds lingered. He walked down to the lake's edge and stood looking across to Citadel, rising dark and sharp against the steamy mists. When his stomach growled, he considered staying in camp for breakfast, but he'd gone hungry often enough in his life to ignore the feeling, and he wanted to consult with Arzosah. Fortunately someone had left a coracle turned upside down on the beach nearby. He dragged it to the water, then paddled across.

Rhodry found the dragon curled up on the roof of the ruined temple. In the rising dawn her scales gleamed like polished gems. When he climbed up, she opened one eye.

"Good morrow," Rhodry said. "I hope you didn't sleep out in the rain."

"I didn't." Arzosah opened the other eye, then paused for a massive yawn. "Not far from here there's a mountain with a cave—a bit small, but I slept well enough. I came back here when the rain stopped." She rose, stretching like a cat, one front paw at a time. "I think it's going to clear today, the sky I mean."

"Good. I want to talk the town council into trying Raena out of doors, so you can testify."

"Splendid idea. I'm still mulling over what you told me last night, that all they plan to do is exile her. We'll have to hunt her down if they do. I can always eat her."

"Not if it brings a Horsekin army down on the town."

"Oh, what do we care about this stinking town? Don't look so grim, Rori. I know it matters to you, but Raena—"

"We may be able to kill Raena with this town's laws for a weapon. That's why your testimony's important."

"Aha! You've been thinking again."

"I have. Now sit down and listen carefully."

Normally in Cerr Cawnen the Council of Five sat as a panel of judges whenever someone broke the laws, but Admi for obvious reasons had to exclude Verrarc. To ensure an odd number, he had asked Zatcheka, whose town had similar customs, to sit as the fifth judge. Just past noon, after a fresh wind had broken up the storm clouds and taken them off to the east, the court convened. The five judges sat at a long table placed just outside the Council House. Guarded by five members of the town watch, Niffa's brother among them, Raena sat on a bench to their left. Dallandra noticed a big blotch of dried blood on her dress, from the dog bites, she assumed. Rakzan Kral and two of his men stood as near to Raena as the guards would allow. Prince Daralanteriel, representing Carra as the injured party, sat to their right with Rhodry next to him. Carra herself and the child had stayed back at the elven camp, out of harm's way.

In front, filling the plaza, stood a good-sized crowd of townsfolk. Dera and her family had found a good place in front, but Verrarc had chosen to stay away, apparently—all for the best, Dallandra thought. The most surprising witness of all, however, came waddling along just as the trial was about to begin: Arzosah, who managed to find enough room for her massive self behind Rhodry. The crowd of townsfolk flowed back to give her plenty of space. Once she got herself settled, Admi stood up. His ceremonial red cloak rippled in the wind.

"There will be silence in the gathering," he called out. "We do assemble here to adjudge a grave matter this day. It is alleged that Raena, daughter of Marga, did last night at the conclusion of the Deciding attack Carramaena, Princess of the Westlands, and her infant child." He waved his arm in Dar's direction. "Her husband has come to so attest and charge."

Solemn-faced, Dar stood up, bowed to him, bowed to the crowd, then sat again. Admi motioned to one of the guards, who came forward with a wood tray. On it glittered a silver dagger.

"This be the weapon that the witness do claim the miscreant did use," Admi said. "We do lay it here in evidence."

The guard laid the tray on the table, then returned to his post by the prisoner. Cradling her injured wrist, Raena sat calmly, her lips twisted, her eyes narrow with contempt.

Admi turned to her. "Prisoner, how do you plead?"

"Guilty, of course." Raena stood up to face him. "Half the town did see, Chief Speaker. Why do you parade fine words and give yourself such pompous airs? Do spare us all, that I may ride out of this stinking town with my new folk, my chosen folk."

Throughout the crowd the townsfolk began muttering to themselves, angry words from the men, the women shocked at her arrogance. Admi once again called for silence and, eventually, got it.

"Very well then," Admi said. "If the other judges do so agree."

The other judges all spoke at once, stating that indeed, they did agree. Dallandra noticed that a fair number of townsfolk looked disappointed.

"So be it," Admi said. "Since there be no other charges against you—"

"But there are!" Rhodry called out. He rose from the bench and strode forward to face the five judges. "I do bring a charge, that she practices witchcraft of the dark sort and foul sorcery."

Raena's face drained white. "You lie!" she snarled.

"Indeed?" Admi ignored her. "Tell me, Rhodry from Aberwyn, have you proof of this charge? Under our laws it be a grave one."

"I have witnesses, good sir." Rhodry bowed to him. "Arzosah of the Lofty Wings, and Jahdo, Lael's son."

When the dragon lumbered to her feet, the townsfolk gasped, swore, and moved back yet another distance while they chattered among themselves. Jahdo left his mother's side and trotted over to stand beside Rhodry. Admi had to call for silence for a good while before at last they fell quiet.

"Raena," Admi said. "Do you deny this charge?"

"I do." Raena's voice was shaking badly. "He does hate me for a supposed wrong I paid him, when never I did such a thing."

"Oh, you've done me many a wrong," Rhodry said. "But not me alone. Jahdo, tell the judges about the woman you saw out in the water meadows."

"I will." Jahdo was trembling a little as he turned toward the table, and he took a deep breath before he could go on. "It were before I did leave our town with Meer the blind bard. I did go among the meadows gathering herbs for Gwira, and I did see Councilman Verrarc. He did talk with a woman all wrapped in a cloak, and here it were a summer day. And I did find a talisman lying in the grass."

Rhodry took a little metal disk out of his pocket and laid it on the tray next to the dagger. "Judge Zatcheka," Rhodry said, "can you tell us what the mark upon this disk means among your people?"

Zatcheka leaned forward, glanced at the disk, and made the sign of warding against it. "It be a foul thing," she said. "The sign of havoc and chaos."

The watching townsfolk stayed dead-silent, straining to hear. Raena made a little sound under her breath, more a moan than an angry cry, Dallandra thought.

"Chief Speaker," Arzosah rumbled, "I have seen this foul woman turn herself into a raven. She's what the Horsekin call a mazrak, and truly, the raven suits her. She's a scavenger like them, and like them, she'll kill a baby in its mother's nest. Isn't that what she tried to do last night?"

"You have no proof!" Raena screamed at her. "It be your word or mine, and none in this town will ever believe me, but you lie lie lie!"

"You claim you don't know sorcery?" Rhodry strode forward. "By your leave, Chief Speaker? Here's the dagger she carried when we caught her." Rhodry pointed at Yraen's silver dagger, lying on the table. "Kiel, all of you—am I right?"

"You are," Kiel said.

The other men of the town watch nodded their agreement.

"Then look at this." Rhodry picked up the dagger and held it high.

A pale bluish light bloomed on the silver and flared like a fire in straw, clearly visible despite the sunlight.

"She's bewitched the metal." Rhodry turned, holding the dagger so all could see. "And for dark purposes, no doubt."

"Curse you!" Raena snarled.

Rhodry ignored her and laid the dagger back down on the table. "One final thing, most honored judges," he went on. "You've heard Jahdo tell of the war against Cengarn, how the Horsekin besieged an innocent city, all to capture the prince's wife and kill their unborn child. Raena was at that siege, and she worked witchcraft for them. I saw her, Arzosah saw her, Dallandra, the prince, all of his archers— need I go on? We'll all swear that she goaded the army on, and all to kill a woman heavy with child."

At that the crowd could endure holding their tongues no longer. Everyone began to talk at once, and no matter how Admi yelled, they went right on whispering, cursing, muttering in fear and anger both. Finally Arzosah threw back her head and roared, a soft sort of utterance as her roars went, but the hush that followed lay deep and profound over Citadel.

"My thanks, good dragon," Admi said. "Raena, come forward. What say you to these charges of such grave import?"

With a toss of her head, Raena walked over to stand in front of the table of judges.

"I can say naught," she said, "for who will believe me no matter what I say? Mine enemies have banded together to kill me with their lies. Should you believe them, they will succeed, and there be naught that I may do but swear my innocence."

Rhodry turned to face her, and he smiled, an arrogant smirk. Raena's face blanched. With one smooth motion she scooped Yraen's dagger from the table in her clumsy left hand and leapt forward, swinging her arm to stab up from below. Admi yelled, Zatcheka screamed, the men of the town watch surged forward—all too late. Dallandra barely saw Rhodry move. He flung one arm around Raena's shoulders and grabbed her jaw with the other hand. There was a sickening sort of crack, and Raena's head flopped back, her neck clean broken. Rhodry let the corpse fall and glanced at the judges.

"So much for that," he remarked. "You're better off rid of her."

For a moment the silence held, then like the first few drops of a breaking wave a woman screamed. Voices followed, crashing down and thundering across the plaza in a babble of confusion and fear. Dallandra realized that Rhodry was leaning over the table and gripping it with both hands. A bright red stain was spreading across his chest and abdomen. The dragon leapt to her feet and roared, a boom of angry thunder that sent the crowd running.

Dallandra rushed forward and reached Rhodry just as Zatcheka hurried around the table to do the same. His face was pale as ice and twice as cold, it seemed, but Rhodry smiled at her.

"Dwarven silver," he whispered. "It burns an elf like me. Ah gods, the hurt of it!"

Between them the two women managed to pick him up and lay him on the table. His head lolled to one side in a faint. His breathing was dangerously shallow. The dragon hurried over with her peculiar lurching walk.

"Save him, curse you!" Arzosah was roaring the words out. "Or I'll take a blood price from Cerr Cawnen that the stinking humans will remember down the long centuries of years! Save him!"

"Don't you think I will if I can?" Dallandra yelled back at her.

For an answer the dragon merely growled, tossing her head back and forth. Dallandra grabbed the bloody edges of the cut in Rhodry's shirt and ripped them back. The wound was a small stab, but she could hear his death in every gurgling breath he drew.

"Did it pierce a lung?" Zatcheka said.

"I think not, but he's drowning in blood all the same. It's the dweomer on the metal, I think, that's doing so much harm."

The dragon roared in rage and grief both. The very earth seemed to shake—no, it was shaking, a tremor deep inside Citadel. Dalla grabbed the edge of the table to steady herself, but the tremor passed as quickly as it had come.

"If he dies," Arzosah snarled, "pray to your gods, elf! I shall call forth fire, I shall make the earth shriek beneath us, I shall drown this wretched city in fire!"

"And will that bring him back to life?" Dalla snarled right back. "Don't disturb me again, you lackwit wyrm! I'm trying to do what you want."

Arzosah crouched and said naught more. Dallandra leaned over the table and put her hands on either side of Rhodry's face. Beneath her fingers his skin felt not only cold but slimy. As she stared down at him, trying to conjure some desperate dweomer to force life into him, he stirred and woke, smiled at her—and in that faint smile she saw the truth, that he no longer wanted to live.

"Rhodry," she hissed. "Arzosah's crying for vengeance. She says she'll destroy the town, and she can."

"Ah gods." His voice was so faint that she could barely hear him. "Call her."

Although the wound oozed, it no longer flowed, at least not outwardly. Deep within his chest it was no doubt drowning him in his own blood; she could only hope it was doing so slowly enough for him to calm the dragon's rage. She turned and gestured at Arzosah.

"Come see him! He wants to talk to you. See for yourself."

Head down, her wings half-raised, Arzosah padded across the cobbles. The enormous black head swung round, the eyes glittering as they sought his face.

"It's such a little cut," Arzosah said, her voice a hiss and roil. "Heal him, elf!"

"I can't. It may look little to you, but it's deep enough for him."

For a moment Dallandra thought that she was about to die with Rhodry. The great head swung up, the jaws dropped, fangs gleamed in the setting sun as Arzosah propped herself up on her forelegs and arched her back. Zatcheka screamed and ran.

"Hush, my little one." The voice came from behind Dallandra and sounded amused. "Mind your courtesies, or I won't even try to save your beloved's life."

"You!" Arzosah's voice dripped hatred. "You! What could you do of any good to anyone?"

"Probably naught," Evandar said. "But mayhap I can try." He glanced at Dallandra. "He'll die here before the sun touches the horizon."

"I know that. It won't staunch, and it's too deep for me to reach with a bandage or suchlike."

Evandar knelt, slipped one arm round Rhodry's unwounded side, and hauled him up with a surprising flourish of strength. With a yell Dallandra darted forward to stop him from killing her patient there and then. Dimly she was aware of the earth shaking as the dragon leapt up and roared. Dimly she felt cold mist wrapping them all round and grass, damp under her feet.

They stood in the last remnant of Evandar's country. Sluggish between deep banks the river flowed brown through dying water reeds. Black trees raised withered arms to the grey sky. Automatically Dallandra clutched at her throat and found the amethyst figurine hanging there. Rhodry himself stood nearby, holding a silver dagger between clasped hands, but he seemed barely conscious, as if he were a child suddenly awakened from deep sleep. He stared this way and that, fingering the dagger hilt for comfort. When she saw the chip on the blade Dallandra realized that it held his life the same way that the figurine held hers.

"Where's Arzosah?" she snapped.

"Over there." Evandar pointed to the riverbank. "Not even I can bring a dragon through with a snap of my fingers, my love, so she used a dweomer of her own."

Dallandra could just make out Arzosah's astral form as a shaft of silvery light, cool to look upon, towering up into the mist. When Rhodry walked toward it, the mist reached out tendrils as if to put an arm around his shoulders. Dallandra—they all—felt Arzosah's voice as a touch of mind upon their own, not as spoken words. Though her rage flowed out as pure as fire, in it swirled hope.

You, sorcerer! Will he live if he stays here?

"After a fashion," Evandar said. "And for a while."

Then I'll stay with him.

"And welcome you are, for that little while." He glanced at Dallandra. "You have a bit of time, my love, to reconcile her to the inevitable. That's all I can do. May it be enough to save the innocents in your world from the venting of her grief."

The dragon had understood. Her roar spread like a flame within the mist.

Heal him!

"I can't. No one can."

Then I shall fly to the mountain and call up its fire. I will drown this city in fire.

"Hold your tongue!" Rhodry stepped forward, staggering a little, as if even here on the astral he felt his wound. "Ah ye gods, leave the town be!"

I will have vengeance! Hush, Rori! Don't argue with me! I shan't listen if you try.

"All things come to their dark, Wyrm," Evandar said, "and he has come to his. Soon, too soon, I know, by the way that your kind measures Time, just as that cut would be but a scratch upon a dragon, but—" Evandar paused, staring into the darkening water of the river. All at once he laughed, a berserker howl much like Rhodry's own. "Such a little cut, isn't it? Rhodry, Rhodry, do you still crave death?"

"Not if it means the death of everyone I fought to save." Rhodry turned to look his way. "If I'd die to save them, wouldn't I live?"

"What I can offer you is life, of a sort."

"I think I understand you. And it'd be a death of a sort as well, wouldn't it now?"

"And a darkness come upon you, as the time demands."

"But could you do that? You're the master of changes, I know, but can you bring about such a change as that?"

Only then did Dallandra understand.

"No!" she snapped. "You can't! Evandar, you just can't. It's impious. It would take him away forever from his own kind. Every race has a life that flows like a river in Time. You've got to ride your own river, not someone else's. Think of the consequences. I can't, you can't, no one can or could predict what such a thing would do."

"A riddle, then, and haven't I always been the master of riddles as well?" Evandar was grinning like a mad thing; indeed at that moment she realized that he'd been mad for years, for all the long years that she'd known him. "Safety for the city, my love. It would buy safety for Cerr Cawnen, and life for all that dwell within, and I do in my heart think it would buy hope for me as well."

"Evandar, you can't! The price—"

"I'll risk the price."

"Easy for you to say, safe here on the astral, free and far from the consequence."

"No longer, my love. A riddle, a riddle for my soul, and I offer it freely. Chains for a riddle, chains for a price. I'll take up the chains and buy his freedom with my slavery."

"What are you saying?"

"I told you. It's a riddle."

When he laughed, she grabbed at his shoulders to give him a good shaking, but he caught her wrists and held her a little away.

"Go down, my love, go back to your own country and then return in your body of light. I don't trust my dweomer to keep you safe in this form."

Before she could protest, he pushed her, tossed her, sent her sailing through the currents of mist. Beyond her power to stop herself she fell, flew, spinning as she soared, down and down, always down, to wake, sick and dizzy, with a ringing in her ears like the sound of iron striking bronze. She was kneeling on the cold stone of Cerr Cawnen's plaza in the deepening twilight.

"Dalla, Dalla!" Someone came running toward her—Niffa, with Jahdo right behind. "Where be they? We did see you all disappear. Where be Rhodry?"

"No time to explain! Guard my body. Let no one near me, no one!"

"Well and good, then."

Jahdo pulled his own silver dagger that once had belonged to Jill. With Niffa guarding her head and Jahdo kneeling by her feet, Dallandra lay on her back and crossed her arms over her chest. She shut her eyes, shut out the outside world, breathed deep, then summoned her body of light. When she transferred her consciousness over to the flame-shape, the etheric plane sprang into being around her, and the physical earth seemed to drop away.

In the silver-blue glow she could see lives teeming, swarming, flashing, and pouring round her, a horde of elemental spirits like the foam and swirl of rapids on a deep river. Never had she seen so many all at once. In the midst of this outpouring of masks and voices she flew, calling Evandar's name like an invocation, until she saw him at last, a frozen flame of gold, a spear against the blue. Before him stood the dragon, more or less in her true form, though made of some golden stuff that billowed or shrank like clouds. Under the shape of a huge wing Rhodry stood, the silver dagger still in his hand. To either side, dull grey, pitiful, stretched the dead meadows by the shrunken river.

"Rhodry!" Dallandra called out. "Don't! Don't do this."

For an answer he tossed back his head and howled, a berserk peal of laughter.

"Dalla, my Lady Death spurned me too long and once too often. She'll have to wait, though she'll have me in the end, for I've found another hire."

"What do you mean—"

"I've always been the king's man, heart and soul. I shall stand guard for him on the border."

"And do you love the king enough to throw your human soul away? That's what you'll be doing."

"Human soul? And when have I ever had one?"

"Forever, Rhodry, maybe forever. That's what you don't understand. I think me you don't understand any of this."

"Oh, but I think I do—well enough." Rhodry flung the dagger into the blue flux of the etheric light. "I'll take the gamble."

Spinning and tumbling it flew straight up, flashed at the top of its arc, then disappeared. As if at a signal Evandar flung both his arms out to the side and screamed a wordless command. Mist, meadow, river, rock—every scrap and remnant of his lands began to break and swirl, began to spin, to flow, turned to a vast and silvery vortex, centered upon Rhodry, the raw etheric stuff to build his new form. Round and round him it spun, but instead of catching him up and whirling him away it shrank, grew thick as water, poured into him, solidified as it shrank, so that for one moment he seemed trapped at the apex of a vast cone of quicksilver, as if he stood upon a sea and a waterspout towered over him.

Light flashed, blinding. Dallandra heard berserker laughter, then mad demon laughter, or so it sounded to her, but she knew the voice was Evandar's. The light died away. The Lands were gone. Riding serene on the billowing blue light hovered a pair of dragons. One had a tiny cut, a mere nick, on his flank under one wing.

"Naught but a scratch," Evandar said, laughing. "To a dragon."

In a roar of joined minds the dragons leapt and flew, swooping away on a spread of wings, seeking out the physical world far below and beyond. As they flew, and in the echoes of that roar, Dallandra heard a voice still human and felt the touch of human gratitude. For a long time she stared at the silvery wake they left behind, until even that disappeared in the constant ebb and ripples of the Light. Yet she could imagine—or was she scrying them out?—at any rate she could see them in her mind, the pair of dragons, the one greenish-black, the other dark silver touched here and there with shadows of blue, flying fast and steadily through the night sky, heading for their home at the Roof of the World.

"Evandar, Evandar!" Dallandra felt half-sick with grief. "What have you done?"

"Time will answer that riddle, for I cannot."

His voice was so spent and broken that she turned fast to look at him. Instead of his solid elven shape he seemed only a flicker of pale light, a boy, really, slender and frail, his arms still flung out from his sides, as if imploring the gods as he hung upon a shaft of silver light.

"I've spent it all, Dalla, all my power, all my strength. Don't you see? I'm going to be born. I'm going to follow my people down, because at last I can. I'm empty and weak and spent, and I shall have the life you promised me."

The silver brightened into white. The current flexed and rolled. Walking on its brilliant wave came a figure, an old man with dark skin, who was carrying an apple in one hand. Even though his astral form looked nothing like the man she once had loved, she recognized him instantly.

"Aderyn!"

"I am. You were right and I was wrong, my love, all those years ago. The Guardians were always part of my Wyrd."

He threw back his head and laughed, then held out his free hand to the child Evandar had become. The child reached out and clasped it just as a flash of golden light broke over them and swept them away. For a moment Dalla saw or thought she saw figures, great beings made of light who were coming to meet the child and the old man in a pouring of the Light that seemed to flow from the very heart of the universe. On one last ripple of laughter they all vanished, though the Light remained.

"It is over!" Dallandra cried out. "It is beginning!"

In answer came three great knocks, solemn, slow, pounding and rolling over her like waves, tossing her, tumbling her, sending her swooping down and down.

She woke to find herself stiff and aching, still lying on the plaza with Niffa still at her post nearby, though dawn was rising in the east. Jahdo was pacing back and forth nearby.

"Did you see them?" Dalla's voice croaked from a parched throat. "The dragons?"

Niffa nodded in silent amazement.

"The black and the silver?" Jahdo sheathed the knife, then knelt beside her. "I did. Where be Rhodry?"

"You saw him."

Niffa stared, then began to shake her head from side to side in a no, over and over. Dalla grabbed her apprentice's arm and hauled herself up to a sitting position.

"He did it to save the town. There was no saying him nay."

Niffa shuddered profoundly.

"It do be a hard thing to believe," Jahdo said. "It—ye gods, what am I, what are we all to think?"

"Think of him as dead. In a way it's true. The Rhodry you knew is dead, and his long melancholy's all over at last, just as he wanted."

"And what of Evandar? The same?"

She hesitated for a long moment, thinking, then smiled though her eyes brimmed tears.

"He's not. In fact, I'd say that for the first time in his long ages of existing, he's truly alive. Now help me up. I've got to have some water, and I've got to have it now."

The North Country

The dweomermaster who would call forth a mighty flood
had best be sure he knows how to swim.

—*The Secret Book of Cadwallon the Druid*

$\mathcal{D}$allandra refused to leave Cerr Cawnen until she knew that Verrarc would mend. Even more than her death, Raena's treachery had sucked the life out of him. He slept late of a morning and went early to bed, his servants told Dallandra. When he left the house, it was only to walk to the ruined temple and sit by the door, as if he expected Raena to come out to rejoin him. He would stay until the middle of the night, then creep back when the servants were asleep.

"The thing is," Dallandra told Niffa, "he has a certain knack for the dweomer. When Raena was working her spells, he could sense their evil, but blindly. Deep down he knew somewhat was wrong, even if he didn't understand what he was perceiving."

"And what was that?" Niffa said.

"She was draining his life-stuff to get power for her workings."

"Ai!" Niffa laid a hand at her throat. "That be an evil way to treat him who loved her so much."

"It was, though not the worst of her evils. Although, I don't know whether to lay the evils she brought to Dun Cengarn at her door or not, frankly. Alshandra stood behind them all."

They were sitting on the flank of Citadel, taking the sun on a wooden bench beside the path. From their perch Dallandra could see over grey rooftops to the lake and the town below, then beyond the walls to the water meadows, lush and green, laced with sparkling lines of water.

"There be one thing I have no understanding of still," Niffa said. "Why the Horsekin did steal Raena's corpse."

"I don't know either," Dallandra said, "but I wouldn't fret about it."

"What if they should find some way to bring her back to life?"

"They can't. When I scryed I found no trace of her etheric double. She must have shattered it deliberately when she realized she was dead. Don't forget, she was expecting Alshandra to come and take her to some marvelous country."

"For that I almost pity her."

"Me too. Almost."

Dallandra found the solution to this riddle when she went to the Gel da'Thae camp to bid farewell to Zatcheka. Her men were laughing and talking as they loaded up the mules with big canvas packs and saddled the riding horses. The two women walked down to the lakeshore and stood watching the sun dance on slow waves, while they talked of this and that.

"You know," Dallandra said finally, "mayhap you could answer a question for me. In all the confusion after Rhodry broke Raena's neck, Kral and his men took her body and fled with it. Is there some rite that Horsekin work over their dead?"

"You might call it that." Zatcheka smiled with a flash of pointed teeth. "They do eat them."

"They what?"

"They do believe that by eating the dead person's flesh, they keep that person with them always. Otherwise, they say, the dead person will wander alone and lost."

"It makes a certain sense, truly. Do they cook them first?"

"They do, and the preparation of that meal and its serving are solemn things, taking a good three days to perform. I do know this because once, many hundreds of years ago, my people did the same. Now we bury our dead."

"And what made you change?"

"Ranadar's curse." Zatcheka looked away, troubled. "If you mind not that I speak of such things."

"Not in the least. Truly, I'm hoping that one day a bard of my people will be able to talk with one of yours. If they could put together what they know of the Great Burning, maybe we could at last understand it. I know Carra would love to—" Dallandra stopped, caught by a sudden thought. "Oh ye gods. If one person died of that plague, and then the others ate—oh by the Dark Sun herself!"

"That be exactly what I did mean." Zatcheka shuddered, as if she were suddenly cold. "It were a horrible contagion, or so the old tales tell us."

"No doubt!"

"But I do admire your thought, that our bards should meet. Now that we have allied ourselves, Cerr Cawnen would be a grand site for that meeting, I should think."

"So it is. And I hope that we shall meet again as well, you and I."

"You do have my word on that." Zatcheka smiled briefly. "One way or other, we will meet again."

That evening, when Dallandra and Niffa visited her family, they found Verrarc sitting at Dera's table. His face was waxy pale, and his hands shook, but he was eating a thick chunk of bread, the first solid food he'd taken in days. Dera smiled over him as proudly as if he'd been a fractious baby newly calmed.

"And a good eve to you," Verrarc said to them. "I did come here tonight to see if Jahdo were willing to become my apprentice."

"Well, that would be a grand opportunity." Dallandra glanced at Dera. "What do you think of it?"

"It would ache my heart to have our Jahdo gone again so soon," Dera said. "But it would ache even worse watching a bright lad like him spend his life in killing rats."

"So I thought, too," Verrarc said. "I do hope that Lael agrees."

"He will," Niffa put in. "He be not the sort of man who hogs his children's lives."

At that, Verrarc actually smiled. Good, Dallandra thought. He'll recover.

On the morrow Prince Daralanteriel led his followers out of Cerr Cawnen on the south-running road. Soon they left the water meadows behind and travelled through fields as lush as velvet with the burgeoning grain. Although Carra rode beside her husband at first, toward midmorning she turned her horse out of line and fell in between Dallandra and Niffa. Elessario slept comfortably, bound to her back with a new kind of leather sling, an invention of Jahdo's aunt, Sirri.

"I'm confused about somewhat," Carra said. "We're going to Cannobaen, right? The lady of the dun there, Rhodda. You said she was Rhodry's kin?"

"His daughter, in fact."

"That means Rhodry must have been noble-born."

"He was that. And I'll ask you to help me keep a secret. His kin think he died many a year ago."

Carra considered this for a long moment. "Let me guess," she said finally. "Many years ago Gwerbret Aberwyn got himself killed hunting, but they never found his body. And his name was Rhodry Maelwaedd."

"You are clever!" Dallandra said, laughing. "But keep it to yourself, will you? At least in Cannobaen. The People know the truth."

"I will, never fear."

"You know, I just realized somewhat. You and Lady Rhodda will have much in common. When Evandar decided to have Salamander brought to Cannobaen, he may well have been doing you a favor as well."

"Really? Why?"

"Lady Rhodda is a scholar, and a famous one among the Westfolk."

Carra turned her head to stare at her, then smiled, her eyes suddenly wide and bright, as if she'd opened an ordinary sack and found it stuffed with gold. "A scholar," she whispered. "A real scholar and a woman both?"

"She is, though her townsfolk don't know what to make of it."

"I don't suppose they do. How long will it take us to get there?"

"Weeks, alas. We don't have Evandar's dweomer with us any more."

"That's true. Do you miss him, Dalla?"

"Of course." Dallandra paused, feeling the bitter truth of it. "I'll doubtless miss him for the rest of my life."

Some weeks after the travelling show left Myleton, Ebañy had a nightmare so strange that it woke Marka. In her own dream she heard him yelling words in some incomprehensible language. They grew louder, she felt something nudge her side, and all at once she found herself sitting up, wide-awake. There was just enough dawnlight in the tent for her to see Ebañy. He'd rolled off their sleeping mat and now lay facedown on the floor cloth. He was talking, still in the unknown tongue, but quietly, whimpering now and again. When she leaned over and laid a hand on his shoulder, he woke, flopping over onto his back. For a long moment he merely stared at her; then he sat up, rubbing his face.

"Are you all right?" she murmured.

"Yes, I suppose." He let his hands fall into his lap. "In the dream I saw terrible things. I can't even remember them now. Monsters, I think they were, in some kind of swamp. But just as I thought I was doomed, someone gave me a message."

"Do you remember it?"

"Go to Luvilae. That's what they said. Go to Luvilae."

"Who were they?"

"I don't know. I just don't know."

All that morning Ebañy brooded, saying not a word to anyone. Finally, Marka asked him what was wrong, but he told her only that he was thinking about his dream.

"We should go to Luvilae," Ebañy said. "If the rest of the troupe doesn't care to go, well, I'll go alone."

"They generally do follow where you lead," Marka said. "But let's tell them and see what they say. It's time for the noon meal anyway."

Luvilae was the southernmost town on Zama Parae, the southernmost island in the archipelago, a trip that would take them weeks. At first the players grumbled and wondered why they were going out so far, where the profit was slender for a big show like theirs, but along the way they did so well and saved so much coin that in the end they were glad they'd decided to indulge Ebañy. The morning before they reached Luvilae, in fact, Vinto and Keeta counted up the proceeds, all smiles, while the others gathered around to watch.

"We don't need a copper more to get back to the north safely," Keeta announced. "And I think Luvilae will toss us more than a copper, don't you?"

The entire troupe cheered. Marka waved her friend over as the rest hurried to strike camp for the day's journey.

"I can't tell you how glad I am to hear that," Marka said.

"Your man's never let us go hungry yet. But I can't help wondering if he's told you why we're doing this."

"Only that he had an omen dream. It was when we were back in Indila. He had a nightmare, and when he woke, he knew that he had to come to Luvilae."

"Huh." Keeta thought for a moment. "It's where we met him, isn't it? It was so long ago now that I can't quite remember."

"I remember. It was Luvilae, all right. I'll never forget that, and my father, and how you saved me from him."

"I saved you?" Keeta raised an eyebrow. "I thought it was Ebañy who pried you off your scum of a father."

"Oh, he made the decision easier. But you were the one who made me see that I couldn't stay. You were right, too. My father would have had me whoring for him, and I probably wouldn't even be alive by now."

Keeta shuddered hugely at the memory. The two women sat down on a rolled tent cloth out in front of Marka's tent and watched others work. Dust and shouts rose high. Carrying three of the children, Nila the elephant ambled past with her trunk curled around a bundle of hay. Nearby Tillya sat on a little carpet and kept Zandro amused, safely away from the enormous beast's feet. Off in the distance, Marka saw Kwinto hurrying back and forth, giving the acrobats orders, while Vinto smiled at him like a proud uncle.

"Your boy's almost a man," Keeta said. "It's time to find him a wife."

"You're right about that. Gods! The years have gone by too fast."

"Indeed. If it weren't for losing my Delya and your babies, I'd say that they've been good ones, but then, the gods never feed anyone honey without giving them vinegar to wash it down."

Since shade trees lined the well-made road, the day's travel went fast and comfortably, or so Marka thought, but Ebañy fretted the entire way. The troupe always travelled as fast as the elephant travelled, no more, no less, and Nila never hurried unless she was terrified of something. Ebañy kept hopping down from their wagon to run back and urge the keeper to make the elephant walk faster. Whoever was riding her would roll his eyes heavenward and ignore him, sending Ebañy fuming back to the wagon.

"I can't believe you're so eager," Marka said, laughing. "The town's not going to run away from us."

"Oh, I know, I know," Ebañy said. "But it's because of the dream. Though I suppose they'll wait for us."

"What? Who?"

"I'm not sure. The dream was very clear about where we should meet them, but I'm not quite sure who they are."

All her pleasure in the green view vanished.

The troupe drove into Luvilae on an afternoon shot with sun and shadow both. As overhead huge white clouds billowed and sailed, the narrow streets and whitewashed houses of the town alternately brightened and dimmed. All along their route to the caravanserai the townspeople ran to greet them and cheer the unexpected arrival of a show to break up the tedium of their days. As usual, Ebañy drove the lead wagon, with Marka sitting beside him and Kwinto next to her, bowing and waving to the crowd in imitation of his father. By the time that the camp was set up, it was well into the afternoon, with the clouds gone and the sun hanging low over the ocean. Marka left the younger children under Tillya's care, then went looking for Ebañy. As so often happened, she knew exactly where she'd find him, standing, in this case, at the edge of the camp by a single palm tree.

The town and the caravanserai at Luvilae both sprawled out along a flat clifftop, overlooking a sandy beach and a gentle sea some thirty feet below. From where they were standing, they could see down to the harbor, some hundreds of yards away off to their right. Ebañy put his arm around her waist and drew Marka close, then pointed to the distant wooden pier.

"No ships," he said. "Not so much as the sight of a boat, coracle, or skiff, even. How very odd. The Lords of Water told me that the ship would come to harbor today, and the Lords are never wrong."

Marka felt every muscle in her body turn tense.

"Who?" Her voice came out all trembling, as well. "Who do you mean?"

"The Lords of Water are elemental spirits, but of a higher degree of developed—."

"I didn't mean them. I meant, who's supposed to sail in?"

"Ah. The ship, of course." Ebañy shaded his eyes with one hand and stared out to sea. "The one I told you about."

"You didn't tell me about any ship."

"I didn't? Well, it's the reason we're here. The one I dreamt about."

"Oh. Oh, I see."

In other words, Marka thought to herself, there isn't any ship to worry about. She patted him on the shoulder and left him there, staring at the horizon, while she went back to camp. She fed the children, discussed buying grain for the horses with Vinto, then noticed that Ebañy had never returned. Nibbling on a chunk of bread, she strolled back out to the cliff's edge and the solitary palm to find him sitting on the ground. When he saw her, he sprang to his feet.

"Look!" he crowed. "They're just pulling in now."

Ice-cold in the warm sun, Marka looked where he pointed. Edging up to the pier under oar came a ship, a long, sleek thing, painted white, and hung with a row of shields that glittered in the sunset. At the prow rose a figurehead carved to look like some sort of beast—she couldn't quite make out which from their distance. She could, however, see the tiny figures of sailors unstepping the mast while others leapt ashore with hawsers in hand. With quick ease they brought the ship in broadside to the pier and tied up.

"The dream was a true one, then." Ebañy was silent for a moment, but she could feel him trembling against her. "Come walk with me, my love."

She took his hand and allowed him to lead her away. Near the edge of the town proper stood a flight of rickety wooden stairs leading to the beach, and they climbed down, watching their footing more than the view, till they reached land safely, close to the pier and the strange ship. An enormous painted eye decorated either side of the prow. For a figurehead, a curling dragon, head raised, mouth open, snarled at the passersby as it rose and fell with the waves. She could also see the sailors quite clearly, as they stood on the deck and the jetty itself.

"They're all so pale! They must be barbarians."

"Not truly, but my kinsmen, nonetheless, though only in a way."

His voice was so soft and hesitant that she spun round to look at him. He was staring at the ship and its crew with greedy eyes.

"So, my people have come for me," he whispered. "Marka, my love, my heart, my soul and the very center of my world, how much do you love me?"

"With all my heart, but what do you mean, come for you? Why? I . . . oh!"

One of the sailors was walking toward them. She could see his moonbeam-pale hair and steely-grey eyes, slit vertically like a cat's, and his long ears, curling up to a delicate point. He was well over six feet tall but slender, with long hands, heavily callused but still oddly delicate. When Ebañy spoke to him, it was in a strange and musical language that Marka had never heard before. The sailor laughed and spoke in the same tongue, then turned to call out to a man hurrying down the pier.

Not another sailor, Marka realized—this fellow was too stooped and narrow-shouldered for that. He had the same pale hair but violet eyes, and his hands looked soft, strangers to ropes and oars. He bowed to Marka, then to Ebañy, and began to speak. Ebañy listened, his eyes filling with tears. All at once she was terrified, listening to them, seeing them clasp hands like brothers, remembering all the many little odd things about Ebañy, and all the many riddling remarks he'd made over the years about his kin and his homeland, far over the seas.

At last he turned to her, and he seemed more stranger than husband.

"Do you remember the Guardian?" Ebañy said.

"No." Marka felt her voice tremble. "Or wait! Do you mean Evandar?"

"That's the fellow, yes. He sent this ship for me." Ebañy waved at it. "And this is Meranaldar. He's come, he says, to help us cure"—he hesitated, then visibly forced himself to push out the words—" my madness."

"Ah! Thanks be to all the gods, then!"

Yet later she would regret her too-ready prayer. Although most of the sailors stayed with their ship, Meranaldar and the ship's captain, Taronalariel, came back to the camp with them. The troupe clustered round, asking questions all at once while Ebañy laughed and tried to answer them without ever mentioning that these strangers had come to heal him. Marka hurried over to Keeta and led her a bit away.

"Ebañy told me they've come to heal his madness, but—I don't know why—but I'm so frightened. I never even knew that there were people like this in the world, and they turn up here in their ship—it's such a peculiar ship, too—and my husband can talk with them, but I can't understand a word."

"All good reasons to be frightened, I'd say."

"And then he said, 'my people have come for me.' It sounds like they're going to take him away."

Keeta turned and watched the troupe, clustering around the strangers. When marka looked, she saw the children huddled together, staring at their father in fear.

"I'd better go to the children," Marka said.

"Yes, I agree. They're very good at picking up feelings and portents, children."

The troupe entertained their guests with a meal that bordered on a feast. The two Long Ears, as Marka was mentally calling them, had beautiful manners when they ate. They also learned the Bardekian word for "thank you" and muttered "gratyas" at everyone who came close. When night fell, some of the other sailors came to the camp; they'd seen the town market opening, Ebañy told her, and wanted their captain to go buy provisions.

"You'd best go and help them," Marka said. "But do they have any Bardek coin?"

"Not a one, which is exactly why you're right. We'll have to argue with the merchants, no doubt, to the point of apoplexy."

When the troupe turned in for the night, Marka rolled the side panels of the tent up a few feet to let in the cool night air. She coaxed the younger children to lie down on their mats, but none of them wanted to sleep. She tried singing, then storytelling, but they lay awake on the edge of tears. At last Kwinto and Tillya came in with oil lamps and sat down on the ground. In the better light Marka could see how frightened the younger children looked.

"Those men," Kwinto said. "What are they?"

"Kinsmen of your father's," Marka said. "I don't know much more than you do, actually. Your father's not told me much."

"Papa looks happy," Tillya said, but doubtfully. "I should be glad, Mama, but I'm frightened."

"So am I."

Kivva did cry at that. When Marka held out her arms, Kivva scrambled up and ran to her. Terrenz and Delya sat up, leaning against one another, while Zandro began to suck his thumb.

"I keep thinking about Evandar," Marka went on. "Do you remember how he talked about your grandfather in Deverry, and how Grandpapa wanted to see your father again? I think this ship must come from there."

"Mama, you're not thinking!" Kwinto said. "We see Deverry ships all the time up on the north coast. They don't look like that, and they never sail this far south, either."

"Well, that's true. I just don't know where else it could have come from."

"I don't want to go to Deverry." Tillya's voice shook. "It's way too far away, and it's full of barbarians. I want to stay here with our show."

"What about you?" Marka looked at Kwinto.

"Well, yesterday, you know? Vinto told me that I'm about ready to take over the acrobats."

Indirect, but Marka understood him all too well. Kivva snivelled with little whimpers, while Delya and Terrenz merely looked miserable.

"Well," Marka said at last. "We don't know yet if Papa's going anywhere."

"But if he does," Tillya said, "we'll all have to go too, won't we?"

"You and Kwinto are old enough to stay here if you want."

"Oh, Mama!" Tillya burst out sobbing. "I'd have to lose you then."

Marka wondered why her own eyes were staying dry. She realized, listening to her children cry, that she was too furious for tears.

It was so late when Ebañy finally returned that the children had given up waiting and gone to sleep without having to be nagged. Marka had taken the lamps outside and was sitting on a ground cloth when he came back alone, walking unsteadily and smelling of wine. He sat down beside her on the ground and smiled, considering her, while dancing light from the lamps dappled his face. She tried to find some normal thing to say, but questions about ship's provisions seemed too ominous to ask. Finally he sighed and held out one hand.

"I can't think of how to put this," Ebañy said, "except baldly. My heart, my beloved, the time had come for us to leave the islands, you and me and our children, and sail away."

"I thought that was coming."

"Did you? Why?"

"Evandar, and his talk about your father."

"Ah. That's true." He pulled his hand back. "Meranaldar is most desirous of meeting my father, you see."

"He doesn't know him?"

"No. This ship—it's not from Deverry. They don't want me to tell you more until we're out to sea, and no one can overhear."

"Overhear? What do you mean? What is this? You want us all to just pack up and go off somewhere with these strange people in a strange boat with barely any time to think?"

For a long moment he sat blinking at her, his mouth slack.

"Well, what about the show, the troupe?" Marka went on. "You worked years to build up this show, and so did I, years and years of performing for coppers in ugly little towns and doing without things and travelling all over, until finally we have what we wanted, the most famous show in all Bardek. And now you want to just sail away from it."

"You're angry with me."

"Well, are you surprised?"

He shrugged and stared at the dapples of light, dancing a little in a waft of breeze.

"Oh by the Wave Father!" Marka said at last. "You haven't even told me where we'd be going!"

"Oh. Now that was a nasty oversight, omission, lapse, and breach of all good manners on my part." He looked up with a sunny grin that made her remember the first years of their marriage. "Across the seas to my homeland. To Deverry or to be precise, to the Westlands at its border."

The world seemed to rise and fall like the waves.

"I don't know why that was so hard to hear," she said at last. "That's exactly what I expected you'd say."

"It's not just a question of seeing my father. It's this—this—madness of mine. Out in the Westlands, there's someone who can help me, Meranaldar tells me."

"Can you trust him? You've never seen him before this day."

"He comes from Evandar."

"So? I don't understand why that should be—"

All at once she realized that tears were running down his face in two silent trails.

"You don't love me anymore," he said.

"What? Why? Just because I don't want to get on a ship and lose everything?"

"We'll take our children."

"Kwinto doesn't want to go, and neither does Tillya. I've already asked them. We should be thinking of getting them married, not running all over the ocean."

"You're the one who doesn't want to." He spoke very softly. "You don't want to come with me."

"I love you. But to leave my children—" Marka paused, gulping for breath. "Why can't the healer come here, and your father too?"

For a long moment Ebañy stared at her. He had stopped crying, and he turned away to wipe his face on his sleeve, leaving dust smeared across his cheeks.

"You don't understand what you're asking," he said at last. "It's bad enough that the good folk of Luvilae have seen this ship and its crew. But if we leave quickly enough, they'll turn the entire thing into a storyteller's fancy, and no one else will ever believe it. But to come back and forth—" All at once his voice dropped, as sonorous as a priest's. "No. It's too dangerous, to let the people here learn of the rich islands in the far south. The omens are all wrong. I see burning and spilled blood."

Marka felt fear clot in her mouth like sheep's wool.

"Besides," Ebañy went on in his normal voice, "it's time for the exiles to meet again. The Lords of Fire told me that. Or maybe it was the voice in the dream. It's so hard, sometimes, to sort it all out."

A night wind swept through the camp, rustling the tents and the trees. The flaming wick dipped dangerously, then died. Ebañy snapped his fingers over the lamp. The flame burst into life.

"Ah ye gods," Marka whispered. "It's true! You do have real magic."

"The dweomer, yes." Ebañy looked up, puzzled. "I told you that, didn't I? I'm sure I did."

She could only nod for an answer. Behind her she heard someone yawn and turned to see Zandro, standing naked at the tent door and rubbing his eyes. When Ebañy held out his arms, Zandro ambled over and flopped into his lap.

"You'll come with Papa, won't you?" Ebañy said.

Zandro nodded and began to suck his thumb. It was at that moment that Marka realized she wouldn't be sailing with the ship.

And yet she argued with herself. It was her duty to go. She was Ebañy's wife, and she should follow where he led, unthinkingly, lovingly, blindly. She was being selfish, wrongheaded, untrue to her womanly nature, to say nothing of depriving her children of their father. And yet like a drumbeat her heart pounded out no no no every time she thought of sailing off north to some unknown country and leaving Kwinto and Tillya behind. Ebañy said nothing more, merely watched her with Zandro sleeping in his arms.

It seemed to her that they must have sat that way for half a night, watching each other in silence, yet it was still long before dawn when she saw lanterns bobbing through the dark camp. They turned out to belong to Meranaldar and two sailors, hurrying through the tents. Ebañy handed Zandro over to Marka and stood to speak with them. She could see them looking at her with puzzled glances. Finally Ebañy turned back to her.

"If you and the children are coming," he started, then let his voice trail away.

"We'd best get ready?" Marka laid Zandro down on the ground cloth. "When are we leaving? On the next tide out?"

"Just that."

In the flickering light she could see his eyes, begging her. She rose, dusting off the back of her tunic.

"I can't." The words seemed to burst out of their own accord. "I can't do it, I just can't. The children—it's too dangerous. What if there was a shipwreck? What if they all drowned?"

"I'd not thought of that."

"No, I don't suppose you did." The venom in her voice surprised her.

"My love, forgive me! I'll come back. I promise you that. No matter how far I go or how long I spend there, I *will* come back for you."

For a long moment Marka merely looked at him.

"I'll go get Zandro's clothes and his little horses," she said at last. "He'll want them."

As she ducked into the tent she could hear the Long Ears, murmuring in their soft language. She found Zandro's tunics and the wooden horses his father had carved him, then stuffed them all into a tent bag with his blanket on top. For a moment she stood in the darkness listening to her other children's slow breathing. Could she really let Zandro go? They all need me, she thought. He'll drain me dry, and then there'll be nothing left for the others. She took a hard deep breath and strode back outside.

Ebañy had picked Zandro up, and he was half-asleep, snuggling into his father's shoulder. When Marka held out the tent bag, Meranaldar took it from her. He pushed out a watery smile and murmured a few words that she recognized, eventually, as "please forgive me" in bad Bardekian.

"It's all right," she said, even though she knew he'd not understand her. "You're only doing what you must."

Yet still he hovered, bowing a little, saying a few words that would then miserably trail away. He cares more than Ebañy does, Marka thought. She turned to her husband and found his face wiped clean of all feeling.

"Just go," she snapped. "Please. Just go and get it over with!"

Ebañy nodded. He settled Zandro more securely, turned, and walked off fast, with the sailors trailing behind. Meranaldar hesitated, then grabbed her hand and kissed it, bowed once more, and ran after the others. Marka waited until they were out of sight, then dropped her face to her hands and wept.

"Mama?" It was Kwinto's voice.

She turned around fast and tried to wipe her eyes.

"You don't have to hide it," he said, his voice shaking.

"I just—well, I just wanted to thank you. I mean, for all of us."

"It's going to be hard at first, without your papa."

"I know. We'll manage. The show's strong enough to hold an audience even without him."

Oh by the Star Goddesses, Marka thought. He really is almost a man, isn't he? Somehow I hadn't noticed.

"You know something," Kwinto went on. "He didn't even come into the tent to say farewell to us. He didn't even kiss the little girls good-bye."

"Ah!" She heard her own voice turn heavy with grief. "No, he didn't, did he? I don't know what to say—"

"Don't even try, Mama. You need to get some sleep."

Marka went to bed then, for a few hours, and cried herself to sleep, but when she woke in the morning, she felt only an emotion so strange that at first she couldn't identify it. She got up and dressed, then slipped out of the tent without waking the children. The dawn had just broken, and the eastern sky spread out in pale pinks and blues, touched here and there by an ivory wisp of cloud. In a cool wind, she walked through the drowsy camp to the edge of the caravanserai, where far below her she could see the ocean and the wooden pier. The only ship in sight was a fisherman's boat, bobbing on the small waves in the harbor.

Standing in sunlight, watching the blue-green waves run up onto the shore, it came to her. She felt free. She would miss Ebañy, but not as much as she was relieved to be free of his madness. She would have a peaceful middle age now, surrounded by her children and her children's children, the undoubted matriarch of the troupe, safe in the travelling life she had always known. With a long sigh, she stretched her arms out to the sunlight. When she walked back to camp, she was smiling.

In his dreams Salamander had sailed on so many wondrous voyages that for most of the journey he had no idea if he were awake or asleep. As the elven longship rode the summer trade winds north for Deverry, he would crouch in the bow and stare out over the ocean. When the sun shone, undines rose from the water and frolicked around the prow. Sylphs swarmed around the mast and sails, and sprites and gnomes danced on deck or let a giggling Zandro chase them back and forth. At night, after he'd put the boy to bed, Salamander would return to the bow and watch waves as black as obsidian glittering in the silver light of enormous stars. At times a moon would rise, all purple and swollen. When the ship reaches port, he would remind himself, you'll have to search for the door, the wooden door bound with iron, and behind it lies the magical book.

Often Meranaldar would come sit with him. At those times, particularly if the loremaster was asking him questions, Salamander would remember that he was awake, that this ship was taking him back to the Westlands, and that Marka had refused to come with him. He would burst into tears and sob until in a flurry of apologies Meranaldar would get up and leave him alone. The rhythm of the waves would seduce him again, and once more he would believe that he slept and dreamt.

He could not keep track of days. Since the sailors often mentioned their good luck in the weather, he could assume that they were travelling fast. They put in at Myleton, on the north Bardekian coast, to reprovision, then headed out due north, sailing mostly by the positions of the stars, or so Salamander heard them say. The days merged into one long stretch of sunlight with his son's laughter for music. The nights melded into a long torment of black sea and the splash of waves, a funeral dirge for his lost love. I *will* go back, he would tell himself. I'll find the book behind the wood door, and then I'll be able to go back to my family. Yet out of the waves would rise silver monsters, all gleaming teeth and red eyes, to mock him and tell him that he'd never see Bardek again.

At last, when the food was nearly gone and the water was running short, in a bright morning seagulls wheeled around the ship and cried out greetings. As he leaned over the bow, Salamander could see an occasional long trail of seaweed in the murky water or the bobbing wood of sea wrack. Humming under his breath, a smiling Meranaldar joined him.

"Almost there," Meranaldar said. "The homeland! Ah ye gods, never did I dream that I'd actually make this voyage, no matter how much I longed for it."

"Are we going to the cities, then?" Salamander said.

"No, we're landing in Elditiña, or whatever it's called now."

"Eldidd."

"Eldidd." Meranaldar rolled the name around his mouth as if he were tasting wine. "Evandar gave our captain a map, you see. There's a cove with a wooden pier, he said, and a town called Cannobaen. Nearby is an island called Wmmglaedd."

"I know them both. You'll like Wmmglaedd. The priests there have books, a veritable treasure-house of lore."

"I'll look forward to going there, then, after we make landfall at Cannobaen." All at once Meranaldar frowned. "I was hoping that Evandar would come to us and perhaps guide us in. But oh well, there's no accounting for the Guardians. They do what they please."

"If we find ourselves off course, all we have to do is follow the coast."

Yet that night, as they stood in the prow and looked forward to a dark line of land on the horizon, they saw a light burning to the north of them, a tiny spark from this distance.

"There's Cannobaen," Salamander said. "I remember now. The Cannobaen light. It marks a treacherous shoal just west of the town."

When morning came Salamander could see the white chalk cliffs and the stone dun perched on top, about the size of his thumb from this distance. The sight of the sandy beach and the pale cliff rising beyond overcame Meranaldar. He stood next to Salamander and let tears run down his face while he muttered an ancient prayer. At Salamander's direction, the helmsman steered toward the east, and soon they saw the harbor, a notch in the coastline, and its long wooden pier. Behind it stood houses, round and thatched, marching up the gentle slope of the town. The captain ordered the mast unstepped and

stowed, and under oars the longship glided in to Cannobaen. Salamander took Zandro amidships, where they'd
be as much out of the way as possible. Taronaleriel, the
captain, took up his place at the bow and watched the
coast coming ever closer without saying a word, but he
was grinning like a madman. Even the sailors bending to
the oars appeared to smile as they worked.

Suddenly the captain broke his silence and sang out orders. The sailors shipped oars and let the longship glide up
to the pier. Carrying hawsers two sailors leapt for the
bleached-silver pier. It trembled but it held their weight.
The normal routine of bringing a ship in took over; men
laughed and called out to one another as they tied the longship up and dropped anchor. Salamander handed Zandro to
Meranaldar, climbed onto the pier, then leaned down and
took the boy, swinging him up to stand beside him. Zandro
was frightened enough to take his father's hand without
fuss. Meranaldar followed them up.

"Look!" Meranaldar pointed. "Someone's here to greet
us."

Sure enough, at the far end of the pier stood a small
clot of people, elven and human both. When he recognized
Devaberiel, his father, once again Salamander believed
himself dreaming. The light seemed all wrong, as well, a
brilliant glitter that washed out colors and danced upon the
pier and the town beyond. Through this ghastly light
Devaberiel strode toward him, followed by a woman
Salamander vaguely remembered as Dallandra. But who
was that young man with them, who walked so straight and
so proudly, with his dark hair ruffling in the wind and his
violet eyes? Around his neck he wore a golden pendant, set
with a sapphire—a figure fit for a dream.

Devaberiel laughed and broke into a run. Salamander
stood dazed as Devaberiel threw his arms around him and
pulled him close. the pressure of his arms, the warmth of his
body, made Salamander realize that he was indeed awake—
awake and back in Deverry.

"Ah ye gods!" Devaberiel said. "My son, my son!" Tears
were glistening in his eyes. "I'm so glad to see you."

"And I'm glad to see you, Father. Here. This is one of your grandsons."

"A fine-looking boy!"

When Devaberiel held out his arms, Zandro allowed himself to be picked up. Behind them Salamander heard something of a commotion. He turned to find the rest of the crew disembarking, calling out, and hurrying forward. Meranaldar and the captain both were staring at the young man. Meranaldar took one step toward him, then knelt with bowed head. Trembling, the captain did the same.

"What?" Salamander said to his father. "Who's that?"

"Daralanteriel tran Aladeldar," Devaberiel said. "You don't recognize him, do you? He was only a child when you left."

"So he was! But what are they doing?"

"I'm not sure." Devaberiel glanced this way and that, saw Dallandra and called out to her. "What's the meaning of this, Wise One?"

Dallandra hurried over, her mouth tight-set in anger. For a moment she watched Meranaldar, staring up at a totally flustered Prince Dar, and once again the scribe was weeping.

"Curse Evandar anyway!" she snarled at last. "He might have warned me. Devaberiel, these men are descendants of our people, the ones who escaped from the sack of Rinbaladelan by boat. They eventually found their way to Bardek. They thought the lineages of the seven kings had all died out, and now here they are, faced with Ranadar's heir."

Devaberiel tried to speak, then merely stared slack-mouthed.

"This is going to change everything," Dallandra said. "Don't you see? For over a thousand years we've lived here, and they've lived there, and we each never knew the other existed. Now we're meeting."

"I do see." Devaberiel recovered his voice at last. "The Westlands border will never be the same."

"Just so." For a moment Dallandra stood silently, watching the ship's crew as they climbed onto the pier. "I don't suppose Evandar even realized what he was setting in motion, but even if he had, he probably would have done it anyway, knowing him." She tossed her head, as if shaking off a painful memory. "Well, there's no use in standing round here. Welcome home, Ebañy. We'll be sheltering tonight with your niece out at the dun."

"My thanks," Salamander said. "It's a strange enough welcome, but truly, it gladdens my heart to be home."

Yet late that night, Salamander looked out of the window of his chamber high up in Cannobaen's broch. The moon laid a silver road upon the sea, a road that seemingly ran south to Bardek. He wept, thinking of his wife and family, so far away. Why had he left them? For a moment he hoped he was dreaming, but the scent of a real sea filled the room, and the stone of the windowsill felt rough against his fingers.

"Alaena," he whispered. "Marka. Will I meet you again someday, my love, when we both have different faces, different names?"

All at once he felt so exhausted that he sat down on the straw-covered floor. He leaned against the cold stone wall and fell asleep, right where he was, to dream that he stood on a mountain peak and called out to a dragon, silver-skinned but touched here and there with blue.